Mj Roë

The Seven Turns of the Snail's Shell

A Novel

MjRoë
October 2011

Copyright © 2009 Mj Roë
All rights reserved.

ISBN: 1-4392-2279-7
ISBN-13: 9781439222799
LCCN: 2008911933

Visit www.booksurge.com to order additional copies.

For my husband Denny and daughter Kirsten (who reminded me in 2008 to "go confidently in the direction of my dreams" à la Thoreau).

DEAD, AND YET ALIVE:
'TIS A DOUBLE STORY.
-TEUCER
EURIPIDES' *HELEN*

ABOUT THIS BOOK

In 1997, Diana, Princess of Wales, was involved in a horrific car accident in Paris. In the year following the accident (the timeframe during which this story takes place), there was considerable suspicion that she was not dead, indeed had not been in the accident at all. Conspiracy theories proliferated around the world. While this is a work of fiction, my intent was never to identify what happened to Diana but to tell the story with that situation as the backdrop.

It is an old Corsican game. All that is required is a set of players and a map. The player who is "it" has three responsibilities: to decide what "prize" is to be found, put it in place, and draw a map for the others. The map, always circular in nature, must have seven turns. Players do not know what they will encounter at the seventh turn. The game has been known to turn deadly.

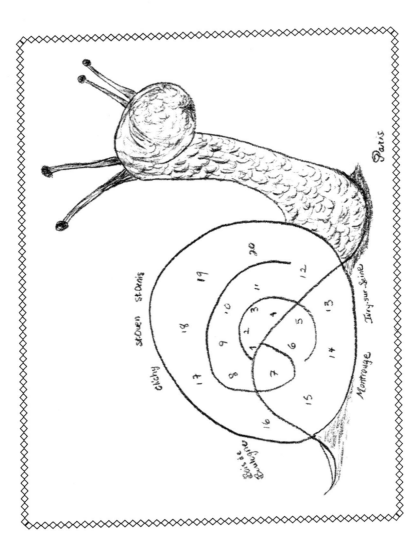

Paris

Ivry-sur-Seine

St-Ouen   St-Denis

Clichy

Montrouge

Boulogne

20
19
11
12
10
3
4
5
13
18
2
1
6
14
9
7
15
17
8
16

Mj Roë

The Seven Turns of the Snail's Shell

A Novel

PROLOGUE

Paris, France, August 1997

Diana, Princess of Wales, was thirty-six years old, desperately happy, and desperately unhappy. Desperate to avoid the media, who at once admired and hounded her. Desperate to keep her life private. It was the end of August, and she could trust no one. There was only one way out. As she reached for the phone, it rang.

"What is it?" she snapped. "Didn't I tell you not to call me at this number again?" She knew that the phone would be monitored.

There was silence on the other end.

"Yes, well, I understand. It's going to be dangerous. I am counting on you to carry this off."

The caller's question took her by surprise.

"No. I have no idea whether we'll see each other again. I suppose it is unlikely. So, good-bye then. *Adieu*."

"It's not like we were ever friends, anyway," she said coldly as she hung up the phone. "I've got to do this, so I can have what I've always wanted. In two days' time, I will be gone from the world. I told them to just wait and see what I would do next. I told them. If only it didn't have to end this way. But I can still change my mind — or can I? What good would it do? No, it has to be carried out...as I planned it. Even if we all end up dead."

She picked up the phone and dialed. "Make sure this looks good. Give them the pictures. It's our only chance for happiness, darling."

The male voice on the other end was softly reassuring.

"Yes, well, I hope so. If all goes well, then we'll be together again shortly. I love you, too."

She tugged at her barren earlobes as she hung up, her face drained but radiant from the sun she had enjoyed on the Côte d'Azur.

"My work will live on," Diana said to herself, "and so shall I."

Then she laughed out loud, her laugh filling the empty room as she recalled the time she had leapt from the balcony into the snow for a night of freedom, but this time the freedom would be guaranteed...forever.

PART ONE

CHAPTER 1

August 31, 1997

The phone rang in the residence above a restaurant on the rue du Gros-Horloge in Rouen. Still half asleep, Jacques Gérard looked at the clock on his nightstand. It was four o'clock in the morning. "Who could be calling at this hour?" he grumbled.

"Listen," the hoarse voice said in the familiar Corsican dialect. Jacques recognized it immediately. It was Diamanté. He felt a sudden apprehension. They had known each other for a very long time.

"We have to get someone out of France... *vite*." Diamanté's voice was gruff. "No one can know about it."

"What are you saying, *mon ami?*" Jacques felt like he was back in the war.

"The situation is very grave," Diamanté explained in hushed tones. He sounded tense and on edge. Jacques heard him take a deep breath. "We will require *Les Amis* and your son."

Jacques froze.

"But what is going on? Why Charlie?"

"I am on my way to Paris," Diamanté continued. "Alert your son that I will be stopping shortly at La P-S to pick him up. The support of *Les Amis* will be needed for the last part of the journey. I will call with details later. *À bientôt.*"

"*Salut.*" Jacques hung up the phone. He had many questions, but it was not the Corsican's way to question intentions. He scratched his head. What was Diamanté involved in this time? Why was a group of former Résistance fighters needed and for what role? Why was his son needed? And how did Diamanté know that his son was at the hospital, anyway? What would be required of him in all of this?

"Diamanté will have his way," Jacques said aloud, shaking his head. Diamanté always had his way. He was stealth itself, quick, tireless, and clever. That's why they called him *le loup*, the wolf. During the second war of the twentieth century in Europe, he and Jacques had been part of the French underground network known as the Résistance. The local group in Rouen called themselves *Les Amis Clandestins*. There were still some of them around. Jacques knew that Diamanté was counting on it.

Jacques Gérard faced a personal dilemma. He had not spoken to his son, Charles-Christian, since his wife, Nathalie, had passed away two years ago. Before that, he had not seen him for several years. They had had a falling out over that girl Charlie was in love with – that American. What was her name? Anna? Jacques spat at the thought. "*Merde.*" His brows furled. He turned on the television in his bedroom and picked up the phone to call Diamanté back. His son must be left out of this.

A live news report was being broadcast from Paris. Jacques watched intently. A serious car accident had happened around midnight in the tunnel near the place de l'Alma. An ambulance of the state-run emergency medical service SAMU (*Service d'Aide Médicale Urgente*) was on the scene.

"Charlie must be left out of whatever this is. Find someone else," Jacques protested.

"You are my friend, the only one who I can trust," Diamanté explained in a calm, low voice. "It will be a difficult trip. We will be in desperate need of someone with your son's skills and experience." Diamanté knew of the gag rule that all French doctors lived under. It would be against French law, rigorously prohibited by the *Ordre des Médecins*, for Jacques' son to discuss any details afterward. That would be of utmost importance.

Jacques put down the receiver and let out a heavy sigh. He was getting old. Charles-Christian was all the family he had in the world. He wanted desperately to resolve their differences. He turned up the volume on the television. Channel TF1 was broadcasting live from the Alma Tunnel. The SAMU ambulance had left the tunnel and arrived, according to the broadcast, at La Pitié-Salpêtrière Hospital sometime around two o'clock in the morning. Jacques' eyes grew wide. Charles-Christian would be in the middle of the event. He was one of the emergency room doctors. They had identified the victims as the Princess of Wales, her bodyguard, the chauffeur, and another man thought to be her current love interest.

"*Nom de Dieu!*" he said over and over as he dialed the hospital's main number.

CHAPTER 2

The sirens of the SAMUs bleated like distressed donkeys in the night. All of Paris seemed to be awake. At La Pitié-Salpêtrière Hospital, the press was everywhere. The emergency room, pitifully understaffed, was in chaos.

Dr. Charles-Christian Gérard felt the vibration of his beeper just as he finished stabilizing a head trauma victim on an emergency room gurney. He picked up a nearby phone and heard the sound of his father's voice.

"Charlie, do you remember, when you were a boy, the bizarre man, the one in the beret with the scar on his forehead, who would show up from time to time at the restaurant? The one you always asked about?" Jacques was speaking too fast; his voice sounded nervous and tense.

"Papa, *écoute*, listen. *Zut*. I am not at liberty to have a conversation with you now. We are extremely busy here tonight. I need to go back to my work."

"*Mais*...but, there is something I..."

"Not now. I...I will call you later. *Salut*, Papa."

As he hung up, the beeper went off again.

Nurse Florence Le Blanc could not help looking at the man who was waiting for Dr. Gérard at the ER desk. His lips were tightly pinched together, and he was obviously in a hurry. His face was furrowed with the years. His black, beady eyes were close to each other and delimited by dark circles and bags. A deep crevice, from an old wound, coiled its way from his right temple and disappeared under a black beret. He stared keenly down the hospital corridor at the doctor walking briskly toward them.

Nurse Le Blanc came forward and put her hand on Dr. Gérard's arm. "*Monsieur le Docteur*, this gentleman insisted on speaking with you. He said it's extremely urgent."

Diamanté stepped forward. He had recognized Charles-Christian Gérard at once: Nathalie's gray eyes, Jacques' swagger.

"*Bonsoir, Monsieur le Docteur.* Loupré-Tigre," he introduced himself, quickly offering his hand. "Did your father reach you?"

Charles-Christian did not know the man immediately, though something about him set off a danger signal in his head. He wished now that he had allowed his father to tell him more on the phone. He took the man's hand, noting that it was bony, and the veins on the back stood out distinctly with age.

"*Oui, Monsieur*, he called just a few minutes ago." Charles-Christian was weary from working through the night, and he intended to get rid of this strange person in the next few minutes. "*Monsieur*, as you can see, we are extremely occupied here in the ER at this hour. I'm afraid this will have to be brief."

"I need to talk to you in private. Is there a room, *s'il vous plaît*? It is most urgent."

Charles-Christian heard the man's distinct Corsican accent, an accent that reminded him of his father's. It had been a long time since he had seen that strange man in his father's restaurant. The man he remembered had dark black hair and black eyebrows that seemed to meet in the middle of his forehead. He rarely smiled. There was something familiar about this older man's wolf-like gaze, though, that reminded him of the mysterious visitor of his youth.

"Are you injured, *Monsieur?*" He had to shout because of the noise in the corridor and sirens "he-hawing" in the street outside the hospital.

"*Non, non.* It is not for me. *Il est nécessaire*, of the utmost importance, *Monsieur le Docteur*, that I talk to you confidentially. Now."

"*Très bien.*" Charles-Christian nodded. "*Par ici.*" He led him down the frenzied corridor into a small, blue-walled room.

Nurse Le Blanc stared after them.

As Dr. Gérard closed the heavy door, he glared directly at the man. "What is this about, *Monsieur* Loupré-Tigre?"

An hour later, in the same arrondissement as the Pont de l'Alma, an unmarked vehicle left the British Embassy on rue du Faubourg Saint-Honoré. Inside the small, white truck were five people: Diamanté Loupré-Tigre and an armed British guard in front, and in the back, the patient, the emergency room doctor Charles-Christian Gérard, and Nurse Florence Le Blanc. The inside of the vehicle had been made into a makeshift ambulance, an ER on wheels.

As the vehicle sped through the back streets of Paris, Charles-Christian wiped his brow and stared at the face of his trauma patient. Ever since he and Nurse Le Blanc had made a decision, just an hour before, to walk out of La Pitié-Salpêtrière, he had been sweating profusely.

Diamanté had explained to them the gravity of the situation and the need especially for the doctor's help.

"Why me?" Dr. Gérard had asked.

"Simple," was the only response from Diamanté. "You are Jacques Gérard's son, *hein?*"

"But I must have at least a nurse to assist me," Dr. Gérard had insisted.

"Very well. But the choice must be made quickly. We have no time to waste."

In the chaos of loading the patient under armed security and the departure of the unmarked vehicle, Nurse Le Blanc had been the only choice. She was young, but willing.

"What else do I have to do but come to this ER every night of my life, anyway? It will be an adventure," she had said to Dr. Gérard with a sort of excited grin.

Inside the makeshift SAMU, the air was stale and smelled strongly of diesel exhaust. It occurred to the doctor that the three of them might die of asphyxiation.

"Give her more oxygen," he directed as he adjusted tubes and checked vital signs. "Her condition is very grave." The patient's blood pressure was dangerously low. She had massive injuries. They were working against time. He looked intently at the young woman's face as Nurse LeBlanc carefully adjusted the oxygen mask. It was not disfigured from the accident. There was a wound on her forehead and a small cut over her lip. One delicate pearl earring hung from her earlobe. She was very beautiful, like a china doll. He sat back and wiped his brow again.

In the cab, an uneasy Diamanté sat staring out the passenger seat window. He caught a quick glimpse of the Eiffel Tower in the early morning light as the vehicle followed the Seine onto the A13 highway which would take them northwest to their final destination, the port of Le Havre, via the city of Rouen, where the next part of the plan would be carried out. He thought about the massive numbers of reporters in front of La Pitié-Salpêtrière, where he guessed a press conference was being held at this very moment.

"Is this as fast as this vehicle can go?" Diamanté asked the youthful British driver beside him. Diamanté did not even know his name. The driver, concentrating with intensity on the road, took a deep breath and ignored him. They both listened intently for any signs of an acute emergency coming from the back.

Once out of the Paris basin, Diamanté relaxed and allowed himself to reflect a bit. He had not been in Normandy for several years. The urban scene gave way to forest and trees. He opened the window and breathed in the fresh country air as he focused on the auto route and watched for any sign of someone earnestly following them from the rear. There was, thankfully, not much traffic on this early Sunday morning. The countryside was lush and sweet-scented, and it reminded Diamanté of the fragrant undergrowth known as the *maquis* in his native Corsica. There, on any hillside, a goat or two might come bounding out at any moment. A train sped alongside the auto route and crossed a bridge overpass.

Diamanté thought about the group that called themselves *Les Amis*. Well, one member of the group was not a friend: Narbon, a Corsican like himself, whose *nom de guerre* had been *l'écureuil*, the squirrel. The two had been bitter enemies, caught up in a triangle of family, love, and war. The woman they mutually loved and the clandestine cause for which they were fighting overwhelmed them. He removed his beret and rubbed the scar on his head. Just then he caught sight of two motorcycles in the rearview mirror. Each of them had a rider riding pillion, and they were swiftly closing in. He quickly replaced his beret.

"Speed up without causing attention," he commanded in a brusque voice. "We are being followed."

CHAPTER 3

Summoned by Jacques Gérard, they gathered, one by one, at the rendezvous point in the wine cellar of Le Canard à la Rouennaise. A familiar odor, the musty combination of mildew and fermenting wine, greeted them.

Léo La Bergère was first to arrive. He had to bend his head to enter the cellar. Jacques motioned to him to have a seat. The retired stockbroker nodded and lowered his bulky frame onto a bench near a wooden worktable.

Pierre Truette was next. The priest, hunched over with age and dressed entirely in black, quickly shook his old friends' hands.

André Narbon, the one they called "the squirrel," entered, much to Jacques' surprise. He had not invited him. Narbon glanced around the room suspiciously, twitching his mouth nervously from side to side. Jacques thought about how much he looked like a rodent. Jacques had always been leery of the graduate of Saint-Cyr École Supérieure de Guerre. Narbon was a man who could kill.

"Haven't seen you in quite some time, André. Several years, in fact. Where have you been?" They shook hands, eyeing each other cautiously.

"Things to be done, mostly in Corsica," the unsmiling Narbon said curtly as he pulled a green-slatted chair from the back corner, placed it at the end of the worktable, and sat down.

The last to join the group was the plump, genial head chef of Jacques' restaurant. Lucie La Forêt entered just as Jacques was beginning his speech. A white-haired woman now in her late fifties, Lucie was merely a toddler when her mother was arrested during the last days of the war in June 1944. Marie-Thérèse La Forêt, now many years deceased, escaped twice from her captors and was considered one of the great heroines of *Les Amis Clandestins*.

"*Écoutez*, listen, *mes amis*," Jacques began. "Our survival during the war was a miracle of luck and bravery. Other members of our escape line—Doctor Lemonier, the hotelier Forestier, the tailor Christophe, the Breton whose fishing boat we used many times, may they rest in peace—are no longer with us. We few, somehow, were spared to be alive today. Alas, there is yet another mission for us." Jacques took a breath and went on. "Our old friend Diamanté will be arriving any minute." He glanced from face to face. They stared at him as if transported back in time. *Young actors,* he thought, *who have powdered their hair and painted lines around their eyes and mouths in order to appear old enough for the final act.* He cleared his throat and continued. "At this moment, Loupré-Tigre is transporting a precious cargo from Paris to Le Havre. We are to provide the cover operation from this point to the coast. A member of the crew who is coming this far with Diamanté will be returned promptly to Paris so as not to raise any suspicion. Léo, that job will be for you.

I cannot tell you any more than that. You will have to trust our old friend." He ignored the razor-sharp gaze Narbon gave him.

"We won't have a lot of time. Narbon, you will take over as the driver. I'm hoping that I can count on you to carry this mission."

Narbon nodded and lowered his eyes. He inwardly congratulated himself on the fortunate move he had made by showing up in Rouen at just this precise moment.

"Truette," Jacques went on, "and Lucie, you two and I will make sure no one is following them and handle any complications."

"*Beh, magnifique!* This will be like old times," La Bergère chuckled, his eyes twinkling.

"Except that there will be no submarines in the Channel threatening to blow us up," commented the soft-spoken Truette. They all nodded. There was no doubt about their support.

"One last piece of information." Jacques paused. The heavyset, brusque man with a deep, growling voice and a commanding demeanor suddenly looked uneasy. "Charlie is with them. Please do what you can to...to assure his safety."

Through his thick, dark, square-framed glasses, Narbon stared into a wall stacked with huge wine barrels. He rubbed the stubble of whiskers on his chin as he thought about how he was going to feel when he saw Diamanté again.

CHAPTER 4

The young man is behind her as she pushes her luggage cart toward the end of the loading platform. The look of admiration is in his eyes as she glances casually back at him. She smiles. At the end of a long journey, she returns. The same man is waiting on the platform for her. He takes her hand. They waltz together. Then, something happens that stops the dancing.

Anna Ellis awoke abruptly. She stared at the unfamiliar, high-ceilinged room, unable to immediately remember where she was. The chamber, painted in a delicate turquoise with white trim, was fresh and summery. A wrought-iron fireplace in the corner was filled with ballooning violet-blue hydrangeas. A crystal vase with fresh-cut pink roses had been placed on the antique writing desk.

Anna stretched and climbed out of bed with a sigh. She threw back the sheer white curtains, pushed open the window, and looked out on the street below. The air was balmy and the morning bright and clear. She was in Paris.

That dream...again. What does it mean? she thought. *Had I maybe handled it differently? Had I come back? Maybe things might have been...*

Monique knocked lightly and peeked in her room. "Ah, good morning, *chérie*. How did you sleep?" Her voice brought Anna back to the present. "Do you want a *café crème*? Sabastien and I have just walked down to the *boulangerie* to get some fresh croissants. Join us in the breakfast room."

Sabastien, the Durochers' gentle Basset Fauve de Bretagne, swished his tail in greeting as Monique winked and quietly closed the door.

Anna looked down from her window perch. She had arrived just the day before and, jetlagged, had not slept at all well. In fact, she had slept fitfully because of the screaming sirens that had started after midnight and continued for what seemed like hours.

She dug through her luggage and quickly changed into a tank top and jogging pants. Then she opened the door and wandered down the wide, darkened hallway with mirrored French doors, peering into the salon with its crystal chandelier, cabochon-patterned carpet, and walls covered in red and gold wall fabric. Two striped, two-tone, gold satin-upholstered antique chairs flanked a white marble period fireplace.

Anna found Monique and Sabastien in the cheerful, mahogany-paneled breakfast room at the end of the apartment's long, L-shaped corridor. The windows, open to let in the fresh morning air, overlooked the ivy-covered walls of the building's inner courtyard. The table linens and dishes were in the familiar violet-blue-green-gold pattern of the textiles of Provence. A brightly colored, hand-painted majolica vase filled with blue irises sat in the center of the table.

"You and Georges have a nice apartment," Anna said as she sat down and helped herself to a croissant. "It's so elegant."

Monique was pouring giant breakfast bowls of coffee with cream. They had known each other since their student days at Paris University IV, the Sorbonne. Monique's husband, Georges, was an executive in the French media industry, and they often traveled internationally. Their apartment, just around the corner from the Arc de Triomphe in an eighteenth-century building with a mansard roof, was charming and filled with *objets d'art* from their travels.

"*Alors*, do you have something in particular that you want to do while you are here, *chérie?*" Monique asked.

Anna ate a bite of her croissant while she stirred a pure cane sugar cube into her *café crème*. "I've got to do some research for my book, and…" she hesitated, staring into her cup, "there's someone I have to find."

Monique lifted an eyebrow and gave Anna a sideways glance. With her short-cut brown hair, long neck, and fine-boned face, she reminded Anna of the French film star Juliette Binoche.

Anna sat back, combed her fingers through her long, dark brown hair, and lowered her chin. Her piercing, dark brown eyes met Monique's. "Do you remember C-C?"

"The medical student you dated? Of course. How long ago was that? Maybe ten years? Charles-Christian, wasn't it?" Monique leaned forward. "Is that the someone you have to find?"

Anna nodded.

"I always wondered what had happened between you two. You seemed so perfect for each other, so in love. Do you remember, in the late fall I think it was, when we were walking in Montmartre? He swept you up and carried you in his arms to the top of the steps. Then you two kissed for the longest time. I thought it was so *romantique.*"

Anna was silent for a minute. She had used a version of that scene in her latest novel. "Yes, well, I guess I never mentioned that I didn't hear from C-C again, did I? We spent our last night together parked in front of the Eiffel Tower, said good-bye at the airport the next day, and I flew home. I never heard from him after that."

"*Mais*...but, since you didn't hear from him," Monique hesitated, her eyebrows knitted, "didn't you worry that something terrible had happened to him?"

"Yes, of course I did. At first I wrote letters. Nothing in response. Then I tried to call his apartment. You remember. The one in the fifth arrondissement? No forwarding address."

"Did you ever try to contact his parents?"

"Yes, but his father wasn't too keen on his son's romantic interest in an American girl, if you remember. He always just hung up on me."

"But wasn't there someone who would have known his whereabouts? A friend?"

Anna shook her head.

"Well, did you just give up then? *Fin de l'histoire?* No more trying to find him?"

"Yes, yes...I guess...I did, finally. There was no use. I was back home in California—a long way away—and I was broke."

"So there has been no one else?"

"No one serious until recently. I've been dating an attorney. Mark. He's sweet and pretty good looking. Keeps himself in shape. He lives in the same condo complex as I do. We have fun together. He's..." Anna bit her lip, "in love with me. He hasn't said it, but I can tell. The problem is that I'm not sure I'm in love with him or that I could even consider marrying him. For some inexplicable reason, I can't let C-C go."

They both sipped their *cafés* and looked out the window. Sabastien came over with his tail swishing and put his paw in Anna's lap. Anna thought about her dog, a golden retriever named Paris, at home in California with her grandparents while she was away. She petted Sabastien and gave him a kiss.

"Do you think it's possible to turn back the clock ten years, Monique?"

Monique considered her question. "Have you ever regretted leaving when you did?"

"Yes, but C-C was still in medical school, and his father was supporting him until he finished. There was no firm commitment. I guess I figured that C-C would remain in limbo until I waltzed back into his life…" She laughed. "Kinda like that dream I keep having."

"I have an idea, *chérie*. Why don't you stay here until the end of September? You can take care of Sabastien while Georges and I are in Los Angeles."

Anna brightened. "I'd love that. We can swap apartments, if you like."

"Deal." Monique smiled at her. Her eyes twinkled.

Just then Monique's cell phone rang to the tune of the French national anthem.

"Oh, *mon portable. Allô? Oui, chéri.*" Monique cupped her lips and whispered to Anna. "It's Georges. He's at the office." The conversation was typical between the couple. From Monique's side, lots of "*Oui, chéri. Non, chéri. Mais non. Mais oui.*" And then a dramatic demonstration of kisses interspersed with "*Je t'aime, Je t'aime, Je t'aime*" before signing off with a quick "*Salut.*" Monique kissed the phone and put it gently back in her pocket as if, Anna mused, it were Georges.

"Georges has to make a last-minute drive today to check out a film location on the coast. We're leaving shortly. Why don't you join us?"

Within the hour, Monique, Georges, Anna, and Sabastien were on their way to the port of Le Havre. As Georges maneuvered the big, black Mercedes onto the A13 expressway, a box truck whizzed past, followed closely by two motorcyclists with riders.

"Why do the French always drive like bats out of hell?" Anna wondered out loud from the back seat. Sabastien was curled up and asleep with his paws tucked under him on the seat beside her.

"Because we're dying to get to heaven," Georges countered in English with a slight British accent. He was older than Monique, handsomely dressed, expensively shod, and his silver gray sideburns glistened in the sunlight streaming into the car.

"By the way, do you two know what all those sirens were about last night?" Anna asked.

Monique and Georges looked at each other and nonchalantly shrugged their shoulders.

"We don't concern ourselves much with the news on Sundays," Monique explained. "It's our day to enjoy each other, *n'est-ce pas, chéri?*

Georges nodded and blew her an affectionate kiss.

"*Oui, chérie,* I only have eyes for you on Sundays."

"Oh, you two. You must have heard the sirens. Aren't you the least bit curious?"

They smirked. "Actually," Georges confessed, raising his eyebrows, "we did turn on the TV a bit this morning. There was an incident in a tunnel near the Eiffel Tower. The Alma Tunnel. The TV announced that Princess Diana was killed."

"Killed? You mean, murdered?"

Georges shook his head. "They said it was an accident."

CHAPTER 5

The unmarked SAMU entered the outskirts of Rouen and followed the quay until it reached rue Jeanne-d'Arc. Two motorcycles with riders followed at a distance. Diamanté watched them in the rearview mirror. Just short of the rue du Gros-Horloge, he instructed the driver to make a sharp turn into a back alley. They pulled alongside another truck and waited. Then, with a roar, the first motorcycle spun around the corner. The man on the pillion held a camera with a large lens perched on his shoulder.

"Paparazzi," yelled Diamanté to the driver. "Hit it."

Lucie La Forêt spotted the truck and the motorcycle. She shouted at her kitchen assistants, who were busy unpacking crates of produce. "*Tout le monde!* Everyone, *vite! Vite!* Toss your crates into the alley behind that truck. *Maintenant!*"

They did as told, and just as the truck passed, the motorcyclists saw a storm of produce and crates, some still unpacked, come hurtling towards them.

Jacques saluted Diamanté and motioned to the driver not to stop. The SAMU zoomed off just as the second motorcycle, its rider hanging precariously off to the side, turned the corner.

Lucie amassed her army behind her. "*Hé, les commis, à la sortie!*"

The small army of kitchen assistants positioned themselves behind the massive body of their head chef, standing in her white apron with her hands on her hips, legs spread apart, frizzy white hair protruding under her chef's cap. Jacques, a rather hesitant Father Truette, and the portly La Bergère joined her.

The first motorcycle plummeted into a sea of wooden crates, and its two riders were thrown into the mess. They lay moaning, covered with cabbages, cauliflowers, leeks, and carrots. The next two arrived, braked, and skidded to a screeching stop just inches in front of the miniature brigade. As they revved the engine and reversed their direction, Lucie motioned to her sous-chef. The man went into action instantly. As the second motorcycle attempted a speedy retreat back down the alley, the sous-chef lowered the loading dock just in front of them. With a crash it came down, and the paparazzi were trapped.

"*Où allez-vous?* What do you think you are doing?" yelled Jacques angrily. He stepped forward, motioning to the army behind him to hold their position. "See what a mess you have made of my Sunday menu? The cabbages for the *chou-croute* are all over the cobblestones."

"And the leeks," Lucie added, her Gallic arms flying. "My leeks for the soup."

"We were so looking forward to the *morilles*." La Bergère shook his head in disgust.

The two who had crashed into the wall finally managed to get up and were picking salad greens out of their clothing. The motley army and the stunned paparazzi faced each other.

In all the chaos, no one had noticed that Narbon was missing.

Narbon was an old man, but in his Résistance days he was the most athletic of *Les Amis*, and he was still wiry and quick. As the SAMU sped out of the alley, he scurried into the courtyard of the hotel next door to the restaurant, crossed it, and arrived in the rue du Gros-Horloge just as the truck pulled around the corner.

Diamanté spotted him. It had been years since the two had seen each other, but the slight profile with the oversized beret and the thick, dark, square-rimmed glasses was unmistakable. He had seen it many times in the shadows, planting dynamite under bridges, behind buildings waiting for rendezvous with escapees, beneath trees in the dark forest waiting for planes. He briefly wondered to himself how André had managed to appear in Rouen at this very moment, but this was no time to question Jacques' decision. He motioned to the driver to halt.

"We can't very well do that, now, can we?" the young man objected. "What do you want us to do? Get out and give a press conference, old man?"

"Your replacement." Diamanté pointed to Narbon, now hurriedly approaching. "You realize your absence will be noted if you are not back at your post in two to three hours." He was correct; the driver was an employee of the British Embassy. It would not be smart for him to be reported missing after his break.

The driver pulled up, got out, and reluctantly allowed Narbon to take over the wheel.

"Go around to the main entrance of the restaurant and wait in the bar." Narbon spoke to him in low tones. "Have a cigarette. Act nonchalant. They are expecting you. You will be driven back to Paris immediately."

Narbon hauled himself into the driver's seat and nodded in Diamanté's direction. "Jacques has everything under control." There was no warmth between them. The SAMU lurched and sped off toward their destination, the port of Le Havre.

"*Alors*, so, *mon frère*, why didn't the Brits get the Yanks to do this job? The CIA or something? They would have been eager to do it."

Diamanté gave Narbon a hard look. "No one will suspect a bunch of old fighters like us. We can be trusted to do this quietly. The Yanks would bring in the big helicopters and artillery, probably a tank or two for good measure. And the whole operation would appear live on the evening news...Hollywood style." He chuckled to himself. Secretly, he liked the Americans, an opinion that he, Jacques, and particularly André Narbon had not shared.

"*Eh bien*, André, what brought you to Rouen just at this moment?"

CHAPTER 6

I have reached the point where the Seine begins...and
ends. Where a story I have in mind begins...and perhaps
will end. I sit on a bench on the quay in Le Havre, the
wind blowing in my face. The sea is gray, angry, troubled.
I taste the salt as droplets of water in the air fall on my
lips.

Anna paused from writing in her journal and stared at a British ship in the dark waters of Le Havre harbor. The quay was deserted. It was misting, overcast, and threatening to rain as a storm approached from the Channel.

Anna tried to make out some activity at the end of the wharf. Breton fishermen, perhaps coming in with their catch. The wind was blowing stronger, and the light was dimming. The British ship, in full view, seemed to be turning around. As it did, it sent a series of waves into the Channel. Anna closed her journal as a small, white, unmarked truck pulled up to the end of the pier. Next, a yellow military helicopter hovered over the truck and landed behind it, its rotary spinning. From the distance, Anna couldn't tell what was being said, but it was obvious that someone was motioning to the driver and yelling to him to get out of the cab. Two elderly men jumped out, both in berets. Without hesitation, they ran.

Anna stared in amazement as they approached her. They didn't look back. One of them seemed to have spotted her. He diverted his path to avoid looking her in the eyes. The two disappeared into the maze of corrugated iron warehouses in the streets that made up the port. Anna looked back at what was going on where the truck was parked. All the action seemed to be on the side opposite from her. In an instant, the helicopter took off and was gone. She couldn't tell where it went because of the storm. It just disappeared into the mist. The truck seemed to have been abandoned.

I wonder what that was all about, she thought as she opened her journal and briefly sketched the scene.

Fate had brought both Anna and C-C to the same harbor on that last day of August 1997. Fate could not, however, arrange their reunion. Destiny intervened.

The only person who saw Anna did not know who she was. With the keen wolf's eyes, Diamanté had spotted the young woman watching him.

In Rouen, Jacques turned on the television in the bar of the restaurant. A press conference was being broadcast live from in front of La Pitié-Salpêtrière Hospital.

> *The princess was pronounced dead at three a.m.*
> *Paris time after failing to survive emergency surgery.*

The phone rang.

"*Allô?*" Jacques said anxiously.

"It was a setup." Diamanté's hoarse voice was lower than usual.

Jacques tensed. "What do you mean, a setup?"

"André and I, we had to escape. I am at the *gare* in Le Havre."

"Where is Charlie?"

"I don't know, honestly, Jacques. I think the nurse was killed. I'll be in touch." There was a sound of footsteps and muffled voices in the background. The phone went dead.

Jacques' chest felt tight, and he was suddenly nauseated.

CHAPTER 7

The following morning, September 1, Anna stepped onto rue Beaujon, uncertain where the day would take her. Earlier, she had admitted to Monique over breakfast that there was one person in Paris who might know of C-C's whereabouts: Elise, the Portuguese concierge who managed his apartment building in the fifth arrondissement. Anna crossed the busy avenue de Friedland. She breathed the familiar mix of diesel exhaust, bakeries, wet streets, and Gitanes. People were beginning to fill the sidewalk cafés, and the vehicle traffic was at its usual frantic pace. As she skillfully dodged an errant taxi that came screeching around the corner, it occurred to her that Elise may not even be still alive. She would be in her seventies by now.

Putrid smells and the familiar ricocheting sounds of the métro assaulted her senses as she descended into the station at the Arc de Triomphe. It was all so familiar, as if she had never left Paris at all. Knowing that she would be spending some time in Paris, she bought a *carnet* of tickets at the *guichet* and plunged into the depths of the labyrinth. As she walked onto the platform, she recalled vividly how in her student days she had always compared descending into the métro to descending into Dante's Inferno. While some of the stations were clean and well lighted, most were not. The whole system reeked of sewage, garlic, and vomit. She waited for the train to slow and the doors to open, then boarded, holding her breath as she noted that the car was full of people. The overcrowded cars always smelled of human sweat and stale tobacco. The doors slammed closed, and the train lurched. She found a corner and stood, holding onto a metal pole next to her so as not to lose her balance. It wasn't long to her stop: Maubert Mutualité. Absorbed in memories, she ascended to the street. She knew the quarter well. She had lived there while attending the Sorbonne. It was where she and C-C had met and spent many hours studying together, where they had browsed for antiquarian treasures in the bouquinist's stalls and, as lovers, walked arm in arm along the quay.

Suddenly, a soft-beige stone building with seventeenth-century details reared up, beast-like, directly in front of her. The monster enveloped her, drew back on its tall, ground-floor windows, then pitched forward. Its eyes became progressively smaller, seeming to squint at her. The tiny mansard windows peeped down from the sloping roof, and the iron railings and protruding sills of the balconies sneered in unison. A huge "No. 4" stared at her from its forehead. Anna blinked. A young man with a cigarette in his mouth stood on the balcony of the *première étage*. Just as suddenly, the monstrosity shrunk and took its place amongst the others just like it on the street; the young smoker disappeared.

Anna shook her head, thinking that she must still be jetlagged, when she realized that she was standing directly in front of C-C's former apartment building. She pressed the main button on the keypad. The heavy, wooden *porte d'entrée* pushed open easily. It wasn't locked; the daily mail apparently had not yet been delivered. She peered into the courtyard, looking for any sign of Elise, who could usually be found humming softly to herself while working in the small kitchen garden outside her apartment.

Elise had lived in the building for over forty years. Her small apartment was on the ground floor, or *rez-de-chausée*, off the flower-filled courtyard. Elise had told Anna once about how she had come to Paris from Portugal and thought that the city was especially beautiful from the Seine.

"My husband, Ferdinand, *et moi*, we lived in this very building," Anna recalled her saying. "It was the *appartement noble*. We had a balcony. We went into partnership with a financier and, with one little decrepit boat, we wished to start a business running tourist boats on the Seine. Ferdinand thought it would be a very good business. *Eh bien*, on the first day out, going only in circles, the boat broke down. *Et voilà*. We were out of business, just like that. Today, the *Bateaux Mouches* line is a successful tourist attraction, but unfortunately, we have no connection to it."

Elise had told Anna that she never intended to manage the apartment building, but when her husband died in the war, she needed a place to live rent-free.

Anna had been inside her apartment only once, but she remembered it well. The interior was high-ceilinged and uniquely decorated with antiques that, Anna recalled, gave off a musty scent that she had liked.

C-C's apartment was on the *troisième étage*, overlooking the street. She and C-C would hang over the balcony in the evenings and peer down into that of his neighbor below. An elderly Russian lady with bad legs and a character to match, she would sit out there and drink her glass or two of vodka, dumping the last drops every so often on passersby in the street, usually pretty young women, and mumble an expletive in her native language. It was rumored in the building that *Madame* Russe, as everyone called her, hardly paid any rent. Anna noted from the street that the apartment appeared to be vacant now. She caught her breath as she looked to the floor above, to the apartment that C-C had occupied. New lace curtains hung in the window, and a child of about six watched her from behind them.

"*Qui est-ce? J'arrive.*" Anna recognized the voice of Elise coming from across the courtyard. She still had a Portuguese accent after all these years in France. She was on her knees by a stone birdbath, pruning some hydrangeas.

"*Entrez.*"

"*Bonjour, Elise,*" Anna called affectionately.

"Anna. *Oh là.*" The petite woman rose from her knees with great difficulty. Slowly, painfully, she wiped her dirty hands on her apron.

The two women embraced, air kissing, *les bis* style, first the left cheek, then the right.

"*Comment allez-vous,* Elise?"

The older lady gestured and shrugged her shoulders. "*Comme ci, comme ça.* Some days, they are better for me than others."

"I'm back in Paris to do research for a book, Elise. I am an author now."

"*Félicitations.*" The old lady nodded.

"I thought I would visit you today." Anna hesitated and drew in a breath. "I wanted to find out if something happened to Charles-

Christian Gérard. I haven't, no didn't, hear from him…" Damn. She was stammering. She cleared her throat. "Let me start again…" Elise stared strangely at her. "When I left to go back to California, Charles-Christian and I were a couple…in love. Do you remember?"

"*Beh, oui.* Let's sit for a bit." Elise took Anna's arm and led her over to a bench under a chestnut tree. She sat down, straightened her apron, and smoothed back stray strands of her salt-and-pepper hair from her forehead with both hands. "I do remember you two coming and going arm in arm. Such a nice young man. He was so… so *prévenant.*"

"Yes, thoughtful." Anna looked up into the tree, feeling a growing lump in her throat. "C-C, as I was fond of calling him, and I used to sit under the cool shade of this tree. We studied here together during many hot summer afternoons. How long did he live here after I left?"

"Oh, a very short time. He paid his rent until the end of the month, but he moved out in a few days. I kept all his mail, thinking that he would come back, but he never did. The only forwarding address he gave me was his parents', whom you know I already knew because of my dear husband's brother. So one day, I bundled up all the letters he had received and sent them to Rouen…to his father, Jacques."

"I wrote him several letters. Not one response. Did you ever see anyone visit Charles-Christian after I left? We did have some student friends that he might have invited occasionally."

Elise shrugged her shoulders and looked up at the window of C-C's apartment, as if to try to remember something. "*Non…non, enfin,* I don't remember. It was some time ago. *Un moment. Oh là.*"

They sat in silence, listening to the birds chirping in the tree above and the slight buzz of bees in the roses along the wall. Then Elise appeared to have thought of something. She put her bony finger on her chin. "*Attends.* There was a young lady who came to see him several times. I think the last time was about when he moved out. She was not French. She spoke English. I think she could have been British or American."

"Do you know who she was? Did you get her name?"

"*Non, non. Enfin,* I don't remember."

"Describe her to me."

"Reddish hair, green eyes, tall, *eh bien*, taller than I am, which is meaningless. *Tout le monde* is taller than I am." She smiled as she waved the back of her hand. "She had a rather well-developed *poitrine*." She wrinkled her nose as she outlined the image of a large set of breasts with cupped hands.

Anna's eyes grew wide. "Reggie? Might he have called her Reggie?"

Reggie was a classmate of Anna's and Monique's. Her boyfriend was C-C's best friend, Bertrand. She had introduced Anna to C-C. Her nationality was British, but she held a South African passport as well, her parentage being split between England and Africa, and her home also shifted between the two countries. She was in Paris to study French but skipped most of her classes to play around with French men. Monique and Anna disliked her intensely. She was a nonstop flirt and bragged incessantly about how she had stolen boys' hearts away from the other girls. C-C's friend Bertrand had been the latest "*victime*," as Monique had put it. Anna had always had a suspicion that C-C was targeted as her next conquest.

"*Oui*," Elise said, hesitating. She looked as if she had divulged a secret.

"Nothing has changed," Anna told Monique later as they entered the Tea Caddy at No. 14 rue Saint-Julien-le-Pauvre. During their student days, Monique and Anna had met often after classes in the cozy *salon de thé* with its linen-covered tables, oak beams, and elegant dark wood paneling.

"*Bonjour, Mam'selle, 'Dame. Vous désirez?*" A waiter in black bow tie and starched white apron stood over them. "*Un café? Du thé?*"

Anna ordered first. "*Un exprès, s'il vous plaît, Monsieur, et le gâteau au chocolat.*"

"*Pour moi, un thé et la tarte du jour,*" Monique clicked her tongue as she turned back to Anna.

"What hasn't changed, *chérie?*"

"Well, this *salon* for starters." Anna looked around the room and listened for a moment to the sweet sound of clicking spoons and whispered conversation. "The atmosphere is still wonderful, and it always smells so good…like fresh-baked pastries and tea and chocolate and coffee. But what I meant was C-C's apartment building, really—the concierge, Elise, and her Portuguese accent, even the bench under the chestnut in the courtyard." Anna leaned forward conspiratorially. "Oh, and *Madame* Russe died. Elise gave me the scoop on everyone who had lived in her apartment building. Bertrand, C-C's friend, remember him? Well, he is stationed in the military somewhere in Africa or Asia. I forget which. And…do you remember Reggie?"

Monique nodded and squinted her brown eyes.

"*Eh bien*," Anna went on, "she came to see C-C after I left for California. She must have made a move on him. She showed up several times, and then he moved out." Anna leaned back as the waiter placed pastries on English Blue Willow plates in front of them. She took out her pen and pretended to concentrate on a map of Paris that she had pasted in her journal.

"You are first time in Paris, *oui?*" the waiter asked, nodding in the direction of the journal. "Can I 'elp you find some place?"

"I am looking for a hospital. *Bon*, well, several hospitals." Anna glanced over at Monique.

The waiter gave Anna a look of grave concern. *"Mais, mais, vous n'allez pas bien, Mam'selle?"*

"*Oh, si, si, Monsieur, je vais bien.* I am fine. I am looking for someone in Paris. That is all."

Monique shifted in her chair. One eyebrow lifted. It was obvious that she was becoming very impatient with the conversation.

"And he is at a hospital?" the waiter persisted.

"*Oui, un docteur.*"

"*Ah oui. C'est normale.* But of course." He set down Monique's hot water for her tea and hesitated, standing by the table until they looked at him inquisitively. "It is often said that a snail's shell has seven turns. Do you know that expression, *Mam'selle?*" he asked Anna as he served her cup of espresso. His intense black eyes fixed on hers.

Anna noted that he was short and rather stocky. She decided that he was probably in his twenties, maybe a university student, or an artist perhaps.

"*Pardon, Monsieur?*"

"With your permission, *Mam'selle?*" He nodded at her pen and open journal. She hesitated and then handed them over to him.

"May I turn the page?"

She nodded.

He carefully laid the journal on the table and turned to a fresh page. On it, he drew a quick, circular drawing.

"*C'est quoi ça?*" Monique asked with impatience.

"*Beh, l'escargot, n'est-ce pas?* The snail?"

"*Oui.*" Anna nodded. There was a slight resemblance to a snail's shell.

Monique squirmed in her chair.

Next the waiter drew a downward-curved horizontal line resembling a frown through the center. "*Voilà la Seine,*" he paused to check to see if they were with him. "It runs through the center of the city, *hein?* And it curves around—*comme ça.*" He extended the line upward and to the left, then completed the circle. Again, he checked on their understanding. "*L'escargot, oui?*"

Anna smiled, nodded, and enjoying herself, she took a sip of her espresso. It looked indeed just like the venerable *escargot,* the snail that the French find a culinary delicacy.

"Now, I show you the good part, *Mam'selle.* You will remember this way all the arrondissements of Paris."

She watched as he put in numbers, starting with numbers one through four, above the line in the very center, and continuing clockwise below the line with numbers five through seven. "Now we are crossing the river again. We are on the Right Bank." He put in the numbers eight through twelve above the line. "We are now dropping to the Left Bank at *La Nation*."Numbers thirteen through fifteen on the Left Bank completed the next turn of the shell. After adding arrondissements sixteen through twenty on the Right Bank, he made a circular motion around the whole with a flourish, holding the pen in his hand as would a maestro conducting an orchestra with his baton. "The *périphérique*, the auto route, goes around the twenty arrondissements." He pointed to the outer curve. "Bois de Boulogne, west, Clichy, Saint-Ouen, Saint-Denis, north, Montrouge, Ivry-sur-Seine, to the south. The outskirts."

"*Parfait. Bravo!*"Anna applauded, and the young man gave a little bow.

"À *votre service, Mam'selle.*"

A customer entered the café and sat down at a table nearby. The waiter handed Anna's pen back to her and hustled off to wait on his new arrival.

Anna looked at the map he had drawn. She tried to count the turns.

"Interesting concept, but I don't see seven turns," she said to Monique.

Monique's neck stiffened, and her head cocked to one side. "Where on earth did he get that strange idea? The seven turns of the snail's shell. I've never heard of such a thing. Anyway, *chérie,* before we were so rudely interrupted, were you implying that C-C moved in with Reggie? I can't believe that. They were friends—but lovers? *Ah, non,* I don't believe it."

"I don't know, Monique. You remember how Reggie was— what sort of girl she was, I mean." Anna's thick eyebrows met in a frown.

"Well, I agree that she was a rather well-endowed little *putain*. I didn't like her much," she added, frowning.

"Monique, she introduced me to C-C, but I just think that she was jealous and possessive of him at the same time. She probably convinced him that I didn't care because I went back to the U.S. Why else wouldn't he have answered any of my letters?"

"But, I'm confused, *chérie*. You are saying that he would have made some kind of commitment to Reggie when he wasn't willing to make a commitment to you?"

"Yes...no...well, maybe. I don't know."

They had emptied their cups, paid *l'addition*, and were strolling through the massive, wooden doors of the stone gateway into the cobblestone street when they heard someone say, "*Mam'selle. Un moment.*"

The waiter was behind them; he had followed them out the door. "*Mam'selle*, the story I told you? About the seven turns?" He spoke directly to Anna, ignoring Monique entirely.

Anna nodded.

"You will find what you are searching for, *Mam'selle*, but beware," he added hesitantly as he wagged his finger at her in a sinister fashion, his closely set, black button eyes looking directly into hers. "It may not be what you want." Then he performed a slight bow, turned on his heel, and scurried quickly back into the café.

"Whatever was that about?" Monique huffed. "The nerve of the fellow."

Anna shook her head.

CHAPTER 8

A small group gathered in front of a television in an electronics store window on the rue du Faubourg Saint-Honoré. It was September 6, 1997. On the screen, millions of people lined the streets of London, watching a funeral cortège. Most of them were weeping. In Paris, the handful of bystanders stood silently in the rain under their umbrellas, participating in the spectacle. Anna stood among them. She had just seen Monique and Georges off to the airport. Their flight to California was due to leave in a couple of hours.

The BBC announcer was speaking in hushed tones of the tragedy that had befallen the British royal family: "More than a million people weep today as they struggle to catch a last glimpse of Diana, Princess of Wales. Flanked by Welsh Guards, Diana's remains are borne through the ancient streets of London on a First World War gun carriage drawn by six black horses. The cortège will arrive shortly at Westminster Abbey, where the funeral service will take place. We have all been touched, in one way or another, by the life of a woman who struggled with her own emotional problems even as she reached out to the victims of homelessness, AIDS, cancer, and land mines."

"*Qu'est-ce qu'il a dit?*" an old lady next to Anna whispered to her companion, who held up his hands and shrugged his shoulders, indicating that he hadn't understood a thing.

The camera zoomed in on the coffin draped in the red, gold, and blue of the British Royal Standard and decked with wreathes of white trumpet lilies and tulips. A white card inscribed with "Mummy" was nestled in a third wreath of white roses. A collective "Ahhhhh..." emanated from the gathering.

The camera panned next to the acres of flowers laid at the gates of Kensington Palace and along the funeral route. The announcer was saying something about so many bouquets being in demand that the florists had declared a national shortage.

The skies were gray, and the rain was falling harder as Anna put her hands in her coat pockets and walked down the street. Everywhere, it seemed, Diana's famous face peered from the thousands of newspaper and magazine special editions being sold to mark the event.

She entered a small café and took a seat at a table next to the window. As she watched the parade of umbrellas scurrying to and fro in the downpour, she thought about how Paris in September was such a different place. The summer tourists were gone. The Parisians had returned from their annual *vacances. La Rentrée*, they called it. Time to resume the routine and take back the city. What everyone does in September in France. With the cold rains arriving, the chestnuts on the boulevards had taken their cue too and were starting to show the first signs of color.

Anna sighed. As much as she loved being in Paris, she was unhappy that she still had no leads as to the whereabouts of C-C. In the days before her departure, Monique had helped her search the MINITEL, the electronic phone directory. They had come up with nothing. When they had searched under *Hôpital Assistance Publique* and discovered twenty some hospitals in the Paris basin, Anna had nearly given up altogether.

"I can't just call every one of these," she had said, looking at the list. "No one will ever talk to me. And anyway, what if he's not even in a Paris hospital at all?"

"Where else would he be?" Monique had said with a shrug. "I can't imagine why anyone would want to live anywhere else. But you are correct, *chérie*. I agree that it would be too easy to dismiss you over the phone. So, there is only one thing to do and that is to go visit all of the hospitals in person. Either that or hire a detective to do it."

Anna had laughed at the thought. "Well, I guess I could play detective myself. Maybe I could even appear in need of medical attention, if necessary."

Anna had arranged the list of hospitals by arrondissement and then plotted them on the waiter's hand-drawn map in her journal. "It will take at least three days," she had told Monique. "Day one—the eighteenth and tenth arrondissements. They're close to each other, close enough to make fewer métro stops anyway. Day two—the fourteenth and fifteenth. Day three—the last two hospitals in the twelfth and thirteenth."

Today, when the two friends had said good-bye, Monique had asked, "So when do you begin your *grand tour de Paris?*"

"Tomorrow. I'll start tomorrow."

It was still raining the next morning when Anna started out on day one armed with her map of Paris and her plan of attack.

At the Hôpital Lariboisière, she claimed to be a former college classmate of Dr. Gérard who had lost track of him.

The woman at the front desk seemed sympathetic, but she was of no help.

"*Non, Mademoiselle*. We have no one on staff by that name."

Near the Gare de l'Est, in the same arrondissement, there were two hospitals: Fernand Poisons on the rue du Faubourg-Saint-Denis and the Hôpital Saint-Lazare.

"*Je regrette, Mademoiselle…mais non…*there is no one here on our staff by that name."

The last, Hôpital Saint-Louis, was located near the Goncourt métro station. She returned to rue Beaujon and called Monique to give her a status. It was late. By now it would be early morning in California.

"Day one down, Monique. No luck—not even a hope," she sighed.

"You sound like you are ready for a glass of wine and a hot bath. Do you think they are telling you the truth? What if this search is useless?"

"Wouldn't they have at least shown some recognition of his name, even if they were trying to withhold the information? I don't know, Monique. They were all relatively small hospitals I visited today. I haven't gotten to the big ones yet."

"How many do you have to visit tomorrow?"

"Oh, let's see. It's the next turn of the snail's shell." She laughed as she consulted her map. "I feel like I'm following a snail's trail instead. The fourteenth and fifteenth arrondissements—all the hospitals are near Denfert Rochereau and the Montparnasse cemetery. Good Lord, there are ten of them! I may have to split the list into two days."

"At least that's a lovely part of Paris to walk. How's the weather?"

"Miserable. It's much cooler."

Anna made one more call before she went to bed. She wanted to check on her grandparents and find out how her dog, Paris, was doing.

"Oh, we are all just fine, dear," her grandmother told her. "Paris is no trouble at all. When do you think you will be home?"

"I don't know, Grandma…in a couple of weeks. When Monique and Georges return. I'll see you soon. Give a big hug to Grandpa for me. I love you both."

When she hung up the phone, she had a sickening feeling in the pit of her stomach, a dark feeling of foreboding she had never felt before.

"I need sleep," she said to Sabastien as she fed him his nighttime cookie. "What say we make that quick trip to the street, and then we can go to bed?" It was raining again, and she held the umbrella over both of them as the little dog completed his final pee of the day.

The following day, in a cold storm, Anna set out in search of the hospitals located in the fourteenth and fifteenth arrondissements. As she entered the métro, she studied her map. There were five hospitals in the fourteenth; one specialized in burns. She could probably count that out. That wasn't C-C's area of specialty. One was a clinic—also probably not. He had wanted a hospital position. Another appeared to be a mental hospital. Again, probably to be discounted. That left two good possibilities—Hôpital Saint-Vincent de Paul and Hôpital Sainte-Anne in the fourteenth. She would start with them. Looking at the fifteenth arrondissement, there were two hospitals on the rue de Sèvres, but one was a children's hospital. She crossed it off the list and also Institute Pasteur. Now she had a more manageable list of three to four hospitals for the day.

Later, on the phone again with Monique, she reported that crossing possibilities off her list might not have been a good idea. "I came up with nothing at all today, Monique. It's discouraging."

"Where do you go tomorrow?"

"I'm taking the morning off to write. I've got to get some work done. In the afternoon, I'm going to just two hospitals. They're the largest. One is in the twelfth, near the Gare de Lyon, and the other is in the thirteenth near the Gare d'Austerlitz."

"Well, I wish you *bon courage, mon amie.* Maybe your luck will turn."

They chatted about Monique and Georges' appreciation for her apartment and how much they loved Laguna Beach, the weather in California, and so on, and so forth. Anna shivered. It was a cold night in Paris.

Too early to call Grandma and Grandpa, she thought. Monique was still on Paris time, so she could call her anytime, but her grandparents would worry if she called them this early. *I'll call them tomorrow evening,* she promised herself.

On the third day of scouring the hospitals in Paris, she finally had the lead she so desperately sought.

"Dr. Gérard? Charles-Christian Gérard?" The administrator at Hôpital La Pitié-Salpêtrière clarified the name after Anna finally found someone in that huge complex who was willing to speak with her. "He is on, how you say it, leave, *Mademoiselle*? We assume he is taking some time to travel. He does a lot of medical work in Africa, you know."

Anna was eager to keep the man talking. "Do you know where in Africa?"

"*Non, Mademoiselle.*"

"Do you have any idea when you can expect him to return?"

"*Non*, again, *Mademoiselle*." He shrugged his shoulders. "I'm afraid that is all I can tell you today." His manner became abrupt and dismissive. His eyes stared at her coldly.

Just great. Where could she go next? Anna went over the conversation in her head as she entered Monique and Georges' apartment on rue Beaujon.

The rain had let up, and Sabastien was begging for a walk, so she slipped on his leash and was just opening the door of the apartment when the phone rang. It was Monique calling from California.

"*Allô*, Anna, can you hear me?" She was crying. "I don't know how to tell you this, but we've just had the most frightening news. It's about your grandparents. They have been in a horrible accident."

Anna's heart stopped. Her grandparents, the only parents she had ever known, were all she had for family in the world.

"What? Where are they?"

"The police came to your apartment. I'm glad we were here. They said that the SAMU, I mean ambulance, took them to a hospital. Just a moment. I wrote down the name. They took them to the UCLA Medical Center. I told them where you were in Paris and that I would call you immediately."

"I need to leave Paris right away. I'll be on the next flight I can get out. Please, Monique, try to find out what their condition is."

"If I can learn anything at all, *chérie*, I will call you."

Anna sobbed as she dialed Air France.

"Oh, please God, don't let me lose them," she prayed.

PART TWO

CHAPTER 9

Los Angeles, California

Only her grandfather was alive by the time Anna's flight landed at LAX fourteen hours later.

She choked back the tears when she entered his hospital room. He had just come out of surgery. His face was as pale as the white bed he lay in. His mouth gaped. There were scrapes from shards of glass on his cheeks and forehead. A plastic tube ran into his nose from an IV stand nearby. The distinctive smell of rubbing alcohol filled her nostrils.

"He is very weak. He sustained critical internal injuries," the surgeon had told her. "He may not make it through the night." They would control the pain, he said.

"Oh, Grandpa," she bawled and laid her face on the pillow close to his.

The old man looked lovingly toward her. His unruly white eyebrows twitched as he blinked back the tears in his eyes. "Your grandma. She, oh God, Anna, she didn't make it," he said. His voice was raspy, his breathing labored. It appeared that he was drawing all his strength to speak. "She and I, oh dear God. We were hit. It came so fast. I couldn't get out of the way. Oh, dear God. Why her?" He sobbed aloud.

Tears welled in her eyes. "Shush, Grandpa, don't wear yourself out. You need to rest." She spoke as calmly and reassuringly as she could, concealing the anguish she felt.

"Anna, there is something very important I need to tell you." She tried to shush him again. "No, no, you must understand something that I have not told you previously." He spoke haltingly. His chest heaved with every breath. "Who your father was, how your parents met…You know I adore you, and you have been the pride of my life. Now that your grandmother is gone…" He choked up again and hesitated. "I need to answer those questions you asked me so many times. Remember? You finally quit asking because I wouldn't give you any information."

Anna nodded and stared at him. Her heart was pounding. She remembered how many times as a child she had asked him to explain who her father was, and he would always tell her that he didn't know anything. Even after her mother died, and she was old enough to understand, he maintained his ignorance on the subject. He was correct about one thing. She had finally stopped asking. What use was pestering? She loved him as a father anyway.

"I thought you didn't know anything about my father?" She kissed his forehead and forced a smile. One of her tears spilled onto his cheek.

"It was a long time ago, but I want you to know now. So you can… Anna, I was shot down over France during World War II, as you know." Anna's grandfather had never shared much of his war experience with anyone, even his wife. "I was rescued by a group of Résistance fighters from Corsica… They saved my life. One of them, a man named Diamanté, became my friend."

Gasping for air, Stu Ellis managed to tell his beloved granddaughter the whole story. Anna was later to remember how time seemed to stand still as he related the details. Diamanté and he had exchanged letters for years after the war ended. They were about the same age. Both of them had returned to their homelands and married. Diamanté had a son, Diamanté *fils*. When Junior was of age, he joined the French military, as was required. One day, Anna's grandfather received a letter from Diamanté that Diamanté *fils* was coming to California to attend an exchange training school with the American Navy in San Diego. Would he entertain him occasionally on weekends, Diamanté asked, so that he wouldn't get homesick for family? Stu Ellis wrote back that, of course, his son was welcome in their home and they looked forward to the young man's coming. As it turned out, their beautiful daughter, Anna's mother, was seventeen at the time of Diamanté *fils*' visit to California. He was there just long enough to sweep her off her feet; when he left, she was pregnant with Anna. Her grandfather told Anna that he didn't believe that her father ever knew because the next letter he had received from Diamanté was several months later. It bore the terrible news that his son had been killed in the war in Algeria and that Diamanté was heartbroken. Stu didn't hear from him again, and he never told him about Anna.

"You must have been born right about the time of your father's death." The old man closed his eyes, exhausted.

Anna sat in stunned silence. Why hadn't she been told this before?

"Grandpa?" When he didn't open his eyes, she panicked. "Grandpa, I can't lose you. Not now."

His eyes opened. "I'm awake, Anna."

"Didn't this Diamanté ever try to contact you?"

"No." His voice faded to a whisper. "I heard from another of the old Résistance leaders that he had moved to the south of France. I had no more news after that."

"What was Diamanté's last name?"

He thought for a moment, holding her hand tightly. "It's funny, Anna. I always just called him Diamanté, but I recall that his last name was Wolf or Tiger, or something like that, in French. The *maquis*…that was the name they all called themselves… I think that the word had something to do with Corsica… They all called him "the wolf" for short. He had such eyes, like those of a wolf." He patted her hand. "His son was very handsome. I see his features in you. It gives you a very European beauty."

Anna sobbed. She was angry with the old man for not telling her all these years, for being in a car accident now, for giving her so much love over the years that it hurt to bear the thought of losing him now. She laid her head on his heaving chest and stayed with him, holding his hand. She told him how much she loved him, that he was safe, that the doctors would take care of him—everything she could think of to comfort him. Sometime during the night, he slipped into a coma, and two days later he quietly passed away.

CHAPTER 10

Anna and Monique strolled through Laguna Beach's Heisler park overlooking the Pacific Ocean. Anna's thoughts went back to her childhood and the good times she had spent in her grandparents' care.

"Tell us a story, Anna." She was eight years old. Her grandfather was smiling at her. He and her grandmother were sitting next to each other in their seaside chairs under a big, purple and orange umbrella. It was August. As a child, she had first exhibited the gift of storytelling when she was in preschool. She would make up stories about her stuffed animals. Grandfather never tired of hearing her stories.

"You have such a gift, Anna. No one else in the family has this gift, sweetie. You will use this to your great advantage someday."

Of course she had, and he had always been so proud of her successes as a novelist. Her story at eight was about how a blue and beige horse named Handee became a sculpture in the park near her grandparents' home.

"Okay, Grandpa." She had hesitated a minute to think up her story. Then the little girl had begun her fable in earnest.

"This is the story of Handee. Handee was a blue horse with tan spots on his back. He also had a tan spot over one eye, which made him look like he had a patch on it. He had big, really big feet, so his horseshoes were huge. He had white patches on his legs all around his knees, which made him look like he had white socks on. Handee enjoyed singing tunes every day as he trotted along the beach. He was a singing horse! He sang horse songs! One day, as he was trotting happily along singing a favorite horse song, he saw a perfectly circular hula hoop standing up between two trees in the park on the hill right in front of him. *That hula hoop is bigger than I am,* he thought, as he cocked his head this way and that to get a better view of it. Just then, he decided to have some fun. He pawed the sand with his big, horseshoed feet and began galloping upward toward the hoop. As he picked up speed, he made a huge leap with his back feet in the air, and he jumped right through that hoop. The weather was so beautiful, like today, and he had such perfect form that he turned around and jumped through the hoop again and again. It was like he was dancing. He was having such a good time that he didn't see a fairy appear. It was a park fairy. The fairy watched him jumping and singing for a while, and she was so delighted at what she saw that she decided that she should cast a magic charm on him. Right then and there, just as he was midway through the big hoop, his hind feet in the air, his tail pointed skyward, his eyes closed in perfect happiness, and his mouth open in song, she froze him for all to enjoy forever after. That is how Handee became one of the beautiful sculptures in the park near our house. The lesson to the story is to jump and sing with all your heart in whatever you do, and you will be rewarded because people will like you forever. The end."

"BRAVO! BRAVO!" Her grandfather and grandmother had clapped, and her grandfather had slapped his knee in appreciation.

Anna bowed in front of them and kissed them each softly on the cheek.

"Can I have an ice cream cone, Mama?" A small voice behind her brought Anna back to reality. Her grandparents were gone. Only their seaside chairs stared at the Pacific now, locked arm in arm like the companions they had been and would be forever in heaven. Anna turned to look back.

"Not now, baby," was the woman's response as she walked along, holding the hand of a little boy. "It's too close to dinner time."

"Can I have a puppy like that one?" was the little boy's next request. Anna's golden retriever, Paris, was sauntering along beside her. The dog gave a lick at the chubby finger as they passed in front of them. The mother smiled at Anna and hurried her little boy along.

"Seems like everything is pink in California," Monique pondered aloud.

The late September sun was setting over the Pacific, shedding a pinkish light over everything in Laguna Beach—the white sand, the tile roofs, sprawling white driveways, and wide sidewalks. Everywhere, pink roses and pink bougainvillea looked as if they had chosen their colors from the sky. A gentle breeze off the ocean whipped the two women's hair.

"Monique, I really appreciate your staying for a while. It has helped with all the sorting out I have to do."

"I'm glad to be here. Unfortunately, I can stay only a few more days. What exactly will you do now?"

"I don't know. I have some unanswered questions in my life." She hadn't told Monique about Diamanté yet.

"Oh, we aren't over that yet, then?" Monique rolled her warm brown eyes, thinking it was C-C to whom Anna was referring.

Anna looked at her directly. Monique's impeccably made-up, fine-boned face and shell-like ears were glowing in the pinkish light. "It's like when I was a little child and I dreamt that I found another room in our house by just opening a door. I have a door in front of me that, when I open it, will lead me into an unfamiliar room in my life."

"And what if that room, as you call it, brings still more pain?"

"Then so be it, Monique."

"What about Mark, *chérie*? You should give him a chance. Besides, I like him. I think he's very handsome and so personable."

"Mark? He's comfortable, but I'm not in love with him, remember?" She took off her dark glasses and looked at her friend. "Come on, Monique, you and I both know that until I see C-C again, I won't be able to set up house with someone else. If I find out that he is married, or has a life of his own, I won't interfere. I just need to know for sure."

Monique shrugged her shoulders. "My advice to you, my friend, is this: get C-C out of your system, once and for all. Forget him. Seize a life, as you Americans like to say." She seemed to take a subtle pride in her new command of American slang.

"You mean get a life, Monique," Anna gently corrected her friend, smiling.

They walked past several pieces of public art on display. The light had turned more bronze now, and the sun was right at the point where the smooth line of the water delineated the western horizon. In a moment it would drop below the surface and seem to disappear forever. Anna contemplated a garden snail chomping its way through a hibiscus plant. She was reminded of the Parisian waiter, his drawing of the arrondissements of Paris and the seven turns of the snail's shell.

"You are probably right, Monique. I'll work on it."

"Promise?"

"Promise."

Monique flew back to Paris at the end of the week.

CHAPTER 11

With her grandparents gone, Anna felt alone, truly alone, for the first time in her life. The day following Monique's departure, she and Paris took a long, rambling walk along the beach.

She sat down on a wooden bench, took off her straw hat, and watched the clouds billowing over the ocean. A seagull swooped down and landed next to her bench. The graceful bird balanced on one webbed foot as it looked at her first with one sharp eye and then the other. The two of them stared at each other until the bird flew off. She watched it as it took wing directly into the wind, soaring far out over the ocean, gliding in a wide circle with its wings spread, then flapping wildly in ascent, to be carried along on a second crosswind. Chee! Chee! Chee! She heard its cries rise and fall across the water as she finally lost sight of it in the haze over the long stretch of coastline. She tried to imagine the absolute feeling of freedom it would be to be able to take to the air like that.

Rejected by her mother as a baby, Anna had grown up to be tough and self-reliant. Her grandparents had raised her. When she was five, her mother had died of a drug overdose, and she never was told anything about who her father was, despite the many times that she had asked her grandparents. Now, because of a terrible accident, she had some information that haunted her. She knew her father was dead, but was there a family somewhere? She had a name, Diamanté, and a nationality, Corsican. A grandfather. Where are you?

Anna had grown up longing to do something interesting with her life. Creative and talented, she had further developed her storytelling ability through her high school years. Her first short story was published when she was a senior in high school. She published a short novel while studying English and French at UCLA. Once she had completed her undergraduate studies, she flew off to study for her graduate degree in Paris, a move that would transform her and profoundly affect how she lived her adult life. She adapted to the easygoing nonchalance of the French and lived a relatively carefree life as a student and writer in Paris in the 1980s. It was during that time that she had met and fallen in love with a young medical student whom she nicknamed C-C. She had not intended for the affair to be serious; he certainly had not, or she would have had a response to her letters. Anna closed her eyes as she leaned back and held her face up to absorb the warmth of the sun. She was back in Paris, standing for a moment looking up and down the rue Saint-Jacques. A sudden and deep feeling of loss flooded her entire being. C-C. Where are you?

"Where are you?" Mark's voice, eerily echoing her thoughts, brought her back to the present. She opened her eyes.

"So, what's the answer? What were you thinking so hard about just now?" Breathless and sweating from jogging along the shoreline, he flung a towel around his neck and plunked his appealing muscular frame down beside her. He stretched his powerful legs straight out in front of him, crossed his arms, and smiled. He had a handsome, boyish face, and his sandy hair was in disarray.

"My latest novel, I guess..." she lied.

"Hi, boy." Mark tousled Paris' big floppy ears. The man had definitely won over her dog. The golden retriever was up on his feet and responding with a wild wag of the tail.

"How about we go get a latte at Starbucks?"

"Okay...sure," she nodded, smiling.

"By the way, there's a package waiting for you at your door. I saw it when I was leaving."

"Hmmm. I wasn't expecting anything."

"Ah well, then we have a mystery." He leaned over, grinning, and nudged her with his arm. "Let's go get that coffee first."

An attorney in his midthirties, raised in Pacific Palisades in a wealthy Hollywood filmmaking family, Mark was what Anna referred to in her novels as the quintessential "Mister Perfect." He had done his undergraduate work at the University of California, Berkeley, then attended Stanford Law School, passed the California bar, and immediately moved to Laguna Beach where he had found a small office above an antique store on Glenneyre Street and opened his own practice. The sign on the side of the building read: "LAW OFFICES M. A. Zennelli, Attorney at Law." He didn't have a lot of clients, but the ones he had seemed to keep him busy processing mostly real estate litigation. He drove a new navy blue BMW convertible, worked out daily, and liked to eat out a lot. Anna had thought that he was a sweet guy the day she had literally run into him jogging on the beach near her condo. They had started dating and, she had to admit, they had fun together, but the relationship had never blossomed, despite Mark's occasional suggestion that it might.

Since she had returned from France, he had been trying to understand what was going on with her. She had been indifferent, aloof. He liked her enough to be patient, telling himself that it was her grief over her grandparents that had caused her to become more distant. So he had come up with a plan. The package sitting at her door represented the initial effort.

CHAPTER 12

Mark and Anna stood in front of the open French doors of her condo. Outside, the shimmering blue-green Pacific Ocean sent sparkling waves crashing to the beach. Mark's hazel eyes reflected the ocean as he watched her open the mysterious package that had arrived that afternoon on her doorstep. It was a large oil painting—one of those Paris street paintings.

"I found it on consignment in one of those small galleries just down the highway. I thought you'd like it," he said. "I guess some old lady had bought it on a trip to Europe decades ago and didn't want it anymore. I know how much you like Paris, and it sort of, ah, reminded me of you." He shifted his weight to his other foot and waited for her reaction.

The painting was a cliché. In the impressionistic style of Paris street artists, it was the often-painted scene of the place du Tertre in Montmartre, the artists' square, with the white dome of Sacré-Coeur visible in the background. In the foreground was the Café Gascogne, with a blurry assortment of people seated at tables under a green awning. A couple walked in the square, the woman clothed in a bright, tulip red. It appeared to be a cloudy day, and the artist had given the street a mirrored effect as if it were wet from a recent rain.

"You know, it's odd, but I've never purchased one of these paintings in Paris, Mark. All the time I've spent there, I've admired lots of the artists' work. I always thought it would be too much trouble to get through customs. This one is rather nice. Thank you." Anna was touched by Mark's thoughtfulness. Her brown eyes glistened. She looked up. "I have the perfect spot for it—over there, on that wall." She pointed to an empty space above the persimmon-colored couch. "It will go perfectly with the colors of the room."

"Anna…" Mark hesitated a moment and then dropped what he was going to say. "I…I'm glad you like it." He put his arm around her shoulders and drew her to him. Without pulling back, she let him kiss her. He was warm and smelled of musk. His strong arms enveloped her small frame. "How about dinner tonight? My place. I'm cooking for a change. Spaghetti *alla Bolognese*. It's a family specialty."

"That should be a treat. Sure."

That evening, after dinner, with Paris at their feet, they lay wrapped in a large beach blanket on the chaise lounge on Mark's balcony. He listened with his arms around her as Anna shared with him the story that her grandfather had told her before he died in the hospital. She told him about the Corsican father she hadn't known who had died as a soldier in Algeria, and about the mother who hadn't cared to know her. She poured out her heart to him about losing her grandparents, all the questions she had now about whether there was a relative, a grandfather, somewhere in the world. The only thing she didn't tell him about was C-C. They sat for a long time in silence, listening to the waves and enjoying the smell of the fresh, salt air.

"Have you ever been in love, Anna?" he asked her as he nuzzled her ear.

The question took her by surprise. She pulled back slightly and looked at him.

"Yes…maybe…I don't know. What is real love, anyway? I write about it all the time. I write passionate love scenes in my books. But do I really know what love is? I don't know."

"If I read one of your books, would I get a clue as to how to make passionate love to you?"

She laughed. "Wait. You mean, like reading one of your law textbooks?"

"Sorta…" His eyes twinkled in the moonlight as he played with her hair. He kissed her neck.

"No, my books are all fiction." She put her hand on his chest. "You'll have to figure it out on your own. You're the smart attorney."

"Is that a summons to court?"

She couldn't speak, but she nodded in spite of herself. Her heart was beating too fast.

"Well then, I'll have to put together a creative motion for this case." He moved his tongue down her neck and smothered his face between her breasts. His right hand slid under her sweater around her ribs, and his left hand slipped under the drawstring waistband of her warm-up pants, caressing her buttocks as he pulled her in close to him.

She felt weak. "Is this how you win cases?" she whispered.

CHAPTER 13

*You could be the woman in the painting with this on. I'd
like to be the man walking at your side. M.*

A world away from Paris, Anna stood on her doorstep, staring
at the card that had arrived with a special delivery package
from one of those glamorous shops on Rodeo Drive. Neatly folded
inside the signature tissue paper was a soft, cashmere sweater in her
favorite color—persimmon.

The gift was a little too personal, a bit too extravagant. It made
her uncomfortable. Yet, it was sensual. She nestled her nose in the
softness of the cashmere. She went into the bedroom and pulled
the sweater on over her head. It had a classic V-neck and small rib-
bing. It was a good color for her, and it fit her perfectly. She looked
at herself in the mirror. She had a nice figure. Her skin was light
olive and healthy looking. Her long, dark hair was shiny. The image
in the mirror stared back at her. What could you have been thinking? A thirty-five-year-old woman? That you could just waltz back
into C-C's life after all this time and take up where you had left off
a decade before? You are insane. You should fall in love with Mark.
Marry him. Have a family. Why not?

She picked up the phone and dialed Mark's cell phone. His voice
message said he was with a client and to leave a message.

"Hi Mark. It's Anna. The sweater arrived. It's just…just beautiful. I'm not sure I deserve all this attention. Stop over for a glass of wine when you get home later so I can thank you in person."

He called back and left a message an hour later when she was out walking Paris. "Hi. It's Mark. How about we meet somewhere? I'm tied up at the office until the wee hours—new client and all that. But I would like to see you. How about a margarita at Las Brisas at say sevenish? *Hasta luego.*"

It was a cool November evening. Anna walked into the popular Mexican restaurant in Laguna Beach. She wore her new sweater with black pants, a melon wool scarf, and high-heeled black leather boots. The colors offset her long, dark hair and stunningly beautiful eyes.

Mark was waiting in the cantina. Showing his obvious admiration, he took her hand and brushed her on the cheek with his lips as he guided her to a table.

"Hi, gorgeous," he whispered in her ear.

Anna gazed at him. Dressed in a sleek, taupe suit with a chestnut beige silk tee that matched his hair, he looked to-die-for gorgeous himself. She squeezed his hand.

The waiter brought them chips and salsa. Mark ordered two of the house specialty margaritas, on the rocks.

"I'm swamped at the office. I've got this new client…very rich, and now my family has asked me to do some work for them also. It involves some travel. I'm leaving tomorrow. I'll be in New York until sometime next week. Will you be okay?"

"Sure. I've got to meet with my agent anyway, explain why my book's not getting done before the end of the year as planned. He's getting a little testy about it."

"Good luck on that. What say we plan a weekend getaway when I get back? We could spend Thanksgiving in Vegas, maybe? My family will be in Europe, so no Mom's turkey feast this year."

She flinched. He really was moving too fast now. A trip together would be a whole new step in their relationship. Was she ready?

He regretted the comment about the Thanksgiving turkey feast as soon as he said it. Anna's face showed it.

"I…I hadn't even thought about the holidays coming up. My grandmother always made a big deal out of Thanksgiving," she said, clearing her throat and shifting in her chair. "Even if we didn't have many guests, she made a huge turkey with all the trimmings and fussed and fussed over the table." She paused a minute to gather herself together. The whole subject made her uncomfortable. "Actually, Mark, getting out of town that weekend might be a good idea." She forced a smile. She could handle it. She needed to get out of her shell.

"Great, then." He heaved a small sigh of relief. "We'll plan on it." The restaurant was noisy. They finished their drinks. "I've really got to get back to work." He looked at his watch. "I have an early morning flight, too, so guess this is good-bye for a few days."

They left the restaurant and walked down the hill toward the beach, lingering briefly along the concrete beachfront footpath. In the moonlit darkness, the ocean waves could be heard lapping against the rocks. He took her in his arms and kissed her. Then he kissed her again, a lingering, passionate kiss that took her breath away. The ocean air was crisp and cool, and the stars shone brightly above them.

CHAPTER 14

"Have you ever been in eastern France?"
Mark called Anna from New York two nights later. The question took her totally by surprise.

"Years ago. Why, Mark?"

"Our meeting today. Legal issues with the European Union. Firm's in Strasbourg. I have to fly over and see what's goin' on. It's a family issue."

"Lucky you. A business trip to France. When do you leave?"

"Not so fast, Anna. I don't speak French, remember."

"Oh, you'll get along just fine."

"I'm not talking about in the meetings. The firm I'll be dealing with speaks English. I'm talking about getting around. Ordering in the restaurants. Asking for directions. You know, the street stuff. Last time I was in France was when I was a little kid. I need a tour guide."

"Most taxi drivers will gladly give you a tour, Mark." She was having fun with him. "They will even provide you with commentary."

She heard him groan, then clear his throat.

"Anna, I want you to go with me." His tone was suddenly serious. "We can stop in Paris, if you like, at the end of the trip. I've already made the reservation—for two, if you agree."

Wait. What was he saying?

"And I called our neighbor Tillie," he rushed on. "She's up to watching Paris while we're gone—that is, ah, if you agree." He hesitated, waiting for some sort of reaction from her, then continued. "Instead of Vegas, over Thanksgiving we'll be completely out of the country. It'll be great! What do you say?"

She was speechless. Strasbourg? And the reservation already made? Wasn't he pushing this just a bit too fast?

"Well, what do you say?" Mark repeated his question.

"It's just…" She tried to collect her thoughts. "It's ah, just, that it's…" she stammered.

"Look, I have to go, and I want you to go with me, Anna."

What should she do? She couldn't explain what she was thinking to him over the phone. "I…I don't…this is so sudden, Mark."

"Okay, Anna. If I'm rushing you, I'm sorry. Let's just sleep on it. I'm tired. I'll call you in the morning, and we can discuss it further. Bye, gorgeous."

In New York, Mark hung up the phone and poured himself a cognac. "Damn."

In Laguna Beach, Anna poured herself a glass of Chardonnay and sat down on the large Persian rug next to her dog. She thought about how much she had liked being in Mark's arms the night before he had left for New York. The way he had held her. How warm he had felt. The scent of musk. Still, it seemed fast. But she had liked it. Liked him. Wanted more of him. What should she do?

It wasn't just his offer that was bothering her. It was the coincidence. In the previous few days, as she had sorted through her grandparents' belongings, she had run across some old, yellowed letters her grandfather had kept in a long-forgotten keepsake box. Among them were two or three perfume-scented love letters her grandmother had sent to him while he was serving in Europe during the war. In another bundle, there were two pieces of correspondence, postmarked from Corsica, from the man he had called Diamanté, one of which was sent in 1960 announcing that his son would be coming to California for military training and another sent in 1962 with the horrifying news that the son had been killed in the Algerian War. She had had a hard time reading those letters, knowing now that the son was her father. There was also an old French Christmas card in the box—a curious card signed "*Joyeux Noël, Guy de Noailles et Nathalie*"—postmarked from Strasbourg, France, in 1950, five years after the war had ended. She had wondered why her grandfather had kept that card and whether it had some connection to the Résistance fighters her grandfather had known during the war. Now, Mark was wanting her to accompany him to, of all places, Strasbourg. Her mind was spinning. Was this Guy de Noailles even still alive? He would have to be very old. If so, what was his connection to her grandfather? Might he even have known Diamanté?

It had been her plan that evening to go through some old photo albums her grandmother had kept. She picked up her grandparents' wedding album, then another devoted to her mother, Lily, as a girl. Finally she picked up her own, which was the thickest, mostly because of her grandfather's growing interest in photography as she was growing up. With a sigh, she went back to the second, her mother's. As Anna carefully turned the brittle, yellowed pages, she wondered what it was about Lily that had made her take up drugs. Was she really that heartbroken that the father of her baby wasn't coming back? When Anna was born, she had been very young and was apparently unable to cope with the changes that a child would bring about in her life. Anna felt such resentment. What right did Lily have to think about only herself and not her child? Why had she just taken off? Anna would never know the answer. Besides, she told herself, it would probably be painful to learn the truth. As she flipped through the pages of the child growing from girl to young woman, she saw lots of black-and-white photos of Lily with boys… on dates, with groups of friends, surfing, boating, in skirted bathing suits on the beach. Then, there was one photo that caught her eye. The photo was shot, probably by her grandfather, on the oceanfront lawn in front of her grandparents' home. Her mother looked to be about the age of seventeen. The young man standing beside her was very European-looking. Dark features, heavy eyebrows, curly black hair, a neck scarf tied loosely in his open shirt, a cigarette hanging from his lips. He was leaning into her, holding her around the waist. She was smiling. Anna stared at the photo for a long time. She carefully removed it from its flimsy, black paper corners and looked at it closely. No writing on the back. No name, date, occasion. She hated it when people didn't write anything to identify the subject on the back of photos. The young man's features resembled Anna's, especially around the nose and chin. She was suddenly certain that this was her father—Diamanté *fils*—the young Corsican who had won her mother's heart, seduced her, and left her with child. Did he love Lily Ellis? It was hard to tell from the photo. But Anna knew she had to find out more. The answer just might be in Strasbourg. She looked at her watch as she picked up the phone. It was one minute to midnight.

Mark's cell phone woke him from a deep sleep. He panicked when he saw who was calling. "Anna? What's wrong? Are you okay? Christ, it's the middle of the night."

"I'll go to Strasbourg with you...on one condition...that I pay my own way. Now go back to sleep. I'll explain in the morning." She hung up.

"It is morning..." he said, smiling into the dead phone. Somewhere along the hallways of the New York Marriott in Times Square, there was heard a loud "WAH HOOOO!" about three in the morning.

CHAPTER 15

Near London, England

"Dr. Gérard?"

"*Oui,*" he said softly.

"You are free to go now. Are you ready?"

The doctor nodded.

"Follow me, then."

Charles-Christian Gérard closed his medical kit and followed the British armed guard from the room. At the end of the long, empty, whitewashed corridor, a scarf was placed over his eyes, and he was escorted a short distance and helped into a vehicle. After what he guessed to be an hour's drive, he was transferred, still blindfolded, to what sounded like whirling blades of the rotor of a helicopter ready for takeoff. The noise was deafening, and a person was holding onto him, forcefully keeping him upright and guiding him so he wouldn't fall in the wind. The air smelled of dampness and diesel fuel.

"You are going home, Doc," the pilot explained to him, once they were in the air. "You can take off that bloody blindfold now."

Charles-Christian removed the scarf and blinked his eyes. He recognized the pilot. He was the same man who had flown them out of Le Havre over three months ago.

"Name's Geoffrey." The pilot leaned over and shook the doctor's hand. "How is she, Doc?"

Charles-Christian looked at him. "I am not at liberty to divulge," he said above the noise and vibrations of the helicopter.

"Understand. Guess that means she's still alive." The pilot smiled as he guided the heavy military chopper over the foggy Normandy coast. "You have done well. Now sit back, Doc. We are going into the Paris basin."

"Do you know what happened to the other two men who were with us? The old *mecs*?"

"Fraid bloody not." The pilot shook his head.

There was no more conversation. Charles-Christian was lost in his thoughts as he watched the brown, lifeless winter landscape of France move swiftly by below them.

He was forty years old, unmarried, and devoted to his work. He was not a tall man, not heavy and thick-boned like his father, but fine-boned like his mother. Slim and graceful with erect posture, he exuded competence and confidence. Soft-spoken and a man of few words, he often came off as curt. He had his mother's unmistakable gray eyes: light and transparent in happier moments, they turned to a stormy, smoky charcoal in times of turmoil. He had attended Paris Université VI, the medical school. His father, Jacques, had funded his education. He had grown up working in the restaurant on the rue du Gros-Horloge in Rouen and living in his parents' apartment above it. Nathalie, his mother, was the hostess, and as he got older he occasionally performed the duties of the sommelier. He was an only child and very indulged, especially by his mother, who adored him. Thus Charles-Christian had grown up to be a self-centered man, focused on his own world. A man with no personal life.

He raked his slightly graying hair as he thought now about his life and the people he had known. He had always been serious, responsible, focused on his profession, but prone to quick decision (not always the right one, his inner voice now told him), and he had pushed people out of his life, shut them out, especially the one woman he had loved. His lips became tight, and his upper lip thinned. Anna. She too was gone from his life.

As the helicopter put down on the helipad at Orly Airport, driving sleet hit the windshield. Charles-Christian wondered where he would go from here in his life. It was not even certain whether he still had a position at the hospital.

"Watch yourself, Doc," Geoffrey told him as they shook hands good-bye.

Charles-Christian nodded and climbed out, wondering what the man had meant by that.

He would soon find out.

CHAPTER 16

The pilot announced their descent into Strasbourg Airport.

"*Mesdames et Messieurs. Nous commençons notre descente pour l'aéroport de* Strasbourg."

Anna looked out the window. It was eight o'clock in the evening, dark. Light rain mixed with snow was pelting the outside pane. The plane bounced around in the turbulence caused by the Vosges mountains she knew they were flying over. Inside the dimly lit cabin, passengers shifted nervously in the narrow seats. A child across the aisle was crying, and his mother bounced him up and down, trying to get him to calm down. An elderly woman in the seat ahead tried to tell the mother that it was because the baby's ears were closed in the descent, but the mother ignored her. A young man with a small dog stuffed in his backpack sat in the seat next to the elderly woman, and she would periodically lean over to pet the dog and coo, "Oooh, *mon petit bebéee!*"

All of this irritated Anna. After so many hours traveling, the seat felt uncomfortable, and her head ached. The air was stuffy. All she wanted was a bed.

Mark was asleep in the seat next to her. His long legs barely fit against the seat, and his blue jeans, navy blue CAL sweatshirt, and flashy Nike jogging shoes made him look more like a college kid than an attorney on his way to meetings at the seat of the European Union. For a man who selected his weekend wardrobe in Los Angeles as carefully as he selected his business attire, this look clearly was out of character. She smiled. He looked so sexy in his sleep. What did sexy mean, anyway? She had pondered that word in her writings, used it indiscriminately, too. She could never decide whether it was an individual interpretation or a cliché, but it was definitely a word that was overused in romantic fiction. Whatever, Mark looked sexy to her tonight. She had hardly seen him in the past couple of weeks. He had been on the East Coast for several days and had been working long hours since arriving home. They had hurriedly packed and headed to Los Angeles International for their direct flight to Paris via Air France.

"I have some good news," she had told him over champagne and dinner as the huge 747 soared over North America. "My agent, Harry, arranged for my last novel, *An Unexpected Turn*, to be translated into several languages. The French version is ready for distribution. I'll finally be able to do a book signing in Paris, if he can schedule it while we're over here. He'll call me if he's successful."

Harry had not been happy with the news of a delay in her latest book, *Pas de Deux*, when they met at Spago in L.A. for lunch on Friday two weeks before. A rotund man with a bulbous red nose, he had worn a pin-striped suit with a garish, bright green tie and looked more like he was a clown auditioning in Hollywood than a literary agent. He had the personality of a joker, too, but he was in reality a serious agent who was known in literary circles, and he had done well by her as her representative. This latest coup, as he had called it, would bring in a sizable sum for them both, and it would fetch her international recognition.

"So, you are going to be famous everywhere." Mark had beamed at her.

After the eleven-hour flight, they had arrived at terminal C at Charles de Gaulle. Four hours later, they had been through customs, exchanged their dollars, had a bite to eat, taken the airport shuttle to terminal D, and were aboard the one hour France Inter flight to Strasbourg.

Mark woke as the plane tires hit the runway and roared to a stop. The airport was deserted, except for a few people having a cocktail at the bar. In no time at all, they were in a black Mercedes taxi, speeding through freezing rain into the center of the old city.

"I found a very *romantique* hotel for us," he had told her. She hadn't known how to react to that comment. In fact, he had finally reassured her, his travel agent had recommended it, and he had no guarantees as to the romantic promise. It was owned by a German-based chain known as Romantik hotels all over Europe and had recently been renovated. What was important to him, he had said, was that the location was near the center of the city so he could easily take a taxi or walk, weather permitting, to his meetings and they would have easy access to restaurants, his other priority.

The Mercedes pulled up in front of a quaint hotel on a quiet street just around the corner from the canal. The entrance was through a small cobblestone courtyard. There was no one in the tiny lobby when they arrived. The breakfast room off the lobby was darkened. Anna pressed the button on the bell at the front desk. A thin, blond-haired woman appeared. Anna guessed that she was in her late forties.

"*Bonsoir, M'sieur,* '*Dame.* Ah, *vous êtes les américains?*" the woman said, taking obvious note of Mark's attire. "*On vous attends. Vous devez être fatigués.* Jean-Michel, *viens toute de suite. Ils sont arrivés, enfin."* Her accent was thick, and she sounded as if she had cotton balls stuffed in her cheeks. Anna remembered from her previous visit to Strasbourg that the regional Alsatian patois had been difficult for her to understand.

"*Bonsoir, Madame. Oui, le vol de Los Angeles a pris du temps.*"

Mark stood by in silence as Anna apologized for their late arrival. A dark-haired young man, Jean-Michel, appeared from the back office and escorted them to the elevator. At the third floor, the doors opened to a long, darkened hallway. Jean-Michel pushed a button, and the hall lights came on. They walked down the hallway to a door at the end.

"This light thing will take some getting used to," Mark remarked to Anna.

"They're on a timer. It's called a *minuterie*. It's pretty common in hotels in France, especially in the provinces. Saves electricity. I think it's kinda quaint."

"Actually, it's not such a bad idea—saving energy, that is."

Their suite was decorated Alsatian-style with a low, wood-beamed ceiling. A large fireplace was surrounded by two upholstered loveseats. A writing desk stood beneath a window that overlooked the street. On a small, round table sat a silver bucket containing a bottle of Moët et Chandon champagne in a bath of melting ice.

Mark looked around, his hands on his hips.

"Umm, there's something missing here. Where are we supposed to sleep? There doesn't appear to be any bed."

Jean-Michel smiled and pointed his index finger straight up. "*Voilà, Monsieur. En haut.*"

Their eyes followed the direction of his finger. Above a small, open stairway, tucked under a large beam, could be seen the corner of a bed in a loft overlooking the room below. Anna climbed the stairs. Her slightly muffled comments floated down as she disappeared into the loft.

"It's got a down comforter and huge pillows. Euro style. Looks comfy." She appeared at the top of the steps. "Where are you sleeping, Mark?"

"Ah," he said, scratching his head. This definitely wasn't going the way he had intended.

To their amusement, the bellman proceeded to demonstrate how one of the loveseats could be pulled out to a full-size bed. "*À votre service, Monsieur.*"

"Er, mercy."

Anna made a mental note to teach Mark how to pronounce *merci* correctly with the accent on the last syllable.

Jean-Michel opened the door with a professional nod.

"*Bonne nuit, M'sieur. 'Dame,*" he said as Mark handed him a tip.

Once they were alone, Mark poured them each a glass of champagne then opened his briefcase and started taking out the contents.

"Oh, no, Mark, you're not going to work tonight, are you?"

"No, it's just that…" he was fumbling around looking for something. "I've got something for you. Ah, here it is." He pulled out a little package. "I bought this for you at the duty free shop in the airport in Paris while you were freshening up. It's to say mercy," he pronounced *merci* wrong again, "for making this trip with me."

The prettily wrapped package contained a bottle of Allure perfume.

"The woman who helped me spoke English." He grinned. "She told me that Chanel is very popular."

She hugged him. "You are a thoughtful man, Mark."

"Haven't you figured out by now that I'm an incurable romantic?" He put his arms around her shoulders and kissed her. "I'm on cloud nine now that you are here with me."

Anna looked up to the loft. The fatigue she had felt on the plane was suddenly gone. What the hell. She was in France again. She threw her arms around his neck.

"Make love to me, Mark," she whispered softly into his ear.

CHAPTER 17

At eight o'clock in the morning, Anna was awakened from a deep sleep by sounds from the street. It was still pitch dark. She wrapped a blanket around her, put on her slippers, and descended from the loft. A market across from the hotel was getting its morning deliveries. Fresh produce was being unloaded from a farmer's truck. *Camionettes*, small delivery trucks, their doors open, lined the street, panels advertising Orangina, Badoit, Perrier, Vins fins d'Alsace. Anna watched the charming and provincial scene with fascination from the window over the writing desk. She heard pigeons softly cooing from their perch on the red tile roof overhang. At dawn the cathedral's bells began to toll. Anna peered into the distance. The outline of the single, tall spire of the great pinkish-red Gothic cathedral dominated the view.

Mark appeared behind her in his sweats. She turned to look at him and put her hands on her hips. "You look rejuvenated."

"I'm going for a morning jog," he announced.

"In this weather? It's bitterly cold out there." Anna glared at him.

"Hey, I'm up to it." He glanced out the window at the canal. "The water doesn't look frozen, and the rain or sleet or whatever it was has quit. Besides," he reassured her, "I've been conditioned.

I've been jogging in Central Park while I've been in New York…in the snow. There were always lots of runners out. Got this winter running garb there."

Anna laughed as she watched him pull on a heavy jacket, winter leggings, and gloves.

"No wonder your luggage was so bulky."

He isn't likely to meet up with a crowd of runners here, she thought. *Hardly anyone ever jogs on the streets in France.*

Out he went, looking for all the world like an athlete in training.

In he came, freezing and grumbling, a half hour later.

"It's impossible to run on those cobblestones. And doesn't anyone ever pick up their dog's poop in this city? It's an accident waiting to happen. I nearly sprained an ankle twice."

Anna laughed. "It's the law that owners are supposed to pick up after their dogs, but the French always ignore it. That's the way the French are."

She had managed to unpack, get a shower, and don a pair of black wool pants and a hunter green turtleneck sweater while he was out.

"You smell good, gorgeous." He snuggled into her.

"It's the new perfume you gave me."

"Mmm…sooo good," he moaned as he nuzzled in closer and kissed her. "Last night was fantastic."

Anna couldn't understand her own emotions. She was drawn to him sexually, that was certain, but was she in love with him? She drew back suddenly, releasing herself from his embrace.

His eyes narrowed. "What's wrong?"

"It's just…oh, nothing." She grabbed his hand. "Come on. I'm famished. The breakfast room is still open."

The cozy, wood-paneled room off the lobby was mostly deserted. Mark and Anna poured generous, oversized breakfast bowls of *café crème* and slathered slim *tartines* and big flaky croissants with rich, sweet cream butter and fresh fruit preserves.

"What say we do some sightseeing today?" Mark said tentatively as he sat down. "I don't have any meetings scheduled until tomorrow, but after that my agenda is pretty full. You said you had visited Strasbourg before?"

"Yes. A few years ago. I was on my way with a friend to visit the Black Forest in Germany for a weekend. We didn't stop over for very long. I think I only saw the cathedral. We had lunch and did some shopping."

"I was in Strasbourg once myself. I was five years old, so I don't remember much, but everything sure seems smaller now. Except for the cathedral. It's still as huge as I remembered it. I came across it in the square this morning. I have the strangest memory of seeing something inside that everyone was oohing and ahhing over."

"The astronomical clock, probably. My friend told me about it. Something about a parade of the Apostles every day around noon. I've never seen it myself."

The friend she had been with was C-C. They had walked around the cathedral square arm in arm, and he had told her about going to see his grandparents who lived in Strasbourg. She was silent for a minute, looking at Mark, but seeing and hearing C-C across the table from her, his gray eyes, not Mark's hazel eyes, staring back at her from years ago.

"Every summer," the gray eyes stared at her as her memory re-played C-C's narration, "*Maman* would take me with her to Stras-bourg to visit *Grand-père*. My favorite thing to do was to go with him to see the astronomical clock in the Cathédrale Notre Dame. This is no ordinary clock like the *gros horloge* over the street in Rouen. This clock was magical to a little boy. Everyday just after noon, the clock literally woke up. I remember it in vivid detail. *Grand-père* and I would walk up the cobblestone street that led to the cathedral. Then we would wait impatiently by the south portal, looking up at the spire, until the guards would let us file in. *Grand-père*, in his soft, low voice, would bend over and whisper in my ear all the details he knew about the clock."

Anna couldn't recall all the rest of the details, but the story had gone on for some time.

"Well, then…" Mark had been watching her face. The expres-sion was different somehow, melancholy. His hesitant voice brought her back to the present. "I…I'd like to see that clock."

"There's something else I've got to do this week, Mark." Anna stared pensively into her coffee. "I didn't mention it before, but there is someone I have to find while we are here."

Anna shared with Mark the story of the Christmas card she had found in her grandfather's keepsakes box.

"I have a feeling that if I can find the person who sent it, if he is still alive or maybe his wife…maybe this is just another piece of the puzzle. I'm not sure what I'll learn, but it's worth an attempt."

"Maybe my contacts here can help," Mark offered. "They're a legal firm. They must have access to all the directory information. I'll get on it tomorrow."

The day was cold and clear. Anna nestled her nose in the soft, fake fur collar of her coat as they stepped out into the cobbled street. They walked past the market, now bustling with Strasbourgeoises purchasing their daily produce, and across the bridge over the canal into the main part of the city.

Immediately, she noticed the difference. In Paris, she was used to blending in. Now she was walking with Mark, who was unmistakably and recognizably American from his Nikes up. She heard the whispered comments as they walked past.

"...*américains*..."

The comments didn't seem malicious, just made out of curiosity, she thought, until a little street kid threw a pile of dirt at Mark and ran away.

"What the...?" Mark wiped his neck. "I'd like to beat that kid to a pulp."

"Check your wallet," Anna said. "The kid's likely a pickpocket."

Mark immediately put his hand on his back pocket.

"Nope. Wallet's still there," he said with a sigh of relief, winking at her.

They rounded the corner, and directly in front of them was the massive pink cathedral. Anna had forgotten how imposing it was. It filled up the entire view ahead of them.

"One of the great Gothic cathedrals of Europe," she said as they went inside. Oddly, it felt cold and unwelcoming to her.

CHAPTER 18

Anna had just powered down her laptop after reading her e-mail when the phone rang.

"Hi, gorgeous." It was Mark calling from the law firm's office in the center of Strasbourg. "I think we may have found your Guy Know All," Mark mispronounced the name, but Anna was getting used to his attempts at French. The other morning he had greeted the blond woman at the front desk in the hotel with a big, toothy "baan jur" to which she had replied in a reserved fashion in perfect English, "Good morning, sir."

"Good news?" Anna held her breath.

"Yeah. Good news. He's still alive. There's a partner here who knows him. Or he did know him. Apparently, this character was a banker for a long time in Strasbourg. Well known, I guess. He retired several years ago. The partner said that he had moved to a small town. Anyway, the admin here found an address for him. It's not far from Strasbourg. I'll get all the information. If you want, we can rent a car on Saturday and drive out. I'll be wrapping up here by the end of the week anyway. I'm game to try driving in France. Couldn't be that much different from L.A."

Anna was ecstatic. She had so many questions.

"Did you catch the name of the town, Mark?"

"Yeah, can't pronounce it, but it's spelled O–B–E–R–N–A–I."

"It's pronounced O-bear-nye. I think it's along the famous Wine Route. I'll get a map and some other information from the hotel and arrange for the car rental. It will be interesting to see the country-side...but there's one thing." She hesitated. "I do the driving, okay? Driving in France is nothing like driving in L.A., even if you are a wild BMW driver."

"Okay, suit yourself, gorgeous. I'll navigate."

CHAPTER 19

On Saturday morning, the sky was gunmetal gray, and the cold promise of snow was in the air. Mark had given up trying to jog in the uneven streets of Strasbourg, but he arose early anyway, put on his warm running garb, and went out for a walk. When he returned, he brought with him hot coffee and croissants. Anna was in bed, listening to her favorite CD: the Vienna Philharmonic playing classic Strauss.

"You are always so thoughtful, Mark." She stretched. "I feel so much better than I have in weeks."

He joined her in bed and cuddled up close to her. She was beautiful, her dark hair lying over her shoulders. Her skin was soft and warm, and she smelled of the perfume he had given her. He nuzzled her cheek.

"I know you don't want to hear this, but I'm in love with you. You realize that, don't you, gorgeous?" He put his arms around her and kissed her. He smelled of fresh air from being outdoors.

"Give me some time, Mark." She ran her fingers through his hair. "I have to admit that I'm getting used to your being around. Besides, you're a pretty good kisser." She lifted her chin for him to kiss her again. "Mmm...say, do you know how to dance? I've never

asked. I mean ballroom stuff, like waltzing. Strauss, for example."
She turned up the volume of the CD.

"Ahhh…the romantic 'Blue Danube' waltz." He gently put his
right hand at the small of her back and took her right hand in his
left, kissed it, and pulled it in close to his chest. "Yeah, I like to
dance," he whispered as he drew her in to him, slightly swaying her
back and forth to the music, "in bed…"

Two hours later, they picked up their rental car, a Le Car.

"Maybe I can ride on top," Mark remarked after moving the seat
as far back as it would go. His long legs barely fit into the front seat.
"My knees are next to my freakin' chin."

"It's the standard rental size. Sorry, Mark," Anna said, laughing.
"I didn't think about that. I should have arranged for a Mercedes."

With Anna at the wheel and Mark still complaining about the
size of the car, they headed out into the drab Alsatian countryside.
Rain mixed with sleet hit the windshield. Anna turned on the wip-
ers and was pleased to see that they worked.

"Hmmm…I'm not used to driving in bad weather. I hope we
don't run into a snow storm." She looked in the rearview mirror.
There wasn't much traffic behind them, so she slowed.

The brown landscape was enshrouded in fog. They passed open
fields and barren vineyards. In the distance, the foothills of the ev-
ergreen-covered Vosges were barely visible in the mist.

Mark studied the map. "According to this, Obernai is only about
thirty kilometers from Strasbourg. At this speed, we'll be lucky if
we make it in time for dinner," he kidded her.

"At least we'll make it," Anna shot back. "Speaking of dinner, we'll have to look for a good restaurant."

"One of the people in the office gave me the name and address of an inn that supposedly has a great restaurant not far from Obernai. He said to try the regional dish...how did he pronounce it? *Chou-croute*. It's supposed to be an Alsatian specialty. He said it's sauerkraut with sausages and ham."

Anna made a face. "I don't much like *chou-croute*. By the way, your French is improving. You said that almost perfectly."

"You're good for me, Anna." He leaned over and pecked her on the cheek. "I'm even starting to like France."

Obernai was picturesque, even in winter. The town was filled with old stone and half-timbered houses, corbelled constructions, most with balconies and bow windows. Ancient wrought-iron signs hung from the buildings.

Anna drove into a central square that was dominated by an ochre-colored building with a carved stone balcony and blue mansard roof.

"That must be the town hall." She pointed to the building. "The Michelin Guide I bought said it goes back to the fourteenth century." The marketplace in front of the building was filled with Saturday shoppers, despite the cold weather. A sign in both French and German advertised the Christmas market in the town center starting on December first and running until the twenty-fourth.

"Let's find a place to park and take a stretch," Mark suggested. "I really need to get out of this car. Besides, we're within walking distance of the address we're looking for."

Anna steered the car down a side street and pulled alongside the curb. There were snow flurries in the air as they got out and walked down the narrow, cobbled street. Anna was silent, thinking about whether Guy de Noailles would be home, and if so, how she would introduce herself. It hadn't occurred to her up to then that he might not understand why she was there or who she was. She almost turned and walked back to the car.

"I really like this town," Mark interrupted her thoughts. "It looks like it's half French and half German, which I guess it is, huh?" He pointed to the leafless skeletons of deciduous trees along the promenade. "They're pretty, those trees, even without the leaves." He looked at her, sensing that she was having second thoughts. "How are you going to know this guy?"

"I don't know." A blast of wind blew snowflakes into her face. She shivered and pulled the faux-fur collar of her coat around her neck and chin. "What if he thinks I'm some kind of nut? I...I..."

Mark put his arm around her. "He won't think you're wacky. Besides, if it turns out to be a dead end, we will have had this trip to the country and our *chou-croute*." He kissed her. "Plus all this kissing I'm so good at."

She smiled. He was right. Maybe she had set her expectations too high.

They rounded the corner. The smoky scent of wood-burning fires filled the air of the quiet street. In front of them was a two-story white stone house with the characteristic half timbers of Alsace. Newly fallen snow layered the pitched roof.

"That's our address," said Mark.

Anna studied the house's details. The brown-shuttered window frames were painted white. Empty wooden window boxes awaited flowers in the spring. Red-checked curtains were visible inside. From the corner of the house at the second-story level hung an object from an intricate, filigree-decorated, wrought-iron bar.

"What do you think that is hanging on that rod? Looks like a bread board with a hole in the middle and a fork and knife crossed inside the hole."

"Probably an old sign for a shopkeeper who lived here at one point. Maybe he owned a bakery or a restaurant. That's how they identified addresses long ago."

They walked up to the heavy, wooden front door. Anna took the knocker in her hand. She looked at Mark. His hazel eyes stared into hers. He nodded his support.

"Okay, here goes." She looked at the Christmas card from long ago, which she held tightly in her hand. "This will be my introduction."

The sound of the knocker resonated on the wooden door. They waited a few minutes. No response. A car passed in the street.

"Doesn't seem to be anyone home." Anna sighed.

Mark encouraged her. "Try knocking again. He's old. Maybe he's a bit deaf."

She knocked twice this time. They waited for what seemed like an eternity. Then they saw one of the curtains move in the window on the floor above. An old man's face peered down at them. Anna held up the card. He didn't move. She smiled. He didn't react. Then he backed away from the window. The curtain closed.

"Oh, what's the use? Let's go, Mark. He doesn't trust us. He's not coming to the door."

"Maybe you could leave your card and that Christmas card with a note by his door. You know, so he could contact you, if he wanted to."

"Actually, that's not a bad idea."

She pulled off her black leather gloves and took one of her business cards and a notepad and pen from her bag. As she started to scribble a note, there was a click. The door opened slowly, with a slight groan, as if reluctant to be budged in the cold.

A small, white-haired man with a handlebar mustache peered at them.

"*Bonjour,*" he greeted them hesitantly. "*Qu'est-ce que vous voulez, Mademoiselle? Monsieur?*" He looked from one to the other.

Anna gathered her confidence. "*Bonjour, Monsieur. Monsieur* de Noailles?" The octogenarian nodded. Anna smiled and apologized in French for the disruption. Then she introduced herself and Mark to him. The old man's handshake was polite and quick. There was an awkward silence until Anna held out the Christmas card for him to see up close. He put on a pair of wire-rimmed reading glasses and took it from her. He paused a moment to study the front, then he opened it. His eyes lit up. He looked up at her and then down at the card again, fingering it carefully.

"But where did you get this, *Mademoiselle?*" he asked her.

"My grandfather was Stu Ellis. An American, from California," she explained. "Did you possibly know him? Maybe from the war? He was a flier. I found the card in his things after he passed away recently."

He looked at her and at Mark. "I think this is going to be a long conversation." He stood aside and opened the creaky door wider. "You must come in, *Mademoiselle. Monsieur*, too. It is cold outside. We will all freeze."

Mark looked confused, not having understood a word.

"He wants us to come in. I think he recognized my grandfather's name, Mark."

CHAPTER 20

Guy de Noailles was a small, thin man dressed neatly in brown wool trousers, a navy blue flannel shirt, and a well-worn, camel-colored sweater with dark brown, suede-patched elbows. He walked with a slight limp, but, for an octogenarian, he was very limber.

He took their coats and led Anna and Mark to a large study just off the foyer. Anna stood for a minute, warming her hands in front of the glowing fire in the fireplace. The room was cozy and inviting. A giant Persian rug covered most of the wooden floor. A painting above the fireplace depicted the great cathedral of Strasbourg with its single spire. On the mantel were silver frames with photos. One wall was lined with bookcases filled with books. A round table in the corner held more framed photos.

Guy de Noailles was soft-spoken, and he had an endearingly polite way about him. He motioned for them to sit on the sofa, then settled himself in a chair by the fireplace. He propped his silver-topped walking stick against the arm and looked at Anna.

"You say Stu Ellis was your grandfather?"

Anna was relieved that his accent in French was easy to understand, and she liked him immediately.

"*Oui, Monsieur*. He and my grandmother were in a horrible automobile accident very recently." Her voice caught in her throat. "Neither of them survived."

"I am very sorry to hear that. He was a good man. During the war, we saved many American fliers who were shot down over our country. I keep the photos as a reminder." The old man waved his hand in the direction of the round table in the corner. Fingering the Christmas card, he said, "This was sent from Strasbourg a long time ago. How did you know where to find me?"

"My friend here." She nodded in Mark's direction. "There is someone he has been working with in Strasbourg who knows you." She leaned over to Mark. "What was the name of the man in Strasbourg who knows *Monsieur* de Noailles?"

"Forestier. Claude Forestier. I think that's how you pronounce it." Mark winked and shot her a grin.

"Ah, I know him. I was a banker in Strasbourg for a long time. Claude and I had many clients in common." Noailles nodded his head and twirled the ends of his white mustache between his thumb and index finger. "How is the fellow?"

Mark was staring at him blankly. Anna realized that he hadn't understood that the question in French had been directed at him.

"He said they had many clients in common. He wants to know how this Forestier is."

Mark cocked his head to one side and grinned.

"You will have to tone this down in translation. Forestier is feisty. He was the most opinionated, obstinate, dictatorial SOB that I have worked with in a long time. But," he added, "I have to admit that he is getting results with our case."

When she had translated Mark's comments, almost verbatim, there was a chortle from deep in the old man's throat, and he said with a twinkle in his eye, "*Pas beaucoup changé, alors, mon vieux collègue.*"

"He said he's not much changed, then." She and Mark laughed.

"Would you like some tea? My housekeeper is out for the afternoon, but I think I can manage." Guy de Noailles got up slowly and disappeared into the back of the house. They could hear water running from the tap and then china rattling.

Anna stood and walked over to the mantel to have a closer look at the collection of family photos. She studied a large, black-and-white photo of a young couple in wedding clothes posed in front of a town hall. Anna guessed that the thin, dark-haired young bridegroom was Guy de Noailles, though, with the exception of a pair of distinctly close-knit eyebrows, the resemblance to the man they had just met was barely visible. There were other photos of the same couple, a year or two later with a little girl between them. The rest of the framed photos appeared to be of the little girl, apparently their daughter, as she grew to adulthood. Then there was a photo of her in a wedding gown. And another of her holding a baby. The last photo on the mantel was in color. It was of an older Guy de Noailles, probably in his fifties, graying and thicker through the middle, holding the hand of a small boy in front of the Strasbourg Cathedral. The photographer had apparently tried to get in the whole cathedral, so the faces of the two were barely visible. *Life's itinerary,* Anna thought.

She moved over to the table. Here, the photos were different, much older, all black-and-white.

Mark was standing over them. "I am fascinated by old war photos," he said. "Look at the uniforms and the faces. Is your grandfather in any of them?"

Anna studied the photos closely. There was one of a large group, not so much posing but standing around in a wooded area waiting for something. They all were looking up. She pointed to a light-haired young man in the back row.

"That man looks a good deal like him. There is a similarity to my grandfather's earlier photos, anyway, but it's too blurry to make out. Wish I had a magnifying glass."

Another photo caught her attention. The inhabitants of this one were male, all certainly French. They appeared to be congregating in a wooden, barn-like structure. A thin, dark haired man of about thirty-five with closely knit eyebrows was seated prominently on a wine barrel. He wore a World War II–era, wide pin-striped suit and a dark aviator's scarf around his neck. His gaze was deadly serious, his eyes black and piercing. He held a torch in one hand. The other hand was on his knee. Anna pointed to the image.

"This has to be *Monsieur* de Noailles. Look at those eyebrows, Mark."

The group varied in age, some not yet twenty, others much older. None of them were smiling. They were scattered about the room and appeared to be assembled for a meeting of some sort. Most wore similar wide pin-striped suits with or without white shirts and neckties and heavy overcoats. The exception in dress was one man who wore a heavy jacket and pants. His boots were splattered with mud. A dark beret was perched low over his forehead. Another man, barely visible in the back of the group by the door, also wore similar dress and a beret.

As they were studying the photo, Guy de Noailles returned with the tea tray and set it on a table.

"Ah, I see you have found the Résistance a fascination. That's quite a group, don't you think? Can you pick me out? It was a long time ago."

Anna looked at his piercing black eyes and the thick, white, knitted eyebrows. "He wants to know if we can pick him out, Mark." They pointed in unison to the figure seated on the wine barrel.

The old man smiled. He nodded in Mark's direction.

"I was about the age of your friend here when that photo was taken. We were scared that night. The Gestapo was very near. It was toward the end of the war, and we were waiting for the Americans. It was the last time that we were all together. Only a few of us are still alive." He heaved a huge sigh.

"Where were you born, *Monsieur?*" Anna asked. "You don't have an Alsatian accent. You sound like you might be from Normandy."

"*Très bien, Mademoiselle*. I am Norman, actually." He poured the tea from the antique teapot into matching china cups, set the cups on their saucers, and handed them to Anna and Mark. Despite his age, his hands were as steady as theirs.

"When I was a young man," he said, "I left the farm in Normandy where I had grown up. I eagerly went off to the war, but I was wounded in the leg and ended up in a hospital in Italy. My leg was so badly mangled that I was no longer any use as a soldier, so I was sent home to France. The war was at its worse for us then. I married my dear wife, and we settled here in Alsace. I joined the Résistance. It was very dangerous, but it was a way that I could still fight the Boche."

Anna took a sip of the tea. It tasted of orange and cinnamon.

"It tastes good. *Merci*." She took another sip and pointed to the bride in the wedding photo on the mantel. "Is that your wife, Nathalie?"

The old man looked up, confused. "Nathalie?" Then he nodded his head.

"Oh, oh…understood. That is my wedding photo, *oui*, but my wife's name was Marguerite. She died very young. Our daughter's name was Nathalie."

"So that explains the card. You signed it from you and your daughter."

"*Oui, Mademoiselle*. I raised her alone. There were just the two of us after my wife died."

"Where is your daughter now?"

The hurt eyes met hers. Anna was immediately sorry she had asked such an intimate question. She knew the French to be very private people, and she had stepped over the line.

"Oh, *Monsieur*, forgive me for prying. I don't know you very well. I didn't mean to…"

"*Non, non, Mademoiselle*," he interrupted. "No need to apologize. It's, it's just that my daughter Nathalie died two years ago." He broke off and rubbed the tip of his nose with a gnarled index finger.

CHAPTER 21

A door opened at the back of the house, and voices could be heard. A fluffy, ginger-colored little dog scurried into the room and jumped into the old man's lap.

"This is Puccini," Guy de Noailles explained to Anna and Mark. "He is my housekeeper's poodle. Ah, Jean-Paul. *Viens*." He beckoned for a short, stocky man, nearly as old as he, to come into the room. "This is Jean-Paul, my chauffeur. He and his wife, Maria, have been with me for a very long time. They are my family. They helped me raise Nathalie."

The chauffeur, dressed entirely in black, took off his cap and shyly shook their hands. From the kitchen came a horrified scream and a crash.

"*Mamma mia! Merda! Santa Patata vergine!*"

"That is Maria. Not to worry. She's just discovered that I was in her kitchen making tea." The old man's eyes twinkled. "Maria, come meet our guests."

Mark leaned over with mischief in his eyes and whispered to Anna, "If I'm not mistaken, I think she just said 'Holy virgin potato' in Italian." They both laughed.

Into the room came a round little woman in a fury, with wisps of wiry, graying hair spewing from under a heavy, woolen hat. She still had her coat on. Seeing Anna and Mark, she stopped in the doorway and put her hands on her ample hips.

"Maria, my apologies. I made my guests tea this afternoon. This is Anna...and her friend Mark. They are Americans. I knew Anna's grandfather in the war."

Maria studied Mark. He was almost a third again as tall as she. Puccini ran back and forth and around them all, wagging his tail. He stopped in front of Mark and sat down.

"Mark and dogs have an *affaire de coeur*, a love affair," explained Anna, laughing. She directed the next remark to Puccini. "He is Italian, also."

With that, Maria's eyes widened.

"Italiano? *Américain?*"

Mark understood that one. "American, *sì, signora*, but my name is Zennelli."

"Ah, *sì*! I know that name Zennelli." She spoke in English with a heavy Italian lilt. "I learn some English from American films. I *love* American films! That name Zennelli famous. You actor?"

"No, but my family is active in film. I am a lawyer."

This time Anna was translating into French.

Maria was in a total state of happiness. She took off her hat and coat and threw them onto a chair, all the time muttering something about being so honored to meet someone from a famous American film family. Then she went over and shook Mark's hand, giving it several pumps, and kissed Anna on both cheeks like they were old friends.

"*Allora*, you must stay for *cena*. I make a special *pollo alla cacciatora* for Marco here." She had christened Mark with the Italian version of his name. Then she caught herself and turned to her employer. "*Monsieur?*"

Guy de Noailles understood her request. He simply needed to make the formal invitation.

"It would be our pleasure if you would be our guests for dinner. Maria is a very good cook. If she is making an Italian specialty, we are all in for a treat."

Anna and Mark smiled and nodded at each other. Of course, they would stay, she said.

Jean-Paul placed a log on the fire. It sputtered and crackled. "The Beaujolais Nouveau has just arrived," he told Guy de Noailles. "We bought a case of it today."

"*Magnifique.* We'll have it with our dinner. I hope it's good this year," Guy said.

With that, the chauffeur and the housekeeper left the room. Pots and pans clanged; dishes and silverware rattled. Maria would sing arias in Italian to the chopping of vegetables all the rest of the afternoon. In an hour, the entire house would be filled with the delicious aroma of chicken and mushrooms and tomatoes stewing in herbs.

Anna excused herself and found *le cabinet*. The small space was painted a deep emerald green, and it had a black-and-white checkerboard tiled floor. A dozen gold-framed engravings of scenes of rural France filled the wall. Anna looked at herself in the beveled, heart-shaped, black-framed mirror. She couldn't help feeling that her grandfather had led her to Guy de Noailles, that maybe he was with her now.

When she returned to the study, Puccini was snuggled in Mark's lap, asleep. Mark stroked the little dog's ear.

"This dog," he said, "even looks like an Italian composer. Look at that shaggy hair." It was true. The dog had not been given the typical coif of the Parisian poodle.

Soft snores came from the chair by the fire. Guy de Noailles too had fallen asleep.

Anna went over to look at the photos on the round table. There was something about the picture of the members of the Résistance movement in the barn-like structure that intrigued her.

The old man coughed in his sleep and awakened.

"Were they all French?" she asked him, pointing to the photo.

He shifted drowsily in his chair and sat up, clearing his throat.

"Technically, yes. Two of them were Corsican."

"Two? Which two?" She studied the photo carefully.

"The two with the berets. The one in front, and the other toward the back. You can't see him very well."

Something told Anna not to let this go. After all, Stu Ellis had also known a Corsican during the war. Maybe Guy de Noailles could provide the clue she so desperately needed.

"Do you have any other photos of the Corsicans?"

Mark was watching her.

"Just one," Guy said. "It's toward the back of the table. The small one in color over there to the right, with the dark frame."

Anna picked it up. There were two men in the photo. They were posed on a hilltop overlooking the sea. The scenery was very beautiful. The older man in a beret appeared to be the same one who was in the group photo. Both of the men were suntanned. They had white shirts open at the collar and scarves tied around their necks. The older man had put his arm over the shoulder of the younger, who had a cigarette drooping from the corner of his mouth. Neither smiled, but they didn't look unhappy.

"Is this the same man as in the other photo?"

"Yes. But it's several years later. He was with his son in Corsica."

Anna looked at it closely. The son's face was unmistakable. She grabbed her purse and took out a photo. "Look at this, Mark. Do you think this is the same person?" She sat down beside him and held the photo side by side with the framed photo from the table.

"I found this in one of my grandparents' albums." She pointed to the girl in the photo. "That's my mother when she was about seventeen. There were no names written in the album and nothing on the back of the photo. I just have a feeling that the young man in this photo was my father."

Guy de Noailles looked at them curiously, not understanding.

Mark studied both photos carefully. After a few minutes, he said, "I believe they are the same person, Anna. In fact, I'm sure they are. There are too many similarities: the black curly hair, the mole under his eye, the cleft in the chin, the way he holds his head."

She held her breath. "*Monsieur*," she said to Guy de Noailles. "What are the names of the father and son in this photo? Do you remember?"

"But of course, my dear. Diamanté is my good friend. Loupré-Tigre is his last name. His son was his namesake. Why would that be important to you?"

CHAPTER 22

Anna didn't know whether to laugh or cry. She hugged Mark. "That's the name my grandfather gave me, but he could only remember the first name and something about a wolf or tiger or something."

Guy de Noailles was watching her patiently.

"*Monsieur*," she said, "from what my grandfather told me just before he died, the young man in this photo of yours is my father." She handed him the photo from her grandparents' album and told him as briefly as she could the story her grandfather had related on his deathbed.

He put on his reading spectacles and studied the two photos closely. Then he took off his spectacles and looked at her face. His eyes narrowed.

"Diamanté Loupré-Tigre has been my friend for over fifty years. We met as members of the Résistance during the last years of the war and have visited each other frequently. I have never heard Diamanté speak of a grandchild, *Mademoiselle*. He would have told me."

"Do you know when this photo was taken?"

"Yes. Diamanté brought it when he visited me after his son's death. He had a duplicate of it that he kept always tucked inside his beret. It was the last time he saw his son."

"Then it could have been taken after Diamanté *fils* had been in California for training. He was possibly never aware of my mother's pregnancy," Anna said more or less to herself than to anyone in the room. The two men were silent, watching her.

"*Monsieur*...."

Holding up his hand, the old man stopped her from speaking. The tone of his voice softened.

"I believe it is time for you to call me Guy. We do not need to be so formal now. My friend Diamanté is like a brother to me. He would be most amazed at this story. I am sorry that he is not here to hear it. If he is indeed your grandfather..."

"Do you know where he is?"

"*Non*. The last I heard from him was in August. He was on his way to Paris. There was something important going on. He was asking for my son-in-law's phone number in Rouen. That's all he could tell me. I have not heard from him since."

"Is that unusual?"

"*Non*, again. He has been known to disappear from time to time. Mostly, it's that he goes back to Corsica. But I have become worried as Christmas approaches. We always contact each other during the holidays."

"Tell me about Diamanté." Anna wanted to learn everything she could about her Corsican grandfather. At that point, Mark leaned over to her.

"Guess it's time to leave you two alone. I'm going out for a walk. Get some fresh air. I'd like to see what that town square looks like lit up at night."

She nodded and watched him put on his jacket and gloves. He opened the front door, giving her a quick, reassuring look as he closed it behind him.

"He's a nice young man," Guy said.

"Tell me about Diamanté," Anna repeated her request.

"His full name is Diamanté Soudain Loupré-Tigre," he began. Guy de Noailles knew Diamanté's story well. "During the war, we all called him *le loup*, the wolf, because of the way he would follow you with his piercing eyes. He's tough, that one, and he has weathered a lot of storms. He is the type of man who never stands by to let events take their course, and he is not afraid of death." He paused and took a sip of tea.

"But I must go back to the beginning, Anna. Diamanté was born in Castagglione, on the east coast of the island of Corsica. He is younger than I am, by more than a decade. He must be almost seventy-five by now. He left Corsica at around the age of fifteen and became a metallurgical worker outside Marseilles. When the war started, he must have been about eighteen. From the very beginning, he helped organize resistance to the occupation. He operated out of the unoccupied zone in the south. Northern France was in the occupied zone. It was virtually impossible for fliers shot down over the Channel or over Normandy to escape via the coast. As the Résistance activities became more critical to the war effort, a group was formed in Rouen—*Les Amis Clandestins,* they called themselves. *Les Amis* worked tirelessly to rescue people who were in danger. They sent the 'evaders,' as we called the rescued fliers like your grandfather, to Diamanté by train. He hid them until the network could supply them with civilian clothes and money and then escorted them to the railway station. The escape line was an elaborate route that took the 'evaders' eventually out of France, sometimes via air, sometimes via boat. Sometimes they were hidden in monasteries for months while false papers were made out. They were taught how to 'behave' and given cover stories to rehearse if they were caught. It was an incredible effort.

"The original name for the Résistance was the *maquis*. It was coined in Corsica after the name for the dense hillside undergrowth that covers the lowlands. There were about two hundred members of the *maquis* in northern France. We fought to the death and were prepared to cut our own wrists to avoid capture and torture that could wring from us information fatal to our fellows.

"Diamanté and I participated together in both escape lines until he was captured. He never talked much about the experience. I only got *un bon morceau*, a tidbit, every so often as a clue." He cleared his throat and fingered the top of his walking stick. "The story I know to be true about when he was captured was that the enemy set out to break him. Enraged at his obstinacy, they threatened to shoot him on the spot. When that didn't work, they locked him in a dark hut with a corpse, then, finally, threw him in a prison. His health was not good for years as a result of the severe beatings he endured during the interrogations. He still bears a scar on his head where he was struck by a rifle butt. Finally, he managed to flee from a hospital where he had been placed under surveillance after attempting suicide. As the war progressed, he assisted in thousands of escapes from France. He should have been one of France's most decorated Résistance heroes, but he went back to Corsica after the war was over. I think he didn't want the notoriety. *Quand même*, he is still well-respected," he hesitated, "among those who remember, for his courage."

"What did he do after he went back to Corsica when the war was over?"

"Ah, now there's a love story for you, Anna. He didn't go back to Castagglione, but to the other side of the island, to the capital, Ajaccio. That's where he met Clotilde. She was a pretty one. Dark hair, eyes like yours. Diamanté would have married her the day he met her, he was so much love-struck. As it was, the Corsican ways prevailed, and they had to wait. He set out to learn the restaurant business, and he worked hard to prove himself to her family. Finally, the marriage was granted, and they were very happy. She died several years ago. I don't recall when, but it was a year or so after their son was killed. They were both heartbroken. He was a handsome young man, their only child."

Guy eased himself out of his chair and went over to the fireplace. He stood for a long time, staring into the fire. He looked up at the photos on the mantel, took the one of his and Marguerite's wedding in his hands and fondled it for a moment, then put it down. He turned around and looked at Anna. His eyes were moist.

"I'm sorry. I was just remembering my Marguerite." He sighed. "Ah, those were such good times back then after the war was over. The country was in ruins, but we had hope and each other. Eventually things got better, and we were busy with the day-to-day work of living. Time goes by fast. Suddenly, you are white-haired like me and..." He didn't finish the sentence. His voice just trailed off.

"Does Diamanté have any relatives?"

"As far as I know, Diamanté is all alone now. He had a brother, Ferdinand, who lived in Paris. He participated in the *Francs-Tireurs et Partisans*, or Snipers and Partisans, in the Paris region. That was the group that organized the uprising against the occupiers the week before the liberation of Paris in August 1944. He is no longer living. His wife still lives in Paris, as far as I know."

"Does Diamanté still live in Corsica?"

"*Non*. He moved again to the south of France a few years ago. His health improved considerably. Recently, he has occupied himself with his own restaurant. I visited him once after he first bought the place. It's in a very quaint village, even quainter than Obernai, about twenty kilometers from Nice. The village had just three hotels, two *restos*, a single *boulangerie*, and a *chocolaterie* in a convent when I visited. I don't know if it has grown since. Probably not. His plan was to name the *resto* 'Ajaccio,' but it didn't have a sign yet when I visited. He specializes in Corsican cuisine, which has a highly distinctive flavor because of the herbs, olive oil, and spices. The food is very rustic—roasted meats, cooked-down stews, and thick soups with white beans. He uses the same herbs in his restaurant that grow in the *maquis*: thyme, marjoram, basil, fennel, and rosemary. Ah, such aromas in that restaurant. And such flavor in the food. And he serves Corsican wines." He put his fingers to his lips. "But I digress." His thick, white eyebrows knit together in worry. "I tried to call him several times recently. He hasn't been seen or heard from since August. Three months is a long time for him to be away without letting someone know where he is."

CHAPTER 23

Guy was just finishing Diamanté's story when Mark opened the front door. His cheeks were flushed from the cold, and his down jacket glistened with drops of rain.

"Ah, Marco!" Maria was at the dining room door. "Come taste the *cacciatora* for me. I need true Italian taster."

Mark's face gleamed. "*Sì, signora*. Be delighted." He hung his jacket on a coat rack in the foyer, winked at Anna, and followed Maria obediently into the kitchen.

Five minutes later, the summons came from Maria in the dining room.

"*Attenzione! Le dîner*, it is served."

Anna and Mark took seats at one end of the table. Puccini settled in beneath Maria's chair at the other.

"Jean-Paul and Maria have been my family for so many years that we always dine together," Guy explained.

They opened the year's new wine, and Guy tasted it, swirling it in his mouth approvingly. "Berries," he remarked. "It tastes like berries this year."

Anna explained to Mark. "Beaujolais Nouveau is released every year on the third Thursday of November. There are signs in all the restaurants which announce its arrival. *Le Beaujolais Nouveau est arrivé!* Then the favorite pastime is to determine what it tastes like. This year, I guess, its taste is like berries."

Mark took a sip. "It does taste like berries. Very light." They all seemed to understand that Mark liked the wine, and they beamed at his approval.

"*Buono appetit,*" Maria said as she served the first course, an Italian meatball soup. As they ate, Maria went on to Mark in English about all the American movies she had seen. He politely acknowledged them, at one point leaning over to Anna and whispering that he had no idea whether some of the titles even existed or not. Maria seemed to mix English with French and Italian in such a way as to make the movie titles seem entirely unidentifiable.

They finished the soup, and Maria got up to go into the kitchen. She returned with a huge platter of ravioli. Next came the *pièce de résistance*: the main course chicken cacciatore served with roasted potatoes and crusty, homemade bread.

"This is so good," Anna remarked, giggling as Mark surreptitiously slipped a tidbit of bread under the table to Puccini.

Salad followed, French style because, as Maria explained, Guy always insisted, and then the dessert, a luscious cannoli.

Over coffee, translation ceased. Mark caught a word here and there, but he was mostly the spectator watching fascinating human dynamics. Jean-Paul, too, was silent, sitting with his fingertips together, nodding his bald head occasionally, smiling. Guy reminisced about how he had come to hire Jean-Paul and Maria, how Nathalie had been such a darling child, how they had all doted over her.

Anna remembered something that Guy had said during the afternoon. "You said your son-in-law is in Rouen? Is that where Nathalie went to live after she was married?"

"Yes. She was only a young girl when the war ended, but my son-in-law had seen her. He came back for her about five years later. They were married in 1952. I was not so thrilled about his crusty temperament, but he owned a restaurant, so I forgave him. She was very much in love with him."

Anna recalled a photo she had seen on the mantel. "Did they have a child? There is a baby in the photo on the mantel."

"Yes, a little boy. We all called him Charlie. Nathalie would bring him every summer to visit me in Strasbourg. Have you ever seen the astronomical clock in the cathedral, Anna?"

Odd question, Anna thought. *Does everyone obsess about that clock in Strasbourg?*

"It's quite amazing." The old man went on eagerly before Anna could reply to his question. "The clock is seven stories tall. In the center is the perpetual calendar, to the right the solar and lunar equations. Above the perpetual calendar pass the seven divinities standing for the seven days of the week. On Sunday, Apollo appears with his sun horses. On Monday, it's Diana with her stag. On Tuesday, Mars with his war horse. On Wednesday, Mercure with his lynxes. On Thursday, Jupiter and his eagle. On Friday, Venus with her pigeons, and on Saturday, Saturn devouring a child." He went on, with a twinkle in his eye, remembering the whole scene in minute detail.

Maria filled his cup and rolled her eyes at Jean-Paul. They had heard the story a thousand times. It was time to clear the dishes.

Not noticing their departure, Guy took a sip of the coffee and continued on as if in a trance, as if the spectacle were right there in front of him.

Mark fidgeted. The question mark on his face reminded Anna that she hadn't been translating. She leaned over to him and put her hand on his knee, whispering, "Remember that clock in the cathedral in Strasbourg? He's describing how it looks."

Mark nodded his head.

"In front stands a celestial sphere covered by thousands of stars," the old man went on. "In the background stands Death, holding his scythe in one hand, a bone in the other with which it slowly strikes the hours." He held up his hands as if to demonstrate how the Death figure looks.

There was something in the way that he told the story that sounded familiar to Anna.

"How did your son-in-law come to see Nathalie during the war?"

He seemed surprised by the question. He blinked his eyes and looked at her. "Jacques was a member of *Les Amis Clandestins*. He was the youngest of the group, not yet twenty years old, hotheaded even then. He is Corsican, born in Ajaccio, birthplace of Napoleon," he added, "and like Napoleon, he is short and thickset." He went on to describe Jacques' bull-like build, his dark eyes, and his heavy hands. "They say we deserve the face we get." He shook his head. "Well, today his face is a mass of deep crevices."

Rouen...a restaurant...Jacques...Charlie...the astronomical clock.

"Guy," Anna asked wide-eyed. "What is Jacques' last name?"

"Why, it's Gérard. My son-in-law's name is Jacques Gérard."

"And your grandson's full name?"

"Charles-Christian Gérard."

Oh, my God. Stunned, Anna thought to herself, *This man is C-C's grandfather.* She tried to rise from her chair, but the room was spinning. "I...I feel like I'm going to faint."

CHAPTER 24

Maria concluded that the reason for Anna's near fainting spell was that she had had too much Beaujolais Nouveau.

"American women," she stated matter-of-factly, "like their wine too much. I have seen that in all the American movies."

Anna did not let on to them, not even to Mark, the reason for her near collapse.

Guy de Noailles looked tired.

"We had better be going," Mark said as they finished strong coffee.

"I want you to have something," Guy said as he went over to a bookshelf and pulled down a large, black box. He opened it, and inside were more photos in silver frames. He sorted through them, mumbling to himself, and then pulled out a small, square, silver-framed, sepia-toned photo. "This is the last photograph I have of Diamanté. It was taken a couple of years ago, just before Nathalie's death, when he came to visit me and we went hunting like in old times. We didn't get anything. We only shot photos." He chuckled and handed it to Anna. "You may have it."

Anna looked at the photo in her hands. The old man in a black beret was staring back at her. His hands, holding a rifle, seemed arthritic. His eyes were piercing, wolf-like, and the look on his face was guarded, cautious.

"I hope I can find him. I want to meet him."

"He will turn up sooner or later."

Anna hugged Guy. Maria embraced Anna and Mark and made them promise to come back to visit again.

It was drizzling heavily outside as they put on their coats. "I insist that you allow Jean-Paul to drive you back to Strasbourg," Guy said. "He has driven that route thousands of times. I don't want you two to risk getting lost in this weather. Jean-Paul can return your rental car to Strasbourg Airport tomorrow. It will be no trouble at all."

Mark was relieved. He insisted on giving Jean-Paul a sizable tip for the effort, put his arms around Anna, and fell asleep in the backseat of Guy's big Citroën during the drive back to Strasbourg.

Anna's head spun meanwhile with trying to put all the details of the amazing coincidence straight in her mind: C-C's grandfather Guy, World War II Résistance fighter, rescuer of American pilot Stu Ellis, her grandfather. C-C's mother Nathalie, Guy's daughter. C-C's father Jacques, Guy's Corsican son-in-law, Résistance fighter, Rouen restaurateur, the one who hated her. Guy's friend Diamanté, Corsican, Résistance fighter, her mysterious grandfather. His son Diamanté *fils*, killed in Algeria, her father. She had wanted to ask Guy about C-C, but with Mark there, she had decided against it. They would be in Paris the next day. *Paris,* she thought. *Was C-C in Paris?*

"Mark," she patted his shoulder to wake him. "We're at the hotel."

CHAPTER 25

Two faxes had been slipped under the door of their suite. The most urgent was for Mark. It was a simple message in bold handwriting from his secretary, Jackie, in Laguna Beach.

Subject: URGENT!!! CHECK YOUR E-MAIL!

Ex parte motion. Hearing MONDAY.

"Oh, Christ. I was so busy wrapping up yesterday that I forgot to check my e-mail."

The other fax was from Harry, Anna's agent.

"Look, Mark. Good news. My book in French translation is due to hit the Paris market just before Christmas. Oh, I like what they did with the title. *L'Affaire Imprévue* sounds so much more sexy." The rest of the memo provided details. Harry had arranged for a couple of book signings in two weeks' time. Could she stay in France? She was so busy reading the memo that she didn't notice that Mark was too preoccupied to listen.

"Damn it, that's all I need now." He quickly plugged in his laptop and tapped his fingers impatiently on the table as he waited for his e-mail to load.

"Shit...of course, the new client, too." He looked at his watch as he picked up the phone. It would be midafternoon in L.A.

Anna heard him responding to a voice message.

"Hi Jacks. Oh, boy, shit. I just now got back to the hotel and found your fax. I'm flying to Paris early tomorrow—Sunday. Will try to get a connecting flight to LAX. Guess I'll see ya bright and early Monday. Bye." He hung up and rubbed his temples, whispering, "Shit, shit, shit." Shutting down his laptop, he turned around in the desk chair. "What's the word for shit in French?"

Anna came out of the bathroom in her robe, brushing her long curls. "*Merde*. Why? Are you planning to start cussing in French?"

He got up and took her in his arms. "Yeah. *Merde*." He smiled. "Hey, that's just about like the Italian *merda*! Anyway, I've got bad news. I won't be able to see Paris with you this trip. I have to be back in L.A. for a court hearing on Monday afternoon. It's an emergency motion. The hearing date couldn't be changed. I've got to fly straight through tomorrow. No one there to cover this for me."

"It's okay, Mark. I have catching up to do with Monique and Georges." She yawned. "I feel like I've had an exhausting day."

"Are you feeling okay? I mean, you almost fainted dead away." He followed her up the stairs to the loft.

"Oh, I'm okay. Maria was right. It must have been the wine."

When they arrived at Charles de Gaulle Airport in Paris the next day, Anna accompanied Mark to the departure terminal for the Air France international flights. As they entered the lounge area, Mark suddenly turned to her with a worried look on his face.

"You will be back in California for Christmas, won't you?"

"I assume so. After the book signings are done. I've got to figure out what to do with my grandparents' home," she added. "Whether to sell it or not. It's not an easy decision. My grandfather bought that land along the Pacific coast after he came back from the war. He was a housing contractor, and he built that house himself. I love it and the view, but it's too big for one person."

"You don't have to rush the decision, you know. Take your time." He took both her hands in his. "Anyway, I want you to meet my parents. They will be home for the holidays, for a change. They've purchased a house in Bel-Air. We have a big, Italian extended family, and they'll probably all be there for Christmas dinner."

"There should be no reason for me to remain in France. But..." Meeting his parents was a new issue. She decided to defer the discussion for now.

"This is not how I had planned the end of our trip, gorgeous. I wanted to spend time with you in Paris, to..." He stroked her hair.

"We'll get another opportunity, Mark. Hey, I need to call Monique and let her know I'll be a bit delayed. Back in a minute." When she returned, they were calling his flight.

"I'll call you everyday. I love you," he whispered in her ear as he hugged her tightly. Then he picked up his briefcase and grinned at her. "Don't worry about the dog. I'll take care of him. Actually, he's moving in with me." Wink. "See you in a couple."

As she watched him walk down the jetway to his flight, she admired his muscular back and slim, sexy hips. No Cal sweatshirt this trip. He had his suave L.A. look back—the blue jeans were topped with a crisp, striped cotton shirt open at the neck and a well-cut, taupe sports jacket. He wore soft, black suede loafers.

She thought about how much she admired his stamina and his style. He wasn't one of those asshole lawyers everyone hated. He was a decent individual with a true sensitivity to others. She knew that he was probably a tough negotiator, but she had never heard him say a harsh word to anyone. He was the kind of man who would make a good life partner. She didn't get the impression that he would ever abandon her. Damn, C-C. Why had she allowed herself to fall in a ten-year trap? It was obvious that he didn't ever want to see her again. It had been three months since she left her card at La Pitié-Salpêtrière.

When the flight had departed and the gate was deserted, she found her way to the main terminal and took the blue airport bus to the Air France terminal near the Arc de Triomphe, a short walking distance from Monique and Georges' apartment on rue Beaujon. It was a peaceful winter afternoon. The sky was clear, the sun was out, and the air was crisp after the previous day's storm. The chestnut trees along the Champs Elysées were leafless skeletons. A few couples walked their dogs along the boulevard. Anna shouldered her briefcase and deliberately took the long way to the side street, rolling her suitcase behind her. She had to think. Tonight, after the expected catch-up with Monique, she needed to spend some time writing in her journal so she wouldn't forget all the details of the story about Diamanté's life she had learned from Guy. Tomorrow, she needed to go to Saint-Germain and meet the owners of the bookstores where she would do the signings. She couldn't help thinking what Guy de Noailles had said about Diamanté: "He has weathered a lot of storms...the type...who never stands by to let events take their course." She rounded the corner and walked up rue Beaujon. The small street was practically deserted. Monique was waiting for her with the door open, and Sabastien leaped in glee as she entered the apartment. It was like coming home.

As the Air France 747 made its way out of European air space, Mark settled into his seat in the forward cabin. No one occupied the seat next to him. He stretched his long legs.

"Would you like something to drink, sir?" the flight attendant asked.

Mark ordered a cognac. From his briefcase he took a pile of legal papers and his Montblanc pen. As he pulled out a file, he felt for a little square box in the bottom of the briefcase. He held it next to his chin and stared out the window at the clouds below. Then he opened the box and carefully fingered the antique, delicately pierced, platinum filigree ring between his thumb and index finger. It had been hand-finished with millgrain edging. At the ring's center was a large, brilliant-cut diamond.

The flight attendant returned with his cognac.

Mark noticed her eyeing the ring. "It's an engagement ring," he explained with a shy smile.

"It's very beautiful, *Monsieur*. The young lady is very lucky."

He smiled at her and took a sip of the cognac. The ring was perfect for Anna. He had envisioned them strolling arm in arm through the place du Tertre near the Sacré-Coeur church, as in the painting he had bought for her. The romantic plan had included him sweeping her off her feet and asking her to marry him right there in that square. He stared out the window, imagining the scene.

"The ring will have to wait until Christmas now," he said aloud to himself as he put it back in its box, buried it in the bottom of his briefcase, and went to work. What was the word? *Merde. Merda.* Shit.

The plane hit some turbulence. The large screen in the front of the cabin showed passengers the flight path. They were over the Channel already. He was having trouble concentrating on his paperwork. He stared out the window again. After their time in Strasbourg, he felt closer to Anna and wanted her more than ever. He had never felt this way about another woman. He knew she was the one. She hadn't told him that she loved him when they said goodbye. There was a barrier between them. Something to do with the Corsican grandfather she needed to find? Damn, he wished he had understood that conversation at the dinner table, too. What had she gotten suddenly so upset about?

An hour later, he was sound asleep, and ten hours later, Sunday evening, the 747 landed at LAX.

PART THREE

CHAPTER 26

Just outside the door of La Pitié-Salpêtrière, Dr. Charles-Christian Gérard lit a cigarette and hesitated for a moment. He felt numb. He was dead tired after having worked the grueling fifteen-hour-plus night shift for two weeks. Because of the harsh December weather, there had been more than the usual number of accident victims in the trauma center during the past twenty-four hours. He had been there most of that time. Now, even to walk the short distance to the Gare d'Austerlitz to catch the métro would take the last of what little energy he had left.

He crossed the darkened street. It was too early for the café on the corner to be open, but, he thought, he was too tired to eat anyway. At the Gare d'Austerlitz, he descended into the métro, crossed through the turnstile, and walked onto the deserted platform. A derelict curled up in a blanket slept on a bench. The station smelled of urine.

An older man, wearing a beret, appeared on the platform as the train pulled in. Charles-Christian flipped the door latch and entered an empty, brightly lit car. He noticed that the man in the beret had entered the car next to his. The doors slammed shut, and the car lurched forward as the train took off again. Charles-Christian sank into a seat by a window, catching a glimpse of his reflection in the mirror-like pane as the car sped through a darkened tunnel. He saw his graying sideburns, his drawn face, an ashen color, the dark circles under his eyes, the stubble of beard from not having shaved for hours. *Not a pretty sight*, he thought, as he ran his hands through his hair and rubbed his temples.

Life had been grueling in the trauma center since he had returned to La Pitié-Salpêtrière. Working long hours had been his life since he had become a doctor, but now he realized that it had desensitized him. Every night, he coped with blood and chaos. Every night, he had to make instantaneous decisions, life-and-death decisions, and there was no time to consider whether they were right or wrong. It seemed people weren't people anymore.

At the Jussieu stop, a young couple entered the car, holding hands. They made their way to the back and sat down. Before the car moved again, they embraced in a passionate kiss.

Charles-Christian heaved a deep sigh and glanced at the seat beside him. Someone had left a copy of last evening's *France Soir,* folded open to the book review section. He picked it up. The lead review was of a book entitled *L'Affaire Imprévue.*

The title intrigued him. He read the first sentence: "If you like tales of romance and intrigue, you'll love this exceptional novel by an American author, newly translated by Sophie La Félisse." He scanned the article for the author's name, and his face flushed as he read it: "Anna Ellis of California has created a good plot and a well-developed set of characters." He clenched his jaw and held the newspaper so tightly in his fist that his hand hurt.

The train pulled into the Cardinal Lemoine stop. An older lady in a black coat and hat got on, clutching a string filet shopping bag. She nodded to him and took a seat facing his.

"You are a doctor?" she asked in a low voice as she eyed his hospital coveralls under his coat.

"Yes," he smiled faintly at her over the newspaper.

"I am on my way to market," she said as if responding to a question. "There will be fresh shellfish today. It's so rare to get good oysters, clams, and green mussels this time of year. I'm going to make a bouillabaisse for my Robert's supper tonight. Robert is my husband. He just left for work. It will be a long day for him. He will like the warm stew for his supper."

Charles-Christian smiled at her again. Taking the newspaper with him, he gave her a nod and wished her "*Bonne journée, Madame*" as he got up to stand at the door. Maubert Mutualité was the next stop, his stop. Several people were waiting on the platform, crushing forward as the car slowed. They were all dressed for work. The morning commute was beginning.

Charles-Christian walked the short distance along boulevard Saint-Germain to rue Saint-Jacques. It was a cold morning, and Parisians emerging from their apartment buildings were bundled in heavy coats and scarves, faces barely visible. He reached his apartment building, not even noticing the man in the beret following him as he entered through the heavily carved wooden door and climbed the dark stairs, slowly, to his apartment.

Once inside, he took off his coat, made himself a cup of hot chocolate on the small stove in the kitchenette, and sat down at the tiny table. He spread the newspaper in front of him and read the entire review of Anna Ellis' latest book. It was not a bad review as book reviews go, he thought. In fact, the reviewer, a woman, rather liked the heroine, though she wasn't impressed with the hero— "too mean spirited," she had written. Charles-Christian wondered to himself if Anna had had him in mind when she wrote that character. He sipped his hot chocolate and went to his desk to get a pair of scissors. As he carefully cut out the review, he noticed a box at the bottom of the page. Its heading read "Book Signings in Paris This Week." Curious, he studied the lengthy list. About a third of the way down was Anna's name—Librairie La Hune, 170 boulevard Saint-Germain, and Librairie Bonaparte, 31 rue Bonaparte. He cut out the notice and sat back, heaving a huge sigh. The first of the scheduled signings was in two days. Anna would have to arrive in Paris shortly, if she was not already here. The thought of seeing her again made him apprehensive. *What if she doesn't recognize me?* he wondered. *What if she's married? What if...?* There was no photo of her with the article, no personal information. He put his head in his hands. His life was lonely. He had no one. At forty, he was certainly not a happy man. He climbed the spiral staircase to the loft and sank onto his bed, too tired to undress or shower, and fell asleep.

CHAPTER 27

It was drizzling and the sky was heavy when Anna stepped from the métro. She knew boulevard Saint-Germain well. She had walked the length of the Left Bank's most celebrated thoroughfare many times. She took a detour past the Sorbonne, crossed the boulevard Saint-Michel, continued past the École de Médecine and the place de l'Odéon to Saint-Germain-des-Prés, the oldest church in Paris, for which the quarter was named. The small bookstore, Librairie Bonaparte, where she was to do her signing, was located just off the boulevard Saint-Germain on the rue Bonaparte in the sixth arrondissement. She turned right from the boulevard Saint-Germain and found the bookstore at 31 rue Bonaparte. The shop was cozy and smelled of old books and dust. There were not a lot of people as there had been in Librairie La Hune. This was more a neighborhood store where the locals came to browse on Saturday afternoons. There were dozens of small bookstores like it along this street. No one seemed to pay much attention to authors who came in to sign their books. But Harry had set it up, and it was an opportunity for Anna to promote her book to the French audience. She would do her charming best.

She greeted the bookstore *propriétaire*, a petite elderly woman with black hair and bright, smart eyes. They had met when Anna

had introduced herself two weeks before. The woman had seemed
tentative about the signing, but had agreed, she told her, because
she had no one else lined up for this particular afternoon. *Nothing
like being wanted*, Anna had thought at the time. From the look on
the old woman's face now, she hadn't much warmed to the idea.
Anna hung her coat and scarf on a coat tree and took a seat at the
table where her books were stacked. No one approached her.
Unlike her experience at La Hune, this was going to be a long couple
of hours. She thought about the excitement that Harry had gener-
ated at La Hune. He was such a clown. At their lunch with the publisher at Brasserie Lipp, across the street from the bookstore, he
had been the life of the party. Flammarion had promised to publish
Anna's new book, which Harry had calmly stated would be coming
out next year. Anna had quietly crossed her fingers under the table
on that point. Well, Harry had departed for California, and this was
the end of it for now. Monique and she had plans to finish their
Christmas shopping in the next few days, and then she would fly
home.

Anna was so absorbed in thinking about the events of the week
before, her Christmas list, and her impending return home that she
didn't notice the man standing in front of her.

"Am I in that book?" The question in French was more a state-
ment than a question. His voice sounded familiar. She looked up.

"Am I in that book?" he repeated. The gray eyes studied her
without showing any emotion. He had taken off his heavy winter
coat. Underneath, he was wearing the white coveralls of an emergency room doctor. He wasn't a tall man, and he was fine boned.
His bearing was the stiff posture of the French. There was a youthful

handsomeness about him, but the first signs of age, crow's-feet extending from the eyes and gray streaks running through his dark hair at the temples, made him an older, saddened version of himself.

"Do you want a signed copy, *Monsieur?*" It was the *propriétaire.* "This is the author."

He nodded, and his lips pursed together. "Don't you recognize me, Anna?"

A tightness caught in her throat. Of course, she did. He was still as slim, elegant, and graceful in his medical attire as the young man who had carried her up those steps in Montmartre and kissed her passionately ten years before. She took a book off the pile in front of her, opened it, and wrote simply:

> *Pour "C-C"*
> *Anna C. Ellis, décembre 1997*

Her hand shook slightly as she handed it to him. "How did you find out I was in Paris?" She had dreamed, even written it in her journal, that when she and C-C saw each other again, it would be like a Hollywood moment, a *"scène classique."*

> *Speechless, each of them frozen in place, they stare at each other for a long moment in recognition and disbelief. Suddenly, tears streaming from her eyes, she runs to him. They fall into each other's arms. She holds his head in her hands, looks into his eyes, her fingers running desperately through his hair, now streaked with gray. They kiss. "What are you doing here? Why didn't you write?" they each whisper a succession of questions breathlessly.*

Hollywood moment gone. That wasn't what was happening now. They were staring at each other across a table piled with books, neither of them smiling. A shiver ran up her spine.

He answered her question. "I was curious. I saw in the paper that you were doing signings in Paris, Anna. I was at the Librairie La Hune, in the back of the shop, earlier this week, but it was so crowded that I left. I decided to try again today. The book is called *L'Affaire Imprévue*. I wanted to know if I am in it." He shrugged his shoulders in the manner French men do when they don't have anything more to say on the subject. He looked an awkward boy of ten.

"No, well, there are of course some situations that you might find familiar." She glared at him, wondering to herself why they were having this bizarre conversation. "But you are not in it, C-C." Her response was curt, angry. Why had he come all of a sudden back into her life? All those ignored phone calls and, in particular, the unanswered letters.

C-C paid the *propriétaire* for the book. He gave the old lady a quick smile. *That familiar, crooked smile*, Anna thought to herself.

"*Merci, Monsieur. Au revoir, Monsieur.*" The *propriétaire* waved her hand over her shoulder as she disappeared into a room in the back of the store.

"*Au revoir, Madame.*" To Anna he simply nodded and said *adieu* as he pulled his coat on and walked toward the door. Anna stared after him. *That same familiar swagger,* she thought again. *Damn that same sexy, self-confident swagger.* A blast of cold air swooshed into the shop as he opened the door and tucked her book under his arm. Anna shivered again. He was a man of few words, but the few he spoke made their point. "*Adieu.*" Good-bye forever. Not "*au revoir.*" Not "see you again." *Am I going to just let him walk out of my life?* she thought as she stood up.

"Wait, C-C. I don't mean to be rude. It's just that all the letters I sent..."

He closed the door and turned partway around, his head down. She could only see half of his face. It had a bewildered look. His eyes narrowed, and his jaw tightened. "Letters?"

"Yes, after I went back to California. I tried to call you. I sent letters, then I gave up because you didn't answer them. I never knew what happened to you." She hesitated as he turned to look at her. "Damn it, C-C, what was I supposed to think?"

A couple entered the bookshop. They were young, bespectacled in bohemian wire-rimmed glasses, and bundled against the cold in heavy coats and gloves. Soft woolen scarves were wrapped around their necks. His was navy; it matched his long coat. Hers was a sage green, which matched a sage green turtleneck sweater protruding under her camel jacket. They both wore jeans and leather boots. The *propriétaire* greeted the couple warmly and introduced them to Anna. It was obvious that they were regular customers.

During the short time that the couple spent in the store, C-C remained inside the door, appearing to stare through the window out into the street. He studied Anna's reflection in the window. She wasn't looking his way. The weather reminded him of the driving trip he and Anna had made through the Alps to Vienna. His throat tightened as he recalled the tender, sweet warmth of her body close to his. It was as if it were just yesterday.

Anna signed a copy of her book and handed it with a smile to the young couple, who departed with promises to the *propriétaire* to return to check on a shipment of *bouquins* arriving the following week. After bidding them *au revoir* and *merci*, the *propriétaire* returned to her desk in the rear room, humming softly to herself. The bookstore was again deserted except for Anna and C-C.

Anna's reflection in the window was turned in C-C's direction. He glanced her way. Their eyes locked. His were a deep, dark, stormy gray, gray as the buildings of Saint-Germain in the chilly rain.

"Look, Anna. A lot of water has flowed under the Pont Neuf since we last saw each other. It's not appropriate to discuss here. I am due back at the hospital, and you have your signing. Can you meet me somewhere this evening?"

Anna felt weak. Her face felt flushed. "Where?"

"Do you remember that little fondue restaurant off the boul' Mich near the Sorbonne that we used to go to a lot?"

"Is it still there?"

"But of course. It's rather still *en vogue* even. It seems to be always crowded. I get off around ten o'clock, provided there is no catastrophe. Is there somewhere I can reach you, in case of a problem?"

"I'm staying with Monique. You remember Monique? My friend from the Sorbonne? She is married now, and she and her husband live in the eighth." She wrote the phone number on the back of one of her cards and handed it to him, looking directly into his eyes. "We can have our talk later, C-C, but answer one question for me: Why didn't you even once try to contact me?" *Even after I left my card at La Pitié-Salpêtrière in September?* "And why didn't you answer my letters?" *And where did you so swiftly move to? And why didn't you leave Elise a forwarding address? And what were you doing in Africa?* There were so many more questions that followed that one.

He came over to the table and leaned into her. His handsome face was inches from hers. He smelled of antiseptic and hospital. He was aging in a familiar way. There was a sudden twinkle in his eye and a slight quiver of a smile at the corner of his mouth. In that moment he bore a wonderful resemblance to his grandfather, Guy de Noailles. Anna softened a bit. She felt a yearning to touch the lines which the years had created around his eyes, but she seemed frozen in place, standing there behind her signing table.

"That's more than one question, Anna." His tone had changed. "I received no letters from you." He stood there for an awkward moment, taking in her face so close to his, smelling her scent. "I have questions for you also." He hesitated for a moment, as if he wanted to say something more. His eyes were fixed on hers. "*Au revoir*. I'll see you later, Anna."

Then he pulled on his leather gloves and held the door for two young women who were entering the shop. He glanced toward Anna once more as he departed.

Outside in the street, the precipitation was heavier. C-C drew his coat collar around his chin and wrapped his heavy wool scarf over his mouth and around his shoulders as he crossed the boulevard and headed for the hospital. He had not at all intended to come off as passive, even dismissive, when he met Anna face-to-face. He had glimpsed enough of her at Librairie La Hune to understand that he wanted to see her again. He had also noticed something different about her. She was no longer the student, no longer the girl. She was an attractive young woman, a professional. Everyone around her seemed charmed by her. There was something else, something he couldn't quite isolate. She had a look about her that spoke softly that someone loved her. He wondered briefly if she would stand him up later at the restaurant. There was the lingering question about the letters. What letters? If he didn't get them, who did? Why weren't they forwarded to him? Who would have gained from keeping Anna and him apart?

CHAPTER 28

When Anna returned to the eighth arrondissement after her book signing at Librairie Bonaparte, it was already dark, though only late afternoon. The rain had let up, but the air was crisp and cold, and the streets were shiny and wet. She caught a glimpse of Monique and Sabastien rounding the corner to avenue Berthe Albrecht. She hurried to catch up with them as they headed in the direction of avenue Hoche. It was Sabastien who first caught sight of Anna following them. The little dog halted and wagged his tail until Monique recognized her. Monique kissed Anna warmly on both cheeks.

"*Salut, chérie*. Sabastien and I are just heading for the Parc Monceau. Want to join us?"

Monique was warmly bundled Parisienne-style with a soft, dove-gray cashmere wrap wound around the collar of her long, black wool coat.

"Sure." Anna bent down and petted Sabastien, who was begging for her attention. "I need to talk anyway."

"How did the signing go?"

"There were very few customers. The store is a small one, and maybe because of the weather, I don't know, there weren't many people out shopping in Saint-Germain anyway. If this had been the only signing in Paris, I think I would have felt like a failure. The *propriétaire* seemed to warm up to me as the afternoon went on. I felt guilty for not generating more business for her, so I purchased a book." She held up a wrapped package.

Monique said, "The big department stores were quite crowded. I could only take a couple of hours of Galéries Lafayette before I gave up."

"Are you up to some more shopping tomorrow?"

"Unfortunately, *chérie*, I have so much to do. We are departing for the south in a week! It's final. Georges said today that he can get away *enfin*. We'll be spending Christmas in our *bastide* in Provence. Isn't that exciting?"

"Yes, indeed."

Monique had spent much of their time together during the past few days talking endlessly about the country home, the *bastide*, that she and Georges had purchased near Grasse. Anna had looked at vast piles of photos of the large, but rather run-down, two-story, ocher-colored home with a tiled roof, green shutters, and wrought-iron decorated façade. The couple had made plans for extensive renovations and were planning to spend their month-long vacation in August there.

The two friends crossed the place du Général Brocard and headed toward the avenue Van Dyck entrance of Parc Monceau. Sabastien paused and lifted his leg to pee on a lamppost.

"Monique, C-C showed up unexpectedly at my book signing today."

Monique stopped and turned toward Anna. "*Oh là là!* Oh dear, *chérie*. You poor thing. The absolute gall of the man. After all this time."

"The strangest thing. He said that he had been to the first book signing at Librairie La Hune, but he never came up to me because of the crowd. I never saw him. You were there. You must not have seen him either."

"No, and had I recognized him, I would have given him my opinion of him, too."

"Well, all of a sudden, this man whom I have not seen in ten years was standing in front of my table at the Librairie Bonaparte this afternoon."

Monique blew air through her lips in disgust. "So, what did you do? Did you ask him if he received your letters?"

"Yes. He said he never received them."

"*Ridicule!*"

They entered the Parc Monceau. The trees, stiff with cold, stood out against the darkened evening sky, and the path was wet. The wind blew slightly. Park lights lit up brown vegetation, and Anna thought the effect was quiet and charming as only a Parisian garden can be in winter.

"Brr. I'm shivering," Monique said. "Sabastien, let's hurry up and do our duty, puppy. I want to go home and warm up. So what happened next?"

"Monique, I nearly let him walk out of my life forever. He bought a copy of my book. I signed it. Then he opened the shop door and said *adieu.*"

"Well, in my opinion, you should have let him walk out forever."

"I didn't. I couldn't. Don't you see? Then I would always have wondered if I had done the right thing. He asked me to meet him for dinner in the Latin Quarter tonight…at that fondue restaurant we always went to."

"What do you think you will learn?"

"If you mean that he's married, has children, has a life without me. Well…"

"Well? What then?"

Anna threw up her arms. "Well, so be it. It's more than I've known for the past ten years, isn't it?"

"But do you really want to know all of the details?"

"Yes. Yes, I guess I do, Monique. Don't you see? Until this afternoon, I didn't even know whether I would recognize him again. I didn't even know if he would recognize me. Until three months ago, I even thought he might be dead. I have to know what's happened to him in the past decade."

They left the Parc Monceau and walked briskly toward rue Beaujon. The streets were surprisingly full of activity. Residents were returning to their apartments for the evening, and guests at the hotel on the corner were hailing taxis. Monique put her arms around Anna's shoulders and squeezed.

"I think you need an *apéritif* and a hot bath, Anna."

Anna looked at her watch. She had missed Mark's evening call.

CHAPTER 29

At eight o'clock in the evening, the phone in the apartment rang. Monique and Georges had already gone out, and Anna was luxuriating in a steaming bubble bath. Her first thought was, *Do I want to get out of this warm bath for a call that is probably for Monique or Georges?* Her second thought was, *Merde, I should get that. It could be Mark.* She climbed out of the tub, wrapped herself in a heavy, white terrycloth robe, slid into her slippers, and ran down the hall.

"*Allô?*" She was out of breath.

"*Allô?*" the male voice hesitated. "Is that you, Anna? It's Charles-Christian."

Anna's heart thumped an extra beat. His voice over the phone evoked deep-seated memories. She took a breath before responding.

"Has…has something come up?"

"Actually, it's really quiet in the trauma center for a Saturday night." He hesitated. "Look, Anna, I thought that maybe I could pick you up in say, half an hour, if that would be convenient? There is something I want to show you."

"Sure. Okay. I guess I wouldn't mind having dinner earlier. I didn't get much lunch. There's a hotel, a Sofitel, on rue Beaujon just off the Étoile, between avenue Hoche and avenue de Friedland. It's just down the block. I'll wait for you out front so you won't have to find a parking space."

"I know the street. Watch for a dark green Renault. *À bientôt. Salut.*" He was gone.

She replaced the receiver. A half hour.

Back in her room, she opened her laptop and sent a quick e-mail to Mark:

> *Sorry, I missed your call earlier. Monique and I were out walking the dog. I tried you on your cell phone. Assume you were out for a jog. Won't be able to talk later. I'm going out for the evening with an old friend from Sorbonne days. Talk to you tomorrow. Bye, A.*

She reread it before clicking the send button. She had tried to sound nonchalant, but it seemed rather abrupt, so she went back and inserted two more quick sentences:

> *Book signing done. Be home soon.*

She also decided to delete the part about being "with an old friend from Sorbonne days." He could assume she was out with Monique and Georges. Click. Message sent.

The dark green Renault pulled up to the curb in front of the Sofitel. Anna stood just inside the hotel door. It was too cold to wait out in front. She wore a heavy, black wool coat and high-heeled, black leather boots. Waving off the bellman, who was making motions of escorting her, she pulled her melon-colored wool scarf closely around her ears and neck and ran to the car.

C-C got out and opened the passenger-side door for her. "*Bonsoir.*"

"*Bonsoir.*"

The car smelled strongly of cigarette smoke. C-C closed the door, climbed into the driver's seat, and pulled the Renault away from the curb without looking at her. "I thought we might take a little drive before dinner."

"And where would that be to?"

"You'll see." He said as he negotiated the typical traffic jam in the Étoile around the Arc de Triomphe.

"Wouldn't it have been better to take the side streets?" Anna inquired about halfway through. There were cars everywhere around them.

He didn't answer her.

As they turned right onto the Champs Elysées, the spectacle was breathtaking. The famous boulevard lined with barren chestnut trees strung with lights was lit up for the holidays. There were crowds strolling the sidewalks, stopping in the shops, and socializing in the cafés and restaurants. At avenue Georges V, C-C turned right.

Anna guessed where they were going. Georges V leads to the Pont de l'Alma, the bridge which crosses the Seine to the Eiffel Tower. The last time she saw him, a decade ago, they had spent the entire night until sunrise parked near the Eiffel Tower. "Are we going to the Tour Eiffel, by any chance?"

"I thought we should start where we left off." He wasn't looking at her.

"But, C-C, it's been so long. A decade. We are both different people today."

"We are also the same two people, Anna."

She watched him as he drove. He still wasn't looking at her. The car crossed the Alma Bridge.

"There was a bad accident here in August." C-C said it more to himself than to her. "In the tunnel, under the bridge."

"You mean the Princess Di accident? I know. I was in Paris. I had just arrived the day before. Monique, Georges, and I drove to Le Havre that day, the day of the accident, and there was the oddest event in the port."

For the first time, he looked over at her. His eyes shone like two icy, gray pebbles in the darkened car. The effect made her shudder.

"What kind of odd event?"

"It was the strangest thing, C-C. I was sitting on a bench, writing in my journal, making notes on what I was seeing, hearing, smelling—you know, for future reference for my book. Monique and Georges had walked down the waterfront. Georges needed to check out something for a movie set. He's in the movie business. Anyway, I was alone, and there was this commotion at the end of the quay. A helicopter and a truck of some sort. Some people yelling at each other."

They had arrived in front of the Eiffel Tower, the Trocadero side. C-C pulled over into a temporary parking spot and lit a cigarette.

"Are you still smoking?" Anna wrinkled her nose in disgust.

"Not as much. Only once in a while. If it still bothers you."

"It does."

He doused the Gauloise in the ashtray. "I mostly have quit. It's *en vogue* in France to quit these days, so I try. But it's a stress reliever for me." He smiled at her for the first time. "Sorry. Tell me more about what you saw in Le Havre." He was astounded at the coincidence. If she was describing the scene as she saw it, that would have put them in Le Havre within a short distance of each other.

"There's not much more to tell. Only two old men running as fast as they could away from the port; then it looked like something was going on with the helicopter, and it took off. It was foggy. I couldn't see what exactly was happening. But I always wondered if it had something to do with the Princess Di accident."

"Why is that?"

"There was a British ship in the port. I suppose there are always British ships in the port of Le Havre, but this one just looked kinda official, like it belonged to royalty, and the helicopter was one of those yellow military ones used for emergency rescues. Anyway, when we arrived back in Paris—with the mourning in England and the funeral—well, I assumed it was just my imagination."

"Did you see where the two men went?"

"No. They just disappeared. I was too engrossed in what was going on. Why?"

"Oh, I was just curious if anyone followed them. That's all."

"No, not that I saw."

"It's a good piece of fiction, Anna," he said. But he thought, *So Diamanté and André Narbon did make it after all*.

"It will appear as a scene in one of my books, probably. Did you ever notice how a helicopter looks like a dragonfly?"

C-C shook his head and gave her a little crooked smile. He leaned over toward her window and pointed to the second level of the Eiffel Tower. A panel of lights spanning the outer balcony read "J-747." It was the countdown to January 1, 2000—the millennium.

"I saw the panel when it was unveiled in April. There were spectacu-lar fireworks. They promise an even better show for the millennium celebration."

"Do you think it was a conspiracy, like they're saying—that Di-ana was assassinated?"

C-C shifted uneasily in his seat. "I couldn't say." The car seemed suddenly stuffy. "I need to get out," he said as he opened his door. "Let's get some air." In seconds they were standing underneath the Eiffel Tower.

Anna stared up through the iron grids. The tower's bright lights sparkled above them in the cold air. "I've always loved it, the tower, lit up at night. It's so magical. Do you remember what we said to each other that last night, C-C? We made promises. I don't remem-ber the exact words. All I recall is a feeling, a special feeling, that we promised each other we would be here again. And I guess we are, but..." Her voice trailed off. She almost felt like crying. She turned to him, but she kept her distance. Their eyes met. "I searched for you when I was here in September." She didn't wait for a reaction. "I went to your apartment building. Elise was still there. She didn't know where you had gone. I couldn't go to your father. So I visited so many hospitals in Paris that I lost count." She paused, heaved a huge sigh, and went on. "I finally found someone at La Pitié-Salpêtrière who could at least tell me you were on staff there but that you were on leave or something. I left my card and Monique's phone number and address."

There was no visible reaction. He just stood there looking at her.

"*Merde*, C-C," she finally said. "Didn't you ever get it?"

He cleared his throat. "Since we're outside, can I have that cigarette now?"

She nodded, put her hands in her pockets, and looked at the ground.

His voice was calm, the practiced calm of an ER physician in the face of panicked friends and relatives. He cleared his throat as he took the cigarette from the packet, and then he said, "Actually, I did get it, and I did go over to the Durocher's apartment. There was no one home. I even asked a neighbor. She said that the occupants were in America. I assumed you had gone again."

"You didn't leave a message?"

"*Non*." He lit the cigarette and inhaled a full breath.

"Why not?"

He exhaled. A white cloud of smoke trailed slowly into the cold air. "I wasn't sure why you had tried to contact me. After all, I hadn't heard from you in nearly ten years."

The realization hit her. He had gone through much the same dilemma that she had. "Then you thought I had ditched you?"

"At first, *oui*, then I wondered whether you had been kidnapped, murdered in America. I didn't have any way of knowing."

"What do you think happened to all my letters?"

He lowered his head, kicked at the dark sidewalk, ran his hands through his hair, and scratched his temple. "I...I never knew about any letters." He looked directly into her eyes. "Honest, Anna. It's a great mystery to me."

"But you never tried to contact me?"

"I...the truth is I misplaced your address, Anna." He looked at the ground again.

"Misplaced?" Anna's eyebrows rose. "Misplaced? How could you misplace an address of someone you cared about?"

"I moved." He shrugged his shoulders. "I looked everywhere for the piece of paper you had written it on. I could still see it in my mind, but I couldn't remember it."

"And you couldn't remember that it was somewhere in California? That there are phone directories to look information like that up in?" She crossed her arms and turned around, her back to him, to look up at the tower again. The wind was blowing, and her toes were beginning to freeze in her lightweight California boots. "You moved in with Reggie, didn't you? That's why you found it convenient not to find my address."

"That's not exactly how it was. I can explain." When Anna didn't respond, he continued. "Yes, I moved in with Reggie. How did you know that anyway?"

"Elise. I asked her if anyone had visited you after I left. She remembered a young lady who spoke English but wasn't British or American. I figured out it was Reggie when she described her. I assumed that she and Bertrand had visited you together, but she told me that Bertrand had gone into the military and was stationed in Africa or Asia. I don't recall which."

"She broke off with him when he left for Asia. Reggie didn't like to be alone."

"So *you* moved in with her?" She emphasized the "you." "Were you lovers, then?"

"Anna, you were gone. I hadn't heard from you in months."

"Did your father approve of the little tramp?" she snapped. She was still standing with her back to him, her eyes staring at the reflections of the tower's lights in the numerous puddles of water the rain had made during the day.

"By then it did not matter. We were no longer speaking. After you..." He touched her elbow lightly. "Look at me, Anna. Turn around."

She swung around angrily.

"Reggie died two years ago. It's a long story. In 1990, after I finished my residency, I joined Médecins Sans Frontières."

"Doctors Without Borders."

"*Oui*, and I went to Africa to work. You probably remember that Reggie was from South Africa. She always had this compulsion to go to Africa to work with the AIDS patients. And I..."

He paused, took a drag on his Gauloise, and said, "It was an adventure for me. The Médecins Sans Frontières work in countries many people have never heard of. It is sometimes very dangerous work for the volunteers. They are often harassed. Some of the AIDS workers have even been kidnapped. Reggie became so fearful that she wanted to go back to her native South Africa. I preferred to stay in the sub-Saharan countries where the AIDS epidemic is the worst. It was when we were working in a hospital in Zaire, the Republic of the Congo that is, that she became ill."

Anna was staring at him, wide-eyed. "With AIDS?"

"No, it wasn't AIDS. It was a viral hemorrhagic fever known as Ebola. The disease is often spread in health-care facilities. There was an epidemic in '95 that affected many hospitals, including the one we were working in. There is no treatment. Researchers do not understand why some people are able to recover from Ebola HF and others are not. Reggie was unable to recover."

"Was it an awful death?"

"The onset of the illness is very abrupt. It is the internal and external bleeding…" He looked down, hesitating. "After she died, I came back to Paris. It was not long after that that my mother passed away. I took leave and went back to work with the MSF in Africa after the funeral."

A couple passed nearby, lovers, arm in arm, leaning into each other as they walked. Anna and C-C simultaneously looked at them and then to each other.

"So you never married Reggie?"

"*Non.*"

Anna had tears in her eyes. "I'm sorry. It must have been awful for you."

He stomped out his cigarette. "Reggie introduced us, remember?"

"Yes."

"Are you married, Anna?"

"No."

"But there is someone, isn't there?"

She didn't answer the question. They walked back to the car, together, in silence, side by side but not touching, keeping their separate rush of memories to themselves.

CHAPTER 30

The restaurant was noisy and smoke-filled, yet warm and inviting. The tables, topped with red checkered cloths, were crowded together and full of patrons, most of them young. A waiter motioned to them to take a bench by the far wall and set an open bottle of Beaujolais Nouveau on their table. There was a little sign on the table next to a flickering candle. "*Le Beaujolais Nouveau est arrivé!*"

"It's the wine of the season," sniffed C-C.

"Oh, I remember that," Anna commented with a wry smile. "The connoisseur of wines himself snubs his nose at Beaujolais Nouveau. I've had some this year. I think it's rather good."

He shrugged his shoulders and helped her with her coat. As irony would have it, the only item of clean clothing that Anna had left was the persimmon-colored, cashmere V-neck sweater that Mark had given her. She had packed it in the bottom of her suitcase, thinking that she would wear it in Paris, but when Mark had had to fly back to Los Angeles, she had decided to leave it where it was. Tonight, getting dressed, she had found a spot on the sweater she was planning to wear, so she had no choice.

C-C took off his coat, hung it on the rack with hers, and held her chair. He looked at her admiringly. "You have not changed a bit, Anna. Chic, as always."

He, on the other hand, looked haggard, as if the weight of the ten years had taken its toll. He seemed harder, too. She could hear it in his voice.

"Do you live in those doctor clothes? I would have thought that you might have had at least a chance to change."

"I am actually officially still on call tonight." He held up his pager. "It's my life."

"Don't you ever get tired of it? The life, I mean?"

"Do you ever tire of writing?"

"Sometimes."

"To your book." He held up his glass of wine. "May you sell many copies in France."

She clinked hers to his. "*Santé.*"

They ordered *fromage fondue raclette* and *fondue Bourguignonne*. A rowdy group of young people was seated at the next table. It was hard to talk without shouting.

The waiter delivered two fondue pots, one filled with boiling wine, the other with melted cheese. Next came a platter of beef chunks and assorted sauces, and a basket of crusty chunks of baguette. They each speared two or three of the beef chunks with long slim forks and set them cooking in the pot. Anna speared a piece of the bread and swirled it in the melted cheese.

"Where are you living now, C-C?" she shouted. To her relief, the noisy group of young people finally got up to leave.

"I moved back to Elise's apartment building recently. I like the location. Do you remember the Russian lady downstairs from my old apartment?"

Anna nodded and laughed. "*Madame* Russe? Of course. She was a real character."

"I inquired about the apartment building recently, and Elise told me that apartment was vacant, so I moved in. It's much bigger and has a double balcony. Elise takes good care of me, like always, even though I'm not home much."

"Elise didn't tell you I had been to see her in September...looking for you?"

C-C was silent for a minute. "Well, she did, actually. I hadn't thought about it until just now." He cleared his throat. "She said something about seeing you, but at the time I thought it was just age talking, that she had mixed up the years, as she sometimes does. It never occurred to me that it was a recent visit."

"Not even when I had left my card at your hospital?"

"I have been very occupied these past months."

The waiter refreshed their glasses of Beaujolais Nouveau. Anna took a sip. "How did you come to know Elise, C-C? Originally, I mean."

"My grandfather knew her husband, Ferdinand, when he was alive." Anna suddenly recalled that Guy de Noailles had mentioned Diamanté's dead brother by the same name, whose wife was still living in Paris. It hadn't crossed her mind at the time that Elise had referred more than once to her departed husband, Ferdinand. Another piece fit into the puzzle.

"Have you seen your grandfather in Alsace recently, C-C?"

"Not for some time. He is very old, almost ninety. He doesn't travel much anymore. I'm sorry you never met him."

"Oh, but I did. Not deliberately. It was purely coincidental. You see, my grandfather and my grandmother passed away a couple of months ago. They were killed, actually, in a horrible car accident."

"I'm sorry." He seemed genuinely sympathetic.

"Yes, they were parents to me. It has been hard for me to realize they are gone. Sometimes I just think I can phone them and they'll be on the other end as always."

"That's how I felt about my mother. Even though she died two years ago, I still sometimes think of her as alive." They were both silent, then C-C's eyes locked on hers. "But, I'm confused. What is the connection to *Grand-père?* You said you met him?"

"My grandfather left some personal items that I sorted through. Among them was a Christmas card that was sent in 1950. It was signed Guy de Noailles and Nathalie. No address, except that the envelope was posted in Strasbourg."

C-C dipped a piece of cooked meat in a sauce. "That would have been when my mother was very young. How did your grandfather know *Grand-père?*"

"During the war. My grandfather was a flier. He was shot down over France and rescued by the members of the Résistance. I didn't know the connection to Guy de Noailles. He never discussed the war."

"Then, how?"

"It's a long story. I thought that maybe Guy de Noailles would be able to help me resolve a question regarding something my grandfather had told me, so I visited him in late November, not knowing at all that he was your grandfather. He was so warm and wonderful and welcoming, C-C. He introduced us," she hesitated, "ah, I mean me, to Maria and Jean-Paul. He remembered my grandfather and showed me photos of the old Résistance group. I didn't have a clue that he was your grandfather until practically after the whole visit was over. I should have seen the resemblance...in looks, though. Actually, he's a rather ancient version of you." She gave him a playful look. "C-C, he even told me the story of the astronomical clock in the cathedral."

"But, this is extraordinary, Anna."

"Yes, isn't it? And there's more. That question I mentioned that I was trying to resolve?"

Just then C-C's pager went off.

"Excuse me. It's too noisy in here. I need to phone the hospital." He got up from the table and went outside to use his cell phone.

Anna took a sip of wine and set some more meat cooking. A new group of university-age young people had filled the empty table next to them. They were celebrating something. Anna couldn't quite make out what, but they were toasting and congratulating a young woman who looked to be about twenty years old.

C-C returned and sat down. "It's an emergency. I'm sorry, Anna. I will have to return to the hospital. I'll take you back to rue Beaujon."

They motioned to the waiter, paid the bill, donned their warm coats, and left the restaurant. Anna was still on hold with her story.

"Tomorrow is Sunday. I will not be at the hospital or on call," C-C was telling her. "Then it's night duty for the next week." They reached the car. He held the door for her. "Would you take a drive with me, Anna? Ten years is a long time. We have a lot of catching up to do." He climbed into the driver's seat and started the engine.

"You haven't seen your father for sometime, then?"

"Not since my mother's funeral."

"Then I want us to drive to Rouen. It's high time that you two made up."

"I'm not sure, Anna."

"I'm not listening. I have made up my mind, C-C. If I was the cause of your falling out in the first place, then I want to get that resolved. Anyway, there's something I need to tell you on the way. It's too long a story for tonight. It has to do with a discovery I've made." *And*, she thought, *I may need some information from Jacques to help me find Diamanté.*

C-C reached over and touched her hand. "I think whoever is in love with Anna is a lucky man." He pulled her hand to his lips and kissed it.

CHAPTER 31

Monique had waited up for Anna. The apartment felt warm and smelled of a wood fire.

"Georges went to bed," she said. "He is coming down with a cold or something, poor darling. He wasn't feeling very well, so we came home from the dinner party early." She handed Anna an envelope. "A letter arrived for you today. I forgot to tell you that I had left it on the table in the hall."

Anna took it, noting that it was postmarked from Obernai. It was from Guy de Noailles.

Monique poured two snifters of cognac and handed one to Anna. "So-o-o? How did it go with C-C? I'm listening, *mon amie*. Come into the salon. I've got a fire going. It's cozy."

"Let me open this first. It may have some news."

The letter was handwritten in blue ink on white vellum stationery in the old man's carefully formed script. He had enclosed in it a card wishing her a *Joyeux Noël*.

> *First of all, ma chère Anna, I must thank you and Mark for the wine that was sent from California. I have not had California wine and was surprised to find out that it is very, very good.*

> *Maria was thrilled with the souvenir Hollywood*
> *scarf that arrived during the past week from Mark's office*
> *in Los Angeles. She hasn't taken it off, as far as I know,*
> *a day since it arrived. She sends multiple big kisses (to*
> *Mark, especially) for such generosity. Finally, I must tell*
> *you that I have not yet heard from Diamanté, but I will*
> *not be very concerned about that unless Christmas comes*
> *and goes without word from him. I promise to let you*
> *know immediately if I hear anything of his whereabouts.*

"He's such a sweet old man," Anna remarked to herself, thinking that she would have to tell Mark about what a hit the scarf had made with Maria. She put the cognac on the coffee table. "I'm going to bed, Monique. C-C had to go back to the hospital. His pager went off. An emergency, I guess. The plans are to drive to Rouen tomorrow. I've got to get a spot off my charcoal turtleneck sweater, or I'll have to wear the same thing I've got on tonight."

"Come sit and have a sip of cognac. It will do you good. You can borrow one of my sweaters for tomorrow. But why drive to Rouen?"

Anna picked up the snifter and sat down on the gold brocade sofa, hugging a throw pillow to her chest. "I should have said maybe we'll drive to Rouen. C-C was noncommittal. He seems distant. He still is estranged from his father. Something has happened to him. He was watching behind him all the time, as if someone were following us. In the car, he kept looking in the rearview mirror. And he's smoking."

"He always did. Quite a lot, if I remember."

"It's not how I had imagined, seeing him again, I mean. It just seems like our lives have taken separate turns. He seems to be so dedicated to his work. He has no family. He didn't mention having ever been married, and he wasn't wearing a wedding ring. In a way, I feel sad for him. I owe it to him to help him straighten out whatever caused the estrangement with his father. He seems to think it had something to do with me. Or at least he hinted at that. Besides, his father is the last one who may have seen Diamanté. I need to talk to that man somehow about that."

Monique gave her a knowing look. Anna had told her about Diamanté and what she had learned from Guy de Noailles. "Did you tell C-C about Diamanté?"

"No. I told him about the visit to see Guy and the surprise when I found out that he was his grandfather. But I didn't have time to get into the rest of the story."

"Do you have a plan to tell him tomorrow, then?"

"Yes. I need to enlist his help in my search for Diamanté. Come to think of it, I wonder if he knows Diamanté."

"Here's to your mission!" Monique held up her snifter in toast.

"And here's to you and Georges and your new *bastide* in Provence!"

"Yes, it's all set. We are leaving next weekend."

And I, thought Anna, *where will I be?* She shivered though it was not cold in the room. In reality, she dreaded the turn of events that tomorrow might bring.

CHAPTER 32

It was early Sunday morning. Anna, not wanting to wake Monique and Georges, quietly closed the door to the apartment and quickly descended the dim stairway. The air was cold and damp, and the dark street looked as if it had rained during the night. The green Renault was parked next to the curb.

"Did you get any sleep?" Anna asked C-C as he held the door for her.

"Only a little. You might have to keep me from falling asleep at the wheel." He grinned and closed the door, positioning himself behind the steering wheel. As he put the car in gear, he looked over in her direction.

"To Rouen? Are you sure?"

Anna noted that he had shed his doctor's coveralls and was wearing a heavy, navy blue mock turtleneck sweater and gray trousers. He was clean-shaven and smelled of soap. There were dark circles under his eyes.

"You look tired," she said.

"I'll be okay."

"Then to Rouen." Anna directed. "I'll keep you awake. En route, I have a story to tell you…an amazing but true story…a story you won't believe. I only told you half of it last night: the part about visiting Guy de Noailles and coincidentally discovering that he was your grandfather. There is another coincidence in this story. Did you know that your grandfather, my American grandfather, and my Corsican grandfather all knew each other during World War II?"

"What do you mean, your Corsican grandfather? I didn't know that you were part Corsican."

"I'm half Corsican, just like you, C-C."

One of C-C's eyebrows lifted in a question mark.

"I didn't know it either until recently. Remember I said last night that there was a question I was trying to resolve?"

He nodded.

"Well, when my American grandfather was dying, he told me this incredible story about a French man who was his friend during the war."

"*Grand-père?*"

"No. He never mentioned your grandfather. He told me about a man named Diamanté."

C-C slowed the car and pulled over to the curb near the Seine. The light of the streetlamps shone into the car. He stared at her. "What do you know about Diamanté?"

"Your grandfather said that your father knows him. Do you know Diamanté, too?"

"Diamanté occasionally visited my parents when I was a child. I remember him only vaguely. I knew he was a friend of my grandfather's. Why would you be interested in Diamanté?"

"Because…you see, he is apparently my grandfather, my Corsican grandfather."

"And your father would be?"

"His son, Diamanté *fils*."

"Where is he?"

"He died."

C-C blew air through his lips, indicating disbelief.

"Look, I need to show you something." She dug the two precious photos out of her purse, the one of her mother and the young man believed to be Diamanté *fils* and the other of the aged Diamanté that C-C's grandfather had given her. She showed the latter to C-C. "Your grandfather gave me this. It's a fairly recent photo of him."

C-C put on the car's overhead light and studied the photo. It was unmistakably the man who had come to get him at the hospital in August. "He looks like the man I remember being Diamanté...a little older."

"What do you know about him?"

"Not much. Whenever they were together, he and my father always spoke in a Corsican dialect. All short, choppy sentences. I couldn't understand a thing. I remember his hands were rough, gnarled, and he was physically very strong, like my father. The most amazing eyes, too—dark...vulpine."

She showed him the other photo. "This is my mother and the young man who I believe is Diamanté *fils*. I found it in an old album of photos of my mother that belonged to my grandparents. It was taken in California in front of my grandparents' home. There were no notes to identify the young man who was with my mother, but the face matches a face on one I saw at your grandfather's...that one was of Diamanté and his son together. Your grandfather said that photo was taken in Corsica after Diamanté's son had returned from California…before he went to the war in Algeria…where he was killed."

C-C studied the second photo. "Your mother was pretty, like you. What happened to her?"

"She died when I was young. My grandfather never told me who my father was, until the end. Neither Diamanté knew anything about me, as far as I know."

"You bear a strong resemblance to both your parents. Anna, did *Grand-père* tell you where Diamanté is now?"

"He doesn't know. He said the last person who may have talked to him, as far as he knows, is your father. Diamanté called in August to get your father's number in Rouen. He was apparently headed to Paris for some reason."

Yes, for good reason. C-C wished now, as he had many times since, that he had not been at La Pitié-Salpêtrière that fateful night. He would never be able to live his life again without looking behind him. Even now, on this drive, there could be a tail on him. He could never be sure.

Outside, the air was brisk and raw, causing the windows in the car to steam. C-C turned up the heater, put the car in gear, and headed for the entrance ramp to the A13. "So, you never told *Grand-père* that you and I knew each other."

"It was all such an overwhelming coincidence."

He again seemed preoccupied as he drove, keeping one eye on the rearview mirror.

"Why do you seem to be looking as if someone were following us?" Anna finally blurted out. "You did that last night also."

"I did?" He looked over at her. "I must have developed a bad habit or two since we last saw each other. You look very nice today."

Monique had lent Anna a beautiful, soft, cashmere sweater in a wine-red color. She had coiled her long hair into a simple, classic, sleek, low chignon and put on large, gold hoop earrings. She knew she looked good.

"You changed the subject on me," she said with a grin. "Oh, well, we probably both have...developed bad habits, that is. Mine is that I'm not as patient as I used to be."

He chuckled. "It's the Corsican blood. When you found out you had it, you became impatient."

"Do you think it would make a difference with your father? I mean, if he learned that I have Corsican blood in my veins?"

C-C pursed his lips. He thought about how his father had treated him when he had taken her to Rouen to meet his parents the first time. He had cut short the visit.

"I think he would be very surprised," he said.

A police car came from behind and sped past them. Following it was a SAMU ambulance. Both vehicles' two-tone sirens drowned out any further conversation for the moment.

CHAPTER 33

When Anna and C-C reached the outskirts of Rouen, the sky was blue and the day was crisp and clear. The winter sunshine coming through the car windows warmed Anna's shoulders.

To C-C, the route was familiar. He followed the quay along the Seine until they reached rue Jeanne-d'Arc. Turning right, he drove north until he was just short of the rue du Gros-Horloge, then made a sharp turn into a back alley. It was the same route the small, disguised ambulance had taken in August. As he pulled up behind the restaurant and turned off the engine, C-C looked at Anna as if to inquire, "Are you prepared for this?"

She read his look. "He is your father, C-C."

Lucie La Forêt was organizing her kitchen staff for the Sunday crowd when she noticed the green Renault that had driven up to the back door of Le Canard à la Rouennaise. She wiped her hands on her large, white apron, patted her curly head of white hair into place, and motioned to her sous-chef to carry on. As she approached the door, she saw the driver get out of the car and go around to the passenger side to open the door for a young lady.

"*Oh, oh, oh, oh là là.*" She cupped her two hands to her cheeks. "*Monsieur* Charlie!" She scurried into the alley, her large hips weaving sideways and the strings of her apron flying behind her. "Oh,

Monsieur Charlie!" She grabbed C-C, threw her arms around him, and kissed him three times in succession on his, now somewhat flushed, cheeks.

"*Salut*, Lucie."

"*Beh*, what are you doing here?" she said in her thick Norman accent as she held his face close to hers. "We haven't seen you in so long. We didn't know what happened. You didn't come back."

C-C motioned to her to not say anymore. He wagged his index finger at her and put it next to his lips.

"*Oh, oui, oui, oui.*" She said *oui* three times in succession from the side of her mouth, bouncing her large head up and down in agreement. It sounded to Anna more like "oy, oy, oy."

C-C took Anna's elbow and drew her beside him.

"Anna, this is Lucie La Forêt. She is the sous-chef of my father's restaurant."

Anna shook Lucie's large hand.

Lucie was the picture of a chef: rotund and rosy-cheeked. Her apron, though it was probably clean to begin with this morning, was already speckled with food stains from the specialties of the day.

"Oh, she is so beautiful, Charlie," she said.

C-C blushed again.

"*N'est-ce pas*," he replied with a quick smile. Then it was Anna's turn to blush.

"Come in, come in, it's cold out here." Lucie ushered them into the restaurant's warm kitchen where the staff was busily preparing dishes and chopping vegetables. The aroma of the combination of duck, chicken, apples, herbs, garlic, and spices cooking made Anna's mouth water. She realized she was hungry.

"Please, take off your coats," Lucie said as she led them into the back dining room of the restaurant.

"This is the family dining room," C-C explained to Anna. "We always ate here so my father could keep an eye on the sous-chef," he said with a chuckle.

"*Monsieur* Charlie, what can we prepare for you for Sunday dinner?" Lucie asked cheerfully as she beamed at them. One strand of white hair had sprung loose and was sticking out from over her temple.

"What's the *spécialité*?"

"The duck will be good today. It is still hunting season."

"Lucie, we are here to see my father. Is he upstairs?"

Lucie's eyes widened. She put her hand to her mouth. "*Oh là là*, Charlie, you didn't know? He left here. After you didn't come back again…" She hesitated, looking at Anna. "I am running the *resto* now, since he left."

C-C looked concerned. "But where did he go?"

Lucie's eyes darted toward Anna again.

Sensing Lucie's dilemma, C-C said, "Anna, would you excuse us, please?"

Anna was confused also. *What was all this about?* She had understood enough of the conversation and the body language to catch on to the obvious—that C-C was not allowing Lucie to ask him any questions. She also saw a look of worry and concern on C-C's face.

"Of course. Point me to the *cabinet*." They pointed down the hallway, and Anna left the room. As she headed to the restroom, the door to the dining room closed softly behind her.

"*Monsieur* Charlie, I'm sorry. I didn't know what to say. We were so worried about you. Your father thought you had been murdered. Diamanté didn't know what happened to you, either. He said he thought that your nurse was killed. Your father was beside himself. He wanted to talk with you that day. He had something for you. *Oh là là là là là là...*" She trailed off in a string of *oh là là là là*'ing and cupped her hands to her cheeks again, tears glistening in her eyes.

"It's all right, Lucie. Sit down." C-C motioned for her to have a seat at the dining room table and took a chair next to her. "I am all right."

"But the funeral...we saw it all on the television. She died? After all that?"

"Lucie, I can't tell you anything. It is the oath I took. You know that."

"Oh, Charlie, *merci Dieu* you are back safely." She traced a large sign of the cross quickly in the air above her forehead. "Were you in danger? Are you still in danger?"

C-C shrugged his shoulders and scratched his head. "I admit I don't know. Tell me, is my father all right? Nothing has happened to him?"

"He is sad, *Monsieur* Charlie, and the heart attack, it was bad for him, but now he is healthy as an old Norman cow again."

"The heart attack?"

"*Oui.* After you didn't come back, he began to have severe pains in his chest. One day, in late October, he just collapsed. We rushed him to the hospital. They said it was a mild attack and that he would recover quickly. It turned out that he was working too hard. That, combined with the stress of not knowing what happened to you."

"I…I didn't know."

"He decided that he couldn't stay in Rouen any longer. I agreed to take over the *resto* for him. I had been doing more and more of the management anyway. I hired the new staff myself." She straightened up with pride as she said that. "And I transformed the menu. Updated it."

"That is good, Lucie. But where did my father go? You must realize that I need to find him? *Oui?*"

"*Oui, oui, oui.* He left for the south. Provence. He is managing Diamanté's restaurant in Castagniers for him."

"Where is Diamanté then? Do you know?" C-C knew he wasn't the only one searching for Diamanté.

"Your father thought that Diamanté probably went to Corsica. We didn't know about Narbon…where he went anyway. We never heard from him. You know, there was always that bad blood between those two."

"No, actually I didn't know that. Between Narbon and Diamanté?"

"Yes. It was a long time ago, over Elise. They never forgave each other. At least, I don't think Narbon ever got over it. It's a long story. In the end, both of them lost to Diamanté's brother, Ferdinand."

"Did Diamanté ask my father to manage his *resto?*"

"Is possible. I don't know. One day your father may have decided that Diamanté's restaurant needed him, since it is a Corsican restaurant, you know, so he left. He calls once in a while to check up on us. I always tell him the same thing. We are doing a better job than he did." She chuckled. "I will give you his phone number." She thought for a minute and lowered her head, shaking it. "You would have laughed at the scene that day in the alley, Charlie. We all stood like soldiers, arm in arm. We didn't let those paparazzi get away until they had had too much to eat and drink. By that time, they had forgotten who they were chasing."

C-C smiled at her kindly. "That's good to know." He got up and walked over to the door. "Maybe we had better let Anna back in now." He opened it. Anna was standing in the hallway. "She's an old friend who is not so patient as she used to be."

Anna gave him a quick, flat grin and walked into the room.

"Will you two stay for dinner then?" Lucie was up from her seat.

Anna looked inquisitively at C-C.

"Lucie, it would be wonderful to have dinner in the *resto*. I wonder if we might see the old apartment before we dine?"

"But of course. It is not locked; go on up. I'll see to the duck. Oh, *Monsieur* Charlie, there is one other thing. Your dear mother left a box for you. It's sitting on the bookshelf where your father put it. He said that if you ever showed up, I should be sure and give it to you."

Anna and C-C climbed the back stairs to the family apartment. C-C's face was somber. "My father is not here, Anna. We have missed him today."

"What was all that secretiveness about? Silencing her, I mean, and closing the door. What happened?"

"It is nothing..."

But Anna's antenna was up. Something told her that there was more to this story.

Anna and C-C entered the apartment via a doorway that opened into a small, square hall painted in a light blue color with a

black-and-white checkerboard-style tiled floor. An antique win-
dowed wooden hutch held crystal and china. Two clean, white
aprons hung on a metal coat rack next to the hutch. There were
two doors off the hall. One opened into a bright kitchen, also tiled
in black-and-white, with white painted cupboards and white tiled
countertops. Well-used copper pots and pans hung from hooks on
the ceiling. An alcove held an outsized wine rack filled with bottles.

C-C led Anna through the second door, which opened into the
main sitting room of the apartment. The room was furnished in
overstuffed, blue, brocaded Louis XIV–style chairs and matching
sofa. A single, antique brass lamp stood on a round pedestal table
between the chairs, and two tall bookcases piled and stacked with
books lined one wall. In a corner, by the lace-curtained window,
stood a bust of Napoleon on a pedestal. Above the fireplace hung a
painting of a couple in bridal attire standing in front of a town hall,
and on the mantel stood a single, framed photo. Anna recognized it.
It was the same one that was on Guy de Noailles' mantel: a sepia-
toned picture of Guy holding a small boy's, C-C's, hand in front of
the Strasbourg Cathedral.

C-C motioned to Anna to have a seat on the sofa. He glanced
briefly into a room to the immediate right, then walked down the
hallway and disappeared into the room at the far end.

Nothing had changed in the entire apartment. It was just as it
had been when C-C's mother was alive. Standing in the middle of
his old bedroom, he noted the warm, red plaid comforter laid over
his bed, his childhood books on the small bookshelf. The carved
wooden pull-toy with red wheels that had been made for him by his
grand-père in Strasbourg sat on the woven rug, and the faded poster

of Johnny Hallyday still hung on the wall where he had placed it as a teen. He stood in the room for a few minutes, allowing himself to be the young boy again for just an instant. So much had happened to him since he had left that room.

Anna was examining the books on the bookshelves when he returned to the sitting room. C-C came up behind her. The box Lucie had mentioned was sitting on top of a large world atlas. He lifted it off the shelf and held it in his hands. It was a square, tin box, ornately decorated with gold and silver, a biscuit tin that had probably originally held *galettes*. A note in stylishly feminine handwriting was taped to the cover: "*Pour Charles-Christian, un jour quand je suis partie*." C-C pointed to the color reproduction of one of Monet's paintings of the Rouen Cathedral in the center of the cover. "That was her favorite painting. It's the cathedral where she and my father were married. She hung a framed print of it in their bedroom over the bed. It's still there."

"What do you think is in the box?"

"Oh, probably just some old photos and mementos of my mother's."

C-C placed the box on the pedestal table. He carefully broke the taped seal and opened the lid. The two of them hovered over it, peering together at the contents, which smelled strongly of perfume. C-C began carefully picking out items. First, there were several old frayed and bent black-and-white photos. Family photos. He placed them carefully on the table. Next, he picked out a small, black velvet pouch. Inside it was a red cord necklace with a square-shaped gold locket. The inscription on the locket in gold on bright red enamel read "*Je t'aime, Maman*."

"I gave this to her for Mother's Day one year," he said, "when I was about nine. I remember that I got it free when my father and I bought her some lingerie."

Another pouch made of white satin held a crystal and silver rosary. The box contained numerous other small objects, memories of his childhood: a blue rubber ball, a well-loved stuffed animal with one button eye missing, a miniature wooden replica of the astronomical clock in Strasbourg. He had just about emptied the contents of the box when he noticed something at the bottom, hidden under a white lace handkerchief embroidered with his mother's initials. He lifted the handkerchief and turned pale. Anna turned pale herself as the two of them fixed their eyes in disbelief on a pile of unopened letters, all addressed to C-C, all postmarked from California.

C-C picked the brittle, dry, and yellowed tissue-thin *par avion* envelopes one by one out of the bottom of the box and spread them on the table. There were twenty-two in all. Some had been sent to the apartment address in Paris and forwarded by Elise to Rouen. Some had been sent directly to Le Canard à la Rouennaise.

"*Voilà.*" He sighed. "*Alors,* I guess this solves our great mystery."

Anna sat down on the sofa. "Why do you think she saved them? What purpose? If she didn't intend for you to have them until after she died?"

"One can only speculate…it's possible she retrieved them from the trash after they had been thrown out."

"Every time I tried to call, your father answered. When he heard my voice, he would hang up. Do you suspect it was your father who threw out my letters?"

C-C nodded. "Who else wanted us apart so badly?"

"Is he that vicious?"

He nodded again. "He is an intense man, a ferocious man when he wants to be. He has a bad temper. My mother loved him, but she knew to rarely cross him. He was good to her. Saving the letters…" he swallowed hard, "it was her message to me…that she hadn't agreed with his decision."

"You mean he actually cut off relations with you because of me?"

"Not exactly because of you. I stood up to him over you. I declared my independence. That's what got it going. Then everything exploded…I mean everything. All the old arguments we had came back. We couldn't stand to be around each other. I stopped coming to Rouen to visit them. It probably broke my mother's heart to see that happen. I didn't see her for years, but she called me when she could…when he was out of the apartment. She knew you and I were still together, but she kept our secret. It never occurred to me until now that she knew you had left France…of course, she had to have known…because that's when the letters started to arrive. I know I didn't tell her you were gone. She never asked me about you after that. I was gone a lot…out of the country…for long periods. Then, all of a sudden two years ago she was very, very sick, and there was nothing that could be done to save her." His chin was quivering. He sat down on the sofa beside Anna and buried his face in his hands. Anna put her hand on his arm. For the next few minutes, the only sound that could be heard in the apartment was the solemn ticking of the grandfather clock in the hallway.

CHAPTER 34

Downstairs, Lucie's kitchen was a flurry of activity. Sunday dinner guests were arriving in the restaurant, and she wanted to make an extra special meal for C-C and Anna. There was something else she wanted to do.

"*Allô?*"

"*Salut*, Léo."

"Ah, Lucie. *Ça va?*"

"*Oui, oui, oui, bien sûr. Écoute*, Léo, are you coming to the *resto* for Sunday dinner, by any chance?"

"But of course, *ma chère*, do I ever miss your Sunday *spécialités*? What are we having today, may I ask?"

"Duck. Can you come early? I have a surprise for you. And bring Pierre with you, too. We will be dining in the family dining room."

"Has Jacques returned?"

"*Non*, better than that. Charlie is here, with a young lady."

"*Oh là là*, but this is great news! We'll be there. *Salut*." Léo La Bergère put down the receiver and rubbed his gnarled old hands together. "Such great news. He is all right after all."

Lucie punched the call button again and dialed a long number. It was several rings before there was an answer on the other end.

"*Allô*, Jacques?"

"*Salut*, Lucie. Don't tell me you have blown up my beautiful kitchen already."

"*Non, non, et non.* Everything is just fine here. The duck will be *superbe* today."

"*Eh bien,* congratulations! Are we just having a friendly Sunday chat, then?"

"You are in a jovial mood. Are you enjoying Provence?"

"*Beh oui.* The rain has quit for the time being. It's going to be a nice day."

"Same here. But cold. *Écoute*, Jacques, I have some good news. Charlie is here."

The phone was soundless on the other end. Finally, Jacques coughed. "He is alive, then. How does he look, Lucie?"

"He looks tired, Jacques, older, but he is okay. I couldn't get any information about what happened. He brought a young lady, a pretty one, with him. He didn't want to talk in front of her. They are upstairs in the apartment. They wanted to see you. I invited them to have dinner. Léo and Pierre will join us."

"*Ah bon.* Take two bottles of that vintage Château Haut-Brion from the back of the wine cellar, and make sure you set the table with the best china and crystal goblets from the hutch upstairs. Now, can you pass the phone to my apartment? I want to talk to Charlie. Oh, Lucie, remember about Nathalie's biscuit tin. Make sure he gets it."

Anna and C-C were still sitting on the sofa, staring in silence at the contents of the biscuit tin on the table, when the phone rang three short rings. C-C recognized the rings.

"That's the kitchen. It's probably Lucie wanting us to descend." He got up and answered it.

"*Allô*, Lucie, we'll be right down."

"It's not Lucie." The familiar voice was his father's. "*Salut*, Charlie. Lucie just told me that you are in Rouen. Are you all right? I was afraid…" the normally deep, growling voice sounded suddenly fragile and trailed off.

"*Oui*, Papa. I am all right. And you?"

"I decided to take a holiday. Running Diamanté's *resto* is a lot simpler than running the Rouen restaurant. We don't have the Sunday crowds—not yet anyway." His familiar, gravelly chuckle came through the receiver.

"Papa, I have someone with me who is looking for Diamanté, coincidentally. Have you heard from him?"

"*Non*. But I would not worry yet. He'll turn up. That's what I told Guy yesterday. He was calling for the same reason. He's worried about him since he always hears from him at Christmas." Jacques' voice changed. "Charlie," he inquired cautiously, "who is this person who is looking for Diamanté?"

C-C was reluctant to tell Jacques that it was Anna. "It's merely someone who wants to meet him."

"*Ah bon.*"

"Are you coming back to Rouen for Christmas?"

"I hadn't made plans. I thought you were…" again the silence, then a cough. "Are you back at the hospital in Paris?"

"Yes. Everything is *normale*, mostly. I'm working long hours…in the trauma center again."

"Are you afraid?"

"Yes. Sometimes. We best not talk."

"*Oui, bien sûr.*"

"I was thinking that maybe we should…would it be possible to get together? I would like to see you, Papa."

"Do you want to come down here for Christmas? Take a little vacation?"

C-C looked over at the contents of his mother's box strewn on the table. *Resolve this before I lose him, too,* he thought.

"I can request it. But the holidays are bad times for the ER."

"Charlie, I'm sorry…about everything. We are, after all, Corsican. For your mother's sake, let's…" His father's voice trailed off. The rest of the sentence wasn't audible. Then there was silence, except for the sound of his breathing.

"Papa?" C-C turned around to look at Anna who was staring at him, her eyes wide.

"*Oui?*"

"Nothing." C-C bid his father *au revoir* and put down the receiver.

"That was your father? Where is he?"

C-C returned to the sofa. "In the south of France. He's running Diamanté's restaurant for him. No one knows where Diamanté is. *Grand-père* apparently called again yesterday asking about him. They've known each other for a long time. They keep saying not to worry. He'll show up."

"I know. I mostly worry about what happens if he does." Anna smiled. "What is he going to think? Will he even believe my story?"

The phone rang again three rings.

"That's Lucie for sure this time." C-C got up to answer it.

"*Oui. Oui. Tout de suite.*" He put down the receiver. "We are wanted downstairs. Apparently there are visitors."

They quickly put the items on the table back into the tin box. C-C placed it under his arm. "Do you want me to read the letters?"

"If you wish. It's all old news now, though. Maybe you should just toss them into the trash...for once and for all."

He didn't answer her.

CHAPTER 35

They were waiting with grins on their faces in the hallway at the bottom of the stairs.

"Charlie!" Léo La Bergère was the first to grab C-C and hug him. "So good to see you!" He shook C-C's hand vigorously.

"*Bonjour*, Léo. It's been a long time." C-C turned to the other man. "*Père* Truette."

The priest took C-C's hand. "It's good to have you home, my son." His voice was soft and kindly.

C-C introduced Anna to them.

"*Enchanté*," they said in unison as they each extended a hand.

Lucie bustled from the dining room. "Léo and Pierre are having dinner with us. Please, everyone, come in and be seated. Jacques specifically ordered that we open bottles of Château Haut-Brion. I chose 1936, a fine year…before the war. Jacques saved them from the Germans and from the bombs, you know." She shooed them into the wood-paneled dining room and pointed to their places at a table set with white linens, fine crystal goblets, silver, and china. A silver candelabra with white lit candles twinkled in the center, flanked by sparkling crystal decanters of dark red wine.

"Too bad Jacques isn't here to enjoy this celebration," Léo lamented as the aperitif was poured. They toasted to good fortune and good food…and then to the young couple. "To Charlie and to Anna."

Lucie took a seat at the table as her staff entered with the first course. "I'm putting my sous-chef in charge for the next two hours," she announced. "I don't want to miss any of the conversation. *Bon appétit!*"

The first course was *boudin blanc*, a delicately flavored fresh sausage made with veal.

"*Spécialité de Normandie.* Ah, there is nothing I like more!" Léo declared as Lucie glared at him. "Except, of course, *la pièce de résistance*, the duck. Did you know, Anna, that this *resto* is renowned for its duck?"

"I assumed by the name."

Léo went on. "Ah, but such a duck! Le *canard à la rouennaise* has a story." His eyes twinkled as he seemed to be warming up to tell it.

"Oh, *non*, not Jacques' story, Léo. Leave it!" Lucie exclaimed. There was a collective sigh as they all anticipated what was coming.

C-C smiled. He knew it by heart. "My father," he said, "entertains anyone who will listen with the story about how the duck is killed by suffocation so that the blood is retained, giving the meat a particularly rich flavor. Each time he tells it, he embellishes it so as to make the meal a memorable experience for his clientele. It's a story of fear and terror, but only my father can tell it!"

Léo feigned a stab to the heart. "*Bon, alors.* Jacques tells it better than I do, anyway."

Anna asked C-C, "Why did your father decide to settle in Rouen?"

"He never talked about it. I don't believe that anyone ever knew."

"He is correct," inserted the priest. "Jacques had an air of *mystère* about him. We only knew him during the war. He was young, only in his teens, at the onset. He helped form *Les Amis Clandestins*. Originally, his interest in the Résistance movement was only in saving France's wine. He joined forces with the local restaurateurs and the winemakers to protect France's treasured commodity from plunder. The wine cellar of this *resto*, in fact, was concealed by a false wall. It held over ten thousand bottles of wine during the war, and it also provided a safe haven. *Les Amis* rescued people who were in danger, particularly American and British fliers who had been shot down. Eventually, Jacques became the sole owner. He only ever talked about his life since he married Nathalie, which also occurred, of course, here in Rouen."

Léo La Bergère couldn't help adding, "Nathalie was a native of Strasbourg. The way Jacques tells it, she spent all of her summers with her Norman relatives because her father, a banker in Strasbourg, originated from Rouen. She met Jacques literally over a *Tarte Tatin*."

"Those from Strasbourg believe that they make the best *Tarte Tatin*," C-C added. "The Normans, of course, credit their apples."

"Exactly!" the rest of them chimed in.

C-C continued. "My mother was a good match for my father. She had a fine sense of cooking herself, being that she always claimed that she originated from the gastronomical capital of France." He looked around the table with a mischievous grin. "A fact that she maintained is corroborated by most French citizens." Around the table could be heard loud objections. "Everyone note!" He wagged his finger at them. "She eventually won out on the *Tarte Tatin*, and it was her recipe, not Papa's, that the *resto* served."

"And still does today," Lucie added. "That's one recipe I won't change."

"*Voilà!*" C-C put both his hands on the table in triumph.

Lucie thought for a moment and then added with a wink as she took them all in, "There's another story about Jacques that we can tell since he isn't here." She hesitated, then began with a dramatic flourish. "Because he enjoyed his own cooking, he was from time to time submitted to *la régime de Madame Gérard*." She emphasized each of the last words dramatically.

A collective "Ahhhhh!"

"This diet that Nathalie claimed to have invented herself consisted of vegetables, lots of water, and no bread, cheese, wine, or sugar!"

A collective "Oh, *quelle horreur!*"

The unified audience's support for Lucie's story was amusing to Anna. She looked at C-C. He seemed to be enjoying himself.

Lucie continued, "This put Jacques in atrociously bad humor, and everyone could tell by the booming of his voice when *Madame* had submitted him to yet another round of her famous *régime*. It was impossible for Jacques to live without his Camembert!"

Collective shaking of heads all around.

C-C looked over to Anna as the conversation paused. "Our Anna here is a *raconteur*. She has published several books. One was just introduced in France."

Admiring glances and a collective "*Ah bon, ah bon! Félicitations!*"

"What kind of books do you write, Anna?" The question came from the priest.

"Novels. Fiction. They're stories. I like to tell stories."

Lucie beckoned to the sommelier to fill the wine goblets. "Tell us a story, Anna."

Anna glanced around the table. They were all looking at her with anticipation. She thought for a moment, made a personal decision, and then cleared her throat.

"This is the tale of three men," she began, "one American, one French, and the third Corsican. Each of them has a story." She paused for dramatic effect. "The American was a handsome young flier during the Second World War. He flew bomb runs over northern France. The Frenchman left his farm in Normandy and eagerly went off to fight in the war in Italy. After his leg was badly wounded, he returned to France. The Corsican also left his native Corsica at a young age and joined the *maquis*. He was said to have a lethal gaze and magical powers of survival. One day, during the worst of the fighting, the American flier's plane was shot down over France. After landing his parachute, he was found and hidden by the Frenchman and the Corsican who were with the Résistance fighters working against the enemy. He called them his liberators. The Corsican became his good friend. They wrote to each other after each had returned to his respective homeland after the war. Each married. The American had an only daughter; the Corsican had an only son. One day, the Corsican wrote to the American that his son was coming to the United States for military training. Would the American entertain junior on weekends so that he wouldn't get homesick, he inquired."

Anna paused to take a sip of the wine. It tasted smooth and rich from decades of aging.

"The American's daughter was seventeen," she continued. "She fell in love with the Corsican's handsome son. He in turn was enchanted by her and returned her love. When it was time for the young man to leave, he promised her that he would come back to get her. But he never came back. Several months later, the old Corsican fighter sent another letter to his friend, the American flier. His son, it said, had been sent to yet another war...the Algerian conflict... and he was killed. The Corsican was heartbroken. So too was the American's daughter, for she had just delivered his baby. The little girl's complexion was light olive. She had black, curly hair, and she resembled her Corsican father. The American flier didn't hear from the Corsican again, and he never told him that he had a grandchild. The granddaughter grew up, tragically without either her mother or her father, and went to study in France, never knowing that she was half Corsican." Anna paused again. The group around the table gave the impression of a photo at a family reunion. They were all looking her way, chewing on their food and listening intently. Finally, the priest spoke.

"But, *Mademoiselle*, you said the story was about three young men? What about the Frenchman?"

"I'm coming to that. Thirty-five years later, after the American flier had passed away, the granddaughter was going through his mementos. As if by magic, an old Christmas card from the Frenchman caught her eye. It had been sent from France five years after the war. The granddaughter set off on a quest. She traveled to France and tracked down the Frenchman, who by this time was almost ninety years old. One day, she knocked on his door. She found out many things about her Corsican grandfather, except his whereabouts. To this day, the granddaughter does not know where he is, but she continues her quest with the anticipation of one day finding him."

C-C was looking intensely at Anna. Her eyes locked on his.

"The moral of the story is, whatever the quest, it is the journey itself which in the end makes the story interesting. The American was my grandfather. The Frenchman is—" she was still swimming in C-C's gray eyes. "I didn't know it before I visited him, but he is Charles-Christian's *grand-père*, Guy de Noailles. And the Corsican? I believe you all know him as *le loup*."

"Diamanté?" They gasped in unison.

Anna nodded her head as she pulled her eyes away from C-C's and looked at the others.

Léo La Bergère was the first to speak. "But this incredible story, it is true?"

Anna laughed. "As with all stories, there is an element of fiction and an element of reality. For example, it is not known whether the young man ever promised to return to California. What is true is that I am the granddaughter with the quest, and Diamanté doesn't know of my existence."

"Whew!" There was a collective wind, and the candles flickered as they blew through their lips in unison.

Lucie looked at her, tears glistening in her eyes. "But this is *étonnant*, an astonishing story, Anna. I hope you find the old *mec*. That fellow's a hard one. We all know that." They all indicated that they agreed with her. "It will do him good to have a granddaughter such as yourself. He could use some softening up."

Anna thanked them for listening to her. She had told the story in French. C-C leaned over to her and whispered, "You told it well."

The meal was just as promised. The duck, strongly flavored and redolent of herbs, garlic, and spices, was superb, and there was apple *Tarte Tatin* for dessert. They were all stuffed and happy as they sipped on strong coffee afterward. The laughter and stories continued, some from the war days, prompted by Anna's story. Finally, Léo and Pierre said their *au revoirs*, and Lucie excused herself to return to the kitchen to check up on her staff.

C-C leaned into Anna. "How about a walk?"

They put on their coats and headed out the front of the restaurant down the rue du Gros-Horloge. As if by habit, as she had done so many times in the past without thinking, Anna slid her arm under C-C's elbow. It was midafternoon, and already the December sun was low in the sky.

"How did Lucie come to be your father's sous-chef? Is there a story there?"

"Actually, *oui*. Lucie's mother, as I understand it, was with the Résistance. She was a member of the same organization with Léo, Father Truette, and my father. There were others, too. Some of them we heard about in the stories during dinner. They are mostly gone now. Lucie was just a little girl during the war, but she grew up hanging around the restaurant, and my father taught her everything. She is quite a natural."

"Certainly seems to be. The food was excellent."

"You can't find any better in Rouen, my father always says." They crossed the street. Directly in front of them was the ancient clock which had been there since 1389 and for which the street had been named.

"C-C, what was all that hush-hush business about?"

"Hush-hush? I don't understand what you mean."

"Secretive. They kept asking you questions about something, and you kept trying to divert the conversation. You were deliberately keeping something guarded. I could tell."

He smiled. "It's a game I always play with them. Since I was a little kid. I don't want them to know everything about me." He kicked a stone into the street. "Did you notice, Anna? I haven't smoked all day."

"You just changed the subject."

He grinned and put his gloved hand on top of hers still hooked in the crook of his arm.

"Did we accomplish anything today?"

"What did you expect us to accomplish?"

"I thought we would resolve the differences with your father. We didn't do that."

"We opened the door. I talked to him."

"Will you go see him?"

C-C looked at his watch. "We should be getting back to Paris."

CHAPTER 36

Anna shivered as C-C opened the door to his apartment and held it for her. Neither had talked much on the trip back to Paris. He had driven directly to his apartment, and she had not objected. Their day together had been easier than she had anticipated. It was as if they had rediscovered an old bond by driving to Rouen.

The apartment was sparsely decorated. It had oak beams and a narrow, wooden spiral staircase that linked the first floor to a room above. There was an outsized sofa in the space by the window, a writing desk next to a bookshelf along an ancient, exposed stone wall with a fireplace, a small empty table with two chairs, and a modern-looking stainless steel kitchenette at the back. A miniature abstract painting hung over the bookshelf, and a CD player sat on top of it. Much to Anna's surprise, the apartment smelled of French soap rather than smoke.

C-C took off his coat and lit the gas fireplace. "This will get you warmed up."

"What's up there?" She nodded toward the top of the spiral staircase.

"The bedroom. A bed and a TV is all there is room for. It's really very small."

He put on a CD. Anna caught her breath as the captivating strains of Strauss' "Blue Danube" waltz filled the room.

"Do you remember our weekend in Vienna?"

"How could I forget it?"

She took off her coat and walked over to look out the French windows to the double balcony where *Madame* Russe had sat a decade earlier. "This apartment is definitely larger than your old one."

"*Oui*, do you remember how we had trouble waltzing in that one?" He laughed as he rearranged a coffee table from the center of a Persian rug in the middle of the floor. When he had moved it aside, he stood in its place and held out his arms to her in invitation. "Dance with me, Anna?"

She smiled and took his hand. She had definitely missed dancing with him.

It had all started with a Viennese waltz. Anna had thought it rather clichéd at the time. Waltzing to Strauss in Vienna had seemed so trite to her that she had laughed aloud. But the memory had permeated their love life when they returned to Paris. They had made romantic modifications, allowing their bodies to move in slow motion together to the music. It had seemed, as the tempo quickened, that they heard only the beat of each other's heart. She closed her eyes now as she remembered the intense lovemaking that always ensued.

C-C put his arm around her back and moved his cheek close to hers. As before, they began to waltz in slow motion, pressing closer and closer together, each aware that they had not been intimate for a decade. His groin touched hers; he was hard with wanting her. He brushed his lips against hers, and then his tongue played with her ear. She let him undo her chignon, and as he did, her hair fell to her shoulders. He slowly maneuvered her to the sofa by the window. She lay back against the pillows. He started to undress her, kissing her cheeks softly. His tongue sought her mouth, and then his hands traveled down her abdomen. He pulled her in close, feeling inside her thighs, and touching her most intimate erotic spots. Her spine tingled. She took his head in her hands, pulling him up to her, kissing him hard on the lips.

"I have missed you so," he whispered as he smothered his face in her hair. "It was never like this…I mean…I never felt the same with anyone else."

She pulled his sweater over his head and kissed his chest.

A car's security system suddenly blared loudly in the street. It didn't stop.

"*Merde,*" he said. Still holding her in his arms, he reached over and pulled the curtain aside so he could see into the street below. "It's the Renault. I'd better investigate."

"Do you have to?"

"Don't go anywhere. I'll be right back." He looked worried as he pulled on his sweater and put on his coat.

"Be careful," Anna told him as he closed the apartment door. She shivered and pulled a throw around her bare shoulders.

C-C saw the dark figure immediately. Someone was tampering with his car. There was very little light, and the street was wet. He maneuvered next to the wall in order to get a better view. Suddenly, everything went black, and then he dropped to the ground.

CHAPTER 37

Downstairs in the concierge's loge, Elise was awakened by the unsettling sound of a car siren in the street. She peeked through her lace-curtained window, which gave her a view of the courtyard, just in time to see the shadow of one of her tenants slipping through the heavy wooden door.

A raspy, heavily accented male voice came from behind her. "What is it?"

"I don't know. *Oh là*! Someone just left the building. It may have been Charlie."

"Did it look like him?"

"Same size."

"Then I'd better have a look."

He was already putting on his jacket.

"Be careful, *Lobo*." Elise watched as he opened the door and moved quietly and stealthily through the courtyard. The Portuguese pet name she had given him suited him well. He was an old man now, but he reminded her of her late husband in so many ways. The way he didn't make a sound when he moved. They both had learned that during the war.

He was too late to save the blow from coming, but he saw it happen in the shadows of the dampened, dark street. The only sound interrupting the calm was the incessant shrieking of the car's siren.

A large, bulky man had hit Charles-Christian on the head with a heavy object, felling him immediately.

For a Corsican, he should have been taught to watch out for himself better, Diamanté thought. Without making a sound, he crept up behind the person tampering with the car, simultaneously kicking the back of the man's knees to bring him down to the ground and taking the man's tool away from him.

"*Salaud!* Get the hell out of here! Or I kill you." He slammed the tool into the thief's head. He couldn't make out a face in the dark.

Reeling from the blow, the perpetrator tried to get up, then staggered down the street after his accomplice. The car alarm suddenly quit blaring.

Meanwhile, unaware of Diamanté's presence and unable to see anything through the blur of blood pouring down his forehead and into his eyes, Charles-Christian braced himself against a wall, pulled himself to his feet, staggered, then turned and ran back into the apartment building.

Diamanté silently followed him through the heavy door, crossed the secluded courtyard, and reentered Elise's apartment.

"It was him. He was hit on the head, but he will be all right," he told her. "He can still move."

Elise was alarmed. "But who?"

"I think just car thieves. Look at this." He showed her the bloody tool. It was an ordinary set of pliers. "But it could be something else. We should keep our watch at the window for a bit longer, just in case they come back."

The old couple watched in the darkness, like worried, protective parents waiting on the end of a child's first date.

Bloodied and holding his head, C-C entered his apartment.

"What happened?" Anna raised her hand to her mouth in horror as she saw the blood spurting from the cut above his eye.

"It's only a minor cut. Not serious. The head just bleeds a lot. We have to get out of here. Get your coat." C-C turned off the CD and grabbed his medical bag, which was sitting by the door. Then he did an odd thing. He opened the tin box that his mother had left him, took out Anna's letters, stuffed them in the bag, and handed the box to Anna. "Keep this for me. We may not be seeing each other for a while." He turned off the lights in the apartment and peered cautiously through the window as he held a towel to his bleeding head.

"But what is going on? I want to know, C-C." Anna was terrified. "Charles-Christian Gérard, what are you mixed up in?"

He turned around to her. "It is not illegal, if that's what you are thinking. I was involved with something having to do with my profession…that I can't talk about. Maybe someday I will be able to tell you. In any case, here's the plan. We will use the back exit to the street, then find a hotel where we can call a taxi. If we're not followed, we'll take you to rue Beaujon. If we are, we'll go to the hospital. You can take a taxi from there."

"But who would be following us?"

"That's just it…I don't know exactly."

It wasn't long before Elise and Diamanté, watching from the concierge's apartment window, saw C-C, holding a towel to his head, guide a young woman through the lower courtyard. The two exited via the heavy back door that Elise always used as her entrance to the building.

"I'd better follow them," Diamanté said.

Elise nodded in approval. "Is there anything I should do?"

"No. Try to go back to sleep," he said, tenderly placing his hand on her shoulder. Then he added as he put on his black beret, "Jacques should have trained his son better."

The street was deserted as C-C led Anna toward a small hotel on rue Saint-Jacques. They caught a rare taxi sitting idle outside the hotel; once inside, they were able to speak.

"Will you do something for me…tomorrow?" C-C asked her.

Anna nodded.

"I don't want Elise to worry. Go back to the apartment building and see her. Tell her I have left for Africa again. Give this to her." He handed Anna a wad of hundred-franc notes. "It will cover my rent for a while."

Anna watched the blur of the buildings racing by through the taxi's window. Her head was spinning. This all seemed surreal. She looked at C-C. His skin was pale, his eyes slightly glazed.

"But where will you go?"

He sat in silence. He was cold, light-headed. His pulse rate was too fast. His hands and feet were clammy. He was diagnosing his own initial symptoms of shock. The towel was soaked with blood. He knew he needed to get to the hospital.

They arrived at rue Beaujon. C-C pulled Anna close, assuring her as he kissed her hand, "This is not *adieu*. We are destined to see each other again. I will get word to you."

"Take care of yourself, C-C," Anna said as she got out and stood by the taxi. She held her hand to the taxi window. From the inside, C-C pressed his hand to the glass against hers. The taxi pulled away, and he was gone. Tears streamed down Anna's face as she stood alone in the deserted street.

CHAPTER 38

"Où *allez-vous, Monsieur? À quelle direction?*" The taxi driver hesitated before entering the mostly deserted place Charles de Gaulle.

In the rear seat, C-C checked his watch. It was just two o'clock in the morning. The first train of the day, he knew, wouldn't depart for Nice until almost eight o'clock. He checked to make sure no one was following them from behind. How many times had he done that tonight, every night? Would he even know if there was anyone there? And what could he do about it, anyway? Run away, like he was doing now? He needed to think clearly. He had to stop by the hospital and get the duffel bag he had kept there in case of just such a situation. He would leave instructions for his patients, too. He knew that he couldn't depart abruptly like he had on August 31. He was severely reprimanded for that when he returned. He had to give the hospital a good reason this time. Maybe he could take the vacation he didn't have in August? But he needed to be careful. What if they were waiting for him there?

Who are "they," anyway?

C-C had grown weary of the endless looking over his shoulder. Then there was the thought of Anna. He could still smell the lingering scent of her.

Maybe I shouldn't leave, he thought.

He looked out the window at the street behind them. The thought of losing Anna again mortified him. He opened his cell phone in his confusion, and closed it again.

What would be the use of talking to her now? What could I tell her?

His head throbbed. A warm trickle of blood ran down the side of his face. He felt weak.

Better get this looked at.

The taxi had not moved.

"*Beh...alors...mais regardez!*" The driver pointed to the ticking meter. "*Enfin.*" The man threw up his arms in aggravation. "*Où allez-vous, Monsieur?*"

"La Pitié-Salpêtrière."

CHAPTER 39

Charles-Christian arrived at La Pitié-Salpêtrière distressed and in pain. He went first to the trauma center, where he found someone to stitch and bandage the wound over his temple, and then he showered and changed into a clean shirt and trousers. He grabbed the already-packed duffel bag from his locker and, noting Anna's book sitting on the top shelf, stuffed it into a side pocket. Next, he went to find the new *Chef* d'*Urgences*. She had recently replaced the former chief who had reprimanded him. He got along well with her.

"It is time for a vacation," he told her.

To his surprise, the woman agreed with him.

"So I've noticed, Dr. Gérard," she said scrutinizing his bandaged head with her close-set, beady eyes. "You have looked stressed and drawn lately. Take some time for yourself. Enjoy the holiday…away from Paris, if you can."

Away from Paris, if you can, he repeated to himself an hour later as he stood in line at the *guichet* of the Gare de Lyon in the twelfth arrondissement. He bought a ticket for the 7:54 TGV to Nice. *Over a thousand kilometers away from Paris.* The *trains à grande vitesse* traveled at speeds up to three hundred kilometers per hour. He looked at his watch. The trip would take over three hours. At least he would get some much-needed sleep. Then he would rent a car and drive the twenty kilometers to Castagniers. He pondered what it would be like to be face-to-face with his father again. He had called Jacques from the hospital phone to tell him to expect him this evening. He bought a Monday morning newspaper and settled himself into a corner seating area in the ornate passenger terminal. He took off his heavy winter coat, put it, his duffel bag, and his medical kit on the seat beside him, and then lit a cigarette and looked around casually.

The first travelers of the day were lined up to purchase *cafés au lait*, croissants, and tartines from a vendor's cart. The station smelled of cigarette smoke, fresh strong coffee, and diesel fuel, all of which were overpowered at times by pungent human smells courtesy of the assortment of derelicts who had made the station their bedroom overnight. Out near the platforms, the orange-colored TGVs awaited their departures for southern France, the Alps, Switzerland, Italy, and Greece.

Charles-Christian opened the newspaper and buried his head in it. It would provide camouflage, if needed, and diversion for the next hour or so until the train's loading time was announced.

A man sat down in the seat next to him. He placed a small, tattered valise on the floor between his feet. Charles-Christian continued reading his paper and ignored him. In the background, loudspeakers announced the times of the first departures of the day in French, English, German, and Italian.

"You should watch yourself, *mon ami*. You should have seen the man before he hit you." The voice was low and raspy, the accent familiar.

Charles-Christian lowered his newspaper slightly and peered over the top. The man was in his midseventies. He was wearing a black beret. His wolf-like eyes were not looking at Charles-Christian, but studying the surroundings as if searching for prey. Charles-Christian's eyes narrowed.

"What? What are you doing here?" he said in a low voice.

"Don't look at me. I made your father a promise. You are going to Nice, aren't you?"

Charles-Christian nodded.

"I am also. I'll find you once we board." Diamanté Loupré-Tigre stood and picked up his valise. As if they had not spoken at all, he wandered off noiselessly.

CHAPTER 40

Exhausted and head pounding from the wound, Charles-Christian boarded the Nice-bound train. He found a seat and didn't even bother to look around the sparsely occupied car. No one sat in the seat next to him.

Further down the platform, Diamanté waited, as always on the alert for signs of anyone following him. When he had reassured himself that it was safe to board, he chose the car behind the one Charles-Christian had just entered.

At the back of the train, a man waited, watching. When he was sure that Diamanté had not seen him, he boarded the train and took a seat in the very last car.

At just before eight o'clock, the cars lurched and the train began to slowly move out of the station. Charles-Christian relaxed a bit and looked out the window at the dark Paris streets. It was drizzling again, and there would be a possibility of light snow during the day. The temperature had fallen overnight. *Au revoir, Paris. Au revoir, Anna.* The gentle, quiet movement of the car rocked him almost immediately to sleep.

When he awoke, it was light outside, a dark gray light. The train was moving fast through the lifeless winter countryside. Rain streaked across the windowpanes. He pulled himself up in his seat and looked around him. The car was still mostly empty. There was, however, an occupant in the seat beside him. Diamanté was looking at him.

"You really should be more alert, *mon ami*. I could have easily robbed you while you slept."

Charles-Christian rubbed his eyes like a small child.

"Do you want something to eat?" Diamanté handed him a bag of pastries. Charles-Christian chose a *croissant au chocolat* and bit into it. He still said nothing.

"I had a call from your father. He told me that you were arriving in Castagniers today. I guessed you would be taking the first train this morning to Nice. It wasn't hard to find you in the *gare*."

"Did my father ask you to tail me?"

"I made a promise to your father...after the events of August 31...that if they let you go, I would protect you. We Corsicans always keep our promises."

"Protect me from what? Whom?"

"Have you noticed anyone following you?"

"No, but I have sensed it. There have been some..." Charles-Christian hesitated, "incidents."

"Like the time your car was forced off the road?"

"How did you know about that?"

"I saw it happen. It was an unmarked car. Hard to determine who was behind the wheel."

"So you have been following me too?"

"Jacques and I have a pact. He agreed to take over the running of my restaurant. I agreed to protect you. When we Corsicans are needed somewhere, we are there. Elise, my brother's widow, has been harboring me in her apartment. I think she enjoys the company. I try to remember to bring her flowers every week."

Charles-Christian had noticed flowers in the concierge's window of late. It had also occurred to him that Elise had seemed happier, more animated, especially recently.

"You did me a great favor when you approached her about the empty apartment in her building, you know," Diamanté went on, chuckling quietly. "It made it a lot easier to keep track of you."

"She emerges from her ground-floor lair every time I leave or enter the building," Charles-Christian said. Diamanté gave him an indifferent look. "She's very vigilant. There's no way to escape without her noticing. Why didn't you just tell me you were in Paris?"

"There was no need to worry you. In a while, if I thought you had proven that you could take care of yourself…"

"But you don't think I can take care of myself."

Diamanté shrugged his shoulders. "You confirmed that last night, *mon ami.*"

"So you have been following me…everywhere? Did you follow me to Rouen yesterday? If you did, I never saw you."

"I was quite a ways behind. Pretty lady you had with you."

Charles-Christian was suddenly reminded of the relationship between Anna and this man. He studied him closely. If he was her grandfather, the resemblance between the two was hard to see.

"Did you know I talked to my father from Rouen then?"

"He told me this morning. I think he is glad you are going to see him. It's hard for fathers sometimes to admit they were wrong. He wants to have his son back. I don't know what happened between you. He never said. We Corsicans don't believe in speaking of personal matters. I don't ask now."

Charles-Christian was silent for a few moments. Something was bothering him. "What did you mean when you said I should have seen the man before he hit me?"

"Just that. You are a Corsican. Your father should have trained you to be more alert. I told him that on the phone this morning. I heard the car siren last night. Elise saw you leave the building. By the time I got outside, you were on the ground, dead out. I chased the two away. You never saw me in the darkness."

"I guess I owe you that. It didn't even occur to me that there would be two of them. I was pretty stupid thinking I could take on even one *mec* by myself, *hein?*"

"Agreed."

"Do you think they were thieves? I guessed they were tampering with my car."

"I don't know exactly. I grabbed the tool the *mec* was using and hit him hard with it." Diamanté chuckled again. "He retreated, *le lâche*. The other one did, too. Just before you came to and ran back into the building."

"I got clobbered pretty good. They put several stitches in my head at the hospital." Charles-Christian rubbed his bandage.

"I hope the *mec* I hit had to have three times as many." For the first time, Diamanté almost smiled at him. His voice softened. "I checked your car. It's all right. Whatever they intended to do to it, they didn't succeed. Doesn't mean they won't try again, mind you. You should get rid of it when you get back to Paris."

A vendor came through the car selling espressos. Diamanté bought one. He took a sip of the strong, black coffee and grimaced. "It was a setup, you know," he said. "Narbon and I went our separate ways. I took the train to Paris. I haven't seen him since. Nor has Jacques. At first I intended to go back to my restaurant, but Jacques was very concerned about you." He took another sip of the coffee. "When we ran, we didn't look back. There weren't many people on the pier. I saw only a young woman. We watched for any news about the incident for days. Nothing. All that was broadcast were the scenes of the accident and the funeral in London."

"Why do you think it was a setup?"

"I don't know. I got this call to activate the old escape line. It was similar to calls I receive from time to time. One doesn't question, but one has to be careful. Sometimes…in my line of work… one can be…well…I let down my guard. *Merde*." He spat.

"Do you have any idea now who it was?"

"*Non. Pas du tout.*" Diamanté shook his head and kept his eyes diverted from Charles-Christian's as he glanced around the car. The train slowed for a moment, then crossed a bridge and speeded up again. "I hope it wasn't too difficult for you," he said.

"They let me do my work, if that's what you mean. I was treated well. It was a while before they allowed me to leave, though. I can't tell you anything else."

Diamanté nodded. "I'm sorry for getting you involved."

Charles-Christian looked out the window at the countryside. The landscape was brown and flat. Barren trees dotted the horizon. In another hour, there would be some green to the terrain and the sun would be warmer coming in through the train's window as they

approached the Côte d'Azur. Diamanté's sudden apology had taken
him by surprise. Corsican men, he knew from experience with his
father, didn't like to apologize. It meant acknowledging their fal-
libility.

"I met her before, you know. When I was working with the
Médecins Sans Frontières in Africa. She visited a hospital where
the AIDS patients were being treated. I was one of the doctors she
spoke to." He paused, for a moment miles away in thought as he
listened to the dull, monotonous drone of the speeding train, then
he continued. "She was very beautiful."

Diamanté didn't answer him.

Does Diamanté know who she really is? Charles-Christian wondered
as he excused himself, got up, and went to the WC.

When he returned to his seat, he had made a decision. "Do you
remember anyone by the name of Ellis from the war? An American
flier. I believe his name was Stu Ellis."

Diamanté seemed taken by surprise. His war memories flooded
him temporarily. He cleared his throat. "Stu Ellis, *ah oui*, my friend
Stu Ellis. He was from California. Why do you know about him?"

"Did you ever see Stu Ellis after the war?"

"*Non.* Unfortunately not. We both returned home, married,
and had children. I believe he had a daughter. We wrote to each
other for a few years. My son visited him." He paused with the
painful memory of the death of his son. "He was in the military, and
he was in California for training. Stu and his family were very good
to him." Eyebrows knitted, he gave Charles-Christian an impatient
look. "But what is all this about Stu Ellis? I haven't heard from him
in a long time."

"Did you ever hear the name Anna Ellis?" Charles-Christian persisted.

"*Non, jamais.*" The old man shook his head, baffled. "Who is she?"

"Anna is Stu Ellis' granddaughter, his daughter's daughter."

Diamanté didn't have a clue as to where Charles-Christian was taking this discussion. "I assumed he would have grandchildren by now," he replied gruffly.

This was delicate. Charles-Christian was trained in delicate situations. He was good when dealing with patients and their relatives, but this was a whole different matter. "Did your son ever mention Ellis' daughter?"

"What are you saying?" Diamanté's black piercing eyes penetrated Charles-Christian's like daggers.

"Diamanté, *mon vieux*, I have an extraordinary story to tell you."

CHAPTER 41

En route to Nice, Diamanté listened intently as Charles-Christian spoke of Anna, about her being an author, about the death of her grandparents, even about the lost letters and the discovery of his mother's hidden tin box. He narrated what he knew of Anna's visit to Guy de Noailles and her revelation when she discovered that Guy was his very own *grand-père*. Finally he spoke of the coincidental discovery that she had been in Le Havre on August 31.

"So you are telling me that the young woman I saw in Le Havre was in reality my son's daughter? Impossible!" Diamanté shrugged his shoulders and threw up his arms. "I cannot believe it. My son would have told me about a baby."

"That's just it. According to what Ellis told her on his deathbed, your son never found out, and Ellis never wrote to tell you. She didn't say whether he explained why to her or not."

"*Incroyable.*" All Diamanté could do was shake his head in disbelief. "She is still in France, then?"

"In Paris, *oui*, but for only a few more days. She was doing a book signing." Charles-Christian pulled her novel from his duffel bag and handed it to Diamanté. "I bought a copy."

Diamanté held the attractively-jacketed novel in his knotted hands. He turned it over to see the photo on the back.

"She's good-looking."

"Yes, very beautiful. She looks like him. Your son, I mean. She has a photograph of her mother and Diamanté *fils*. She compared it to an old photo that *Grand-père* has, the one that was taken of you and your son in Corsica before he shipped out for Algeria. It's unquestionably the same man."

Diamanté rubbed the scar on his forehead. He opened the book and squinted at the inscription Anna had written.

"She calls you C-C?"

Charles-Christian shrugged his shoulders and smiled his crooked smile.

Diamanté handed the book back to him, unsmiling. "I need some time to think about this."

CHAPTER 42

The train pulled into the Nice station. As Diamanté and Charles-Christian descended to the platform, Diamanté glanced behind him. He saw a dark figure waiting in the shadows of the last car, watching them.

CHAPTER 43

Paris

T he young man is behind her as she pushes her luggage cart toward the end of the loading platform. The look of admiration is in his eyes as she glances casually back at him. She smiles. At the end of a long journey, she returns. The same man is waiting on the platform for her. He takes her hand. They waltz together. Then, something happens that stops the dancing. He turns around suddenly and runs away. She tries to run after him. Something prevents her from moving. There is a glass window between them. She puts out her hand and cries out.

Anna woke herself screaming an endless, frantic "*Nooooooo!*" Sitting straight up in bed, her heart pounding, she looked around the room. It was the old dream, but it had changed. This time, there was a face: C-C's face. She lay back against the pillows. The tin box with the Monet painting of the Rouen cathedral sitting on the night table beside her bed caught her eye, and the nightmarish events of the past evening flooded her mind. She was not one to easily give in to tears, but they were streaming down her face now. Damn, C-C. Why did he have to come back into her life? And now he'd left again, just like that. His abrupt departure had a dark, frightening aspect that troubled her.

"I'm through with him…for good, this time," she told herself, wiping her cheeks with the heel of her hand.

The apartment was quiet, and leaden light came through the sheer window curtains. Anna looked at the clock. It was half past ten. She pulled back the white, down comforter and swung her bare feet to the side of the bed. The floor was cold. She found her slippers and shuffled over to the window to look out. The sky was a thick blanket of low stratus clouds, and it was pouring rain. Below in the street, the tops of umbrellas rushed back and forth. Even in the bleak weather, the view of bell towers and domes sprouting from a mass of roofs never ceased to fascinate her. She opened the bedroom door. The wide, mirrored hallway with eighteenth-century boiserie paneling was dark. A tray with a thermos, china cup and saucer, silver dish filled with natural sugar cubes, and a basket of assorted breads accompanied by jam and sweet butter had been placed on an antique demilune table just outside. She sniffed the single pink rose in a silver bud vase that adorned the tray. Sabastien jumped from under the table and wagged his tail when she acknowledged his presence. She bent down and patted the little dog's head as he licked her hand.

"Good boy! You have been waiting patiently, haven't you, for me to get up? So, where has everyone gone, heh?"

There was a note on the tray, written in Monique's distinctive, and very small, rounded cursive.

> *Didn't want to wake you,* chérie. *You must have come in very late. I didn't even hear you! Have some coffee—that is, if it's still hot.* Sinon, *Jeanne can make you another pot. She is in the apartment doing some final dusting and polishing this morning before she takes off on holiday. Georges and I will be out most of the day. Let's plan on dinner together this evening, all of us.*

If you are free, that is. I'll have Pierre prepare something special for the occasion. I want to hear everything! P.S. Your petit ami, *Mark, called three times. The last was just after midnight. I had to tell him that I was going to bed and you weren't back yet. Didn't know what to say, really. He seemed extremely anxious to talk to you. I think you should call him,* chérie. He is so sympa!

À ce soir,

Monique

Anna poured herself a cup of coffee and plopped two cubes of sugar into it. She took a sip. It was lukewarm, but it tasted good.

"Come on, Sabastien, let's see if Monique has any orange juice in the fridge." They wandered down the long hallway and found Jeanne in the salon, dusting a collection of enamel vases on the white marble mantel above the period fireplace.

"*Bonjour, Mademoiselle.*" The girl nodded politely to Anna. She was young, pretty, no more than twenty, and was wearing a traditional black maid's dress with a starched white collar and cuffs and a starched white linen apron.

"*Bonjour, Jeanne.*"

The girl noticed that Anna was carrying the china cup and saucer. "*Est-ce que le café est toujours chaud, Mademoiselle?*"

"*Oui, tiède, mais ça va.*" Anna smiled at her, indicating that she needn't feel compelled to make her a new pot of coffee.

Anna walked into the turquoise-green tiled kitchen. A half-empty bottle of Perrier sat on a white, marble-topped table with chrome legs in the center of the room. It was a small room, low-ceilinged, mostly functional, with sparse white cupboards and modern stainless steel appliances. The outstanding feature of the kitchen was a sculpture of a large, golden snail, its body and muscular foot fully extended from its coiled shell, which took up the entire countertop in front of the frosted glass window. Monique had explained that it had once been a sign that probably hung over a snail monger's shop. She had found three of them in a flea market somewhere and had placed the other two as if they were marching one after the other along a wall in the apartment's long corridor.

Anna opened the small refrigerator. As usual, it was mostly empty. Like most Parisians, Georges and Monique tended to eat out, and when they did occasionally stay in for dinner, their chef, Pierre, always brought fresh ingredients with him. When Anna had stayed alone in the apartment in September, she had stocked the fridge with bottled water, orange juice, yogurt, and an assortment of cheeses, patés, and fruit.

"Hmmm. No orange juice. Guess this Orangina will have to do." She plucked out a small bottle of orange soda and found a crystal tumbler in the cupboard. Balancing it, the bottle of Orangina, and her china cup and saucer, she wandered back down the darkened hallway past the other two golden snails toward her bedroom. Sabastien followed at her heels and found a comfortable spot for himself on the woolen rug at the end of the bed. Anna reread Monique's note. "Wonder what Mark was so anxious to talk to me about?"

She booted up her laptop and brought up e-mail. "Whoa!" There were eighteen new messages, half of them spam. Two were from Harry, including the most recent. She opened it.

> *Hi, Anna. Thought I'd pass this opportunity on to you.*
> *Hollywood is looking for a good story on this, and I*
> *thought, well, with your background and all, you might*

want to take a shot at it. I think you were there in Paris
when it happened, right? Anyway, consider it and let me
know. Wouldn't be too bad to have a book advance with
film rights already built in! Good news on the sales in
France. You'll have a nice check for the holidays. See you
soon. H.

There was also an attachment, a letter from a producer. The subject of interest appeared to be Princess Diana's "assassination."

"Interesting choice of wording," Anna said aloud as she saved it in a file to look at it later. "Maybe I can use that scene in Le Havre harbor somehow." She did a quick reply to Harry, thanking him and telling him that she would be back in the U.S. soon and would give him her thoughts on it then.

She next opened Mark's most recent message.

Hi, I just tried to call again. Monique said she's going
to bed, so guess I had better quit bothering her. Call
when you get in. Just wondering...where have you been
anyway? M.

Another e-mail from Mark piqued her interest. It contained an HTML link to a Parisian apartment real estate site. The link pointed to the specific address of a posh-looking apartment in the seventh arrondissement near the Eiffel Tower. Anna studied it for a moment. There were photos of the interior and the view of the tower.

"Mmm...looks nice...expensive." Anna stared at the screen. Why was he sending her this? She looked at the time as she dialed his number. It was two o'clock in the morning in California.

"Hi, ah, Mark?"

"Anna! Christ, where have you been?"

"Did I wake you?"

"No. Shit. I've been worried sick about you. How could I sleep?"

"I'm sorry, Mark. I ran into this old friend. We took a Sunday drive."

"*Old* friend?" He emphasized the "old."

"Well, not *old*, old. I mean former friend," she stammered. "We were friends a decade ago when I was studying at the Sorbonne. It's long story, Mark. I think it can wait until we see each other." She hesitated and waited for a reaction. When there was none, she added as brightly as she could, "Which won't be too much longer now." Still no reaction. She didn't need this. "Look, I can explain, but not now, not over the phone."

"I'm sorry, Anna. I should have known you could take care of yourself. It's just that, damn it…" he hesitated. "You're so freakin' far away. I felt helpless."

"I'll be home soon. Monique and Georges are leaving at the end of the week. They're giving all the help the holiday off and closing up the apartment. Basically, they're kicking me out."

"So, have you booked your flight home yet?"

"Well, no, not yet. I was planning to do that today. I have to run a few errands this afternoon." She had totally forgotten until then the promise to deliver C-C's money to Elise.

"Did you see that e-mail I sent about my parents' fancy new apartment in Paris?"

"Oh, it belongs to your parents? So that's what you were so all-fired anxious to talk to me about last night?" She took a croissant from the breakfast tray and dabbed it in the apricot jam.

"Well, yeah. What would you say, gorgeous, if I told you that my parents want me to oversee it for them for a while?"

"What do you mean?"

"We didn't think the deal would go through so soon. Real estate purchases in France can take a long time. They want me to make sure all the paperwork is in order, manage the delivery of the furniture my mother picked out, etcetera. Mom can't be in Paris because of all the preparations for Christmas, and they're planning on traveling to Europe in January, so the place has to be ready for occupancy."

"So when are you going to accomplish all that?"

"That's why I was wondering if you have your flight booked yet. How about if we make up for that lost weekend in Paris we didn't get?"

"What?"

"I mean it. I'm clearing my calendar for a week so I can fly over. We can spend the weekend and fly home in time for Christmas. I promised my mother we'd be back by then."

"This is so…so sudden."

"Yeah. Sorry about that. So, what do you say, gorgeous?"

She didn't answer him.

"I'm not sure whether we'll be able to stay there," he went on. "It will depend on whether there is furniture. Mom insists that it's in a Paris warehouse, ready for delivery. She purchased it in Italy, most of it, when they were there recently, and had it stored in Paris. She's a whirlwind when it comes to decorating and furnishing her houses. You'll be amazed at what she's done with the new mansion in Bel-Air."

"I bet I will. So let me get this straight. You are arriving end of the week? Really?"

"Anna, remember that square in Montmartre? The one in the painting I gave you?" He was suddenly serious.

"Yes," she said, sudden panic setting in.

"I still want to walk there with you," he said invitingly, thinking to himself, *and there's some unfinished business to tend to with regards to a certain engagement ring.* When Anna didn't react, he cleared his throat and added, "Well, okay, we can discuss our itinerary after I get there. I'm just anxious to see you. Call you later?"

"Sure. Bye, Mark."

Anna hung up the phone and stared into space. She had a gut-wrenching feeling that someday she would be forced to decide between Mark and C-C.

CHAPTER 44

An hour later, Anna walked past C-C's green Renault, which was still sitting in the street in front of his apartment building. She stared at it with a shiver, wondering why it was still there if a car thief had wanted to steal it just the night before. As she pushed open the wooden door to the courtyard, she looked up to the window of his apartment, lingering for a second, allowing herself to be swept into his arms, if only in memory, one last time.

Elise spotted her from her apartment window and hustled to open the door. "Anna? *Oh là, mais, entre, ma chère*. I didn't know you were in Paris."

"*Bonjour*, Elise." The two women embraced.

Elise closed the door to keep the cold air from entering the warm apartment. She appeared younger than she had when Anna had visited her in September. She was wearing makeup, her naturally wavy hair, salted with gray, was pulled back in a smart coif, and a pair of gold earrings sparkled in her earlobes. The spectacles were gone, replaced by fashionable reading glasses hanging from a beaded chain around her neck. There was definitely something that had occurred in her life that had prompted a positive change in her appearance.

"Only for a few days, Elise. I came for a book signing," Anna replied.

The old woman made approving clucks of the tongue. "*Ah bon, ah bon. Eh bien,* let me take your coat." She hung Anna's coat on a rack next to the door, then motioned to her to sit on an antique, brocade-upholstered loveseat. The apartment was quaint, old-fashioned, and spotless, just as Anna had remembered. Like Elise, there wasn't a thing out of place.

From her handbag, Anna pulled out the wad of hundred-franc bills that C-C had given her in the taxi. "C-C wanted you to have this," she said, patting Elise's hand. "It's to pay his rent while he is away."

Elise looked puzzled as she took the money, and then her clear blue eyes grew wide. She knew. "It was you, then? You were the woman with him last night?"

"You saw us?" Now Anna's eyes were wide.

"*Oui, oui. Nous…*" then she hesitated, not knowing whether she had divulged something she shouldn't have by using the first-person plural. "We…that is, *bon*, I mean, I was watching out my window there after I heard the car siren." She motioned toward the front window of her apartment. "Then I saw Charles-Christian and a woman leave through the back exit, the one I always use as an entrance."

"Elise, he doesn't want you to worry." Anna tried to sound calm and reassuring. "He'll be all right. He has gone to Africa again…to work."

Elise cocked her head sideways, squinted her eyes, and wagged a bony finger in Anna's face.

"In the middle of the night?" Her thoughts turned to the frantic call from Jacques first thing this morning and the hasty departure of Diamanté.

Anna sat in silence. What could she tell her? Yes, in the middle of the night. She diverted her eyes through the arched doorway leading into a small dining room. A mahogany china hutch filled with antique crystal and china sat against the far wall, and a wrought-iron and crystal chandelier hung above an oval table covered with a crocheted table cloth. In the center of the table sat a round crystal bowl filled with fresh fruit.

"I...I really don't know," she finally said shaking her head. The event had seemed surreal to her also.

"*Ma chère,*" Elise said gently. She understood more than Anna could have anticipated she did. "I will let Charlie explain when he returns. Would you like something to drink?" She got up to go into the kitchen. "Some wine, maybe?"

Anna nodded. Some wine would taste good. She spotted a large bouquet of mixed flowers on an oval pedestal table in front of the window.

"Your flowers are beautiful, Elise," she said.

"Oh...that...well," Elise smoothed her hair back in a girlish gesture as she disappeared into the kitchen. "I have an *admirateur.*"

"Did I just hear what I thought I heard? An admirer?" Anna whispered, smiling to herself. *These French*, she thought. *L'amour is not just for the young in this country*. She studied the romantic arrangement framed by the lace curtains. There were lots of roses in it. *Her "admirateur" is quite serious, I would say*.

Elise returned after a few moments, carrying a silver tray with two small, etched crystal goblets half filled with port. She put the tray on a rectangular footed ottoman between them.

"So does your *admirateur* have a name?" Anna asked as she took a sip of the port.

Elise seemed slightly coquettish. "Oh, I just call him *Lobo*. It's my Portuguese pet name for him."

"Well, *Lobo* is nice to give you flowers."

"He brings me a bunch every week." The old woman's nose wrinkled up into a smile.

They chatted about the upcoming holiday and Anna's plans to return to the United States, and they finished their wine without Anna discovering anything more about the admirer named *Lobo*. She finally got up and put on her coat and scarf.

"Well, I've got to go, Elise. I'll come by again before I leave Paris, if I can."

The two women embraced, and Anna waved as she walked through the barren courtyard, past the bench under the leafless chestnut tree, and through the heavy wooden door.

Strange, she thought. *Elise didn't ask any more questions about C-C. Concierges always make it their business to know everything about their tenants.* She put her hands in her coat pockets and glanced over her shoulder at C-C's apartment window as she walked down the narrow street, pondering the conversation she had had with Elise. What was the Portuguese pet name Elise said she had given her "*admirateur?*" *Lobo?* Anna knew the meaning of the word in Spanish. Was it the same in Portuguese? She made a mental note to remind herself to look it up.

CHAPTER 45

Diamanté and Charles-Christian arrived midafternoon in the handsome little village surrounded by hills. Diamanté parked the car in front of his still signless café and woke Charles-Christian with a slap on the shoulder.

"*On arrive, mon ami. Voilà Castagniers.*" Diamanté motioned with his upturned hand. "*Et voilà le resto.* I call it Ajaccio, but it doesn't have a sign yet."

Charles-Christian studied the small, weathered stone and brick building. A dark green awning extended from beneath the red-tiled roof. Clear plastic had been hung along the sides and front of it to protect café diners from the winter rains. Wrought-iron tables and chairs spilled from the front out onto the square, but no one was seated at them and the umbrellas remained unopened. He looked around the deserted square. Barren trees lined the perimeter. In the center sat a lone, artichoke-crowned fountain that had been drained for the winter. Directly across from them stood the *mairie* or town hall, its *tricolore* flag thrashing in the wind above the entrance.

Diamanté and Charles-Christian walked into the restaurant. With the exception of a handful of old locals playing cards at a corner table in the bar, it was empty of customers. The place smelled of olive oil and herbs. Lively Corsican dance music played in the background. In the kitchen, they could see and hear Jacques noisily chopping vegetables with a huge kitchen knife.

The café dog, a mixed breed with long, floppy ears and soulful eyes, came from behind a well-worn, galvanized bar. The dog stretched, recognized Diamanté, and loped over to greet him, his bushy tail making windmill circles in the air.

"*Salut*, Max." Diamanté bent down to rub the dog's ears and was awarded multiple wet, sloppy licks on the face. "Go ahead. I want to inspect the wine cellar," he said to Charles-Christian, nodding his head in the direction of the kitchen. Then he whistled to the dog to follow him, and the two of them disappeared through a heavy, wooden door behind the bar.

Charles-Christian paused a moment at the doorway to the kitchen and watched his father deftly chopping vegetables into perfectly thin, julienne-sized pieces. He had not seen him in two years, but he was surprised at how dramatically his appearance had changed. At age seventy, Jacques Gérard appeared at least a decade older. He seemed shorter and more stooped. His face, like an old piece of weathered wood, contained deep furrows and wrinkles on his forehead and around his mouth. The curve under the brow ridge between his coal-black eyes had deepened, and the upper eyelids sagged. His bulbous nose seemed to have grown larger, the crook in it more pronounced. His graying hair, though still quite thick, had begun to recede, and his eyebrows had become more unruly.

"*Shuh vous aid-ah, Monsieur?*"

The accent was unmistakably *provençal*. Charles-Christian turned to face a young woman standing behind him. She appeared to be in her early twenties, dressed in skin-tight blue jeans, high-heeled black leather boots, and a bright lime-green, snug-fitting, low-cut sweater. Her brassy red hair was pulled back in a high ponytail, and her emerald eyes were heavily outlined and accented with sea green eye shadow. Multiple silver pierced earrings of various sized hoops protruded from her ears. She carried at shoulder height a tray filled with bar glasses.

The sound of the young woman's voice drew Jacques' attention. It was then that he caught sight of his son standing in the doorway. He put down the kitchen knife and wiped his hands on a towel.

"Martine, this is Charlie, my son."

Martine smiled at Charles-Christian and extended her right hand while balancing the tray of bar glasses with her left. "Martine Dubonnet." She shook his hand with one firm shake.

"*Enchanté, Mademoiselle.*" He smiled.

Jacques was now standing next to Charles-Christian, his hands on his hips, his black eyes studying the son he had not seen since his wife's death.

"*Salut*, Papa."

The two men stood motionless for an awkward moment, and then they embraced and held each other in the way only a father and son can when they have previously been alienated by conflict and grief.

In the wine cellar below, Diamanté poured two glasses of *marc*, set them on a small wooden table, and awaited a visitor.

CHAPTER 46

A quarter of an hour after Diamanté and Charles-Christian arrived in Castagniers, André Narbon joined Diamanté in the wine cellar of the Ajaccio. From behind Diamanté's wooden stool, Max expressed his discontent with an uncharacteristic onslaught of low, menacing growls. Diamanté grabbed the dog by the collar and ordered him to stay.

"I was expecting you," he said, staring at the man whom he had seen descend from the rear of the train in Nice. "What are you up to, André? What are you doing here?" The man's sudden appearance in Castagniers was unsettling to Diamanté. "So it was you then, following Charlie in Paris all this time. Who are you working for?"

André Narbon swirled the thick liquid in his glass and took a sip. His mouth curled in a twisted, mocking grin. "Will he stay in Castagniers?" he asked.

Diamanté studied the man's eyes, magnified to at least twice their size by bottle-thick lenses. He thought how they never changed; they always looked malicious.

"I don't know. What he does with his life is his business. He is a grown man. He will have to assess the situation for himself, and then make his decision. A lot will depend on his relationship with his father."

"And with the woman in the convent."

Diamanté was taken by surprise at that comment. No one, except himself, he had thought, knew about her.

"I am told that she is still very ill," Narbon went on.

"André, how do you know all this?"

Narbon's eyes were hard; he showed no emotion. "The nurse should have been killed; she could finger us all," he said.

Diamanté removed his beret and scratched his forehead. It was a reaction one could expect from André Narbon. He was the one among them who could kill.

"She won't trouble any of us." Diamanté downed the rest of his *marc*.

"When do we deliver him?"

"We? *Non*, André, I will take him by myself. Tomorrow morning will be soon enough. Your role is finished."

The two men's black eyes locked like angry bulls setting up for a fight.

With both hands, André Narbon slowly removed his glasses. His eyes narrowed. He had waited a long time for the day when he and Diamanté would meet again.

"I heard that you moved in with Elise in Paris." His tone was hateful. "*Félicitations*. You finally got in the door with her, you old fool."

"Look, André, she didn't choose either one of us originally. We had that ridiculous fight over her, but she chose Ferdinand in the end." Diamanté refilled their glasses. "And then Ferdinand was killed. He was the strongest and the bravest of us all. He took the hit that saved the rest of us."

He stopped talking and swallowed hard as he recalled the scene so long ago when members of the *maquis* were setting dynamite charges on railway tracks under a bridge. The German soldiers had discovered them and opened fire. His older brother, Ferdinand, was the closest. He held them at bay with his rifle, motioning to Diamanté and Narbon to escape. When he thought it was clear to run himself, a lone shot rang out. Diamanté had gone back for his brother only to discover him lying in a pool of blood, the back of his head blown away. He had died instantly.

"*Putain de merde!*" he said. "Goddamn it. Shit. She made a life for herself without either one of us...or Ferdinand, for that matter. It's all water under the Pont Neuf now." He spat into a copper bucket that was used for wine tasting.

"To Ferdinand." André held up his glass in mock toast. "He loved her. That was obvious." He paused. "She sure was a pretty lady."

Diamanté met his toast. "Still is, *mon frère*. Still is. Petite, delicate hands, eyes blue as periwinkles. She's a live wire, too. She has such vitality." His eyes sparkled despite his efforts to conceal his emotions.

The two men stared at each other for several minutes until Diamanté put down his glass and folded his knotty hands between his knees, rubbing them to relieve the arthritic pain. "I'm going to ask her to marry me, André," he said. "I'm not sure that she'll have me, but I'm going to ask. Once things settle down here. I have fallen in love all over again."

Narbon studied his eyeglasses, then snatched a handkerchief from his pocket and began to wipe them. He took his time, not looking at Diamanté. Finally, he slowly placed the spectacles back on the bridge of his nose. His thick eyebrows rose slightly. "*Eh bien*, I wish you well," he sniffed as he carefully folded the white cotton square and returned it to his pocket, still not looking at Diamanté.

"I don't suppose you are going to tell me why you're here, André."

Narbon gave Diamanté a hard, cold stare.

Whatever it is, Diamanté thought, *it can't be honorable*. He knew from experience that André Narbon was a dangerous man. He just hoped that it didn't involve a dead body somewhere.

CHAPTER 47

The morning after their arrival in Castagniers, Diamanté, Charles-Christian, and André Narbon sat eating brioches in silence at the breakfast table in Diamanté's apartment above the Ajaccio. In the kitchen below, Jacques was already at work preparing the day's menu.

Charles-Christian studied the large room, envisioning guests enjoying the warmth of the small bed and breakfast in Provence, in winter. A striking crystal and gold chandelier hung from the high ceiling. Two overstuffed chairs with ottomans and two large sofas were arranged around low, square coffee tables on an outsized Persian rug. Conversational groupings of smaller, similarly upholstered chairs and mahogany game tables with various types of antique lamps lined the wall near the windows.

"Do you intend to run a *chambre d'hôtes* eventually?" he asked Diamanté.

"*Non, non*, not at all," Diamanté responded. "I only wanted the bar and restaurant. The inn was very small. Just these few guest rooms, as you can see. I converted the largest bedroom suite into this apartment by combining it with the central salon and the library." He pointed through a doorway to a room lined with shelves of books and more overstuffed chairs with reading lamps. "The previous owner passed away and had no one to leave his furniture and books to, so I got it all with the purchase price." He cocked his head to the side. "*Pas mal* as real estate deals go. I have closed off the rest of the guest rooms for now."

At the chime of his pocket watch, Diamanté stood and put on his beret. "*Bon.* Get your medical bag, *mon ami*," he said to Charles-Christian. "We are going to pay a visit to someone who is in need of your attention."

Charles-Christian was taken by surprise and somewhat mystified. Why would someone suddenly need his medical assistance the day after his arrival? Who could even know he was here?

"Isn't there a doctor in Castagniers?"

"Not presently. The nearest clinic is in a neighboring village five kilometers away."

Still wondering why he was being asked to tend to a medical emergency, Charles-Christian dutifully donned his overcoat, picked up his bag, and followed Diamanté through the restaurant and out into the square. André Narbon, who had said nothing to either of them at breakfast, trailed a few feet behind. A strong wind was blowing. White lights that had been strung for the holidays in the barren trees around the place de la Mairie danced in the wind.

"Another mistral is brewing," Diamanté said as he anchored his beret lower on his forehead and pulled his jacket collar over his ears to shield his face from the cold gale. "It blows for a hundred days a year here."

The stone fountain in the center of the square had been newly filled with fresh evergreen branches. The three men paused a moment to admire a large crèche nestled amongst the evergreens and paid their compliments to two women from the village who were populating the nativity scene with giant versions of hand-painted terracotta *santons*.

Surrounded by hills, the small village stretched out along one long, paved street. Christmas trees were stacked in bundles on the corners, and the few shops along the *rue* advertised with handwritten signs their specialties for the traditional Christmas Eve meal, *le réveillon*.

Diamanté stopped suddenly, turned abruptly in Narbon's direction, and said, nodding harshly, "Here is where we separate, André."

Narbon acted as if he had not understood.

"As we discussed, André." Diamanté stood firm. He glanced in the direction of a stone walking bridge. The entrance was framed by two sandstone pillars crowned by ornate wrought-iron crosses. Behind, on the hill overlooking the entire valley below, stood an imposing complex of large, pink stucco buildings with tile roofs surrounded by tall Italian cypress trees swaying in the wind. Above the buildings rose a slim, two-story-high carillon tower with arched openings and a cross on top.

"The convent where we are going," he said in a low voice to Charles-Christian, nodding in the direction of the buildings. "Cistercian."

The three men remained motionless, frozen in place. Charles-Christian could detect that there was considerable animosity between the two old-timers, who were staring at each other. Finally, André Narbon turned on his heel, deliberately not shaking hands with either of them, and walked back to the Ajaccio with a scowl on his face.

"What was that about?" Charles-Christian asked Diamanté.

"It is not your concern," Diamanté said as he watched Narbon retreat. "André will be departing Castagniers in the next hour or so."

Diamanté and Charles-Christian crossed the bridge, climbed the pathway up the steep hill, and entered the statue-studded grounds through an archway. A sign beside the main entrance read:

> *Nous avertissons nos visiteurs que notre accueil monastique est actuellement fermé pour cause de travaux de restauration dans les bâtiments de l'Abbaye. Avec tous nos regrets.*
>
> —*La communauté de Notre Dame de la Paix*

"The convent is closed for restoration?" Charles-Christian asked.

"*Oui*, for at least a year," Diamanté responded. "It was badly in need. The main building, the old monastery, is over a hundred thirty years old."

"This person who needs medical assistance is, I'm assuming, a *religieuse* here in the convent? What exactly is the matter?"

Diamanté rang the bell at the huge entrance door.

"I was asked simply to deliver you. I shall wait for you here," he said.

Charles-Christian didn't have time for another question. The portal opened slowly, and a diminutive woman, her face framed in a black veil, peered at them through tiny wire-rimmed glasses.

"Oh, *Bonjour. Entrez.* We have been expecting you." She opened the door just enough to let Charles-Christian through and nodded to Diamanté.

"I am *Soeur* Sulpice. *Soyez le bienvenu.*" She extended her hand in welcome to Charles-Christian.

He took her hand. It was bony and felt cold. The nun was about sixty years of age. A wide, black belt fixed the black and white fabric pieces of her penguin-like habit together at the waist, and she wore heavy, flat, black sandals. A large, ornate filigree cross hung on a long, silver chain around her neck.

"*Enchanté, Mère Abesse*," he said.

"Oh, *Monsieur*, I am not *la mère abesse*," she said in a soft voice. "The abbess is away. Please follow me." She turned quickly and quietly escorted him across the dark courtyard, through an archway, and into the largest of the buildings. There appeared to be no one around. The only sound was the slight rustling of Sister Sulpice's habit as she walked. Her soft sandals made no sound at all on the tile floor. Charles-Christian became aware of the echoing clack-clack of his own heels as he followed her down a long corridor with closed doors on either side. They came to the end, turned the corner, and entered a shorter hallway.

It was then that he noted the strong odor of antiseptic.

"This is Saint Bernard," Sister Sulpice said as she bowed her respect to a statue in an arched niche in the wall. The bronze monk was seated at a table, writing. "He is the most famous of all the Cistercians," she continued. "We celebrate his *fête* every year in August."

Charles-Christian suddenly became aware that a single doorway just like all the others, halfway down the hall, was being guarded by two men. He recognized one of them as they approached. It was the helicopter pilot who had flown him to Paris. Sister Sulpice nodded to the two guards and knocked quietly at the door. "Take your time. I will wait here to escort you back to the main entrance," she said as the door opened a crack.

Two brown eyes appeared, then grew wide. The door opened. Nurse Florence LeBlanc slipped through it and silently but emotionally hugged the doctor.

"I am so glad you have come," she whispered, pulling him in to the room and closing the door again behind them. "She will be so happy to see you."

The outside shutters had been closed to buffer the howling of the wind. Charles-Christian squinted his eyes as he tried to make out the contents of the room in the limited light. Against the wall was a single bed with someone lying in it under a heavy coverlet. Alongside the bed, lights blinked, accompanied by beeping sounds from an extensive electronic panel for medical monitoring equipment. The only other furniture was against the opposite wall: a chair and a small table with a low lamp. The aroma of chlorine and disinfectant permeated the room. *The hospital smell*, he thought.

Nurse LeBlanc motioned to him with her hand. He put down his medical bag, opened it, and took out his stethoscope. As he did so, he caught a glimpse of Anna's letters still stuffed inside the case. A sudden panic seized him. Would he be detained again, here in this convent?

Calm down. He told himself. *Feel her forehead, check her vital signs, listen to her heart...you are a doctor.*

CHAPTER 48

At the end of the hall, Sister Sulpice waited patiently. When Charles-Christian and Nurse Le Blanc finally emerged from the room, they spoke in hushed tones just outside the door.

"Her condition has obviously improved since I last saw her," he said. "The signs of recovery are evident. She knew me."

"She has been asking for you daily," Nurse LeBlanc replied. "We flew her in by helicopter yesterday—when we knew you were on the way to Castagniers, at last. *Soeur* Sulpice will explain everything briefly to you when she shows you out." She smiled at him. "I have decided to stay with her, indefinitely, if you want to know." She glanced over Dr. Gérard's shoulder at the two British guards beside the door and winked at one of them. "That one's my fiancé. It happened after you left." The one Charles-Christian had recognized as Geoffrey kept his stern composure but winked back at her.

Charles-Christian smiled and nodded to the young soldier. "It is a small world. Is she...are you...staying here permanently in Castagniers, then?"

"It depends on you. Yes, she wants to stay here until she can recover fully. It is secluded, and very few people know where she is. She is still very ill, but she will recover. A strong woman." The nurse's voice trailed off as she accompanied him down the corridor to the waiting nun.

As Sister Sulpice led the doctor back through the corridors to the main entrance of the abbey, her head low, hands folded into the sleeves of her habit, she articulated the proposed arrangement in hurried, hushed language.

"It is hoped, *Monsieur le Docteur*, that you will consider staying in Castagniers as the village doctor. There is no current local physician for the population, which is over twelve hundred inhabitants, as you may know. If you should choose to stay...you understand that you are not being forced to. It is entirely your freedom to depart, if you wish. This is what is proposed: you will make a daily visit to the convent, ostensibly to check on the conditions of some of the older nuns who are ailing, of course. During that time, you will do what is necessary to assure the recovery of the woman, your primary patient."

They reached the exterior door. She took his hand in hers. "She will decide when she is well enough to depart. Until then, we have agreed to keep quiet. That is the reason for the restoration period for the convent, which is being funded. You also will be well reimbursed for this arrangement, *Monsieur*, should you decide to stay on indefinitely. I hope to see you again. Bless you." She bowed her head in respect as she opened the door for him.

Diamanté was seated on the bench just outside the entry, his arms folded over his chest and his beret pulled down over his eyes. He rose quickly as Charles-Christian, his face pale and his eyes glassy, appeared on the doorstep.

"I think you could use a glass of *marc*," Diamanté said, putting a fatherly hand on Charles-Christian's shoulder.

Infuriated, the stunned doctor pulled away. Diamanté noted at that instant how much the son resembled his father, Jacques. His brows were knit, his eyes charcoal gray, his jaw set firm, his whole body rigid in a great effort to control his anger.

"You knew about this, didn't you? You...you set it up," he snapped.

Diamanté put his hand up as if to halt the conversation. "I can explain."

"What about my father? Have you involved him in this?"

Diamanté shook his head. "He knows nothing. He is not even aware that she is here."

"And he shall not be told. Understand?"

Diamanté nodded.

Charles-Christian said, "I have a lot of questions for you, then."

The wind was blowing so hard that they could barely hear each other.

"I need to take a walk first," Charles-Christian bellowed as he turned his back and tramped down the hill toward the village.

Diamanté looked at his pocket watch. It was noon. The cypress trees that rose over the convent tossed and turned in a dance with the cold wind, but the monastery's bells were silent.

CHAPTER 49

Working through his anger, at times with his back to the cold wind, at times facing it, Charles-Christian wandered the narrow streets of the several small settlements which made up the village—*les Moulins, la Grotte, la Garde, le Vignon, le Cabrier, le Carretier.* He thought about the things he should have done in his life and yet somehow never did, the lost opportunities he had let slip by. True commitment in most everything hadn't come fast enough—or at all in the case of Anna. His only devotion had been to his profession. As he found his way into the Masage quarter with its archways and ancient houses dating back to the nineteenth century, it occurred to him that the woman who had entered his world under such terrible circumstances in August was now asking for a commitment, too, one which would require a drastic change.

C-C quickened his pace as he took out his cell phone and dialed Elise's number in Paris.

"*Allô?*" He heard Elise's soft Portuguese accent on the other end.

"*Salut*, Elise. Charlie."

"*Oh là*, Charlie. *Bonjour. Comment vas-tu?*"

"*Bien. Merci. Dis-moi, Elise, est-ce que...eh, c'est que, je suis curieux, Elise, si Anna Ellis t'as visitée recemment?*" He tried to sound nonchalant in asking if Anna had visited her.

"*Beh, oui, elle était là hier après-midi, vers deux heures, si je me rappelle. Elle m'a donné l'argent. Merci, mais c'est trop.*"

Good, he thought. *Anna delivered the money.* He told Elise that it wasn't too much, despite her objections, explaining that he may have to be gone for a while. She wished him well, and they hung up. *Interesting,* he thought after the call. *Elise didn't inquire as to where I am.*

A few minutes later, Martine answered the phone at the Ajaccio. "*Oui, un moment, Madam-ah...*" She laid down the receiver and hollered in the direction of the kitchen. "Diamanté! *Au téléphon-ah! C'est Elis-ah!*"

Diamanté ascended to his apartment, picked up the receiver, and waited for the click that meant Martine had replaced the receiver in the bar below.

"*Salut, chérie, ça va?*"

"*Oui, c'est que Charlie m'a donné un petit coup de téléphone tout à l'heure.*"

Diamanté and Elise had spoken just this morning. He had not shared with her C-C's story about the possibility of Anna's being related to him. He still wasn't able to believe it.

"Charlie called? What did he want?"

"To know if Anna had been here. Of course, I told him she had delivered the money."

"Did he ask you any more?"

"No, and I didn't tell him anything. Of course, I don't know anything, either. Anna said she would maybe come by to see me before she leaves Paris; that is all I know."

"*Bon.* I'll be leaving for Paris in a day or two. Elise, if you see Anna again..." he paused.

"*Oui?*"

"Don't mention anything about me to her."

"*Oui, c'est fait. A tout de suite, Lobo.*" There was no reason for Elise to consider his request unusual. After all, Anna didn't know him.

When Charles-Christian finally returned to the Ajaccio, Jacques and Diamanté were working together in the kitchen, speaking loudly and rapidly in the Corsican dialect. Wondering what they were discussing, he removed his coat and scarf, hung them on a coat rack, then took a bench seat by the bar and lit a cigarette. As on the previous day, the assembly of old men had gathered to play cards at the table in the rear. *Probably boules players in nice weather*," he thought. The big, brown café dog lumbered over and plopped himself down for a snooze beneath his table. Narbon was nowhere in sight.

From behind the bar where she was polishing glassware, Martine spotted Jacques' son.

"Would you like something to drink?" she inquired, winking at him in a slightly flirtatious manner. She wore a brightly colored, tight-fitting, ginger-red sweater and snug blue jeans with black leather boots just as she had the day before.

"A bottle of rosé, *s'il vous plaît, Mademoiselle.*"

The young woman frowned at him. The *provençaux* only drank rosé wines in the summer. It was the middle of the winter. "It will only make you colder," she warned wagging a finger at him.

"It is not as cold here as it is in Paris," he replied, a crooked, cheerless smile on his face. "I have not had a good rosé since the last time I was in Provence."

"Very well, then. We'll pretend the mistral isn't blowing, that the leaves are on the plane trees and the flowers are in bloom, that the tourists are gathered at the outdoor café, laughing and drinking *pastis*, that the square is shimmering in heat and the fountain is bubbling," she said wistfully, cheerfully, her back to him as she disappeared through a doorway behind the bar. In a minute she returned from the wine cellar and produced the desired bottle. "Voilà, *pour Monsieur*, a perfectly chilled *vin rosé*, dry, fruity in flavor, product of Provence." She popped the cork and poured a taste into a slightly canted glass and handed it to him.

He held the glass by the stem, checked the wine's reddish pink color, appreciated its aroma, tasted it, swirling it in his mouth before swallowing, and finally nodded his head in approval. It was a ritual he knew well. As the sommelier for his father's restaurant in Rouen, he had performed it many times.

"*Merci, Mademoiselle.*"

"To the sun!" She smiled at the thought of the warm weather and bright blue skies that would be returning after the mistral had blown itself out.

"Martine. *Vite!*" Jacques was calling her from the kitchen.

"End of reverie. I am needed *tout de suite*. Bye-bye." She winked and was gone.

The doctor took another sip of the wine. He opened his medical case and pulled out all the letters from Anna, spreading them on the table in front of him in chronological order as if they were playing cards. He hesitated. Were they better left unopened? No, he decided, He would read them all. He next pulled out her book. Then he would read that, too. On a sudden impulse, he fished his cell phone from his jacket pocket and called Monique and Georges' number in Paris. The housekeeper answered.

"*Monsieur et Madame* Durocher?" she responded. "They are presently out, *Monsieur*. I don't expect them back until later."

Charles-Christian inquired if the woman staying with them was available.

"*Non, Monsieur. Mademoiselle* Ellis has departed."

Would she take a message for *Mademoiselle* Ellis, he inquired.

Well, she could take a message, but she couldn't deliver it.

He extinguished his cigarette in the ashtray. Why was that, he asked.

"Because *Mademoiselle* Ellis has left," the woman repeated, a bit out of patience. Then she clarified that the young lady had bid *au revoir* to *Madame et Monsieur* this morning.

Déjà vu. Anna was gone again. Just like before. He sighed.

He left his name and cell phone number and requested, nevertheless, that Monique return his call as soon as possible. He slowly placed the cell phone on the table beside him, lit another Gauloise, and picked up the last of the letters. It was written in blue ink in Anna's finely formed cursive and dated November 1987. "*Mon amour*," it began, "the leaves of the liquid amber trees are turning yellow here in California. The way the leaves swing to and fro in the breeze reminds me of the chestnuts in Paris…and of you."

Anna's C-C looked at her novel sitting in front of him. He picked it up. For ten years she had been gone from his life. Had she really wanted to find him again? He took out his pack of cigarettes and shook another one forward. As he pulled it out of the pack and put it in his mouth, the dog under the table raised its head, put one paw over C-C's foot, and gently nudged his knee with his big, brown nose. Remembering Anna's objections to his smoking the evening under the Eiffel Tower, C-C took the unlit cigarette out of his mouth. He studied it at length. The dog watched him intently.

"You're both right," he said as he tossed the whole pack of cigarettes into the trash can by the bar.

CHAPTER 50

It was after New Year's when Monique finally returned C-C's call.

"Anna has announced her *fiançailles*, her engagement," she told him in a cool, unfeeling voice. "Don't attempt to contact her again."

PART FOUR

CHAPTER 51

Southern France, Eight Months Later

Anna steered the rental car, a Peugeot with no air conditioning, from N202 right onto the D614. The hot, dry *provençal* wind blowing through the open windows smelled of lavender and herbs. Beside her on the seat rested Nathalie's tin biscuit box. On top was the letter from Guy de Noailles, which she had received at the beginning of August. She had reread it several times, enough so she knew it by heart. In her mind, she went over it again.

Dear Anna,

> *I am writing to you from Castagniers. It is the month of August, and I decided to have Jean-Paul drive me to the South. Maria and Puccini have gone to Italy to visit her family. Jean-Paul will join her there, then come back to drive me home to Obernai at the end of August.*

> *How are you, and how is Mark? I see that your next book has been introduced in France. Félicitations!*

> *Now, the good news from Castagniers. It is with great pleasure that I report to you that Diamanté has returned to his restaurant. I was quite astonished to find out that he had been here for some time and had not informed me, but I forgive him. He has been busy falling in love. Yes, in love. The old "con." Elise has moved here from Paris, and*

she and Diamanté are planning to be married the third Sunday of the month. Too old for that, I tell them, but they insist that they are good for each other. She calls him "Lobo" (Portuguese for "wolf"). And, I might add, she has given a wonderfully feminine touch to the restaurant.

My son-in-law, Jacques, manages the restaurant. It is called "Ajaccio" after the capital city of Corsica.

The other surprise I received was that my handsome grandson, Charlie, is here also. Having decided not to return to the hospital in Paris, he has become the town's only doctor. I don't know the reason, but I think that it is better for him being here.

Forgive me if I ramble. I am an old man, too, but not so foolish as to fall in love anymore. There are many things I want you to know. First of all, I am sure that you are wondering about whether I have told Diamanté about you and your visit to Obernai. The answer is yes. But the surprise to me was that he already knew about you. My grandson, who I was pleasantly surprised to learn knew you (not that you needed to have told me), had informed him of your whole story, at least what he knew of it. I understand that Diamanté was quite taken aback at first and not sure whether he was up to meeting you at all. He can be a hard one, but now, I think my old friend has changed his mind. I believe that if you were to come for the wedding, he and Elise would be delighted. I too would be delighted to have the opportunity to see you again. Consider it seriously, ma chère.

There is something I have to confess, Anna. When I recounted your visit to Obernai, I accidentally let slip about your nice young man, Mark, being with you. Charlie was visibly unnerved by the news. He is not one to show his emotions, as you must know, so I felt compelled to discuss it with him privately afterward. He told me the story about Nathalie's tin box, the lost letters and losing you...twice, as he put it. I only tell you this because I am sorry to hear about the tragic nature of your relationship. Jacques should not have discarded your letters. (Incidentally, Charlie told me that his father has apologized to him for that and other affronts as well. They have a good relationship now, a respectful one.)

That is the news from the south of France, dear Anna. If I don't see you here, then perhaps you will come visit me in Obernai again soon.

I remain, respectfully, your old friend and admirer,

Guy de Noailles

D614 had become narrow and winding. "Serpentine" was the word Anna thought of to describe it as it twisted and climbed on its way to Castagniers. There was not a lot of traffic. Anna came to a bend in the road, pulled over, and got out of the car. She looked out over a dramatic vista softly visible through the summer haze. Below her was a sheer drop to a ravine. Beyond it, tranquil villages with terracotta roofs dotted the soft green hills, and vast acres of lavender planted in long parallel lines filled the valley.

"I hope this phone still works up here," she said to herself as she punched in Monique's telephone number on the cell phone she had rented at the airport in Nice. Monique and Georges were spending the month, as expected, at their *bastide* near Grasse, not far from Nice.

"*Allô?*"

"Monique?"

"Anna! Have you arrived, *chérie?*"

"Yes. I'm almost at Castagniers. It's so beautiful here. So peaceful."

"When will we see you?"

"I'll call you."

"Anna, wait, there's something I have to tell you, now that you are so close to seeing him."

"What's that?" The reception was not good; there was a lot of static.

"He called the apartment in Paris the same day that you left in December."

"Who did?"

"C-C."

"C-C called? And you didn't tell me? What did he want?"

"I was out. The housekeeper answered the phone. She said that he asked to speak with you. She told him that you had already departed. He left his cell phone number with a request that I return his call. I didn't call him back until after the first of the year. When I did…it was after you had announced your engagement to Mark, *chérie*. *Alors*, I told him not to attempt to call you again."

Anna was silent, thinking.

"Monique, did you tell him I was engaged?"

"Yes, of course. You know I never liked him. I really wanted to wound him, you know, like he had wounded you. I'm afraid I was playing the anti-heroine. I really was *cruelle*."

"Why didn't you tell me about this sooner?"

"I know I should have. I'm truly sorry. It is not like me to keep such things to myself. I've had insomnia for months over it. I didn't think it would matter, until…well, now that you are going to see him again, you should at least be aware that he did try to contact you." There was more static. Monique's voice was barely audible.

Anna was forgiving of her friend. "You're cutting out, Monique. I appreciate how difficult it must be for you to tell me this now."

She could barely hear Monique say, "I hope everything works out, *chérie*. I'll be thinking about you. *Bonne chance!*" and she was gone completely.

"*Au revoir*," Anna said to the dead phone as she lobbed it onto the passenger seat.

A soft breeze tossed her hair as she stood for a moment, soaking up the sun. It had been almost a year since she had arrived in France to search for C-C. She had finished the book *Pas de Deux* since returning to California in December. It had been released to the market quickly. Harry had taken a risk and had several hundred copies in English shipped to Europe with the first printing. They had all sold. *That*, she reflected now, *is the only good thing about my life that has happened since Mark and I broke up*. Their relationship had seemed so perfect when he had presented her with the beautiful engagement ring on a stormy December evening in Paris. They had had a romantic few days, after which they had flown home and announced their engagement to his family. Everything was going well for them. She was working feverishly on her book. It seemed like life couldn't get better.

Then, in June, things had started to unravel. She was on a whirlwind book tour in Seattle, the next-to-the-last stop before returning to California. She had called Mark before going to bed. The subject of a date for the wedding came up again. He had been pressing her to fix a date. Now his mother was in on it also.

"Mama wants to know if October is good. She's wanting to begin the planning." It was understood that the wedding would be at his parents' immense Bel-Air estate. Anna had wanted a small, intimate wedding, but the Zennelli clan was large, and Catholic. A big Italian gathering would be required, she had been told.

"I…I don't know, Mark. I'm tired. Let's talk about it when I get home."

"Christ, Anna. You keep putting me off every time I bring it up lately. One would think that you don't want to get married."

"Oh, Mark. I just don't want to talk about it now."

"It's because you're not sure, isn't it?"

"Look. I mean it. Let's not talk about this over the phone. I'll be in San Francisco tomorrow. Harry's got dinner lined up for the evening. It'll be late, so don't expect me to call. Can you pick me up at LAX at noon on Thursday?"

There was silence, then he said, "Sure, course."

Things had gotten more heated when she arrived in Los Angeles. When the subject of the wedding came up again, Mark accused her of holding back on him.

"There's something you haven't told me, Anna," he had said. "I've sensed it ever since Paris."

"What…what is it that you've sensed?"

"I thought it was because you hadn't found your grandfather, that you were preoccupied with that."

"Well, that's part of it. It's …it's just that I…"

"You what?"

"I don't know precisely how to tell you." She hadn't meant to hurt him.

"Tell me what?"

"That there was someone else. Someone before you."

Mark had looked confused. "Someone. You mean a man?"

"Yes."

"Whom you were in love with?"

"Yes, I guess…"

"You guess?"

"Mark, let it go. It was a long time ago."

"In France?"

She hadn't answered him. He had understood, she now realized. She had deceived herself into believing that she was having trouble making the commitment because she was tired from the book tour and the business arrangements for her new book. Harry and she had been talking seriously about the subject of her next book, the so-called "Lady Di assassination." They had submitted a proposal to the publisher that was under consideration. Harry was sure she was going to get a sizeable advance to proceed.

"Yes, but it's over. Mark, it's just that there's so much pressure on me right now. Harry's pressuring me on the new book. Give me time. I'll look at the calendar. Seriously." But every time she looked at the calendar, she backed away from a date. The subject became more and more heated between them.

"Maybe we ought to forget the whole wedding thing for a while. Just live together," she had suggested at one point. That had met with a deadly silence. She knew he wanted more than anything to get married and start a family. It's what she thought she had wanted, too.

"You've got to get over C-C," Monique had told her.

"But I don't know what happened. I don't know where he is," she had whined. "He was into something dark. I know it. The way he ran that night. He was frightened. I called Lucie in Rouen. She didn't seem to know anything. I couldn't reach Elise in Paris. He seems to have just disappeared."

"Time to get on with your life, *chérie*," Monique had told her.

One day in the midst of yet another argument over wedding planning, Mark had asked her, "Were you with your freakin' French boyfriend that weekend in December when I couldn't reach you?"

She had never told him where she had been.

"It was a college affair, a decade ago, Mark. We saw each other again briefly in December. Yes, it was that weekend when you were trying to reach me. He had seen in the newspaper that I was doing book signings. We had dinner. The next day we took a drive into the country. That's all. It's over. I haven't heard from him since. I don't even know where he is, and that's the truth."

"Christ, Anna. Do you still love him?"

"I don't know."

"Do you love me?"

"Yes, I guess."

"You can't have two lives, Anna. You have to make a choice."

She had hesitated at that comment, knowing he was right.

"Maybe we should break off the engagement for a while," she had finally said, not believing her own words.

He had looked devastated.

"Oh, shit. Anna, I'm sorry," he had said, pounding the table with his fist. "If it means postponing the wedding for a while, I won't rush you. I love you too much for you to be unhappy with me."

"I need to be sure," she had told him, after which he had thrown up his arms in frustration and stomped out of the room.

Then the letter from Guy had arrived with the confirmation that Diamanté had been Elise's "*admirateur*," and she was on her way to Castagniers to meet him, finally. And there would be C-C. He had actually called her in December? Anna searched her soul. Would it have turned out differently had she still been in the apartment that day when he called? C-C had always been like a magnet, drawing her back to him, even when she hadn't heard from him. In many ways, she had to admit, she was no less attached to C-C for having met and fallen in love with Mark, but Mark's presence, all-embracing as it was, couldn't make up for C-C's absence.

"This time," she said to herself, "I know the reason C-C didn't try to contact me. This time it was Monique who told him not to, not his father." What must he have thought? Guy de Noailles' letter had provided the only information about his whereabouts since then. She was crazy, she told herself, to believe that there would be any chance of the relationship working this time. For all she knew, he had found someone new. Heaving a huge sigh, she climbed back into the small car, put it in gear, and wound her way toward Castagniers.

CHAPTER 52

Although Anna had researched it on the Internet, she was still unprepared for how lovely the small village was. The information on the Web site had been brief: population 1226, three hotels, two restaurants, a single *boulangerie*, and a *chocolaterie* in the Abbaye Dame de la Paix Cisterciennes' convent. There was a photo of one of the two restaurants. She had wondered if it was the Ajaccio. Well, she would soon know.

It seemed different, so remote, this world. In the center of the sun-drenched square was an elegant, stone fountain crowned by an artichoke and surrounded by flowers. At one end of the square was the *mairie*, the eighteenth century town hall, with the French flag flying over the front entrance. The café was directly across from it. A green awning on the old building looked new, "Bar Tabac Restaurant Ajaccio" printed in bold, white letters on its overhang. It was indeed the restaurant she had seen in the photo on the Internet. Several patrons were seated under the shade of umbrellas at outdoor tables. Anna parked the car in the velvety shade beneath a plane tree. She took a deep breath and got out. The scent of herbs and olive oil coming from the restaurant struck her immediately. Lively folk music blared from loud speakers.

Elise was outside, arranging small bouquets of bright gold sunflowers in blue glass vases for the tables. Her vivid blue eyes sparkled, and she looked ten years younger. "*Oh là! C'est* Anna! Guy! *Lobo*!" She called inside as she hastened towards Anna, her arms wide. "I knew you would come. I told Guy you would come."

Anna smiled. "Elise, you look wonderful." The two women embraced, kissing each other on both cheeks.

Guy came from the restaurant. He was speechless. When he took his turn embracing Anna, his eyes were moist with emotion.

"I received your letter. *Merci beaucoup* for letting me know, Guy."

He found his voice. "I'm so happy you came, Anna. I was hoping you would. Elise and I both were." He nodded to a beaming Elise.

Behind Elise stood a man with dark, piercing eyes who appeared to be in his seventies. A deep scar extended upward from his right temple and disappeared under a black beret. It was unmistakably Diamanté. He came forward with a shy smile on his face. "I appear to be the only one around here who doesn't know you," he said in a thick accent as he offered his hand. "I am Diamanté Loupré-Tigre. *Enchanté*. It seems that your grandfather, *enfin, c'est moi*."

Anna's eyes teared. She wanted to hug him, but she held back, not knowing how he would feel about her. Instead, she embraced his hands gently.

"I have come for your wedding. I am so happy for you and Elise."

C-C had arrived on the other side of the square just in time to watch the scene unfolding at the café. He could only see her from the back, but he knew at once that it was Anna. He sighed, unable to move; his heart pounded. She was tan; her hair was longer than when he had last seen her, pulled back at the nape of her neck. She wore a short summer sundress in a soft tangerine color with matching high-heeled sandals. He studied her figure: the soft shoulders, the long legs, the sensuous area of her bare back.

Elise spotted him next to the fountain. She lightly touched Anna's arm and pointed toward C-C.

Anna glanced from Elise to Guy and then to Diamanté. Each of them nodded their head in C-C's direction. Holding her breath, she turned and walked slowly toward the man whom she had feared she would never see again. He didn't move as he watched her coming toward him.

She stopped within a few feet of the fountain. "Hello, C-C," she said, studying him. He was dressed in a light shirt and casual beige trousers. His head was cocked sideways, and his arms were crossed in front of his chest. The gray hairs at his temples radiated in the sunlight. "I came for the wedding. Guy wrote me that you were living here. I brought your mother's tin box."

"I'm sure everyone is pleased that you have come, Anna." His voice was cold, his demeanor removed.

"Yes. Yes, they seem to be." Anna crossed her arms in front of her and looked around at Guy, Elise, and Diamanté, who were all watching her.

C-C dropped his eyes and kicked at the ground with one foot. "Monique told me that you became engaged. *Félicitations.*"

Anna uncrossed her arms and took a few steps closer to him.

"C-C, I didn't know where you were until the letter from Guy came about the wedding. I only learned today why you didn't call or write during the past eight months. At least I think it's why you didn't try to contact me," Anna corrected herself, hesitating. "Monique told me what she said to you. I never knew that you had called the apartment the day I left. She never told me. It was hard for her to admit her deception to me. She feels terrible." Anna yearned to put her arms around C-C's neck, but he still didn't move. He continued to look at the ground. "I'm not engaged, C-C. Not anymore anyway."

He looked up. His hands dropped to his sides, and his shoulders relaxed. There was a flicker of a smile in his eyes. "I read all your letters…and your book, too."

"You should have thrown the letters away." She shook her head. "Anyway, what did you think of the book?"

He shrugged his shoulders and smiled. "You lied. I was in it."

She laughed nervously, remembering the scene in the bookstore.

"Everyone sees themselves in my books."

"Your letters inspired me to write to you. I wrote you once a month. Unlike you, however, I didn't mail anything."

She grinned at him. "I hope you saved those letters."

He nodded. "Are you sure you want them?" She thought she saw a slight blush. "They were love letters."

Suddenly, nothing mattered to her. She wanted only to be in his arms again. "At this moment, I have never wanted anything more in my life, C-C," she said as she moved closer to him.

C-C embraced Anna, catching his breath at the scent of her.

Anna ran her fingers affectionately through the hair at his temples. "You're turning gray," she whispered with a smile.

"From missing you, *amour*."

Their lips met; the world around them disappeared.

The crowd of people in the outdoor café, who had been watching the couple intently, erupted into wild applause and cheers at their tender embrace.

The uproar brought Jacques out of the Ajaccio's kitchen. Knitting his eyebrows into the deep furrows of his forehead, he gave Guy de Noailles an inquisitive look.

"Our Anna has arrived just now," Guy explained with delight. "It would appear that Charlie is very happy to see her."

Martine stood behind Jacques, her arms crossed, her brassy-colored hair redder than ever in the sunlight. "Humph," she grumbled, "that's why I couldn't get him to sleep with me. And I've been trying for at least six months, too. I thought he was joining the convent." Swirling around expertly on her four-inch-high red stilettos, she went back to waiting on tables.

Jacques chuckled and glanced at Diamanté standing with his arms around Elise as they watched the young couple's prolonged kiss in the sun-drenched square. The wide smile on his face was one that Jacques had not seen for a very long time.

"This is embarrassing. What are we going to tell them?" Anna whispered, all of a sudden self-conscious. "Oh God, your father is standing there."

"He will be all right. He knows now what he didn't know before."

"That will make a difference?"

"*Beh, oui*. You are Diamanté's granddaughter. You won't have to explain. It has all been discussed. He will accept you now."

"Do you want him to accept me?"

He nodded.

"There is no one else then?"

"Only you." He kissed the back of her hand.

Shoulders touching, they turned and walked together toward the Ajaccio.

CHAPTER 53

Anna had frequently practiced telling Jacques off over the years. She told herself that she wasn't going to be easy on him. If she ever saw that man again, she would let him have it for all he had done to destroy a relationship in which he had no business interfering. Now she stared at the old man as he took her hand and kissed the back of it. All that she could have said came out in a simple greeting: "*Bonjour, Monsieur* Gérard." The transition from words you say to yourself to those you speak aloud isn't always straightforward.

"Welcome to the Ajaccio," he said in thickly accented French. After years spent in northwestern France, his Corsican lilt had taken on a Norman accent. "My father-in-law tells me that he and Elise have been conspiring to get you to Castagniers for the wedding."

"I am happy to be here for it. I have wanted to find Diamanté for some time." She looked over at Diamanté and Elise.

"I think this reunion calls for a toast. Uncork the champagne, Martine," Jacques yelled toward the zinc bar. He looked over at his son and nodded. C-C smiled at him and then at Anna.

Anna left C-C's side and went over to Diamanté. Not knowing how he would react to her, she offered her hand.

"Where do we begin?" she asked cautiously, wondering how one launches a relationship such as this.

He accepted her hand and touched his lips to it in a gentlemanly gesture.

"We begin with today," he replied with warmth in his raspy voice.

Anna saw in his black eyes the look that had been described to her many times. What was the word C-C had used? Vulpine. Yes, they were vulpine, but there was something more there. She had wanted to meet him, but now, she yearned to understand him.

"May I call you *Grand-père*, then?"

"If you wish. It would be nice, I think." The old man's face flushed slightly. He looked suddenly shy, speechless, self-conscious.

Elise, Jacques, C-C, and Guy had watched their exchange. Elise came to Diamanté's rescue, touching him gently on the shoulder. In an amused voice that showed love and understanding, she said, "My *Lobo* is not used to being called *Grand-père*, especially by such an attractive creature. It will take some getting used to."

Martine arrived with a tray of crystal flutes filled with sparkling pink wine and passed them out. The crowd on the terrace watched, their faces quiet in anticipation.

Guy was the first to toast. "To Anna's arrival! *À la vôtre!*"

"*À la vôtre!*" They held up their glasses to Anna and took a sip.

Jacques was next. "To the wedding! *À la vôtre!*"

"*À la vôtre!*" They raised their glasses again, this time towards Elise and Diamanté.

C-C was next. "*À l'amour! À la vôtre!*" He looked in the direction of Anna.

"*À l'amour! À la vôtre!*" A wild clapping of hands and cheering came from the exuberant crowd on the terrace as they joined the little group in a resounding repetition of C-C's toast.

Anna turned to Diamanté. She raised her glass to his. "To family!"

The crowd erupted in cheers as Diamanté raised his glass. "*À la vôtre!*"

The flutes emptied, Jacques returned to the kitchen. Diamanté joined him. The restaurant was full. Martine raced around, serving everyone drinks. Elise excused herself to go upstairs, saying she would see them all later for dinner. With a twinkle in his eye, Guy sat down at a table by the bar to read the evening newspaper, deliberately leaving C-C and Anna alone.

C-C took Anna's hand. "Come take a walk with me before dinner. We never eat until after the crowd subsides a bit so my father can join us. Besides, I want to show you something." He led her out into the open square where a long line of hungry people awaited tables. "It's been this way ever since the beginning of August," he said. "Diamanté had to hire extra staff. It will last all month. Then it will be a quiet little village again."

The summer evening was warmed by a brilliant yellow sun in a tranquil sky. Gentle breezes ruffled the leaves of the trees, and dusk hovered on the horizon.

Anna clung tightly to C-C's arm for support on the rough pavement. "These sandals aren't designed for walking on these uneven stones," she said. "If we're going very far, I'd better get some different shoes."

"It's just on the outskirts of the village. I want to show you my house."

"Why not take the car, then?"

C-C laughed. "It won't be necessary." They had reached the Peugeot.

She fetched her carry-on from the trunk, reached into the pocket, and pulled out a pair of flat, white sandals. After changing from her high heels, she retrieved Nathalie's tin box from the front seat.

"Think I'll bring this, too," she said of the carry-on. Suddenly feeling the effects of the very long day she had put in since boarding the flight at LAX, she added, "I could sure use a bit of freshening up. You do have a bathroom, don't you?"

C-C laughed again as he took her bag. "With indoor plumbing *quand même.*"

As they strolled through the village square, Anna noticed that a decorated platform had been erected at the far end, and little white lights glittered cheerfully around an area cordoned off for dancing.

"What's going on?"

"A *fête.* All the villages in Provence hold at least one in August. Then the inhabitants of the surrounding villages attend. Many tourists come as well. See, they are buying souvenirs." He nodded towards the crowd wandering through stalls that had been set up by the local artisans. Above them, residents of the village peered from their open windows, and in the park a group of seniors played a game of *pétanque* on a sandy lot under some shade trees.

As they moved on, Anna became aware of a large, brown dog with floppy ears and devoted doggy eyes lumbering along at their heels.

"Is he your dog?"

"No, that is Max, the café dog. Diamanté told me that he just appeared one day and never left. Ever since I arrived here in December, he has been my constant companion. Follows me wherever I go, waits patiently outside the door, snoozes, then we go together to the café to be fed."

Anna laughed. "Where does he sleep?"

"That's just it. I don't know. He's always waiting outside the door in the morning when I come out, but he's not there during the night. I've looked."

When they reached the outskirts of the village, C-C pointed to a two-story house with terracotta-tiled roof and a sun-drenched, yellow façade. Light sage green shutters framed the windows.

"That's the house I bought in January."

"It's charming, C-C," Anna exclaimed.

They entered the front garden through a wooden gate. The pathway leading to the front door was lined on each side with red roses interspersed with lavender. It wasn't what she had expected at all. On the carved wooden door was a simple sign above the brass knocker. The sign read "*Soins Médicaux, Docteur* Charles-Christian Gérard." C-C opened the door for her. With a sigh, Max plopped himself on a mat by the door to wait.

"The interior was pretty ramshackle when I bought the house. The path was all weeds. I've made the front part of the house into my doctor's office for now."

The all-white foyer with a black-tiled floor just inside the door obviously served as the outer waiting room. It held only a couple of curved wooden chairs that were upholstered in black leather, a small antique oval end table with a lamp, an iron umbrella stand, and a bookcase filled with medical books. A framed poster leaning against a wall advertised the work of Médecins Sans Frontières. Through the adjacent door, Anna could see an all-white room. The only piece of furniture in it was a small reception desk with a PC.

"It is sparse, but I don't see that many patients here," C-C's voice echoed in the empty space. "There is one examination room and space for another, but I haven't finished it, and so far I haven't needed it."

Anna saw no one around. She asked, "Do you have a receptionist?"

"No. I don't need one. I can keep most of the patient records on the PC myself. There aren't that many."

"What about a nurse?"

"There is a nurse nearby, if I need her. So far, I have only had to call on her a few times, to help with the delivery of a new baby or to assist with an emergency tonsillectomy."

"So it's a one-doctor operation then?"

He answered matter-of-factly. "Yes, and I like it this way. I have more time with my patients. In Paris, in the hospital, there was always chaos. There was no time to spend with the healing process of the whole individual. It was just boom, boom, boom, get the patient through the system and out the door."

"You don't have many emergencies, then?"

"Not many."

He led her to the back of the house where there was a large kitchen. It was low-ceilinged, well-equipped, and the walls and cabinets were painted a soft celadon. The wall above the gray marble work counter was covered with antique tiles. A large wooden table and four chairs filled the center of the room. An antique copper chandelier coated with a greenish blue patina hung above the table.

"It doesn't look like anyone has been using the kitchen," she remarked.

"It's progressing. One of the village handymen has been doing the work, on and off. I don't know when he'll finish, if ever, but I don't have much use for a kitchen anyway." He looked at her sheepishly. "I eat most of my meals in the restaurant."

"I can't say that I blame you." Anna looked through the French doors to the back garden. "What's that?" She pointed toward a quaint, two-story building with a mansard roof that sat near the back wall. The single French door which served as its entrance was surrounded by potted plants. A shaded open window with a small iron railing and a window box full of flowers jutted out from the roof above the door. Windows on each side of the small building held boxes overflowing with salmon pink geraniums.

"It's the caretaker's cottage. His name is Clo."

"Claude?"

"No, Clo, C-L-O. He's Cambodian. I hired him shortly after I bought the house. He keeps the grounds for me and helps me with the plumbing, too."

"He lives in it? It looks so small."

"It's quite nice now. I told him he could live there if he could make it habitable. He has outfitted it with a small kitchen and comfortable salon downstairs, and his bedroom is upstairs. He says he's alone and that's all he needs. His wife died several years ago. You will like him. Come, let's go upstairs. I want to show you the rest." He picked up her carry-on and took her arm.

They climbed the varnished wooden staircase to the second level. Anna paused at the top of the stairs, her breath taken away by the sight of the elegant room with parquetry floor and carved dark wood wall paneling in front of her. A large, gilt-framed mirror hung over the mantel of a massive marble fireplace. The room's single piece of furniture, a split chaise lounge upholstered in brown and gold brocade, sat on a tapestry rug in front of the fireplace.

"The chandelier and the mirror came with the house," C-C explained when he saw her studying the multifaceted globe that was suspended over the center of the room from a sparkling crystal chandelier.

Anna walked through a curtained doorway to the left of the salon. The adjacent room, also paneled in carved wood, was carpeted in soft midnight blue. A vast, four-poster bed dominated the space. Against the opposite wall stood an antique Bartholdi desk with black lacquer diamond inlay on its center. A gold-framed oval mirror hung between two ceiling-high French windows.

"My bedroom," he said, watching her as he placed her carry-on against the wall under the oval mirror. "It's the only other room that's finished. The rest of the house is closed off for now."

The breeze wafting in through the windows carried the scent of lavender and roses from the back garden. The room was cool in spite of the intense heat of the day.

"It's a handsome house," she exclaimed as she placed his mother's tin box on top of the desk. On the gold-tooled, black leather writing surface, two piles of correspondence caught her eye. Tied neatly with string that looked suspiciously like suture thread were the letters she had sent him a decade before. They had been opened and carefully returned to their envelopes. Next to them lay a small stack of soft pale blue envelopes, unaddressed except for a large "A" in C-C's handwriting on the front. The book that she had signed rested under a pewter framed sketch to the right of the letters. She picked up the frame. The drawing was hers, a self-portrait in pencil.

"I…I had forgotten that I sent this to you."

C-C moved to her and placed the tips of his fingers gently on her bare, perspiration-dampened back, touching the irresistible area between her shoulder blades.

A shiver ran through her as she turned around to face him.

He wrapped his arms around her, drew her in close, kissed her on the forehead, and said softly, "I am so happy you are here, Anna."

She was still holding the framed sketch. "Are you sure that you aren't just still in love with the girl in this sketch? I've changed a lot since those days."

"You are more beautiful." He nestled his nose in her long hair. "I would like to discover the changes." His tongue encircled her earlobe and slid into her ear, causing her whole body to react.

Anna closed her eyes and moaned, took in a deep breath, then pushed him away. "Give me some time to…to freshen up."

"*Bon.*" He dropped his arms to his sides. "*Voilà le cabinet de toilette.*" He nodded towards the bathroom. "You'll find soap and towels in the armoire. Take your time. I need to make a house call. Be back in about a half hour." He hesitated as if to say something else. Instead, he gently took the framed sketch from her hands, placed it carefully back on the desk, turned, and walked out of the room.

CHAPTER 54

A nna heard the front door slam. She rubbed her temples and combed her fingers through her hair.

"Well, let's see that bathroom," she said aloud with a sigh. "If it's anything like the rest of the house..." When she entered the room, her voice trailed off, and her eyes widened at the sight of the large, modern bathroom tiled in gray marble. A massive porcelain tub sat at the foot of steps leading to an etched-glass enclosed shower. She opened the raised panel doors of the solid cherry armoire and found soft midnight blue monogrammed towels and an assortment of hand-cut olive oil, almond, and lavender scented soaps. She undressed and stepped into the shower, wondering fleetingly how C-C had found the means to afford all this luxury.

Twenty minutes later, snuggly wrapped in C-C's thick, pale green, terry-cloth robe, Anna stood before the oval mirror that seemed to invite a person to step right through. It reflected the room behind her, which optically became the chamber in front of her.

What, she wondered, *would happen if I stepped into it now?* She drew the collar of the robe to her cheek and inhaled C-C's lingering scent. A familiar tingling of desire ran through her lower back and buttocks. Both she and C-C had changed, yet she was certain that the attraction between them remained. She went over to the desk and picked up one of the unsealed, pale blue envelopes. She lay down on the bed, stretched, and allowed her head to fall back into the softness of the pillows as she unfolded the pages filled with C-C's handwriting. "*Mon amour...*" the letter began.

C-C arrived at just that moment. He stood quietly, watching her from the curtained doorway, imagining her body touching the inside of his terry robe. He caught his breath, overwhelmed by an irresistible longing to be enfolded in the robe with her. "I see you have found your letters," he said.

Anna jumped. "You startled me. I didn't hear the door downstairs."

"I came in from the south rose garden. I wanted to bring you one of these." He bowed slightly and presented her with a single tea rose, the color a creamy ivory tinged with pink apricot. "Clo tells me this one's name is Anna."

Anna accepted it and held it under her nose. Its scent was light and spicy. "It's a beautiful rose," she said softly.

"It reminds me of you."

"You don't mind if I picked out one of the letters to read, do you?"

He seemed surprised at the question.

"No, they are yours."

"I've only read the first paragraph of this one. You weren't going to write again, were you?"

"Not if you didn't come for the wedding. Eight months is a long time. I couldn't go on forever."

She fingered the fine, pale blue, linen-textured stationery. "You really never intended to send them to me?"

"*Non. Bien sûr que non.* I thought you had married. You wouldn't have wanted letters arriving from a French lover, would you?"

She smiled and rolled seductively on her side. One bare tanned leg slid from under the robe. "Well, no." Hesitantly, she asked, "Have you been with anyone, C-C?"

He shook his head. "I've been too busy with this house, my practice."

"Not even Martine? I saw the way she looked at you."

He laughed. "Martine? She's a big flirt. I think I've been a huge disappointment to her." He came over to the bed and leaned over her, positioning his hands on the pillows above her head. "Are you refreshed?"

"Yes, much better. This robe feels so luxurious."

"You look better in it than I do," he said as he turned off his cell phone, laid it on the end table, and began unbuttoning his shirt.

"In that one," he nodded to the letter in her hand, "I explained how I would feel if you were here in this room with me."

Anna watched him as he pulled the belt from his pants.

"I also describe what I would do," he said seductively as he disappeared into the bathroom.

"You do?" she called after him as she heard the shower turn on. Two minutes later, the water quit running, and C-C was standing in the doorway with a towel draped around his waist.

Anna propped herself on one elbow and studied him thoughtfully. He was long-waisted with no visible hips, slim, but not extremely muscular. "You look to me as if you could use a few days lying in the sun," she said as she eyed the tan line on his arms that gave way to pale skin everywhere else. Then she added, licking her lower lip, "Let the towel drop. I want to see all of you."

Obediently, the bath towel fell to the floor. His body gave away the desire he was feeling. He shrugged his shoulders and put his hands out from his sides. "*Me voilà.*"

She spoke in a soft voice as he came over to the bed and leaned over her. "What does the rest of your letter say?"

"If you came to me, *amour, eh bien,* I would carry you to this bed."

"But I'm already here. What next?" She ran her fingers lightly through the graying hair at his temples.

"I would undress you, *bien sûr.*" He laughed.

"Well that is done, too." She brushed his bare chest with her fingers.

"A slight modification in sequence is all that is required." He kissed her lips, his tongue teasing hers as he undid the tie around her waist and positioned his naked body next to hers. Gently, he kissed her shoulders, then her neck and behind the ears. The tongue moved down her body. When he reached her toes, he slowly drew them into his mouth, licking them one by one, and then he began inching his way up her leg until he reached the inside of her thighs, murmuring to himself as he gently aroused her. He touched her most erotic spots, unhurriedly, methodically, until he reached her lips again, his tongue sliding hungrily into her mouth. She moaned and pulled him into her, yearning for the sensual feel of his body as he came to her. Every inch of her wanted him.

They were finding each other all over again. This time there was no interruption.

Their desire fulfilled, C-C and Anna lay in each other's arms. "Will you stay here with me tonight?" he whispered. "Diamanté will have no rooms left anyway. Lucie, Léo, and *Père* Truette should have arrived by the time we get back to the restaurant for dinner."

"So there's no room at the inn?" she teased.

"No room."

"Okay, but only if you promise me a repeat of what we just did."

He kissed her cheek. "*C'est promis.*"

By the time Anna and C-C returned to the place de la Mairie, the square twinkled in bright lights, and a horde was dancing to the raucous music of a local rock band. The few lingering diners on the Ajaccio terrace listened to the music as they enjoyed an after-dinner liqueur.

C-C looked at Anna lovingly. She had changed into a white linen skirt, white sandals, and a fuchsia tank top. Her long hair fell in cascading curls that covered her shoulders, and large, silver hoop earrings hung from her ears. "You look *ravissante, amour,*" he said, and he kissed the back of her hand.

The music suddenly changed. The band switched from rock to a blues version of "*La Vie en Rose,*" at which point the couples on the dancing platform assumed an intimate stance.

C-C slid his right arm around Anna's waist, stared into her eyes, and drew her to him as he raised his left hand in invitation to dance.

Anna took his hand, and they joined the crowd on the platform.

Above the Ajaccio, from an open window, Elise nudged Diamanté with her elbow. They had been watching the dancers and enjoying the music.

"Look, over there." Elise pointed out C-C and Anna. "I think they have been making love," she said with a certain air to her voice.

"Now, how, *chérie*, do you think that?" Diamanté teased her, putting his arm around her shoulders.

Elise's nose wrinkled and seemed to draw up into her forehead as she smiled into Diamanté's face.

"See how they are looking at each other as they dance? I know these things, *o meu Lobo*." My *Lobo*, she called him now, because he was hers after all. "I have lived for a very long time."

"Not as long as I have." He chuckled and hugged her. "But I think you may be right. Come, let's go join the others. Everyone will be sufficiently famished by now."

CHAPTER 55

C-C and Anna left the dancers and followed the side pathway to the private back garden of the Ajaccio. The air was cool, and a chorus of croaking frogs greeted them in the darkness. From the restaurant's kitchen came mouthwatering aromas that filled the soft evening air.

They found Jacques, Diamanté, and Elise seated at a long, rectangular table under the soft glow of a six-candle, wrought-iron, scroll chandelier hanging from a low branch of a towering plane tree. Tall glasses of *pastis*, the licorice-flavored aperitif, sat in front of them. White ironwork *jardin* chairs with green cushions were set around the table and, in the center on a white linen tablecloth stood a huge blue and green ceramic vase filled with tall, bearded irises.

"Ah, *les voilà,*" Jacques said. "Lucie has arrived, and she has kicked me out of the kitchen for the night." Indicating that he was helpless to do anything about the situation, he shrugged and held up his hands.

"Well then, we will eat well for a change," C-C teased. "I take it the restaurant in Rouen is closed?"

"Yes, not much business in August anyway. She wouldn't miss an opportunity to come down here and show me up, either."

"Oh, Jacques," Elise scolded him, patting his hand lightly. "You know she's delighted to be of help to us. You looked so tired tonight. You've been overdoing. Besides, she wouldn't have missed the wedding for anything."

Diamanté had been quiet, but he couldn't resist adding, "*Moi,* I'm looking forward to that duck!"

"Lucie will prepare the duck, *mon vieux ami,*" Jacques retorted pointing to himself, "*mais, c'est moi* who will tell the story."

A loud groan came from behind them. It was Léo La Bergère, the jovial *bon vivant* who was Jacques' great friend. "Ah *non, non, et non enfin,* Jacques. We can't have that duck story, not tonight. It is too bloody for a celebration." He kissed Elise on both cheeks and shook Diamanté's hand. His face lit up when he saw Anna. "Ah, our beautiful *américaine* has returned to France. Or didn't Charlie ever let you leave?" He kissed her on both cheeks. "*Eh bien,* I see you have finally found your *grand-père.*" He glanced over in Diamanté's direction. "What do you think of your granddaughter, heh, *mon vieux?*"

Diamanté bowed his head in her direction. "She is much more beautiful than I am." Everyone laughed.

Pierre Truette was behind Léo. The quiet-spoken priest from Rouen greeted everyone and shook hands around.

"*Père* Truette will perform the marriage ceremony on Sunday," Elise told Anna as Truette sat down beside her. Elise patted his arm. The bride-to-be had changed into a vivid blue silk dress that matched her eyes. A shawl of the same color was draped over her shoulders.

"*Oui,* and I am delighted to do so. This is a special occasion for all of us," said *Père* Truette, respectfully.

They all took their places at the table, and Martine served *pastis* to the new arrivals, brushing against C-C as she passed him. Then she announced to the group, flashing a discreet wink in C-C's direction, that she was off for the evening and heading for the dance platform and then bed. He squirmed a bit. Anna gave him a knowing look through her lowered eyelashes, which he did his best to ignore.

"What is the schedule for the wedding?" Anna asked just as Guy joined them. She noticed that he was walking less energetically than he had the last time she saw him.

He kissed her warmly on both cheeks and took the chair next to hers. "Oh, *ma chère*, I forgot to include that information in my letter, *n'est-ce pas?*" He nodded toward Elise, who was busy chatting with the priest. "Elise, explain the grand plan."

Elise looked up. "We were just finalizing the last-minute details. The civil ceremony will be at *la mairie* beginning around four o'clock in the afternoon. Afterwards, we will have a little procession to the religious ceremony, which will be held in the *abbaye*. There will be a reception at the Ajaccio following the religious ceremony, and then, in the evening, we will have a fabulous private dinner, just for our special guests, in the back garden. Lucie and Jacques are in charge of the menu."

"And it will be a nine-course extravaganza!" Jacques added.

Everyone in the group put their hands to their stomachs and blew a little air through their lips in wonderful anticipation of the culinary experience.

"Are you sure you are up to that grueling schedule?" C-C asked Elise.

"I'm planning on closing the shutters and taking a long siesta beforehand," Elise answered, wrinkling her nose at him as she smiled.

"I think I had better have a siesta also," Anna whispered to C-C. Returning her smile, he gently brushed her hair away from her cheek with the back of his hand.

Lucie came out onto the terrace. She looked even larger to Anna than when she had seen her in Rouen. C-C rose from his chair to greet her.

"Charlie!" The woman enveloped him in her arms and shook him back and forth as she kissed him on both cheeks.

"*Bonsoir*, Lucie. *Comment vas-tu?*"

"*Patapouf*," she said with gusto. "Fatter than ever. I like my own cooking too much." Then she spotted Anna. "Anna!"

Anna got up to greet her and was wrapped in the pair of meaty arms as well. "*Bonsoir*, Lucie. It's good to see you again," she said when she had finally got her breath.

"Heh, Lucie, are we going to eat tonight or *non*? Are you still picking out the duck?" Jacques clucked at her.

"Oh, Jacques, *attends*, be patient. I've just come to announce that the first course will be served shortly."

"And it will be?" Léo inquired with his eyebrows lifted.

"*Truffes* in puff pastry," Lucie announced.

"Ah, that's it!" exclaimed Jacques. "She's been out in the hills picking the wild mushrooms."

The evening waiter, an extra whom Diamanté had brought from Nice for the month, entered with a tray and began serving them.

Twenty minutes later, Lucie returned to announce the second course, an herb soup.

"It's called *l'ourteto*," she informed the group. She explained to Anna, "It's an old *provençale* soup. The name means *petit jardin*, little garden."

Anna tasted it and nodded her head approvingly.

A salad of *haricots verts* and green hazelnuts was next, followed by *la pièce de résistance:* thinly sliced duck breast *au romarin*, draped over a mound of ratatouille-like vegetables and served with violet asparagus, small zucchini flowers, and miniature potatoes.

"*Eh bien*, Lucie has finally outdone herself," Léo announced as he savored the show-off dessert: an earthy, elegant, and mysterious concoction that consisted of a fresh pear tart topped with candied baby eggplant and lavender-scented ice cream. They all nodded in agreement.

Coffee and glasses of Calvados followed. By the time they had finished eating and drinking, it was after midnight, the band had finished, and the square was quiet.

"It was such fun," Anna said to C-C as they, followed by Max, walked to C-C's house in the darkness.

"They are quite a group when they get going."

"I had to laugh when Jacques passed on telling his duck story. Actually, I thought he was going to tell it when he launched into that booming," she lowered her voice and tried her best imitation of the Corsican accent, "And now I will tell the sad story of the duck." Then she laughed, "But he caved in with all the hissing and booing."

"He was in rare form tonight."

They had reached the house. As C-C opened the door for her, she said, yawning, "Doesn't Diamanté ever take that beret off and keep it off?"

"Not that I've seen. He gives the impression that he was born in it."

"I wonder if he sleeps in it?"

"One thing is certain: he'll probably die in it."

"Oh, C-C," she said, shaking her head.

CHAPTER 56

Anna awoke late the morning after the dinner welcoming the wedding guests. Jet-lagged and slightly hung over, she rolled over and yawned. The side of the bed where C-C had been was empty. On the nightstand, tucked under a vase with a fresh rose, she found a note: "Gone to check on a patient. Back around eleven o'clock. There are tea bags in the kitchen. *Je t'aime.*"

Anna swung her feet off the side of the bed and looked at the clock. Eleven o'clock was a half hour away. She went into the bathroom, washed her face and brushed her teeth, then found her gray running shorts and a white tank top in her suitcase and slipped them on. As she descended the staircase barefoot, she peeked toward the front of the house. Not a soul in sight. Good. No patients waiting in the foyer.

In the kitchen, Anna found a felt-lined, mahogany tea chest on the marble counter. As she filled a copper tea kettle with water from the faucet, she eyed the gas stove. It was one of those stunning *mi-professionnel* stoves she had read about, made of cast-iron and with elegant, polished brass hardware and painted with the same hard enamel used on car finishes. This one, a glossy *aubergine* to match the color of the intricate detail in the antique tiles above the work counter, had beautiful oven doors, and its top was brushed stainless steel. She set the tea kettle on one of the six gas burners. The medallion in the center of the backsplash read *La Cornue*.

"Whew!" she whistled. "This one's the top of the line. Wonder why he spent so much money on a stove he doesn't even use?"

When the water was boiling, she found a china cup and saucer in the cupboard, selected a chamomile from the assortment in the tea chest, placed it in the cup, and poured the hot water over it.

The scent of roses and lavender coming through the open French doors drew her into the back garden. The sun beat down from a flawless blue sky, and the air was hot and still. She plucked a fresh mint leaf from a pot on the terrace, sniffed its distinctive aroma, then placed it in her cup of tea. Except for the grasshoppers and cicadas, the garden was deserted. She wandered around to the south side of the house, where Clo the gardener had created a paradise of multicolored roses, all in full bloom. A small pathway led to a bench by a birdbath under a rose arbor at the back corner. The white roses on the arbor extended to cover the entire wall of a small building. As she studied the tile-roofed structure, Anna took a sip of her tea, savoring the sweet flavor of the mint followed by the cool aftertaste. There were no windows, only a large garage door with a small door beside it. She tried the handle on the smaller door. It was unlocked. The light spilling in from the outside fell across a sleek black roadster, the distinctive three-pointed Mercedes star on the back of its trunk flanked by SL55 and AMG.

She whistled again. If this was C-C's car, something bothered her. She knew doctors in France didn't make the kind of money that they do in the U.S. C-C certainly didn't earn enough to afford all this as an ER physician in Paris. She recalled what he had said about not having very many patients here. How then? This handsome house? The expensive renovation? A caretaker for the grounds? This car? Her eyes narrowed. She closed the door and wandered back through the garden and into the kitchen. A few minutes later, she heard the front door open and close.

C-C crept up from behind and pulled her to him. "Did you sleep well?"

"Yes, but I'm still jet-lagged. And I think I had a little too much Calvados."

"I see you found the tea."

"Yes. I drank it in the rose garden. It is so beautiful out there."

"It's Clo's life. He will be happy to hear you appreciate it."

"I'll tell him myself when I meet him. C-C, I noticed a building that looks like a garage next to the garden. What's in it?" she asked innocently.

"My car."

"Do you use it often?"

"*Non*. Occasionally I go to Nice or into the mountains. But I don't get much time off to go any farther than that."

"It doesn't sound like you. You, the traveler that I remember."

"I guess you discovered another thing that's different." He nuzzled her ear, speaking softly. "Diamanté and Elise have invited us for a late lunch. He wants to get to know you better. I promised them we'd be there by one o'clock. We've got two hours, *amour*. Let's go upstairs."

As they walked slowly up the staircase arm in arm, Anna asked, "Does your PC in the reception room have a connection to the Internet?"

"*Oui, pourquoi?*"

"Do you mind if I use it someday to check my e-mail? My agent mostly communicates with me that way. I didn't want to bring my laptop since I declared this a vacation, but I promised him I would find an Internet café or something to pick up any urgent e-mails he might send. I don't suppose there is an Internet café in Castagniers?"

"No, not yet anyway." He stopped at the top of the stairs and kissed her passionately, and then he said, "You are welcome to use the PC whenever you want. Except, not now."

Anna's concerns of the morning vanished. The anticipation of lovemaking was delicious; his lips tasted delicious. She told herself it was C-C's business how he could afford all this, not hers. Maybe he had inherited or borrowed the money. There had to be an explanation. She would most likely find out.

They lay down on the bed together. He pulled off her tank top and kissed her breasts and bare stomach. She pulled him to her and caressed his back. He was hard and ready, but he took her slowly. "We've got two hours," he whispered.

CHAPTER 57

Lunch was in the tranquil shade of the garden in back of the Ajaccio, where the celebration the evening before had taken place. Martine greeted C-C and Anna and invited them to be seated at a small table covered in a pale green, linen cloth and set with china and crystal. In the background, they could hear the constant hum of cicadas singing with gusto, their unique, high-pitched hissing and whirring filling the air in the heat of the day.

"I will let Diamanté and Elise know that you have arrived," Martine called over her shoulder as she hurried back into the kitchen.

"She's on her good behavior today," Anna remarked with a wry smile as she fetched her camera from her handbag. "She stayed at least a foot away from you."

C-C was absorbed in examining the label on a bottle of wine cooling in a silver bucket next to the table. Anna snapped a photo of him. At the sound of the camera click, he looked up at her with a seductive grin.

Diamanté appeared just at that moment. "How about a photo of the two of you together?" he suggested. Anna handed the camera to him and walked over to C-C, who turned her gently, placed one arm lovingly under her chin, and squeezed her to his chest. Diamanté moved in close and took the photo.

"Now your turn," Anna said as Diamanté handed the camera to her.

"Should I remove my beret?"

"I thought it was glued to your head," she teased.

"*Pas du tout,*" he said stiffly as he removed it and held it to his chest. Anna was surprised that, instead of smiling toward the camera, he looked off into the distance, as if deep in thought.

Elise came through the open French doors onto the back terrace. She embraced Anna, brushing her on each cheek, then graciously offered her own cheeks for C-C's kisses.

"So I see you two have survived last night," she said.

Anna blushed and looked at C-C. Elise was immediately apologetic. "Oh, my dear! I meant the dinner party. I myself was exhausted."

Diamanté came to her rescue. "And she says she is going to dance until after midnight on our wedding night."

"I am, too. You just keep up with me." She poked him in the chest with her bony finger.

"Come, you two lovebirds. Stand together so I can take a photo of you." Anna stood with her camera ready as Diamanté replaced his beret and folded his arms around his bride-to-be.

"*Magnifique!*" Anna said as Elise wrinkled her nose in pleasure.

They seated themselves at the table. Martine poured chilled rosé wine and served the first course, a goat cheese tart with baby artichokes.

"Who's in the kitchen today?" C-C asked Diamanté.

"Both of them. Jacques allowed Lucie to have it all by herself last night, but he couldn't stay away today. There are many tourists in the region, and it is the weekend. The *resto* will be busy all day."

"*Waoui*," Martine piped in. "But, you should hear them arguing! *Nom de Dieu!* The stories they tell on each other. You would think that they would be taking the cutlery to each other's throats any minute rather than to the vegetables!"

Diamanté chuckled as he passed a basket of thickly sliced, hard-crusted bread while Elise served them a summer salad of zucchini, tomatoes, and black olives tossed with olive oil and sprinkled with lemon juice and fresh mint leaves.

"How long are you planning to stay in France, Anna?" Diamanté asked.

Anna looked in C-C's direction. "I'm on vacation until the first week of September. I have friends not too far from here whom I am planning to visit. They purchased a *bastide* last year near Grasse and have been restoring it. I haven't seen it yet."

"Are they Californians?"

"No, Parisians. I have known them for a long time."

"You should turn in your rental car," C-C said to her. "You can take my car to visit them."

"I haven't seen a car rental agency in Castagniers."

"There is one in a neighboring village that is a little larger than ours," Diamanté said, trying to be helpful.

"I'll think about it. It's not costing me that much. Anyway, I may be visiting Monique and Georges for several days, and you might need your car," she looked intently at C-C, "in case of an emergency, that is."

He shrugged his shoulders, and their eyes locked. "It's your decision," he said.

What a strange suggestion, Anna thought. They had not discussed any plans following the wedding.

"Let's have some coffee, Martine," Elise commanded when they had finished helping themselves to a dessert platter of Madeleines and miniature candied apples. "Then I will have to excuse myself for the afternoon. I have so many things to finalize before the wedding tomorrow, not the least of which, my coiffure." She patted her hair.

After Elise had departed, Diamanté turned to Anna and said, "Come up to the library. It will be cooler, and we can have a nice talk."

C-C excused himself as they got up. "I have a patient to attend to," he said as he kissed Anna lightly on the cheek.

"*À très bientôt,*" she whispered in his ear.

Diamanté took C-C's arm firmly above the elbow, saying in a low voice, "Can I have a quick word with you before you go?"

C-C nodded, and they strolled to the front of the restaurant together. When they were safely out of hearing range, Diamanté said in a low voice, "*Écoute*, Charlie, I have intelligence that Narbon disappeared two weeks ago. There's been no sign of him since."

C-C gave him a questioning look.

Diamanté shrugged his shoulders. "You and I must be careful. We are the only ones left who know."

"There's also the nurse."

Diamanté nodded in agreement. "But she's married to the bodyguard now. What's she going to give away? Heh? Just watch yourself, my son. Be alert." Diamanté put his hand on C-C's shoulder and gave him a piercing look. "Like a Corsican."

C-C walked off in the direction of the convent. Ever since he had arrived in Castagniers, he had wondered why Narbon had been involved. Who was he? What was his role anyway? C-C had felt safe in Castagniers, his security assured. He put his hands in his pockets and kicked at a stone. Narbon missing could only mean one thing: that they were all in danger. The old fear that he had felt in Paris suddenly seized him.

CHAPTER 58

The book-lined library above the Ajaccio was darkened and cool despite the heat of midday. Anna and Diamanté settled into soft, overstuffed chairs, facing each other.

"I'd like to hear about my father, your son," she said nervously as she took a photo from her handbag and presented it to him. "I have only this one picture."

Diamanté switched on a lamp and carefully placed a pair of half-inch-thick reading glasses on the bridge of his nose. "It is Diamanté *fils* all right," he said as he moved his fingers slowly over the photo.

"My grandfather refused to tell me anything about my father, until the dreadful night of the car accident, that is, when he was dying. Afterwards, I found that photo in an old album in my grandparent's home. I didn't even know who the man with my mother was, but I guessed, just looking at them."

"I can see a resemblance in you to both of them," he said looking keenly at her. "What happened to your mother?"

"She died when I was very young." Anna hesitated, then decided to spare the old man the sordid details of her mother's life. "I was raised by my grandparents."

"In California?"

"Yes, in Laguna, where I now live. Have you ever been to the United States?"

"No, but I would like very much to visit one day."

"Guy told me some of your history when I visited him in Obernai."

"How did you find him?"

"I discovered a card in my grandfather's personal items. It was sent after the war, postmarked from Strasbourg. A friend of mine helped me locate him through business associates in Strasbourg. I took a chance. I didn't think he would want to see me."

"He is a good man, Guy. He has become very fond of you."

"And I of him."

Diamanté placed the photo on the coffee table between them. "Did you know he was Charlie's *grand-père* when you visited him?" She sensed distrust, or was it just Gallic reserve?

"No, I didn't, not until the end of the visit, that is, when he told his story about the astronomical clock. It was so familiar that I had to ask, but I didn't tell him that I knew C-C." She looked down at her hands. "The circumstances were, well…I had my reasons."

They both fell silent. The only sound in the room came from the faint hum of the ceiling fan slowly whirling above them.

"It is none of an old man's business," he said awkwardly as he eased himself from his chair and walked over to stare out the window. After a moment, he said, "It looks like we may have a storm brewing. It will arrive during the night, most likely. They always do. Don't be surprised at the fury of our storms, Anna. There will be wind, cracks of lightning followed by booming thunder, and torrents of rain. Sometimes we even get hailstones. But it will be all over by morning."

She was watching him intensely. "Tell me about your son…my father," she said, repeating her earlier question.

Diamanté stood looking out the window for what seemed to Anna a long time before he cleared his throat and began to speak. Without turning to face her, he said hesitantly, "My son met his death mere days before the cease-fire ended the Algerian war. He was a patient young man, generous," he chuckled lowly to himself and cocked his head sideways, "a bit stubborn, but so exuberant for life. He was a great storyteller, even as a youth."

The old man walked slowly to one of the bookshelves against the wall behind where Anna was seated. She noted how quietly he moved.

From a shelf, he pulled a worn, black leather journal. His hand shook with age and emotion as he handed it to Anna.

"I have only this of his from Algeria. It was shipped back to me after his death. So many anecdotes. He must have had a premonition that something was going to happen to him. Read the last entry, written the day he was killed." He wiped his eyes and blew his nose loudly into his cloth handkerchief as he sat down across from her.

Anna carefully opened the timeworn book and rested her fingers on the yellowed pages, as if she were gently touching the hand of the father she would learn to know through them. The cursive was small, traditional, in the French style, wedge-shaped letters, broad at one end and pointed at the other, but unique all the same. The entirety of it had been written in dark green ink. It was obvious that care had been taken in the beauty of the penmanship as well as the words. She turned to the last entry, dated March 15, 1962, and began reading the French aloud.

> *La guerre, c'est l'enfer. L'enfer. La guerre.*
>
> *The atmosphere of Algiers is extremely depressing. The hot, dry sirocco wind blows constantly across the desert.*
>
> *I have lost my spirit. Some in my unit have committed suicide. The morale is very low.*
>
> *Today, the "reign of terror" climaxed. There are puddles of blood everywhere. Trucks on the road are riddled with bullets. Every exit is guarded by soldiers with machine guns. We ask everyone to show us their identification cards. Some do not make it past the checkpoints. We search houses. The inhabitants are all scared of us, and we are scared of them.*
>
> *I have written my father a letter. I told him how much I love him and admire his courage in another war. I ended it with adieu for if I get out of this war alive, I do not intend to return to Corsica. Instead, I shall go straight to California, to my beloved Lily, if she will forgive me.*

There was nothing after that. Anna closed the journal with a sigh and looked up at Diamanté.

"He was quite handsome," Diamanté said. "I identified his body. He was a victim of a drive-by shooting. The insurgents. He died on the street. He had been shot many times, but not once in his face. We buried our son in Corsica, in a cemetery in the village where he was born. His mother passed away the next year. Her heart was broken. She lies next to him. He was our only child." He shook his head. "I never received that letter he refers to."

"So we'll never know what he meant by that last comment," Anna said sadly. It was a clue, though, that she would always wonder about. Perhaps something that had happened between them had been the cause of her mother's problems.

Diamanté looked at her kindly. The tension between the two of them had eased.

"He would have been proud of you, being a storyteller, too." For the first time since she had met him, he used the familiar "*tu*" with her.

A sudden gust of wind came through the open window.

"Ah," he said. "It is announcing its intention, our weather."

C-C entered the convent's hospital corridor. When he turned the corner by the statue of Saint Bernard, he came upon the nurse and her new husband in a passionate embrace.

"Oh, *pardon*," he said.

The newlywed couple, still holding each other tightly, simply turned their heads and smiled at him with their cheeks touching.

"Hello, Doc."

"Hello, Geoffrey. *Bonjour*, Florence. I seem to have appeared at the wrong moment."

Geoffrey winked at him. "We were just taking a bit of a break."

"Mind if I talk to you in private, Geoffrey? I've a concern I need to discuss with you."

The British security guard nodded. Florence smiled at her new husband, gave him a quick love pat on the behind, and went inside to tend to her patient. Geoffrey and C-C walked along the corridor toward the courtyard.

"What's your concern, Doc? We've tightened it up pretty well around here."

"I've just learned that someone who was involved in all this—his name is André Narbon—is missing. According to Diamanté, it's been about two weeks since anyone has heard from him. He's apparently completely disappeared."

Geoffrey's eyebrows knit together, and he scratched the back of his neck. "Diamanté mentioned something about being wary recently, but I thought he was just reminding me of my duties. You know, since Flo and I have been a bit distracted." He chuckled. "I thanked him for his concern, and I didn't think much more about it. Is this Narbon a possible victim or a security threat?"

"Don't know. Diamanté seems to think that we're in danger, nevertheless. He was concerned enough to warn me."

"If you want, I'll run it by headquarters. They might know something of the bloke's whereabouts. Probably nothing to worry about."

"Diamanté's wedding is tomorrow, as you know."

"Right. We've got it covered. You won't even know we're there."

"*Bon.* There's one more bit of information I'd like," C-C hesitated. "Keep this confidential, for now, if you wouldn't mind. I'd like to know more about Narbon's background. All Diamanté told me was that he was dangerous and that they had had 'some differences' over the years, as he put it. There's still something that bothers me about him. I'd like to know if he's on our side."

"Sure, Doc. I'll see what I can dig up through Interpol."

CHAPTER 59

The storm awakened Anna and C-C just after midnight. As Diamanté had predicted, it was fierce. First there was the wind, then the rain came in sheets, pounding the windows.

"It will be all right," C-C insisted. "The storms in Provence always seem violent." Just then, a lightning strike hit a nearby tree, and they heard the crash of a branch falling against the side of the house.

Anna screamed and then cried, "Oh, C-C, what about Max? He's outside. We have to find him." She flew down the stairs and opened the front door. The drenched and terrified dog ran into the foyer and immediately shook himself off.

The three of them waited out the storm in the hall under the stairwell. When it was over, they left Max to sleep in the foyer for the rest of the night, and then they returned to bed, energized and unable to resist yet another opportunity to make love before they fell asleep, exhausted in each others' arms.

The next morning, the air was pure and fresh and smelled of ozone. From the bedroom window, Anna, in C-C-'s terry robe, observed the caretaker in the garden picking up debris from the storm. He appeared to be in his early fifties and walked with a cane.

"What's wrong with Clo? Why is he limping?"

"He lost his leg in Southeast Asia. A land mine. I met him when he came to me with a problem. He couldn't wear his prosthesis any longer, and he had sores which were badly infected. I arranged to get him a new one. At the same time, I offered him the cottage to live in, and he took me up on it."

"Was he homeless?"

"You might say that. He lived very meagerly."

"You are kind to have given him a home, C-C."

"I'm not kind. I'm very selfish. You know that. He is helpful to me in return." C-C came up behind her. He was fresh out of the shower, naked, smelling faintly of almond soap. Pulling her against him, he untied the tie of the robe and wrapped her in his arms. "What do you want to do today? We have a few hours until it's time for the wedding."

"If you are implying that we should spend the day in bed, that's out." She rumpled his still-damp hair. "How about a drive? You keep mentioning how picturesque the neighboring villages are. I'd like to take some photos."

"Good idea." He grinned. "Second best, but good. We can have lunch somewhere other than the Ajaccio for a change."

"But we have to be back in plenty of time to get dressed for the wedding."

"And for a little siesta. Remember?" The twinkle in his eyes gave away his thoughts.

"Oh, you. I'll wager that the wedding couple isn't doing it as often as we are."

"They don't have ten years to make up for."

Anna laughed. "Maybe they do. How did they get together, anyway?"

"It's a fairy tale, really. Once upon a time…during the great war, Diamanté and this guy Narbon were both in love with Elise. They fought viciously over her and hated each other for years afterward. What I don't know is how Ferdinand, Diamanté's older brother, won out, but he did. Elise married him, and then a short while later she became a widow. Why Diamanté waited so long after his own wife's death to seek Elise out is also a mystery. He must have never stopped loving her. But now, all is well. They live happily ever after."

"Did he ever make up with the Narbon guy?"

"Not that I am aware of." C-C shrugged, making a mental note to check with Geoffrey on the Interpol search.

CHAPTER 60

In the tradition of all weddings in small French villages, the civil ceremony was conducted in the mayor's tiny office in the Castagniers town hall. Anna, C-C, Guy, Léo, *Père* Truette, Jacques, and Lucie crowded into a tight semi-circle behind Elise and Diamanté as the short, fleshy mayor, dressed in a black suit that didn't fit him very well, read from the time-honored script. When he finished, he cleared his throat and posed the question all in the room were waiting to hear. There were smiles and moist eyes among the group as Elise answered with a quiet "*oui*" and Diamanté, suddenly emotional, merely nodded his head. Everyone clapped their hands as the mayor pronounced, "*Je vous déclare maintenant mari et épouse.*"

"That was quick," Anna remarked to Guy as she walked arm in arm with him in the small procession to the abbey. "The ceremony must have lasted less than ten minutes."

"It's merely a formality." He shrugged.

Anna noticed that Guy was having some difficulty walking, and he seemed more frail than usual. "Is your leg giving you problems, Guy?" she asked.

"It's the old injury. It's telling me I've been overdoing. That is all."

C-C caught up with them. He, like the other men in the wedding party, was dressed to match the groom in a black suit, white shirt, and white tie. He leaned into Anna and whispered by her ear, "You look beautiful, *amour*."

Anna turned to him, her eyes meeting his. She thought how handsome he looked and how happy she was at this moment to be with him. "*Merci, mais c'est rien, une vielle robe*," she said modestly, shrugging her shoulders. Then she kissed him tenderly, allowing her soft lips to linger against his. In reality, she had spent a small fortune on the knee-length, classic, pistachio green, silk Armani dress she was wearing with matching chiffon shawl, encrusted with multicolored beads.

Ahead of them, Elise and Diamanté were being greeted by well-wishers from the village. Elise's dress, a light taupe with lace insets in the long sleeves, was embroidered all over in delicate white flowers, and she wore a white lace shawl over her shoulders. Her long hair, parted in the center and waved, had been pulled back into a smart chignon and adorned with a spray of fresh white rosebuds in the center back.

"Did you see, Anna? Diamanté is sporting a new beret," Guy said as Anna studied her grandfather's soft wool beret. She snapped a photo just as the little procession began moving again.

C-C put his arm around Anna's waist and helped her to negotiate the cobblestones in her dressy, high-heeled sandals. When they reached the entrance to the abbey, the heavy wooden doors were wide open, and there was a small crowd already seated in the back pews.

"Who are all these people?" Anna whispered to C-C as they escorted Guy to a front seat.

"Villagers mostly. And a few tourists who came out of curiosity. The religious ceremony is not private." He chuckled quietly. "And, of course, afterwards they know that it is customary that they will all be invited to the *vin d'honneur.*"

The church smelled like all French churches, Anna thought to herself, of a musty combination of incense and lit candles. There were huge bouquets of white roses and fresh lavender on either side of the altar. As the string quartet seated to the left of the altar began to play the processional, everyone stood and turned to watch Elise and Diamanté, followed by Father Truette in priestly vestments, proceed down the center aisle. Truette took his position at the altar, and Elise and Diamanté stood on the step below, facing him. The ceremony lasted only an hour, after which, as C-C had said, all were invited to the reception at the Ajaccio, where wine and hors d'oeuvres awaited them.

That evening, the restaurant closed and the back garden was set up for a joyful celebration. Anna listened as the string quartet that had played at the church, now seated in a corner of the patio, warmed up with a mixed medley of Corsican dance tunes. Additional lights and lanterns were hung on the trees and along the hedges, and two long tables, set with white linens, fine crystal glassware, china, and silver, were festooned down the center with lavender, bay, and rosemary cuttings interspersed with glowing votives and vases filled with roses from Clo's garden. It was still light, and the candles twinkled as the setting sun began to cast evening shadows across the mountains. The vegetation smelled fresh and washed after the rain of the night before, and the aroma coming from the lamb roasting in the barbecue pit at the back of the garden made Anna's mouth water.

She sneaked a peek into the Ajaccio's kitchen. The private dinner, the nine-course extravaganza that Jacques had predicted, was in progress, and the kitchen was in chaos. Jacques stood in the center of the room, putting last-minute touches on the first course. While he worked, he barked instructions to Martine on how everything should be served. Over by the massive stove, Lucie gave her own last-minute directions to two *commis* who had been brought in to help with presentation of the courses so that she and Jacques could be part of the wedding party. No one noticed Anna as she took photos of the chaos.

The dinner began with toasts all around to the married couple. When it was his turn, Jacques hauled himself to his feet and lifted his glass dramatically.

"A toast," he thundered. His deep bass voice commanded silence. "To the duck!" Much to everyone's delight, and Léo's chagrin, he explained, "Since tonight we dine on Rouen duck, I am going to tell my infamous duck story."

"The pressed duck is one of the glories of French cuisine, a classic," Jacques began, and then he paused to make certain that he had everyone's attention before he continued. "The recipe commences with the instruction to 'strangle a duck.' Now, mind you, this is no ordinary duck! This recipe requires a special breed of duck, a large and elegant Rouen duck..." Jacques' eyes widened, "a duck of fine French descent that has been killed, if possible, in the region of the Seine Valley in Normandy. The important thing is that the duck must be dressed in the proper fashion—that is, it is never decapitated, never," he wagged his finger at them. "It is strangled, so as to retain all of its blood! That's what gives the meat a dark red cast and a special flavor."

Eyes rolled, a loud clucking sound was heard from Léo's direction, and Elise shifted uncomfortably in her chair.

"In my restaurant in Rouen," Jacques went on, gesturing grandly in Lucie's direction, "we have a magnificent duck press the likes of which you have never before seen!" Lucie's large head wagged up and down in confirmation.

Jacques went on for several more minutes. By the time he was done, he had described in excruciating detail the expensive, half-meter-tall, brass-plated gadget known as the "duck press," the crushing of the bones in order to extract all the blood from the carcass, and the resulting juices that ultimately become the thick sauce, which he proclaimed with authority, "must be beaten without interruption for twenty minutes or so." Finally, he described the resulting sauce, "the color of melted chocolate," which is poured over the thinly-sliced duck breast and served.

"Each duck prepared in this manner is registered, and the diner is given a gilded placard stating the duck's personal registration number," he said with pride. Then he raised his glass with a flourish and said, "*Et voilà!*"

At that point, there were great roars of appreciation and laughter. Léo rose to his feet, pushed his glass in the air, and bellowed, "To all the blood-soaked, strangled Rouen ducks that have met their demise by torture for the ultimate satisfaction of Jacques' diners." Glasses clinked, and the group became once again noisy and animated.

Anna looked at C-C. "I'd rather not have known all that. I think I'm going to be sick," she said, secretly hoping that the first course would be seafood.

She was in luck. The first course consisted of crab meat decorated with tiny periwinkles, which prompted another toast as Diamanté noted that the periwinkles matched the color of his bride's eyes.

Then came fresh prawns with *girolle* mushrooms and tarragon mousse, tiny escargots in parsley cream, and stuffed scallops, *provençal*-style, all followed by the notorious duck, *le caneton à la rouennaise*, which Anna decided to pass on.

When they all thought they would burst with any more food, Elise rose, signaled to the string quartet that it was time to begin the dancing, and offered her hands to Diamanté. The quartet launched into a lively, traditional Corsican dance.

"Ah, it's a *Scultiscia!*" C-C whispered in Anna's ear as Elise pulled Diamanté onto the piazza. Everyone rose from their seats and began clapping in unison to the music.

Anna's eyes lit up. "They're dancing a Schottische!" she said as she held out her hands to C-C. Out onto the piazza, the two went to join the dance.

When the *Scultiscia* ended and all had returned to their seats, a refreshing sorbet was served, followed by the *pièce de résistance*, the truffle-dusted, spit-roasted lamb with rosemary potatoes. A salad of red mullet sautéed with baby artichokes and rosy garlic, and a lavish selection of cheeses were next placed in front of the guests, prompting Léo to raise his glass in toast to "the dueling chefs," as he called them. "We have all benefited from their talents these past few hours."

The group danced between courses to a variety of traditional Corsican waltzes, mazurkas, and polkas until well after midnight when the *croquembouche*, a pyramid of crème-filled pastry puffs drizzled with a caramel glaze, was finally served with small glasses of an after-dinner *digestif.*

"What is this?" Anna asked as she tasted the sweet, thyme-flavored liqueur.

"*Farigoulette*, from Provence," C-C explained. "Do you like it?"

She wrinkled her nose and shook her head. "Umm...*non.*"

"Aren't you going on *un voyage de noces?*" Anna asked Diamanté and Elise as she hugged and congratulated them before saying goodnight. "A honeymoon trip?"

"In September, *oui*," Diamanté responded. "We are going to Corsica."

Elise gently placed her hand on her husband's arm and looked into his face. Then, turning to Anna and C-C, she said, "Come to the Ajaccio for lunch tomorrow, my dears. There will be plenty of leftovers."

Anna thought to herself how truly happy the couple looked.

On the way back to C-C's house, Anna asked, "Who was that man off in the shadows?"

"What man?"

"He was standing back behind the barbeque pit, not participating in any of the festivities."

"What did he look like?"

"An older man, with thick, square, dark-rimmed glasses. He was creepy."

C-C lowered his forehead, and his eyes narrowed.

"What is it, C-C?"

"It's nothing. He was probably just a curious old villager."

But Anna had seen the look on his face.

When they reached C-C's front door, C-C closed and double-bolted the door behind them. Anna did not recall him doing that the previous night.

CHAPTER 61

The morning after the wedding, Anna brought up her e-mail on the PC in C-C's outer office, finding numerous messages from her publisher. Groaning at the thought of the myriad of mandatory interviews, cocktail parties, and luncheons that would be waiting for her upon her return, she decided to look at them later. One was from Harry, her agent, and then another from Mark, sent Saturday. She opened Harry's e-mail first. The book proposal had been accepted. The check was literally in the mail, it said.

She slowly pecked away at her response on the unfamiliar French keyboard. "G-R-E-A-T N-E-W-S comma H-A-R-R-Y exclamation point. I W-I-L-L C-A-L-L Y-O-U W-H-E-N I G-E-T B-A-C-K period A period."

"Hmmm…" she stared at Mark's e-mail. It wasn't marked urgent. The subject was "Misc." He was taking care of the dog and helping her with the sale of her grandparents' house. Maybe she had better open it. Click. It came up. As always, the same greeting: "Hi, gorgeous." She scrolled down through it. Some news, mostly that the dog was fine. The real estate agent had a pretty serious buyer for her grandparents' house in Laguna Beach. The offer was expected by the time she got back. Then he dropped the bombshell. His parents, he wrote, were at the apartment in Paris. They were going to be there for a couple of weeks. He was thinking about flying over to see them. Could she meet him in Paris at the end of her trip? He wanted them to have a second chance. Maybe Paris would do it. He ended with:

> *How is the reunion going with the old guy anyway? I*
> *hope, for your sake, well. Take care of yourself, Anna. Hope*
> *to see you soon in the "city of lights." Love always, M.*

Anna sat back in the chair and sighed. She hadn't told him much about the trip except that she was returning to France for a vacation and that she was planning to attend Diamanté's wedding in southern France, after which she would be visiting Monique in Grasse.

Wonder what he would think if he knew that C-C is here, she thought, frowning, as she replied slowly, painstakingly, that she didn't have her PC with her and that she was checking e-mail via the Internet. She told him that she wasn't stopping in Paris on her way home, so sorry about not being able to meet up, and that the reunion with her grandfather was going... She stopped typing and looked out the window. C-C and Clo, followed by the dog Max, were just coming through the front gate. "Let's just say, better than expected," she said aloud, clicked on "Send," and quickly closed the e-mail window.

The front door opened. Anna got up from the desk and went into the hall. C-C's face was grave.

"We have a plumbing problem," he told her. Clo brushed past her with a quick nod and a "*Salut,*" his black, Cambodian eyes focused on getting to the back of the house as quickly as possible despite his artificial limb.

"What's the matter?" she asked C-C.

"A pipe has burst. It's an old house. It has happened before." He followed the caretaker.

Anna shrugged and went back to the PC. Another message popped up. *He must be working late*, she thought as she looked at her watch. She swallowed hard and opened it:

> *Hi, Good to hear that it's going "better than expected."*
> *I assume Guy is there for the wedding? Say* bonjour *to*
> *him for me. I don't understand why you can't stop off in*
> *Paris. Maybe you could call me, if you get a chance, and*
> *we could discuss it? Unless of course, you're planning to*
> *be with* him?

With whom? What are you implying, Mark? she thought, knowing full well what he was implying. She responded with a single question mark in the subject line.

Two minutes later, there was another e-mail from him:

> *Ah, got your attention. You are still online then.*
> *Good. I was joking, of course. A dumb ref to your* former
> *French lover.*

"This is ridiculous," she said aloud. "Okay, absolutely the last response." She typed, "You're working too late. Go to sleep."

Anna knew that Mark frequently had insomnia and would stay up until way after midnight working at his computer, so she expected that she'd get another response. Five minutes passed. She read and responded as enthusiastically as she could to some of the publisher's e-mails.

Then, more out of curiosity than anything, she minimized the e-mail window and looked at the icons on the main screen. A French software package for managing a small medical clinic had been installed. She clicked on the icon. A screen came up demanding a password. She tried the one C-C had given her for Internet access. It wouldn't let her in. Well, at least C-C was security conscious. Being PC literate, Anna checked the size of the database. There couldn't have been many entries. She scanned for the last time an update had been made to the scheduler. Two weeks ago? He hadn't scheduled a patient in two weeks? *That's strange*, she thought. Everyday since she had arrived, though, he had announced that he had to make a house call to visit a patient.

Another e-mail arrived. Mark again:

> *Okay, so if you are still online, Anna, I'm sorry.*
> *I promise to not mention you-know-who ever again. It's*
> *just that I'm missing you so much. I love you, and I want*
> *us to get back together. I won't mention the "M" word*
> *either. I'm groveling now. Won't you please just meet me*
> *in Paris? Or at least call me to discuss it? I do love you.*
> *You do know how much I need you, don't you? I'm yours,*
> *always and forever, M.*

Anna put her fingers to her lips as she reread the e-mail. Mark had once accused her of wanting to have two lives. Maybe he was right. It occurred to her that C-C had not mentioned the future, had not even asked her a question about her plans. Mark, by contrast, was always talking about how he wanted to be married and have a family, how he needed her. C-C had told her that he loved her, but he had never once mentioned the future. Even his house was beautiful and comfortable, but it was so much him, so masculine. There was never any mention of making room enough to accommodate a wife or a family. They had been absorbed in the moment since she had arrived. *What if*, she wondered, *in two days, I just packed up and drove to Monique's? Would he just let me leave him again?* Anna had to admit to herself that she really didn't know him very well. He was and he wasn't the same person. She pondered their relationship. Maybe she didn't really love him anymore. Maybe it was nothing but a scintillating physical attraction, just an affair that would run its course. Then what would be left? C-C had come between Mark and her, now more than ever. Would he always be between them?

A door opened and slammed in the back of the house, ending her contemplation. Suddenly needing to be alone to think, Anna shut down the PC and ran out the front door.

It was a hot, dry, airless day. She wandered down to the park where the *pétanque* players were having an argument about the placement of the little wooden *cochon*. As she seated herself on a green, slatted chair in the shade of a plane tree to watch them, she felt suddenly claustrophobic in this small, rural community, pretty and charming as it was. She missed the ocean breeze, the freedom of being able to walk along the cool, sandy beach for hours. She opened her cell phone and dialed Monique's number, wondering if there would be service in this remote village.

"*Allô?*" Monique's voice was barely audible because of the static.

"Monique? Anna."

"Anna! I've been thinking of you. How did the [hissing sound] go? Are you having a good [crackling noises], *chérie?*"

"The wedding was lovely. They seem to be such a happy couple. [snapping sounds]" Anna winced and held the phone away from her ear. "I took lots of photos."

"And when will we see you? [more hissing and crackling noises]"

"Soon. When are you going back to Paris?"

"Georges is leaving on the thirtieth. I'll stay longer, so you and I can have a good visit."

"I should be there by the end of the week."

"*Bon*. It's all set then. How long can you [inaudible]?"

"What? I think you just asked how long can I stay. A week or so. I don't know really. It will depend on…" Anna hesitated.

"On what?"

"On C-C."

"Do I dare ask how it's going with him?" They were now listening to static interference from another cell phone conversation.

"Go right ahead."

"*Bien*, how's it going with C-C?"

"Since you asked…" As she talked, Anna walked toward the town hall hoping that the reception would be better. "Can you hear me better now?" Monique said she could. Anna then explained the reason for her call. She described the house, her suspicions, her doubts, Mark's e-mails.

Monique listened without interruption until Anna had finished her long discourse. Then she said, "Well, *mon amie*, you have a dilemma, don't you? Let me know when you figure it out."

"Monique!" Anna was irritated. "I was hoping for some good advice from you."

"Not this time, Anna. Call me whenever you need an ear. I'll listen, but I want to keep your friendship too much to try to give you advice. I've interfered enough already. Besides, you have to decide what is best for you."

Anna let out a sigh.

"I heard that," Monique said. "You know, we French have a saying: *Coeur qui soupire n'a pas ce qu'il désire.*"

"What? The sigh I just let out proves that my heart isn't satisfied?" Anna paused and sighed again. "Oh, maybe you're right about that."

"I am, *chérie*. I've got a feeling."

CHAPTER 62

When Anna returned to C-C's house, she found the kitchen in a mess and Clo mopping water from the floor. Above the sink, there was a huge hole in the wall where the antique tiles had been. Protruding from the opening was the rear end of a man, obviously a plumber, whose upper body seemed to have disappeared into the hole. He was pounding loudly on a pipe. Anna picked up one of the broken tiles and looked at C-C with a frown.

"It's all right," he said. "I bought extras. The wall will be repaired."

"What caused the pipe to burst?"

"I expect the extra strain. We've been using a lot more water. The bathroom is directly above." He flashed his disarming smile at her.

Anna turned and ran up the stairs, tears welling in her eyes. She sat down on the bed. It was a bad sign. Even the house couldn't accommodate more than one person.

C-C entered the room. He saw her face.

"Is something wrong?" he asked.

She didn't answer him.

"Did I say something to offend you?" He came over to the bed and sat down next to her. "I was just joking about the water usage.

It has happened before with just me here." He tried to put his arm around her.

"It's not what you said…it's just…" She brushed him away as she stood up and went over to the window. She crossed her arms in front of her and turned to look at him. "It's what you haven't said."

C-C was puzzled. He said, "I don't understand."

"Where is our relationship going? What's the end, C-C? You never talk about anything but how much you missed me, never anything beyond this moment, today, lunch, dinner. Did it ever occur to you that there might be a tomorrow? That the day is coming that I might leave again? What would you do if I left today? Right now? This minute?" She caught herself. It was a rerun. A decade ago she had brought up a similar conversation. Her words had been met then with the cold, icy stare of non-commitment. She had flown back to California shortly afterwards. Her voice lowered as she added a snappish and abrupt, "Well?"

The room was silent. A slight breeze blew gently from the window. Neither of them moved. What Anna saw in C-C's sea-deep, gray eyes this time was neither cold nor icy; it was an emotional storm.

A door slammed downstairs. A voice in the foyer yelled, "*Monsieur le Docteur?*" C-C seemed to be in a haze. "*Monsieur le Docteur? Venez tout de suite! C'est urgent!*" C-C ran his hands nervously through his hair, got up, and went over to the top of the stairs. "*Qu'est-ce?…*"

"*C'est ma femme. C'est l'heure.*"

"*J'arrive.*" C-C turned to Anna. "I have to leave. A woman in the village is having a baby. That is her husband downstairs come to fetch me. She will have a difficult time. I expect a cesarean will be required. It will take some time. Maybe all night." He was changing his clothes quickly as he talked. He turned to look at Anna, his eyes the full register of the grays of the sea. "You have every right to ask those questions. I promise you we will talk about the future... when I get back." With that, he raced down the stairs, the front door slammed shut, and he was gone.

Anna, disappointed and humiliated, stood for several minutes by the window with her arms crossed.

She mumbled aloud, "What is wrong with me? I shouldn't have said those things to him." She found her journal in her carry-on and went down the stairs. Creeping cautiously through the kitchen so as not to disturb Clo and the plumber, who were in heated discussion, alternately scratching and shaking their heads, shrugging shoulders, and pointing to the hole in the wall, she slipped out the back door and followed the small pathway to the back corner of the rose garden.

Seated in the shade on a bench under the rose arbor, Anna wrote about how she felt meeting her grandfather and seeing C-C again. She described the wedding and the festivities following it, the village, the Ajaccio, Clo, and C-C's house. Two hours passed quickly.

"*Excusez-moi, Mademoiselle.*"

Anna looked up. The caretaker was standing, slightly bent over, directly in front of her. He had removed his cap and was holding it to his chest as if in worship.

"*Désolé, Mademoiselle.* I afraid bad news. The pipe, it not be fixed today. *Monsieur* call a little while ago. He at hospital in Nice. He wanted talk you, but I think you gone out." He cleared his throat nervously. "I no realize you still here. I just now came through garden to my cottage." He paused, shaking his head. "Since there no water in house, *Mademoiselle*, *toilettes* no operate. *Monsieur* suggest you go to Ajaccio for night."

"Do you have water to your cottage, Clo?"

He looked uncomfortable. "*Oui*, but it too small for two."

Anna nodded and smiled. He had misunderstood her question. "The Ajaccio will be fine." She thanked him, closed her journal, and went into the house to pack her bag. The letters C-C had written her were still lying on his desk, unread. She folded them into the inside pocket of her journal.

CHAPTER 63

Anna's eyes moved back and forth behind closed lids as she followed the action of her fitful dream.

The young man is behind her as she pushes her luggage cart toward the end of the loading platform. A look of admiration is in his eyes as she glances casually back at him. She smiles. At the end of a long journey, she returns. The same man is waiting on the platform for her. He takes her hand. They waltz together. Then, something happens that stops the dancing. He turns around suddenly and runs away. She wants to run after him. A glass window between them prevents her from moving. She pushes it, and it shatters into a thousand pieces. When the air finally clears, she is suddenly on the quay in Le Havre. There are two platforms in front of her. One is as steep as a hill; the other is pebbled with cobbles. At the end of the steep, uphill platform stands a man she recognizes from an old photo. It is her father. As she watches him, he smiles at her and points downward to a man who is standing at the end of the cobblestone platform. But she can't see who he is, only that his is a male figure. There is fog and mist surrounding him. "Anna?" Rain begins falling heavily. "Anna? Is that you?" It is a familiar voice. She turns around. C-C is walking across wet sand toward her. She takes a step forward, and as she does so, the sun suddenly shines so brightly in her eyes that she is blinded. She can't move, can't see. Someone takes hold of her gently from behind and pulls her back away from the platform. The arms feel strong and familiar.

*She can't turn around to see who it is."Who are you?Where are you pulling
me to?"she cries out.*

Anna awoke and looked around her. She couldn't remember
where she was. The room looked like any one of hundreds of old
hotel rooms in France. In this one there was a chair. Now she recalled. She was in Castagniers, at the Ajaccio. She looked at her
watch. It was two thirty in the morning.

* * *

In Laguna Beach, California, Mark jogged along the beach
with Paris off the leash and outpacing him by twenty feet. At five
thirty that afternoon, it was low tide, and the warm August evening had drawn many people to the Pacific shore. They passed a
group of teenagers playing volleyball in the sand, and the dog found
a lone seagull to chase until a wave doused him and the seagull
flew away.

"C'mon, boy," Mark called as he turned around. "Let's go
home." He checked his watch. He still had three more hours before
his father would be awake in Paris. After he had had no response
from Anna to his last e-mail, he had left a message for his father,
asking him to use his connections in France in order to get a cell
phone number for Georges Durocher. He needed desperately to
reach Anna through Georges' wife, Monique.

After Anna had told him that she was going to meet Diamanté
Loupré-Tigre, Mark had run a background check on the man. The
first brief search through all the normal channels had come up with
nothing, not even an address. Next he had contacted his EU sources

in Strasbourg, the ones who had helped him locate Guy de Noailles. They found the usual statistics: a July 1924 birth date in Castagglione, Corsica, an address in Marseilles, France, fifteen years later, and a notation about Diamanté's being a member of the French Résistance movement during World War II. There was a record of a marriage in Ajaccio, Corsica, and the birth of a son, Diamanté Jr., with notations (son deceased March 1962, Algerian War; wife deceased 1963). They could find no current listed address other than a record of some real estate that had been purchased in the south of France in 1996, and no information about any living relatives. What had concerned Mark most was that his EU contacts had told him that the world's preeminent police organization, Interpol, had placed a security lock preventing any further access to Diamanté's records by unauthorized personnel. Despite their EU status, they were not authorized access.

* * *

In Castagniers, Anna got out of bed and walked over to the open window. It was a pretty night with a bright moon and a gentle, warm breeze. The village was asleep. She hadn't had the dream in eight months, not since the last time she was in France. It was so surreal, in all its variations. She turned on the lamp on the bed stand. Its light shone on C-C's letters sitting below it. She picked them up and climbed back onto the bed.

The letter on the bottom of the pile was sealed, the envelope addressed to A. Ellis, *confidentiel*. Anna opened the envelope, carefully removed the pages, and began reading.

January 1998

Anna, ma chère,

This letter contains the story of how I made the decision to stay in Castagniers. I don't intend to ever send it to you as the contents must be kept a secret. If you are reading this letter, it is because I have given it to you in person and we are together again. If that is the case, then you can be assured that I am at present the happiest man alive.

Remember that night in Paris when I was hit over the head on the street in front of my apartment building? Of course, it was the last time I saw you. Do you recall as well that I thought I was being followed? Well, now I can tell you what I couldn't then. Yes, yes I was being followed, my love. It's a long story.

* * *

Mark took off his running shoes and opened the door to his condo, commanding Paris to stay outside until he could get a towel to wipe the sand from the dog's paws. On the entryway table, he spotted the framed photo of Anna and himself at the restaurant the night of their engagement celebration with his parents. Anna, her bright, dark eyes sparkling, her one bare shoulder and arm exposed by an off-the-shoulder, classic black silk dress, her hand adorned with the engagement ring he had given her in Paris, their hands entwined, both of them smiling.

The phone rang, jolting him from his reverie.

"Hi, Mark? Got that number, son. What's so all fired important that you needed it in the middle of the night, anyway?"

Mark said apologetically, "Sorry, Dad. I have to reach Durocher first thing this morning. I was willing to wait until you awoke, though."

"I had insomnia. Always do when I'm over here. Can't get used to the time change. Never could. Anyway, it wasn't difficult. I got Durocher's cell phone number for you. He and his wife are, like everyone else here in France, hah, *en vacances*, as they say, out of town on vacation until the end of the month, so good luck in reaching him."

"Thanks, Dad."

"There's some other information I have for you. In response to that concern you had? I've sent you an e-mail. I think you had better look at it."

"Sounds mysterious."

"It is, as a matter of fact. I'm not sure what to make of it. It's all I could get, for now, but I'll keep trying. Anyway, so are you coming to visit us in Paris?"

"Don't know. I'll let you know in a couple of days."

* * *

There is a young woman within the confines of the walls of the convent in Castagniers. She is recuperating from a horrible accident in Paris last August...August the thirty-first, to be exact. She is my patient.

Anna gasped and put her hands to her mouth. "This is absurd, C-C," she said aloud. "Are you telling me that your patient is Diana, *the* Princess Diana?" As if he had anticipated her reaction, he continued:

> *No, if you are now wondering, it is not Lady Di but her double, officially employed by the British government to act as a decoy anytime the Princess wished her to do so. It was always Diana's decision when and where. They traveled often together. She recalls nothing of that night in August. The only memory she has is that it was decided that she would take Lady Di's place in the Mercedes. She has no recollection of where the Princess went. When the Mercedes crashed in the Alma Tunnel, it was she (the decoy) who was badly hurt. Her carotid artery was torn, and she suffered a stroke. The British Embassy contacted their trusted old friend from the war, Diamanté—yes, your grandfather—to help get the decoy out without the paparazzi discovering the switch. My father called me, and very soon after the call Diamanté appeared at La Pitié-Salpêtrière to enlist my services with the patient. A makeshift SAMU transported us from Paris to Normandy—Le Havre, to be exact—where we were taken aboard a helicopter. I was blindfolded. The only thing I knew is that we arrived somewhere in the U.K. without Diamanté. I only learned that Diamanté had escaped safely because of the scene you witnessed in Le Havre.*

A bird rustled in the tree outside the window, startling Anna as she visualized the scene on the quay in Le Havre. From a distance came the sound of a dog barking. She took a deep breath and continued reading.

I have since learned that it was Diamanté who was following me in Paris. He was living with Elise in her apartment, and I didn't even know it. The old stealth never let me see him, but he was always in the background. He even followed us to Rouen, and it was he who scared away those two thieves who were tampering with my car that night. And, furthermore, he was on the train to Nice with me the next morning. That's when I told him about you.

I know this sounds absurd, Anna, but it is the truth. You must be wondering what happened next and why the woman and I have ended up in Castagniers. I didn't have a clue that she was being transported here when I took the train. You see, she is still an employee of the British government, but she can't ever go back to England. She would be targeted. Everyone would think that she is Lady Di come back to life. So she had to decide what was best for her. Diamanté took me to the convent the day after I arrived. I was given a choice. I was free to leave, or I could stay and become the village doctor so as not to raise suspicion. I finally decided to stay when I learned from Monique that you had become engaged. There was no life for me anywhere else. Alors, the woman now has two bodyguards, a nurse, and me. I won't tell you her name. You must remember, Anna, that as a doctor in France I took an oath. I am sworn not to divulge anything about a patient. I can only say that she will never recover fully.

> *Her right side is paralyzed, but she is talking better and*
> *improving daily. It has not been all that bad an arrange-*
> *ment, really, for me. The funding was part of it. I invested*
> *most of it in the house, a comfortable living arrangement*
> *for my father, and the car.*

The letter ended abruptly. It was as if he had decided that he had already written too much. It was unsigned.

* * *

It was near midnight in California when Mark placed the call to Georges Durocher and his wife Monique in France. The phone rang several times before it kicked into voicemail. Georges' message was long—first in French, then in English. Mark waited for the beep and said that he was Anna's lawyer in California, that he was in urgent need of locating her as soon as possible. Then he repeated his name and phone number twice and hung up.

Dammit. They probably won't give a crap who I am, he thought as he studied the contents of the e-mail his dad had sent. *Christ. I have to warn her about this, ASAP.*

Mark Zennelli's father, Romano, or "Zenn" as he was called in Hollywood circles, was well-connected. If anyone could find someone to get into the content of the new Interpol CIS database, it was Zenn. The e-mail, flagged highly confidential, read:

> *Diamanté Loupré-Tigre, né 1924, Castagglione,*
> *Corsica. First entered France (Marseilles) 1939. Active*
> *leader in Résistance movement (Marseilles) World War II.*
> *Secret security clearance granted by Interpol Paris 1946.*

Secret security clearance granted by British Security Service (MI5) 1997. Involved currently in top secret British covert operation in France (information highly restricted; written authorization required by British Secret Service). Purchased hotel/restaurant/bar (Alpes-Maritime 06, France) 1996. Last known address: Paris. Red Notice: half brother (name withheld) wanted by Interpol (specifics available; written authorization required by Scotland Yard and/or Police Nationale, France).

***

Anna finished the last of C-C's letters, took a deep breath, and sighed deeply. The sun was up. She looked at her watch. She had just enough time to bathe and dress for breakfast.

In the tub, she lay back in the warm, soapy water and pondered the phantom double. *Then where is the real Princess Diana?*

CHAPTER 64

It was market day. A throng had gathered early in the Castagniers town square.

After breakfast, Léo and Pierre bid everyone *au revoir*, and Diamanté announced that his plan for the morning was to drive them to the train station in Nice, pick up some items he had ordered for the restaurant, and return around lunchtime. After the three men had departed, Elise, Guy, and Anna sat down at a table on the terrace under the shade of an umbrella to watch the shoppers in the square. Martine brought them large mugs of *café au lait*.

Anna opened her journal to the back section, a sketch book. She had been working on a pencil drawing of Elise and wanted to finish it while Elise was sitting there with her. Guy looked over her shoulder.

"That's a good likeness of Elise. Did you study drawing?"

"I've never had any formal training, but I just really like to sketch people's faces."

"Do you have some more in that notebook of yours?"

"Yes." Anna flipped back a page and rotated the sketch book for him to have a look. "I've done two others since I arrived. This one is of C-C." It was a close-up of C-C looking directly into her eyes.

"Oh, he is a handsome one, my grandson, isn't he?" Guy smiled approvingly.

She flipped the page to a rather stern drawing of Jacques. "And this one is of his father."

"You really portrayed the old Corsican. Look at this, Elise."

Elise moved around behind them so she could see the drawings. She smiled. "That's Jacques' usual expression, all right."

Anna turned to the previous drawing. It was a likeness of Diamanté. "I did this one from the hunting photo you gave me, Guy," she said as she flipped back another page. "And this is you." She watched him. It was obvious that he was touched.

Anna showed them a caricature sketch she had done of Harry. "That's my literary agent."

"He looks like a clown!" remarked Elise.

"He is, sort of." Anna laughed. She showed them the rest of the sketches, starting with the first one of her dog. Guy recognized the sketch of Mark and remarked how Monique and her husband Georges looked just like movie stars.

Just then the phone rang behind the zinc. Martine answered it. "*Oui, elle est là...Attends...*" She put down the receiver and came back out to the terrace. "*Pardon,*" she said interrupting the conversation. "Anna, the phone, it is for you. It's Charlie. You can take it behind the bar, if you wish."

Anna thanked her, went inside, and picked up the phone. "Where are you?"

"Still at the hospital. I'm just leaving now. I should be home by lunchtime."

"Were you up all night? Did everything go all right?"

"Yes. I'm exhausted. The population of Castagniers has just grown by one. Did you sleep well?"

"Not well. I read your letters."

"You did?"

"Yes, all of them. That first one about why you decided to stay in Castagniers—is the story true? About your patient in the convent, I mean?"

"Yes."

"C-C, I'm sorry about what I said to you yesterday."

"*Amour*, you have every right to expect something more from me. Particularly now. I want you to know that I have made a decision."

Her breath caught in her throat. "What kind of decision?"

"We will talk about it this evening."

There was silence.

"Okay," she said. "I guess I'll have to wait until this evening."

"Anna?"

"Yes?"

"*Je t'aime.*"

Anna put down the receiver. Suddenly, she had a sickening feeling in the pit of her stomach, the dark feeling of foreboding she had felt only once before in her life, just before her grandparents had died.

CHAPTER 65

Diamanté was heading home to Castagniers, having delivered Léo and Pierre to the Nice train station and picked up his restaurant supplies. It was a warm, hazy morning, and the countryside smelled of lavender. He thought about the past few days. Anna and their friends had all been part of the wedding, the start of the new life that he and Elise would now make together. It was comforting to him.

As he turned onto D614, the road became narrow and precipitous. At the end of August, vacationers were in the last days of their month off, and there was more traffic than usual. He was within just a few kilometers of Castagniers when the traffic slowed and finally stopped completely. Diamanté could see in the distance that a long line of cars was jammed in both directions. A SAMU with its lights flashing was in the oncoming lane, trying to get through the traffic. Several police vehicles and a tow truck, all with flashing lights, were parked along the side of a sheer cliff that fell to the valley below. Diamanté got out of his car and joined a group of onlookers.

"What's going on?" he asked.

A woman answered. "An accident, *Monsieur*. The tow truck is pulling a car from the bottom of the ravine. They just loaded the driver into the SAMU."

Diamanté tried to move closer to the edge to get a glimpse of the car. It was a black Mercedes. He couldn't make out the model or license plate. He went over to a policeman and asked what happened.

"Only one car involved. The poor *mec* must have fallen asleep at the wheel and gone over the side."

"Do you know who the driver is?" Diamanté asked, his heart pounding.

"The identification in the vehicle said he was the doctor from Castagniers."

"Is he going to be okay?"

"*Non*," said the policeman, "he was killed. Chest crushed. Must have died instantly on impact." The car was clearly visible now just a few feet from the top of the cliff. It was horribly smashed. The policeman left Diamanté and went over to aid the tow truck driver.

Diamanté sat down on a boulder by the side of the road and put his face in his hands.

CHAPTER 66

At the Ajaccio, it was well past lunchtime, and neither C-C nor Diamanté had arrived.

"*Oh là…* I wonder what could be keeping my *Lobo?*" Elise worried aloud to Jacques as she placed freshly-cut, bright orange sunflowers in clear glass vases for the evening service. "He hasn't called, either."

Guy had gone up to his room for a nap. Anna had completed her drawing of Elise and was in the square taking photos of the vendors and shoppers in the marketplace. She zoomed in and shot an upclose photo of the bell tower of the convent, visible high over the trees in the distance. Silently, she planned how she would ask C-C to take her along with him later this afternoon when he would most certainly visit his patient.

She paused at an artisan's table spread with handmade pieces of pottery. As she admired a large, contemporary pitcher with a bold, dark blue pattern, the potter approached. He was middle-aged with a balding head and scruffy red beard. His olive skin was tanned like a piece of shoe leather, the result of hours in the sun, and his large hands were caked with clay from working the potting wheel.

"It is made using the traditional methods," he told her in a sing-song *provençale* accent. "You will not find another like it anywhere, *Mademoiselle*. It is a unique piece."

"How much are you asking?" Anna inquired, knowing that she would have to bargain.

"One thousand francs, *Mademoiselle*." There was a suggestion of a glint in his eyes.

Anna mentally calculated the exchange rate. That was a little over two hundred dollars. "Ah, but I can't take it with me," she said. "It is too big for my suitcase." She put it back down on the table, shaking her head. "I'm afraid *non, Monsieur*."

"Eight hundred seventy-five francs, *Mademoiselle*. Then you can surely find room in your *valise*." He tilted his head sideways, his arms outstretched.

"But it will cost me at least two hundred fifty francs to ship it to my home in the United States. I'll give you six hundred twenty-five francs for it, *Monsieur*."

Then came the expected maneuver: "I am a poor potter, *Mademoiselle*," he said with a puff of the lips. "I'll sell it to you for six hundred fifty francs. No less."

Anna reluctantly agreed to the price and handed him the bills. He carefully wrapped the pitcher in brown paper and tied it with a piece of raffia.

Just then, Diamanté's car appeared in the square. Inside the Ajaccio, Elise heaved a sigh of relief. "Ah, *le voilà!*" she said. She hurried out to the terrace to meet him but stopped short when she saw his ashen face as he got out of the car. "*Beh, qu'est-ce que c'est?*"

He quickly bussed her cheeks. "Where is Jacques?"

"In the kitchen. Why?"

He didn't answer. He was already through the door of the restaurant. Elise followed him.

From across the square, Anna saw Diamanté arrive. She looked at her watch, wondering what was keeping C-C. With the potter smiling and waving after her, she zigzagged slowly through the mass of shoppers and finally reached the Ajaccio. A few late diners were finishing their *cafés*, but the restaurant had quieted considerably from lunchtime. As she entered, she looked to see where Diamanté and Elise had gone. What she saw alarmed her. In the kitchen, Jacques and Diamanté were hugging each other, not in friendly greeting, but rather they seemed to be emotionally consoling each other. She couldn't see Jacques' face, but Diamanté's was drained of color. Elise was standing by the closed door.

"What's going on?" Anna asked her in alarm as she placed the wrapped pitcher on a table.

Elise shrugged her shoulders in frustration. "I don't know. My *Lobo* wouldn't let me go into the kitchen with him."

As the two women watched, Jacques, his face a sea of sorrow, took off his apron, threw it on the countertop, and, nodding to Diamanté, walked out the back door.

Diamanté came through the doorway where Elise and Anna were standing.

"Go upstairs, Elise. Find Guy and meet me in the salon. I'm going to close the restaurant for the rest of the day. I'll be up in a minute."

"But what has happened?" Anna remembered her feeling earlier after talking to C-C. She grabbed his arm. "Something has happened, hasn't it? Is it C-C, Charlie I mean? Tell me."

Diamanté looked at her and then turned away. His eyes were moist.

"Let me close the restaurant, Anna," he said to her in a soft, kindly voice. He went over and spoke quietly to Martine, and then together they approached each table and announced to the stragglers that the restaurant was closing. Anna watched the scene but didn't see it. She was trembling.

After the last customer had departed, Martine placed a "*FERMÉ*" sign in the window and shut the door.

"Martine, you had better come up also," Diamanté said to the young woman as he took Anna's arm and guided her up the back stairway. When they reached the salon, Guy and Elise were waiting for them.

"What is it, Diamanté?" Guy asked, his face white and drawn.

Diamanté looked at Anna. "Everyone, please sit down," he said. "It is Charlie."

Anna put her hand to her mouth.

"I don't know how to tell you this. I was coming back from Nice. There was a horrible traffic jam just at the bend on D614 where the road begins to get steeper. His roadster went over a precipice and into a ravine. I asked the police what happened. They said they thought he had fallen asleep at the wheel."

"Is he badly injured? Is he in the hospital? Is that where Jacques has gone?" Anna tried to contain her terror.

Diamanté put his elbows on his knees and held his forehead in his hands. He couldn't look at any of them. For a moment he was quiet, and then a huge sob came from deep in his throat. When he lifted his head, he said, "Charlie is dead."

CHAPTER 67

How many tears can these eyes produce? Anna wondered as she stood weeping in the middle of C-C's bedroom. She walked over to the bed, knelt, and rubbed her cheek against the sheets. In her grief, she hugged his pillow to her chest. His scent lingered in the soft fabric. After a while, she replaced the pillow and shuffled into the bathroom, where she wet a washcloth under cold water, wrung it out, and placed it over her eyes. The flood of tears wouldn't subside.

Downstairs in the kitchen, Diamanté was delivering the sad news to Clo.

Anna finished packing and put her luggage at the top of the stairs, and then she went back into the bedroom to retrieve her letters, neatly tied, still sitting on the desk. Distraught, she put them in her purse.

No use leaving these behind. No one will have any use for them, she thought. She opened Nathalie's tin biscuit box and placed the framed drawing of herself inside. She closed the lid and rubbed her hand gently over the cover thinking, *Jacques should bury this with him.*

Diamanté climbed to the top of the stairs and entered the room. He looked emotionally drained.

"Did Clo take it hard?" Anna asked him.

"Yes. Charlie was very kind to him."

"I want to go see where C-C died."

"I'll take you there. I want to have a look at the tire tracks myself."

"Do you think maybe he was deliberately pushed over the cliff?"

He looked at her curiously. "Why do you say that?"

"Oh, I don't know. In December, when we were in Paris, he was always glancing behind him." Anna's voice broke. "He phoned the Ajaccio this morning." Then, through a sob, she murmured, "I guess I was the last one to talk to him." She paused a moment to gather her composure. "He told me he was just leaving the hospital after being up all night. He was exhausted. Maybe he did fall asleep at the wheel."

"Charlie has fallen asleep at the wheel before. Did you know that?"

She shook her head.

"He said once he was driving to Salzburg in the middle of the night and fell asleep, but he woke up in time before he went off the road. Then another time, again on a long driving trip, to Brussels I believe, he said it happened to him again."

"One would have thought," she choked, "that he would have known then that he was capable of doing it again..." she wiped the tears from her cheeks and muffled a sob, "when he hadn't slept all night."

"Yes, one would have thought."

Diamanté picked up her suitcase. They descended the stairs and walked past the kitchen. Clo was repairing the wall where the pipe had been fixed. He didn't look at them.

As they went out the front gate, Anna turned to look at the house a last time. Holding back her tears, she said softly, "When he called, he said he had made a decision…about us, I mean. We were going to talk about it this evening. I guess I'll never know…" She touched the gate. "You know, I was so suspicious of him."

Diamanté stopped. "Suspicious?"

"I couldn't understand how he was able to afford all this, in this small village, I mean, until I read the letters."

Diamanté put the suitcase down and placed a comforting arm around her shoulder. "What letters are you talking about, Anna?"

"He wrote me letters that he didn't mail. He gave them to me—my God, was that just four days ago?" Her eyes flooded again. "I read them all last night. The first one was written in January. In it, he explained why he decided to stay here."

Diamanté had a concerned look on his face. His eyes narrowed. "How much did he tell you?"

"You mean about *the* patient?" She looked at him through her tears. "He told me everything. Well, not her name, but what happened. About you. About the nurse. Even about Le Havre. The letter was several pages in length. I actually thought the story was absurd. I mean, a phantom double? I asked him on the phone this morning if it was true, and he said it was."

"Anna," Diamanté took her by the shoulders, "the story is true, but you must burn that letter, and you must never mention to anyone, ever, anything about its contents. Do you understand?" His black eyes pierced hers. "Charlie was sworn to confidentiality. He took an oath not to divulge anything about any patient. If anyone ever knew he wrote that to you…well," he hesitated, "you, we…all of us could be in grave danger."

"Jacques, too?"

"He has been kept mostly out of it. He knows very little. Charlie wanted it that way."

"Didn't he have suspicions?"

"Not that I knew of. Jacques is Corsican. If he had had any suspicions, it would not be in his nature to ask questions, even of his son."

"And the nuns? Aren't there nuns in the convent? Wouldn't they know something?"

"It is a large convent. The section where the patient is is presently closed for restoration. Very few are allowed access." He abruptly picked up her baggage. "Let's get these to the Ajaccio. I need to make the convent my next visit."

"I want to go with you."

"You can walk with me, but I won't allow you to go in. After that, we'll drive out to where his car was pulled out." He turned to look at her. "Promise me that you will burn that letter."

CHAPTER 68

The sun was just setting in an eruption of soft peach and pink light when Anna and Diamanté arrived at the scene of the accident. They got out of the car and peered over the precipice to the valley below, where C-C's car had landed. The air smelled fresh, and the gentle cooing of pigeons mixed with the loud shrilling sound of cicadas in the early summer evening.

Diamanté removed his beret, massaged the scar on his head, and studied the road carefully for several minutes. Finally, he said, "There are no skid marks. It doesn't look like he applied his brakes. Look there." He pointed to the edge of the road where fresh tire tracks had mown down the vegetation. "It's where he went over the side. He missed the curve entirely." He pointed further on at some tracks of other vehicles alongside the road where a deep swath had been torn by the tow truck as it raised the car from the ravine. "There's where the emergency vehicles were parked when I came upon the scene."

"How far down do you think it is?"

"No more than five hundred meters, but the car hit a big boulder."

"Do you think someone could have followed him? Forced him off?"

"It's hard to tell." Diamanté walked down the road a few yards and came back several minutes later. "There would be broken glass or parts if another car had been involved. I can't find anything. We have to assume that the police were correct, that he fell asleep at the wheel."

The two of them stood together for a long time, watching the sun set. When it became too dark to see, they climbed back into the car.

"Anna, I think that you should consider leaving France immediately," Diamanté said during the drive back.

"Will there be a funeral?"

"I doubt it. Not here anyway. Jacques' words to me were that he would be taking his son back to Rouen. Guy will go with him."

"What will you do?"

"I may close the restaurant indefinitely. With August over, the tourists leave. There won't be much business anyway."

"What about *her*?"

"Who? You mean the woman in the convent?"

"Yes."

He thought for a moment, then cocked his head and said matter-of-factly, "There will always be another convent, another doctor."

"I still don't get it. Where is the real Princess Diana? She couldn't have vanished, just like that."

"That's just it. I don't know."

"What were you running from that day I saw you in Le Havre, you and that other guy?"

Diamanté had thought about that moment for some time. "It's a long story. The deepest regret I have, now more than ever, is that I involved Jacques' son in the whole tragedy."

"He had trouble making commitments," Anna mused. "Maybe this was after all a true commitment for him. He didn't seem unhappy."

Diamanté parked the car alongside the Ajaccio and put his hand gently on hers. "He seemed the happiest after you arrived, Anna. I am so sorry that you had to lose him so soon after your brief reunion. If he told you about the patient, then he took you into his confidence. I believe he loved you. It was obvious to Elise and me."

Anna couldn't speak; she was sobbing again.

CHAPTER 69

The restaurant remained closed all week. Martine was dismissed, and a sign was posted on the door that the Ajaccio would be "*FERMÉ JUSQU'AU FIN DE SEPTEMBRE.*" After Jacques and Guy departed for Rouen, Diamanté and Elise began making plans for their trip to Corsica, and Anna made plane reservations for her return to California.

"Both of you have shown me such warmth that I feel as if I truly have grandparents again," Anna told Diamanté and Elise at dinner the evening before her departure.

Diamanté smiled at her. "I didn't trust it, you know. I thought that you were an imposter. I didn't believe Charlie when he told me. I wanted nothing to do with you…ever."

His coal black eyes almost frightened Anna.

"Then you arrived," he went on, softening a bit. "I still didn't believe you, but I was willing to accept that you sincerely thought that you were my granddaughter. Then you said something. Do you remember? You said, '*Quelle coïncidence!*' that night of the wedding when you and Guy were talking about how you met. It was the way you said it, not the exact words. You looked exactly like my son in that instant, exactly like him. Had he said those words, he would have had the same look. I knew then that you were not a fraud, after all." He tapped the back of his knuckles on the table.

Elise wrinkled her nose in a smile.

Anna said, "I had no idea. I guess we could arrange a DNA test to verify that we are related, if you still have lingering doubts."

He shook his head. "Not any more."

Anna smiled. "I guess blood is thicker, as they say, after all. I hope I have made him proud."

"You have, indeed you have. The Corsican, Anna, creates for those who come after, and that is just what you are doing. I am proud to have you as my granddaughter."

Diamanté produced a slim, gold coin from his pocket. "I carry this always. It was given to me by a friend who was in Algérie as an advisor to the French airborne troops. In January 1962, when Diamanté *fils* had just arrived, the population was hoarding gold coins. A young Muslim boy, whom Diamanté *fils* saved during a massacre in which his entire family was wiped out, gave him this coin. Diamanté *fils* was intending to adopt the boy after the war. He writes about that in another part of the journal. Diamanté *fils* handed the coin to my friend and told him that if he didn't survive the war, he was to make sure that I…" he lowered his head as he handed the coin to her. "I…I want you to have it…for luck."

Anna took the coin into her hands. "I…I don't know what to say," she said uncomfortably. "This is all so overwhelming."

Later that night, unable to sleep, Anna considered Diamanté's advice to burn C-C's letter about the patient in the convent. She drew a shawl around her and descended the back stairway of the

Ajaccio. Finding some matches on the kitchen countertop, she went across to the corner of the garden where the old stone barbeque pit stood. In the darkness, she set fire to a corner of the letter and watched it burn before throwing it into the fire pit. One by one, she added C-C's other letters to the growing pile of ashes, recalling to herself as she did so the substance of each. They were letters written from his heart, and she was glad that she had read them, that he knew before he died that she had read them. Finally, she removed the suture that C-C had tied around the old pile of yellowed letters that had been buried at the bottom of Nathalie's tin box for a decade. Her letters. The letters of a young woman who thought she was in love.

"No meaning to anyone now," she said aloud. She tossed the whole bunch of them into the little fire all at once. The paper, thin and brittle, was reduced to ashes in seconds.

As she stood staring at the flickering ashes, she had an odd sensation of someone watching her. She turned around. There was only the sound of the croaking of frogs. The light from the full moon cast shadows on the back wall where the tiny white lights had glowed earlier. A cool breeze swirled around her. Anna shivered and pulled her shawl around her shoulders. Then she saw him. At first she thought it was her imagination playing tricks on her, but the shadow moved ever so slightly.

"Is someone there?" she said aloud. "Max, is that you?" She had not seen the dog since C-C's death. The shadow didn't move. *If it is Max*, she thought, *he will come to me*. She moved closer to the wall. Suddenly the figure crept away, taking the side garden pathway along the Ajaccio and disappearing. He made no sound as he moved, but it was unmistakably a man, an older man, slight of build, and agile. He wore an oversized beret on his head.

Alarmed, Anna ran back through the kitchen and up the back stairs. A light shone under Diamanté and Elise's bedroom door. She rapped lightly. Diamanté opened the door. He had on a long night shirt, and his bare head sprouted wisps of disheveled grayish yellow hair.

"What is it, Anna?"

"It's...I...I'm sorry to bother you. I was down in the back garden just now, burning the letter, as you advised, and there was a figure. I thought at first it was Max, but it was a man in the shadows. He disappeared when I called out. He went along the garden path by the side of the restaurant."

"I'll go down and lock up. I'm sure it's just some old transient. We get a few of those from time to time. Go on to bed, my dear." He grabbed his beret and put it on his head.

Anna thought what a funny figure he made in his nightshirt and beret as he closed the bedroom door. "He moved so silently," she called after him. "I wasn't sure it was even a person, but Max would have come to me."

The look on Diamanté's face changed. "He moved silently?"

She nodded.

He turned and walked down the hallway. Anna noticed that he too walked noiselessly, and she was suddenly aware of her own loud footsteps as she started toward her room. She had just opened the door when she heard voices coming from the garden, low voices, male voices. She took off her shoes and descended the stairs in her bare feet so as not to make any sound. When she got to the kitchen, Diamanté and another man whose back was to her were standing in the moonlight opposite each other on the back terrace just beyond the open set of French doors. Anna positioned herself inside where she would not be noticed. The man Diamanté was talking to was definitely the same man whom she had seen lurking by the back wall. She shuddered, wondering how long he had been watching her as she burned C-C's letters. He was around Diamanté's age but more slight of build and wore thick, square-framed glasses. His voice was raspy, and though she could barely make out what he was saying, he sounded hateful.

Anna heard Diamanté say, "Why didn't you do it sooner? In December when we first arrived? Why did you wait?"

"It was the (inaudible)..." Anna strained to hear the rest. "Besides, I had something to accomplish in Corsica—a little unfinished business, I should say."

Anna heard Diamanté ask something, but his voice was so low that she couldn't make out what he said.

"I couldn't risk getting caught here." The man spat as he raised his voice slightly. "It was done perfectly, too; no one knew who the assassin was. I was (inaudible)," the man lowered his voice again and chuckled beneath his breath, an evil, derisive laugh that sent chills running down Anna's spine.

"It's the game all over again, Diamanté. *Toi et moi.*"

Anna closed her eyes and prayed for strength. She somehow knew she had to do something to help Diamanté. She tried to

think logically. Then she heard the man mention Charlie, her dead
C-C, something about "that pathetic dead doctor." Tears came to
her eyes.

"Remember the cat?" she heard the man continue. "It will be
like that for Elise. She will be the one to discover that you are the
prize," he laughed aloud at his own joke. Then he pulled something
shiny from his pocket. His voice became clearly audible as he spoke
slowly and deliberately. "Yes you, Diamanté, I thought your death at
this time would make a perfect wedding gift for her." He was holding a gun, and it was pointed directly at Diamanté.

"*Salaud*, bastard," Diamanté yelled.

Anna put her hands to her lips, stifling a scream. From just behind her in the dark kitchen, a dog growled. Anna's heart jumped
into her throat as she turned and saw Max, his fangs bared in a snarl,
barking frantically.

"Oh, God," she screamed, horrified, as the dog launched himself through the air. The man swung around at her scream, pointing
the gun in the direction of the dark kitchen. At that moment, he
saw her behind the French door. Their eyes met as Max charged
and sank his teeth into the man's thigh. The dog held on as the man
frantically tried to beat if off. Anna heard a muffled "pop" as she
spun around and ran into the kitchen to look for a knife. Another
"pop" and the dog let go and staggered backward. His legs trembled,
his head drooped, and he fell into a whimpering heap. Diamanté
grabbed the man's hand at the same instant and tried to wrestle the
gun away from him.

"Oh God, oh God," Anna was screaming as she frantically
searched for Jacques' cleaver in the pitch-dark room. Then she

stopped in cold terror as a muffled shot echoed from the garden. Her mouth went dry as she saw the man with whom Diamanté was wrestling fall forward against him, then slump to the ground.

At the edge of the garden, Elise stood motionless, holding a small, derringer-style pocket pistol.

"Are you okay, my *Lobo?*" she said in a low voice, still pointing the pistol at the fallen figure.

Diamanté tossed the man's gun into the barbeque pit and bent down to check the lifeless body. After a moment he said, "André's dead. You put a bullet hole right through his temple."

Elise let her pistol fall to the ground and rushed to Diamanté. He put his arms around her shoulders.

Anna stood over Max, crying and trembling. She dropped to her knees and touched the mutt's quivering paws. His brown eyes looked up at her pleadingly, and his tongue hung out. He was bleeding badly and panting heavily.

"It's so unfair," she said, tears spilling from her eyes. "Max shouldn't have to die because of that evil, evil man."

"He saved my *Lobo*'s life," Elise said as she looked lovingly at her husband and patted his cheeks with both her hands.

"I could barely hear the conversation," Anna said to Diamanté. "Who was he?"

"André Narbon, my half brother. He was a killer."

"*Oh là*," added Elise with a heavy sigh. "I'm glad it's finally over. This has gone on for too long."

"Where did you ever learn to shoot like that?" Anna asked.

"When you live through a war, my dear, you have to be prepared for anything." Elise walked over and picked up the small, jeweled derringer. "Many years ago, my husband Ferdinand taught me to use a pistol. This pistol was given to me by my Russian tenant. It has come in handy, once or twice."

"It saved all our lives tonight," Diamanté said. "I have no doubt that André intended to kill."

"I saw him before," Anna said. "It was during your wedding, at the evening festivities. He was standing over there." She pointed toward the kitchen garden in back of the barbeque pit. "In the shadows. I thought he was creepy with those thick, square glasses."

Diamanté and Elise looked at each other. Diamanté shrugged his shoulders. "I didn't see him."

"Nor did I," Elise said.

"I mentioned it to C-C, but I couldn't read his reaction."

Diamanté took off his beret and rubbed his scar. "I told Charlie to be careful." He shook his head. "I told him to watch himself. André intended to get rid of him, too. He said so just now. He was following Charlie when he went over the cliff. Said he didn't even have to do a thing and laughed as if he were delighted that Charlie had done his job for him."

"It's not your fault, my *Lobo*." Elise patted his arm.

Anna walked to Diamanté and put an arm around his shoulders. "Why would anyone want to kill you?"

Just then came the throaty voice of an old woman from the other side of the fence. "Ah, Diamanté, I heard something. Still after the critters stealing your tomatoes, *hein?*"

Diamanté responded in a nonchalant voice, "Ah *oui*, *Madame* Boulot. I think I got the culprit this time. Go back to sleep. Sorry to disturb you."

"*Ah bon! Bonne nuit, alors.*" There was silence.

"She's very old and a bit *sénile*," Diamanté said, tapping his temple with his index finger. "Every time she hears a noise in the middle of the night she thinks I am shooting 'the critters,' as she calls them. She won't remember anything in the morning." Then he turned to Elise. "You had best pack. I'll take care of the body." He looked sadly at his loyal mutt and corrected himself. "Bodies. We'll leave at dawn and take Anna to Nice Airport, then we'll head to Corsica."

Elise nodded and went back into the kitchen. They could hear her slowly climbing the stairway.

When Elise was out of earshot, Diamanté said to Anna, "My half brother had a longstanding vendetta with me. That is where it started. You know that letter you told me about? The one Charlie wrote to you and I insisted you burn?" Anna nodded. "Well, other than Charlie and myself, the only person who knew the truth was André. An unlikely combination of events had put us all together in that strange situation. Charlie knew that he was being followed. I suspected André, but I couldn't prove it. And furthermore, I couldn't catch him, though I tried. Sometimes I even followed Charlie myself at a distance."

"What about that night in the street outside the apartment in Paris? C-C was so afraid. It's what drove him to leave."

"I know. I departed on the same train. We arrived here together. André followed us. I'm amazed he didn't try to get rid of us then. I asked him that tonight. He said…" Diamanté's voice broke.

"I heard what he said to you. About the wedding gift for Elise. What a cruel man."

"Anna, I do not believe that you are in any danger. Even André Narbon didn't know of your existence."

"But he was watching me tonight…when I was burning C-C's letters."

"Did you say anything aloud?"

"I don't think so. I don't know."

Diamanté was considering what she had just said when he saw the dog move ever so slightly. He bent down on one knee and put his ear close to Max's nostrils. "I think this old fellow isn't done with this world quite yet," he said as he picked up the limp-limbed canine. "I know someone who might be able to help nurse him back to health." He turned to Anna and saw the tears in her eyes. "Try now to get some sleep, my dear. I've work to do before daylight."

CHAPTER 70

The next morning, the sky was azure blue, and a few fluffy, white clouds danced merrily in a soft breeze. An emotionally and physically exhausted Diamanté was just putting the last piece of luggage into the trunk of the car when he was startled by a loud vibrating noise.

From behind the convent, a yellow helicopter rose like a dragonfly, rotors gleaming in the sunlight. In a moment it was circling low over the village square, looking for something.

Diamanté watched with keen, black eyes as it hovered above the Ajaccio for a moment, kicking up dust and scattering the outdoor furniture. He put two fingers to his forehead in salute. The pilot returned his salute, and then the dragonfly pulled up and was gone.

The monastery's bells rang for the first time in months.

Diamanté glanced at Anna in the back seat as she stared after the disappearing helicopter. He smiled and whispered to himself, "They are safe."

CHAPTER 71

As they drove out of Castagniers, Anna, exhausted and numb, stared at the back of Diamanté's beret from the car's backseat. She hesitated, then decided to ask a question she had been brooding over throughout the sleepless night. Clearing her throat, she began, "I am curious about your half brother. You said last night that he was a killer. How did he get to be that way?"

Diamanté gazed straight ahead in silence. It seemed to Anna that he was agonizing over the answer. She immediately regretted having asked him.

In the front passenger seat, Elise was watching her new husband. "She should know the truth, *Lobo*," she said finally, putting her hand on his right arm. "*Enfin*, after all, she is your only blood relative now, your only legacy."

Diamanté gently took her hand. It would be ten more long minutes before he spoke.

Finally he said, "Have you ever heard of a game, a child's game, called "The Seven Turns," Anna?"

"No."

"It's a game we played in Corsica, my brothers Ferdinand, André, and I. One player, the one who is it, gives a map to the others, a map with seven turns. It is always circular in nature, and at the seventh turn, often very near the starting point, there is a prize. The game's name comes from an old expression: 'the snail's shell has seven turns.'"

Anna bit her lip. "Actually, I've heard that expression before, in a different context. A waiter in a Paris café once drew a map of the arrondissements for me. It looked like a snail's shell. He called it 'The Seven Turns of the Snail's Shell.' I just thought it was a clever way of remembering the numbering scheme of the arrondissements because I never could figure out where there were seven turns on that map."

"It's not that there are always exactly seven turns, Anna. It can be seven twists, or seven circles, or seven changes of direction or, as in the case of Paris, it could even be seven roundabouts or squares. The important thing is to reach the prize or discovery."

"Oddly, I told that waiter that I was looking for someone. C-C, actually." Anna paused as a feeling of overwhelming emptiness temporarily overtook her. Elise looked back at her sympathetically. "Do you think that the waiter could have been Corsican then?"

"Quite possible. There are thousands of Corsicans who live and work in Paris."

"At least he seemed to be aware of the expression, but why would he have warned me? He said something to the effect that I would find what I am searching for, but to be forewarned that it may not be what I hope for."

"It is because it can be a very macabre game. Between my brothers and me, it was to see who could surprise or, in André's case, horrify, the finder of the prize. I dreaded playing when André won the opportunity to draw the map, because every so often I knew that he would kill or maim something. You asked how he became a killer. I think the instinct came to him early. Once Ferdinand and I found a dead rabbit; another time a strangled baby bird; yet another time a puppy with a broken leg, which Ferdinand and I nursed back to health. When I found our beloved family cat, skinned, at the end of one game, I ran to our mother, but André lied and told her that I was the one who had killed the cat. We were only about seven or eight years old.

"He was evil from as far back as I can remember, my half brother André. He and I were not quite a year apart in age—eleven months, to be exact. Ferdinand was the eldest by two years. Our father, Jean-Pierre Dante Loupré, was killed by robbers in the interior while on his way home to Castagglione from Ajaccio. That was just before I was born. Our mother was young, beautiful, and unable to support herself and two young children. There was a wealthy landowner by the name of Narbon who had taken a fancy to her before my father won her away. She didn't love him, but she had no recourse. She married him two months after my birth, and André was born nine months later.

"André Narbon and I grew up hating each other. He was the rich one, athletic, wiry, and quick, always plotting. He beat me up a few times, but I became tough and learned to fight him back. His father, old Narbon, sent him away to a fancy prep school in France when he was thirteen. He learned languages, was well educated, and had money. Ferdinand and I, on the other hand, were very poor, uneducated, and extremely unhappy. No one, except for our mother, cared what happened to us, but she was helpless. Her husband abused her."

Diamanté looked over at Elise. "Ferdinand left home first. Ambitious, he was a hero to me, and I loved him. I couldn't stand it after he left. When I was fifteen, I too decided to leave Castagglione for good. I kissed my mother good-bye and took the ferry to Marseilles, where I lied about my age and got a job working at a metallurgical plant. It was hard work, and the workers were brutal. I became hardened during those years. Then the war broke out. I was only eighteen."

Diamanté fell silent, remembering.

Anna said, "Guy told me about your being captured and tortured during the war."

"Yes, well, I was glad when those terrible years were over." He smiled gently toward Elise. "The only good thing was that I met Elise during the war years." He looked at Anna in the rearview mirror and added, "And good friends like Stu Ellis. Did Guy tell you the story of how I added *Tigre* to my name, Anna?"

She shook her head.

"A close friend of mine from Marseilles joined the army and was killed in the early combat. He called himself *Le Tigre*. I took his name as my *nom de guerre*. I became Loupré-Tigre.

"It was during the war that André and I saw each other again. By then he was wearing those thick, square, dark-rimmed glasses because his eyesight had been partially destroyed from a grenade attack. We were both members of the *maquis*. He was the one who did the killing. He enjoyed it; he even laughed as he blew the enemy's brains out. There was no remorse, no feelings, in André. He was just as he had been when we were children and he had skinned our cat. I hated him. Then he wanted Elise." Diamanté looked at his wife tenderly. "You see, Anna, André became interested in Elise when he learned that I was in love with her." He reached over and pulled Elise's hand to his lips. She smiled and wrinkled her nose. "He and I fought bitterly, as we did about everything, but in the end she chose Ferdinand."

"What happened to Ferdinand?"

Elise answered Anna's question. "Ferdinand was a hero," she said simply. "He died saving many lives, including that of my *Lobo*."

Diamanté continued, "After Ferdinand was killed, I didn't see André again for a long time, but I knew what he was up to. You see, after the war ended, I was recruited by Interpol to keep an eye on him."

Anna gasped. "You mean spy?"

He nodded. "During the years following the war, there were many assassinations in Europe—collaborators, in particular, and political figures who had carried out Nazi orders. The violence was incredible. In Corsica, there was an upsurge in vendetta-style feuds. And André was in the middle of it all, but we could never pin anything directly on him. Until recently..."

Diamanté stopped speaking and slowed the car. They had reached the point along the route where C-C had driven off the cliff.

A great sob rose in Anna's chest. She willed it away and closed her eyes. The area, once so breathtakingly beautiful, was now too achingly painful to look at.

When they had passed the site, Diamanté went on, "In February of this year, I knew for certain that André was a terrorist and an assassin. I was working with the British on another secret project when Interpol alerted me that the prefect and *de facto* governor of Corsica had been shot dead on the streets of Ajaccio. I had last seen André in December when he passed through here at the same time Charlie arrived. I learned he went to Ajaccio after that and was involved with a terrorist group, the very one suspected of killing the prefect. No one took responsibility, but I knew it was André who had done it. Interpol has had him on its 'Red Notice' wanted list for months. He as much as admitted to the deed last night, boasted about it even."

Diamanté was driving very fast now.

Elise cried out, "Please, *Lobo*. These are dangerous curves."

"*Pardon, ma chère*. Corsican drivers," he reminded her as he slowed the car a bit, "tend to treat all roads as if they were a Le Mans qualifying event."

A sudden thought occurred to Anna. She asked, "Do you think your half brother was involved somehow in the Princess Diana accident?"

"I don't know," he said. "André appeared in Rouen within hours of the accident in Paris. It did seem suspicious to me at the time. When we arrived in Le Havre, the Brits recognized him. The only way for me to keep my cover was to flee with him."

"That's when I saw you."

"And I you. André got away from me, but I knew he would surface, and he did, once Charlie was back. I did my best to protect Charlie—but in the end, he screwed up."

"Do you think he really fell asleep at the wheel?"

"André was tailing him, but he said last night that he didn't force him off the road. His exact words were: 'It wasn't the seventh turn.'"

"What was the seventh turn, then?"

Diamanté considered his answer for a moment. "André had likely contracted for an assassination job in August, but the target had switched places at the last moment. Somehow, I don't know from what source, he learned I was the one who had been contacted. He knew to head to Rouen because I would most certainly involve *Les Amis*. Jacques said André just appeared out of the blue that morning in the wine cellar of the café. It was perfect, you see, from André's standpoint. I was in the way. André had his opportunity to do what he had always intended to do—get rid of me, and get even with Elise for rejecting him. The game was over, and I was to be the surprise, the dead surprise."

Diamanté pulled up to the arrivals gate at Nice Airport. He helped Anna out of the car and pressed his son's Algerian War journal into her hands.

"Your father would want you to have this," he said. "When we see you again, Anna, I will tell you some stories about him. You must come visit us. Corsica is a most beautiful island, amazingly varied and constantly surprising."

"I promise to do that. Take care of yourselves," Anna said tearfully as she embraced her grandfather. They held each other tightly for a long while. In time, Anna stepped away and walked to the terminal. Before entering, she looked back. Diamanté held a handkerchief to his eyes. Elise waved. Anna turned and entered the building.

CHAPTER 72

Monique was waiting for Anna when she walked through the airy, open doors of the terminal. The two women embraced.

"I'm so glad you were able to meet me here, Monique," Anna said, her eyes still moist. Then, with a halfhearted smile, she handed her friend the wrapped pitcher and said, "This is for you…from a potter with an attitude in Castagniers."

Monique looked worried for her friend. "I think you should have come to Grasse for at least a couple of days. It would have been good for you after all you've been through."

"Oh," Anna sighed, "I'll see the *bastide* some other trip. I just want to get home."

"I couldn't believe that C-C died like that. I'm so sorry, *chérie*. How horrible it must have been for you."

Anna's eyes watered. "He's gone, Monique. I'll never forget him. He'll always have a place in my heart." With the heel of her hand, she quickly wiped a tear from spilling down her cheek.

They took a seat in the waiting area.

"What would you have decided had C-C lived? Would you have stayed in France?"

"That's a difficult question. I was definitely having my doubts about the future, and I was claustrophobic in that little village, pretty as it is, even though I had only been there a few days. I don't know whether I could have stayed permanently. And I'm certain he would never have left France to live with me in Los Angeles." She paused as loudspeakers announced the departure of an Air Inter flight.

"A man who loves a woman would go anywhere she wanted, it seems to me, *chérie*. If he loved you…"

"Diamanté and Elise believe that he loved me," Anna said, thinking about the huge personal dilemma leaving Castagniers would have caused C-C. "I don't know…will never know for certain what C-C had in mind on the day he died. In reality, he might never have been able to fit into my world, and there was a strong possibility that I could never have fit into his. Maybe that's the conclusion he had come to."

"And so…what were you, are you, going to do about Mark?"

Anna frowned. "Mark has been pretty clear about his intentions."

"He somehow got Georges' cell phone number and left an urgent message wanting to know how to reach you."

"He did?"

"Georges didn't return the call, not knowing what to tell him. So we decided to wait until I talked to you."

"I'll call him."

Before she boarded her flight, Anna called Mark's office, knowing that it was too early for him or Jacks to be there.

"Hi, Mark," she hesitated. "Anna. I'm arriving early afternoon at Tom Bradley: Air France Flight 62 from Paris. I know it's a few days earlier than I originally anticipated. Don't worry about picking me up. I'll catch a shuttle. See you soon. Bye." She paused and then finally hung up. What she wanted to say to him she couldn't put in a voice message.

CHAPTER 73

The gleaming, white Air France 747 made its approach into Los Angeles International Airport. Anna, gazing through the small window, caught a glimpse of the white block letters of the famed Hollywood sign streaming past the window. She was almost home. It had been only a week since she had arrived in Castagniers. Only a week since her reunion with C-C. Five days since Diamanté's wedding. Three days since C-C's death. A fresh wave of sorrow washed over her. It seemed a lifetime had passed in those few days.

As the plane touched down and taxied to the gate, the passengers were given the usual instructions in French and English about passing through U.S. Customs. Anna gathered her things, exited the plane, and followed the swarm of new arrivals through the long corridor that led to the baggage claim. She had been through customs many times. The agents routinely waved her through. This time, it was no different. She slowly pushed her baggage cart up the ramp to the passenger welcoming area where a small crowd watched eagerly for familiar faces among the arriving passengers. She stopped, glanced halfheartedly through the throng. No Mark.

"Oh, well," she mumbled aloud as she focused her eyes on the soiled carpeting at her feet. "He's probably not certain how I'd treat him either. Can't blame him." Turning on her cell phone, she pushed her way through the mass of bodies to the main lobby, noticing as she did the newspapers in the vending machines. Diana's picture was on the front page of all of them. The headlines were mostly a version of the same wording: "A Year Later, Mystery Still Surrounds the Tragic Death of Princess Diana." She bought one copy of each, placed them in the outer pocket of her carry-on, and headed for the doors. A warm breeze brushed her cheeks as she stepped out onto the sidewalk in front of the terminal. Just then, her cell phone rang. The display showed Mark's number.

"Hi," she said quietly.

"Turn around," he said.

"What?"

"I said turn around."

A few yards behind her, parked next to the curb, was Mark's BMW. The top was down, and her dog was standing in the backseat, wagging his tail. Mark had made the effort to pick her up after all.

Anna forced a smile and walked toward the car. Mark popped the trunk and got out to help her lift her suitcase into it.

"Thanks for picking me up, Mark." Anna slid into the passenger seat and tousled Paris' ears. The dog licked her face in delight.

Mark closed his door and leaned over to briefly kiss her on the cheek. He was dressed in his jogging clothes, his hair was more unruly than usual, and his face was unshaven.

"Are you not feeling well? You look pale," she said.

"I'm okay," he harrumphed, glancing over at her. "You don't look so hot yourself. Must have been some vacation you had." He wasn't smiling.

Anna took a deep breath. She knew she looked haggard, having caught a glimpse of herself in the plane's restroom mirror. She had black circles under her eyes, and her hair badly needed washing. "I've been through quite an ordeal, Mark. It's…it's, well, I'll…" Her voice trailed off.

He frowned at her. "I was trying to reach you."

"Monique told me you called them. What was so all-fired urgent, anyway?" She hadn't meant to sound so curt.

Mark bit his lip and then finally said, "I got some intelligence on Diamanté. I was hoping to warn you about something I found out."

"Why were you checking up on Diamanté, anyway?" she snapped.

"Oh, Christ, Anna. Don't get touchy about it. I just had a tracer run. I hadn't figured on anything to be concerned about, but there was something in the information that troubled me."

"And that was?"

"He's got a brother, a half brother that is, who's wanted by Interpol. That's pretty serious stuff. I mean, really serious, Anna. He's a suspected terrorist. I couldn't find out what exact crime he was wanted for, though, because I didn't have his name. It's apparently a different last name from Diamanté's."

"Yes, and I know some of the story about that terrible man. I wasn't being touchy, Mark. It's just that…" She shuddered, remembering the night that André Narbon had shown up in Castagniers to kill Diamanté. "I'll tell you about it one day."

"Well, at least you're home safe." He stared in front of him for a moment. "There's, ah…something else has happened that I need to tell you about." He sounded mysterious.

"What do you mean?"

He turned to her and pulled off his dark glasses. "You're probably not going to believe this, but…"

Just then an airport security guard yelled at them to move away from the curb. Mark nodded, replaced his glasses, and put the car in gear. Anna's hair blew wildly in the wind as he accelerated the BMW into the fast lane of the I-405. After a few minutes, they sped across three lanes of traffic and exited the freeway at Rosecrans. In the back, the dog lost his balance and fell off the seat as the BMW came to a screeching halt in the parking lot of an In-N-Out Burger. Diners at the outdoor tables of the fast-food restaurant stared at them.

Anna was alarmed. She had never seen Mark so agitated. "What is it, Mark? What's going on?" she shouted. "This just isn't like you."

He turned off the ignition, pulled off his dark glasses, and heaved a big sigh. "Okay, dammit. Here goes. This guy showed up at your condo yesterday asking about you. He made our neighbor Tillie nervous because he wouldn't give his name, so she called me. It was early evening, just around sunset, so I made an excuse to leave the office for a little jog on the beach before dark. When I got to the condo complex, Tillie pointed him out to me. Never seen the guy before. Handsome dude. He was just hanging around on the beachfront, looking like he was casing the joint or something. Dammit, I didn't know what to think, so I just walked over to him and asked him what the hell he was up to."

Anna felt sudden panic. Could someone somehow know what C-C had told her? Was Diamanté right after all that she could be in danger? "What did he say to you?"

"He spoke English, but he had an accent. A French accent. I wondered whether he might be one of your long-lost relatives. All he said was that he was waiting for you to arrive home, that he had some urgent business with you. Wouldn't tell me anything more. I asked him how he knew you, but he didn't answer the question. I couldn't decide what to do. If I called the police, what could I tell them? This guy, this French guy, was loitering on the beach? Wouldn't have been any reason for him not to be there. Hell, it's a public beach."

"So what did you do?"

"I told him that he should move on, that you weren't expected home yet and that I didn't know when you were coming, which is true. It was then that he told me who he was—well, not who he was exactly, but who he is today. I guessed the *was* part."

"Mark, you're not making any sense. Who was he?"

Mark gulped and turned to look deep into Anna's eyes. His face showed no emotion. He hesitated and then said finally, "I met your C-C."

CHAPTER 74

Anna stared at Mark. Her mind raced as she tried to remember whether she had ever mentioned C-C's name to him.

"C-C is dead," she exclaimed. "He died in a car crash three days ago. You're scaring me, Mark. Diamanté warned me that I could be in danger. This person has to be an imposter."

"Anna, this guy that showed up yesterday isn't an imposter. Well, not quite." Mark raked his hair as he tried to figure out how to explain the unbelievable story C-C had told him, how his death had been staged and he had been given a new identity with a chance at a new life, that he was in love with Anna and would stay on that beach for days waiting for her.

"Hell with it. See for yourself, Anna." He gunned the car and sped out of the parking lot.

Anna scanned the beachfront as they pulled into the side alley of the condo. *It has to be someone who knew. But who?* she thought, trembling with fear. Mark didn't know anything. She couldn't let him get involved. Tears welled in her eyes.

In front of them the Pacific Ocean sparkled in the afternoon sunlight.

Mark turned off the ignition. "Well, this is it, gorgeous," he said wearily. "Like I said, he's a handsome dude, and he sure loves you."

At that moment, a figure appeared from around the side of the building and walked with a familiar swagger towards the car. Anna put her hands to her cheeks and screamed. She opened the car door and leaped out, her head spinning.

ACKNOWLEDGMENTS

My sincere thanks to Peter Berkos, Robert Fertig, Lillian Balinfante Herzberg, Byron Earhart, Lorin Nails-Smooté, Morry Shechet, Karl Bell, and the late Aaron Hock, all members of the Rancho Bernardo Writers' Group in San Diego, California, whose tough critique, diplomatic suggestions, and sound advice made this story better. A special thank you also to Jewell Hill and Harriett Staats, who so graciously read and provided extensive comments on this work, and to my daughter Kirsten who provided honest feedback along the way. Last, but most important, I owe a debt of gratitude to my husband Denny for his unwavering support, encouragement, and belief.

Made in the USA
Lexington, KY
29 May 2010